Praise for the novels of Osten Ard:

"Building upon the revered history of *Memory, Sorrow, and Thorn,* Williams has outdone himself by penning a 700-plus page novel that is virtually un-put-down-able. . . . Williams' grand-scale storytelling mastery is on full display here. Not just utterly readable—an instant fantasy classic."
—*Kirkus Review* (starred)

"Tad Williams is a master storyteller, and the Osten Ard books are his masterpiece. Williams' return to Osten Ard is every bit as compelling, deep, and fully-rendered as the first trilogy, and he continues to write with the experience and polish of an author at the top of his game."
—Brandon Sanderson, *New York Times*-bestselling author of *The Way of Kings*

"Williams' latest is a story about pride coming before a fall so big that it shakes the foundations of empires. . . . [*Brothers of the Wind* is] recommended for fans of old-school epic fantasy and anyone who remembers Williams' 1988 classic *The Dragonbone Chair* with fondness."
—*Library Journal*

"[*Brothers of the Wind* is] a fascinating prequel for one of the modern classics of epic fantasy, a story that will take lovers of the original straight back to Osten Ard, and will hopefully carry a new legion of readers off to those faraway shores."
—Reading Reality

"The narration has a sense of weight, history, and inevitability, which plays well with the obvious Tolkien influences that have long informed this series.... [*Brothers of the Wind*] will be best enjoyed by series fans looking to understand the backstory of this intricate world."
—*Publishers Weekly*

"Devout Williams fans will be thrilled with this return to his spectacular high-fantasy world, which continues to captivate as the preceding trilogy did decades ago, and readers new to Osten Ard will quickly be absorbed by the political intrigue, rich description and complex characterization that makes the author stand out in a sea of writers inspired by his work."
—*RT Reviews* (top pick)

"It all adds up to a complex juggling act that a lesser storyteller might fumble in any number of ways. But Williams keeps his balls in the air so masterfully you begin to wonder if he even knows that what he's doing is supposed to be hard. Not one of *Empire of Grass*'s plot threads ever feels shortchanged, nor any of its hundreds of characters unwelcome."
—Tor.com

"An engrossing epic, mixing adventure, intrigue, magic, and some fascinating new characters."
—*Locus*

TAD WILLIAMS

BROTHERS OF THE WIND

A Novel of Osten Ard

DAW BOOKS, INC.

DONALD A. WOLLHEIM, FOUNDER
1745 Broadway, New York, NY 10019
ELIZABETH R. WOLLHEIM
SHEILA E. GILBERT
PUBLISHERS
www.dawbooks.com

First Paperback Printing, June 2022
1st Printing

Dedication

This book is dedicated to our dear friend Cindy Yan, who left us in 2020 after a years-long struggle with cancer. Some in our community knew her as "Blue" or "Cyan", but to everyone who knew her, she was a wonderful friend. Her energy and wicked sense of humor, as well as her determination to wring as much out of life as possible, ensured that even though she lost that life far, far too soon, she did not waste a moment of the time she had.

What it comes down to is this: Cindy made herself an important part of our world, and also a big part of the world of many, many others around her. The joy of that, our good fortune, became even more clear when she left us. Farewell, brave and beloved. We will never stop missing you.

I also want to share this dedication with Cindy's friend and roommate, Mark Gambal, who took such good and selfless care of her during her last months. On behalf of Cindy and all the friends who loved her like you did, thank you, Mark.

Acknowledgments

All of the Osten Ard books I've written since I came back to the place after many, many years of absence have benefited more than I can tell from the work of a wonderful group of people who have propped me up through the process (occasionally after correctly knocking me down) of returning to this world I might have originally invented, but which they actually knew better than I did.

(Authors, this one anyway, do not tend to brood over their previous inventions. It is always "On to the next story!")

So to the extent the new Osten Ard books follow seamlessly from the originals, they deserve most of the credit. I will take the rap for any egregious diversions—although sometimes a writer just has to invent new stuff.

In any case, the list could be almost endless, but I will acknowledge those most guilty of the sin of Tad-enabling:

The Official Canoneers: Ylva von Löhneysen, Ron Hyde, Angela Welchel, Jeremy Erman.

My Book-Constructin' Support Team: Deborah Beale (wife, editor, and Official Beloved), and publishers/publisher-affiliated All-Stars Betsy Wollheim, Sheila Gilbert, Josh Starr, and Marylou Capes-Platt.

Other Important Enablers of Tad: Lisa Tveit (tadwilliams.com administrator) and the kind, helpful, patient people on the TW Message Board and my social media accounts, who are definitely not baying for my blood at the long waits for new volumes. (They've actually been super-patient and sweet.)

A thousand thanks are not enough. A million thanks, while closer to what is deserved, might mean you'd never get to reading the story, so I'll leave it at a thousand.

Blessings on all of you.

Nakkiga

Hikehikayo

THE SNOWFIELDS

Ravensperch

SUN-STEP MTS.

Mezutu'a
(Silverhome)

Hernsland/M'yin Azoshai

SKYGLASS
LAKE

Snowdrift
(Birch Hill)

SERPENT'S
VALE

Da-Yoshoga

Kementari

OLDHEART
FOREST

Enki-e-Shao'saye

Sesuad'ra

Asu'a

LANDFALL
BAY

Timik'oro

Great Redwash

Little Redwash

THE WHISPER WASTE

NABBAN

Nabban

Kwan-To-Po

THE VASTMIRE

N

the world of
BROTHERS of the WIND

Part
One

The Black Worm

I now undertake to tell my master Hakatri's story, or at least the parts of it that I myself witnessed, but even before I have begun I am already full of doubts. I cannot tell my master's tale without telling some of my own, but I am not the same person who journeyed so long at his side. The things that happened to us changed me almost as much as they did him, and I can scarcely remember now the person I was then. Still, this Pamon Kes will do his best to tell of what that Pamon Kes saw, heard, and felt during that fateful time.

I have no idea who will read these words, but I feel I must set them down. The years are passing; death will eventually close my eyes and still my tongue. The knowledge of such important events does not belong to me alone, but to all the heirs of the Lost Garden.

Still, it is a painful thing to tell unhappy truths, even from behind the shield of honesty. Many will scorn my words because of what I am— Tinukeda'ya, though we are often called "changelings" and thought by many to be a lesser kind of creature than our Zida'ya masters. But I beg those who might be angered by my tale to understand that despite all that happened, I still feel loyalty to the House of Year-Dancing and the people of Asu'a. The only way left for me to demonstrate that loyalty, and to celebrate my master, is to set things out just as I remember them, without care for the unhappiness that some might feel at seeing them revealed.

"Duty is honor," my stern father often used to tell me. *"And honor is all."*

But I would amend his saying. I have learned that our first duty is to truth, because without truth, honor itself is hollow.

It was in the last days of the Serpent Moon, early in the Season of Renewal, just as the weather began to turn. Everything seemed ordinary for that time of year: the sky was cold but bright above the city, as it had been for several days, and many birds sang.

After I had arisen and offered a prayer to the Lost Garden, I went to the great palace stables to oversee the care of my master's horses and watch the morning feeding to see who was fit and who was nursing some woe or wound. It seemed like any other day. All around me Tinukeda'ya of lesser rank and status than mine, mostly grooms and stable hands, hard at work even after the horses had finished eating; busy currying the beasts' fine coats, walking them out to exercise on the white sand of the great courtyard, and ministering to them in a hundred other small ways. The stables of Asu'a are filled with old, proud bloodlines, and those who tend them are proud, too.

Yohe, armiger to my master's brother Ineluki—what the mortals of the south would call a "squire"—was the only Zida'ya in the stables when I arrived. Yohe was lean even for her slender race, strong-fingered and practical, wearing her hair always close-braided so it would not interfere with her work. She was singing quietly as she introduced a nine-season foal to the moth bridle. Our eyes met, but she gave me only a curt nod of greeting. I was an armiger, just as Yohe was, but none of the Zida'ya squires ever wasted much time being courteous to me, though Yohe would at least acknowledge my presence. She also had an excuse for her less than friendly greeting: the first time introducing a young horse to the bridle is a delicate moment. Our mounts do not like having anything on their faces, even a restraint as light as a moth bridle. (I have never understood how mortals can put a bit in their horses' mouths. Our Asu'a steeds would never put up with it.) I watched for a moment as Yohe raised and lifted the "wings" of the moth with each gentle pull on the reins. The foal shuffled a little, but Yohe had a light touch and the foal remained calm, lulled by her ancient song. I returned to inspecting my master's horses.

As I was removing a stone from pale Seafoam's hoof and wondering whether to have the bronzesmith make her a new shoe, a young Tinuke-da'ya stable hand came running in from the courtyard. It was Nali-Yun, his face flushed with excitement.

"Master Pamon, there are mortal men in the palace!" he announced loudly.

Yohe turned on him. "Are you witless?" she hissed at him, trying to soothe the startled foal. "Roaring like some animal! Have a care, change-ling!"

I pulled Nali-Yun aside. "When are there *not* mortal men in the palace?" I asked him quietly. "They line up at the gates before dawn every day with things to trade or sell. They lurk around the Visitors Court creaking like crows at everyone who passes by, hoping for an audience with the Sa'onsera and the Protector—an audience they will never get. We can scarcely take a step out of the inner palace without stumbling over some mortal or other. Why do you shout about such ordinary things?"

"You are as stiff as a stick, Pamon Kes," he complained. "My news is nothing ordinary."

"Neither is shouting in the stables." But I disliked chiding another Tinukeda'ya in front of Yohe—she and the other Zida'ya squires already thought little of our kind. "So tell me, why is the arrival of more mortals anything unusual?"

"Because it is a whole *company* of mortal men from the west. They have come seeking an audience—and Lady Amerasu has granted it to them. It will begin when the morning bell rings. You must go swiftly!"

"Do not make me ask for quiet again," Yohe warned him sternly.

I did my best to keep my temper with the young groom. "Why should I rush? To see a few mortal men? That is nothing new."

"Well, you still might want to hurry," he said with a grin. "Because your master Lord Hakatri wants you to come to him in Thousand Leaves Hall."

"You fool." I was truly irritated now. "You should have told me that first."

I immediately cleaned myself as best I could and hurried to the great hall, but the groom's nonsense had delayed me. By the time I reached the antechamber of the great hall the other folk of the court had already begun filing in. The largest number of them were golden-skinned Zida'ya like my master, but I could see a few bone-pale Hikeda'ya—the Zida'ya's sister clan—among them. (We Tinukeda'ya also have golden skin, but it has a less robust hue than that of our Zida'ya masters, like wine that has been watered.) The Hikeda'ya were now scarce in Asu'a—most of them had followed their self-styled queen Utuk'ku north to her mountain city of Nakkiga—which only made those remaining, with their eyes like black onyx and their skins pale as scraped parchment, stand out from the rest of the crowd. The Hikeda'ya who stayed had chosen their lives in Asu'a among the Zida'ya over blood ties, and though their northern relatives might despise that choice or even think them traitors, the Hikeda'ya of Asu'a still mingled freely with my master's folk, as if the great separation of the two clans had never happened.

As I entered, the day's first light shone from the high windows of Thousand Leaves Hall, splashing down on the myriad hues worn by the Zida'ya, both in their clothing and in the fanciful shades of their hair. Far above our heads, the light also struck brilliant gleams from the wings of the countless butterflies clinging to the sides and slender roof-beams of the sacred dome known as the Yásira as they slowly stirred into morning life.

On the daïs beneath the open-air dome sat the leading members of the House of Year-Dancing —most of them, that is. Pride of place of course belonged to Sa'onsera Amerasu and Protector Iyu'unigato, my master Hakatri's parents. My master's wife Briseyu was there too, holding their little daughter Likimeya, who did not seem to want to be held. Even my master's younger brother, Ineluki, had arrived and joined his family. The only member of the Year-Dancing root and bough not on the daïs was my master himself.

As I craned my neck to look around the great hall—Hakatri was usually the soul of promptness—I finally noticed the half-dozen figures kneeling at the foot of the daïs, gazing up at the masters of the Year-Dancing Clan like prisoners of war hoping for mercy. These mortals were tangle-haired and bearded, as was common among the males of that folk, dressed in rough garb made from wool and animal hides. In truth, between their unkempt hair and thick furs, I thought they looked little more than animals themselves.

The one I guessed to be their leader looked young, but he was as shaggy and unshaven as the rest, and his eyes seemed small and secretive compared to those of my master's folk—or to those of my own people, for that matter. His hair and whiskers were a fiery shade of red I had seldom seen on a mortal before, so bright it might have been dyed. I also thought I saw something open and inquisitive about his face—an unmistakable intelligence that belied his savage appearance.

Amerasu Ship-Born was also observing the newcomers, her expression calm and benign, like someone at prayer. The Sa'onsera wore her usual modest robes, gray as rain clouds or the velvety breast of a dove, but they did not make her invisible—far from it. Even her husband, great Iyu'unigato, chief protector of all the Zida'ya clans, seemed to recede into the shadows beside her. Amerasu's wise, gentle face drew the eye like a candle flame in a dark room.

Then she raised her hand and those gathered in the hall fell silent. "We give you welcome, men of the west." Her voice did not seem much more than conversational but it carried across the great hall. "You are guests in our house and need fear no harm." She then turned to the mortals' young leader. "Tell us your name and your errand."

The chief of the delegation bowed his head. "Thank you, Majesty. We are grateful that you and your husband have agreed to hear us. It is a great honor to come before the king and queen of the Zida'ya."

Amerasu's smile was gentle, but those who knew her might have recognized a flicker of discomfort. "Those are mortal titles, young man, not ours. My husband is the Protector of Year-Dancing House, and I am the caretaker of its rituals. Our rulings have only as much power as the respect they earn."

The mortal bowed again. "Forgive our ignorance, my lady. It has been long since any of my folk were here in great Asu'a, and we are unfamiliar with your customs. Only our terrible need brings us to trouble you today."

"You still have not told us your name or your home," she prompted him.

"What do they want?" asked her husband, who often seemed to be thinking of other matters, even with all of Asu'a gathered before him. "Do we know yet?"

"Forgive me, Lord and Lady." The mortal blushed, a strange sight to my eyes, as if someone had built a fire inside him that glowed through the skin of his cheeks and his long neck. "I am Prince Cormach, grandson of

King Gorlach, of the line of Hern the Great. Our kingdom is in the place you call M'yin Azoshai at the edge of the western mountains—as you know well, my lords and ladies, since that country was given to Hern's folk as their freehold by your own people."

I knew this ancient story only vaguely, but Amerasu nodded in agreement. "Yes, the gift of those lands to Hern the Hunter was confirmed by my mother and father," she said. "But that does not tell us what brings you to our court today."

"Do not hesitate to tell us your business, mortal men," said Ineluki, smiling broadly. "Perhaps you have found the weather unpleasant on Azosha's hill and wish to give that country back to the Zida'ya."

My master's brother was fond of jests, although he could also be quick to take offense when he was the target of someone else's wit. "Or have your sheep wandered away from you and into our lands?"

The mortal named Cormach appeared uncertain whether he was being mocked and turned hurriedly back to Amerasu. "Neither of those things is true! We rode here to kneel at your feet, Lord and Lady of Asu'a, because our present situation is dire. We came for no other purpose."

"Do not be troubled," Amerasu said. "My younger son is pleased to make a sort of jest." She gave Ineluki a look that, though it contained affection, also showed she did not approve of teasing guests, mortal or otherwise. "Tell us truly what brings you to us, Prince Cormach. I promise you that you will be heard with courtesy from here on."

Like the others watching this unusual audience, all my attention was fixed on the gathering at the daïs; when someone clutched my elbow, it was all I could do not to cry out in surprise.

"I have been looking for you, Pamon," whispered my master, Hakatri, who had appeared beside me as noiselessly as a shadow. "Where have you been?"

"Here, as Nali-Yun told me that you requested."

Lord Hakatri shook his head in annoyance, then smiled. "I told that young rascal I would meet you *outside* the hall. I waited there no little time."

"I am very sorry, my lord. If you wish, I will help you catch him and beat him. He is as feckless as a cricket, that one."

"Ah," said Iyu'unigato from his seat atop the daïs. "I see the last of our family has arrived. Hakatri, come and join us."

"We will talk later, Pamon," my master whispered, then wove his way through the gathered crowd to join the rest of his family. The mortal men watched him respectfully as he passed, which was no surprise: my master was known to many of them, at least by reputation. In person, he made an impressive figure, tall and graceful, more his mother's child than his father's. Ineluki, by contrast, looked much like his sire Iyu'unigato, with an expressive face and wide eyes that could seem innocent or mischievous. With Ineluki, though, neither expression could be completely trusted.

"I am glad you could join us, my son," Amerasu said as my master took a seat near her. "The heralds tell us that the question these envoys bring is no small matter."

"My apologies," Hakatri said. "There was a confusion of messages."

"We are all here now—but why?" asked his father Iyu'unigato. "We still do not know what these mortals want of us."

"We crave your help, my lord," answered the mortal prince. "We come on behalf of our people—Hern's people—to whom you gave the lands that once belonged to Lady Azosha. And I fear we are the bearers of foul news." He hesitated, as if he did not want to speak the next words. "One of the Great Worms has come down again from the north."

At his words, many of those gathered in the hall looked at each other, disquieted.

"A Great Worm?" said Iyu'unigato. "Are you certain?"

"More likely it is some trifling spawn of the elder dragons," said Ineluki with a dismissive gesture—*small matters made too large.* "Some slithering hatchling that has frightened mortals who have never seen anything like it before."

"I beg your pardon, my lord," said Cormach. "But though we are indeed short-lived compared to your folk, we Hernsmen are old in lore, much of which comes from the teachings of your own people. This is no mere hatchling. This is one of the Great Worms—one of the old blood. In truth, I have seen it with my own eyes. It is a cold-drake, black as a beetle's shell, and if it is a handsbreadth less than two dozen paces from nose to tail-tip I will give away my sword and shield and become a priest. We say it is the beast you call *Hidohebhi*—the Blackworm."

A whisper of surprise—yes, and apprehension, too—swept through the great hall at the description of such a large worm. The long conflict called the War with the Dragons had ended many Great Years before, though the struggle against the wormspawn still continues. None of the oldest, most terrible of the beasts had been seen south of the Snowfields since Aisoga the Tall and a hundred warriors from Asu'a and Anvi'janya had destroyed the mighty White Drake of the northern waste back in Senditu's day.

"That is unlikely," Ineluki declared. "That foul creature has not been seen in a hundred of your mortal years or more, and even then it never roamed south of the Snowfields. No, I doubt very much that Hidohebhi still lives."

"I have seen the monster we call *'Drochnathair'* in our tongue," said Cormach, frowning, "and I cannot doubt it is Hidohebhi of legend in all particulars. Any other thought is even more fearful—may the gods forbid there should be more than one of such a beast!" He shook his head. "Several moons ago the dragon arrived and made its lair in a gorge along the Silver Way, at the eastern edge of our lands—our people now call the place Serpent's Vale. The worm has emptied the nearby hills of life and ventures farther every day in search of prey. Our grazing animals, our precious cows and sheep, are vanishing even from high meadows leagues away from that cursed valley. All of our people have fled the lands around it, and they fear even to walk or ride on the Silver Way. The coming of this beast has cut our small kingdom in half. I fear that if nothing is done to kill or drive away the creature, it will destroy my people."

"But why do you bring the news to us here in Asu'a, so far away?" asked Iyu'unigato, frowning a little. "What of Lord Enazashi and his Silverhome Clan? Mezutu'a is only two day's journey from where you say this creature has its lair. Enazashi is a great lord with thousands of his own folk. What of them?"

Cormach shook his head again. "Lord Enazashi will not see us. He and his kin have no love for mortals, especially my folk. He and his people are safe inside the mountain walls of the Silverhome and that is all he cares about."

Iyu'unigato already seemed weary of the matter. My master's reticent father has never much enjoyed the demands of governance, preferring to spend his days in contemplative retreat. "But what is all this to us?" he asked. "You still have not told us why you have come to Asu'a."

"I think he has," said Amerasu, but her words seemed to go unheard.

"Is it not plain to see, great Protector?" pleaded Cormach. "The lords of Asu'a, your sires, gifted us with those lands. Now we beg your help to defend them, because this threat is beyond us. Who among our mortal kind has ever killed or even survived a fight with one of the Great Worms?"

"We still have only the word of mortals that this is such a beast," said Ineluki with a careless flick of his fingers. "Mortals who confess they know little of dragons, Great Worms or otherwise."

The mortal prince turned to him. For a moment this Cormach seemed near to losing temper, but when he spoke his voice was even. "A man does not need to be stabbed, Lord Ineluki, to know that a knife is sharp."

Iyu'unigato raised his hands in frustration. "This arguing is without point. Hakatri, my son, you have been silent through all this talk. What do you think?"

I guessed that my master had been silent because the conversation troubled him. He stood and said, "I think it is a question that requires thought, my lord. My grandparents did support the mortals' claim to Lady Azosha's old lands—none here can dispute that. More importantly, if this beast is truly Hidohebhi—or any of the Great Worms—then it is a risk to all people, not merely mortals. But it troubles me that Lord Enazashi wants nothing to do with the matter."

"Enazashi is like one of those crabs who takes up a shell that others have discarded," said Ineluki. "If he is protected, he cares for no one else's safety."

Amerasu gently reproved him. "The Lord of Silverhome has proved his bravery many times over, my son. He has slain giants by his own hand, with no weapon but a spear. The courage of Enazashi and his folk is not in question here. What remains to be decided is what responsibility Year-Dancing House bears to Hern's mortal descendants in the lands my mother and father ceded to them."

"If you say so, Lady." Ineluki stood and bowed toward her. "But to me this argument over responsibility seems foolish. We are told a worm has come to the Westmarch and hides in the Seaswell Hills." He spread his arms as if accepting an honor. "I will ride back with these mortals and dispatch the creature with my own hand. That seems a suitable task for a scion of the House of Year-Dancing." He turned to Prince Cormach. "We will set out tomorrow, mortal men. I have a spear of my own, and though it has not yet brought me glory"—he looked briefly to his mother, as if her defense of Enazashi had annoyed him—"it seems a good time to test its mettle . . . and my own."

"Sit down, Ineluki." His father the Protector did not hide his frustration. "This is no time for heroic boasting."

"It is not a boast if it is fulfilled." Ineluki had been caught up by one of his strange moods: his smile seemed little more than a show of teeth. "Do you not trust me, Father? Do you not think me capable of such a feat?"

"The very word you choose proves that you do not understand the matter." Iyu'unigato had finally been roused to full attention. "Slaying a Great Worm is not like hunting a boar or even a giant. Now, seat yourself while I confer with your mother."

My master's younger brother sank back onto his chair, but it was plain to see that Iyu'unigato's words had not cooled Ineluki's indignation but rather stoked it. His handsome face was tight, jaw clenched and bright, golden eyes narrowed. He looked, I could not help thinking, as if a handful of tinder might burst into flame if it touched him. Beside him, my master appeared untroubled, but Hakatri was always better at hiding his feelings than his younger brother.

"Let those gathered here now disperse," Iyu'unigato announced. "Take these mortals to the Visitors Court and make them comfortable there. The Sa'onsera and I will take this up again tomorrow and render a decision then."

After the audience ended, I found Hakatri talking with Tariki Clearsight, a friend of his own generation who was closer to my master than any other except his brother Ineluki.

"As you know, Pamon, we leave on a hunt of our own tomorrow," Hakatri said as I joined them. "A family of giants have descended into the Limberlight and are haunting the forest on the far side of Shi'iki's Wood. Are my horses ready?"

"Yes, my lord. Seafoam was a little lame yesterday, but I think it was only a rock in her hoof. Still, I think you should ride Frostmane instead."

"I wish my armiger was as conscientious as yours," said Tariki with a laugh, and I confess to feeling pride at hearing that. "Perhaps I should have a Tinukeda'ya of my own."

Hakatri clapped his hand on my shoulder. "There is only one Pamon Kes," he said, "and he is mine. First of his race to be granted an armiger's banner."

As I basked in this praise, my master's small, fierce child Likimeya ran toward us, swinging a stick like a sword as she chased a bird. My master caught her up and pressed his face against her cheek even as she struggled cheerfully to escape so she could chase birds again. His wife Briseyu of the Silver Braids arrived and took the prisoner from him, then she and Hakatri touched fingertips. Outside of Asu'a, Briseyu is famed mostly for her great beauty, but she is in all ways a good match for her husband, both in her wisdom and her even-handed manner.

"Perhaps you should put off your hunt, husband," she said. "At least for a few days until this embassy from the mortals is answered. Your brother seems much upset, and I will confess I fear the rumors of this worm myself."

My master's friend Tariki excused himself to leave them to their private talk. I could not leave so easily without my lord's permission, and I failed to catch his attention.

"Beloved," he told Briseyu, "if I had to put off my duties every time Ineluki conceived some strange fancy, I would never accomplish anything. We both know my brother will fret and seethe for a while at being corrected by my parents, but he will cool soon enough. He always does."

Briseyu shook her head—not quite in disagreement, I thought, but disquiet. "I hope you are right, but that is not why I ask you to wait. I do not have your mother's gift of foresight, but Ineluki's talk about the worm gave me a pang such as I have not felt before." She allowed little Likimeya to climb down from her arms. The child crouched at her father's feet and began playing with the cords of his boots.

"A pang?" he asked.

"A moment of fear, but as real as anything that happened today. I almost dropped our child, it froze my blood so."

"And what do you fear?"

"I do not know precisely, husband—I am no prophet. But I fear for your brother, and I fear this worm."

Hakatri tried to smile. "You fear for Ineluki? That is a change. Usually your forebodings are for me."

She shook her head. "Do you not understand how strong this pang was?

And how could anything that happened to your brother not touch you too—and me, and our child?"

I felt like an eavesdropper, but there was nothing I could do about it. I watched as my master took her hand in his. "Do you think I would let something happen to him, beloved? And do you think I would stand by and let something happen to you or our daughter?"

"Not by choice."

"Then quiet your fears if you can and have a little trust in your husband . . . and in my parents. They will make no rash decisions. And a worm is only a worm, no matter how fearsome. Our people have fought many."

She shook her head yet again, and this time it seemed to speak of resignation. "I do not fear the dragon itself. I fear what may come of it."

"You have lost me," he said, looking around the room. "You will have to explain this riddle of your fear more clearly. But speaking of lost . . . where is our daughter now?"

Briseyu looked up. "There she is, at the top of the stairs." She let out a sigh. "If I do not fetch her back, she will be down splashing in the Pool of Three Depths in moments. But we should speak more of this."

"Of course." He watched her leave in pursuit of their child, her movements graceful as windblown mist. "I think my beloved has forgotten that we journey only as far as the Limberlight," he said to me a moment later, but his gaze never left Briseyu's retreating form. "We will be home within two or three days at the latest."

"Then we will still ride out tomorrow?" I asked.

He nodded. "Even if there is a new and dangerous worm in the Westfold, we still must teach the giants not to wander into our lands. Meet me at the stables in the hour before dawn, as we planned. See that all is ready. We will need our boar-spears."

"And your brother, my lord?" I asked. "Will he accompany you and the others on your giant hunt?"

Hakatri looked across the room. His younger brother was showing no obvious signs of dismay at having been chided by his father. He had gathered a group of his friends and was amusing them with playful demonstrations of his dragon-fighting prowess. But I thought Ineluki's eyes seemed over-bright, his laughter forced. My master shook his head. "Seeing how much of that spiced black wine he has already downed—and with the sun still a long march from noon!—I rather doubt it. But my brother is head-strong and always changeable, as you know. It would not go amiss to suggest Yohe should have Bronze ready for him, just in case."

I bowed then and left. I had much to do if my lord was to go giant hunting with the rising sun.

It is hard to speak of my master Hakatri without also speaking of his younger brother Ineluki. In many ways they seemed like two halves of a single thing. They were nearly inseparable during their youth and under-stood each other's thoughts so well that sometimes I saw an entire conver-sation take place between them in a single exchanged glance. As youths, they would race their horses side by side out of Asu'a's gates, laughing as their steeds matched each other's pace, the riders' pale hair unbound and their cloaks billowing behind them. Seeing them, the people of Year-Dancing House would call out, "There go the Brothers of the Wind!" And indeed, at such moments they did seem like creatures far beyond the rest of us, even to their own kin.

But as close as they were, they were also very different. Lord Ineluki, the younger, was as changeable as the wind. His angers were sometimes so im-mediate and powerful that they seem to threaten all those around him; his moments of high amusement were only slightly less alarming. Ineluki was a creature of sudden fancies and strong passions, lively as a flame, and his shift-ing moods could set everything around him ablaze, either for good or ill. My master's humors, though, were like the embers of some sacred, eternal fire, their glow often hidden but never extinguished.

Hakatri was broader in his face and limbs than his brother, and though many admired my master's face and form, no one in Asu'a would have called him the fairer of the two. But it is Hakatri's eyes I always think of first, especially the touch of earthy brown in the gold that deepened their color and gave weight to even his briefest glances. I must also speak of his kindness. He was always generous to me beyond his obligations, but his greatest gift was that of his time and his attention, though few of his folk thought my people to be worth such generosity. He always treated me well and never broke a promise. Most of all, he taught me the meaning of honor.

In truth, it sometimes seemed to me that my master's entire family was haunted by their sense of honor—a strange word to use, but apt. My master Hakatri wore his like a heavy crown, but without complaints. His father Iyu'unigato leaned upon his like a staff, and it was hard to tell sometimes which one was supporting the other. Ineluki could be almost mad with it at times, ready to ride at once to prove true to its charge, but then the wind would change and he would scoff at it and make outrageous jests, as if honor were only a fable for children. And Amerasu Ship-Born, the mother of my master and his brother, the heart of her great clan, was so composed of honor that she could tell only the truth, letting neither courtesy nor tradition silence her when she felt something must be said. Amerasu saw truth even when no one else could recognize it.

So I felt then, and so I feel now, but how much can one of the long-overlooked Tinukeda'ya—a mere changeling, as some would call me—truly understand about his ageless masters?

Before dawn the next morning, with the sky purple-dark and the star called Night-Heart still floating above the horizon, my master appeared at the stables with his friend Tariki. I was surprised to see Hakatri so early but glad for him to find me already there, looking after Seafoam's hoof, which had healed with gratifying swiftness.

"Have you seen my brother?" Hakatri asked me, and the way he said it immediately plunged my heart down into my belly. I hurried across the stable to the stall where Ineluki's horse Bronze was kept and saw that it was empty. The bad feeling in my middle grew colder and heavier.

"As I feared," said Hakatri when I told him, "he has left Asu'a. May the Garden forgive his foolish pride!"

"Perhaps he is just out riding," Tariki ventured. He was called Clear-sight, and indeed he had eyes as sharp as a soaring hawk. But he also saw only the best in those around him, which is why he was one of my master's closest companions while not his most trustworthy counselor. "Ineluki often does that when he is unhappy with your parents."

"Taking his armor and his hunting spear?" Hakatri shook his head. "I spoke to the stable guards before I met you. He has gone and told no one of his plans. What do you think that sounds like?"

Ineluki's armiger Yohe trotted up, hair unbraided and eyes wide. "Is my lord with you?" she asked my master. "I cannot find him anywhere."

"He seems to have taken Bronze and rode out by himself before sunrise," Hakatri said. "Hurry to the gate and ask the watch there if they saw him. Then go to my lady Nidreyu, his heart-friend, and learn if he said anything to her that would explain his absence."

Yohe turned and hurried out.

"He would not . . . he would not go after the worm alone, would he?" I asked.

"If he feels his bravery has been mocked? I do not doubt it." I could see the deep unease beneath Hakatri's irritation. He did not always show it, but he loved his brother fiercely. He sent me then to the Visitors Court to discover whether the mortal men were still there, and if they had heard anything from Ineluki.

I hastened across the palace, through the Court of Fowls, the Dancing Pavilion, and the lingering night-shadows of the Smoke Gardens, coming at last and out of breath to the Visitors Court. I found no evidence of Ineluki there, and the mortals themselves were still asleep. The one called Cormach returned with the guard I sent to them, his face flushed with either worry or embarrassment—at the time I knew little of mortals and could not recognize the difference. "I swear we know nothing of this, my lord," he told me. "We were told to wait until your monarchs have decided whether to help us or not."

"I am no lord," I said. "And neither are Iyu'unigato and Amerasu our monarchs. They are our wisest elders, deep with foresight and lore." But even those wise elders, it seemed, had not foreseen Ineluki's sudden departure. "In any case, I apologize for disturbing your peace."

"But is there something we can do to help? Our horses are rested. We could help you search for him."

I almost smiled at the thought of mortals and mortal-raised horses being able to run down one of the Brothers of the Wind. "You are kind, but my master has enough help. Wait for your audience. May fate smile on you."

When I returned to the stables, I was dismayed to find that Yohe's search had also been fruitless, that Lady Nidreyu had not seen Ineluki since the previous day. Lord Hakatri, knowing his brother had a running start, had already set the grooms to preparing both of his horses. It made me superstitiously uncomfortable to see someone else do the work that was mine to oversee, but I understood my master's haste.

"Armiger Pamon," he told me as he donned his witchwood armor, "you will ride Frostmane. I will need fleet Seafoam if I am to catch my brother." The rest of my master's companions had arrived and were getting ready to set out. They already seemed to know that their giant-hunting trip had been eclipsed by something more important and even more perilous: their faces were grim, and I heard none of the banter that usually accompanied preparations for a hunt.

At last, as the first rays of dawn began to brighten the sky, we set out, with me riding Hakatri's powerful charger Frostmane. I did not expect to keep up with my master and his friends, since what Hakatri wanted most was to catch his brother. My master and the rest of his hunting companions did indeed set out at a blazing pace, and soon left the rest of us far behind. The other squires, all young Zida'ya, lesser scions of Year-Dancing House, must have heard something of the unusual nature of the day's chase from Yohe. They did not speak to me about it—the other armigers spoke to me only sparingly at the best of times, and were it not for my master's exalted status, I doubt they would have acknowledged my existence at all. But I saw them murmuring among themselves and their gestures were full of confusion and concern even as Hakatri and his comrades sped away from us along the shore of Landfall Bay, galloping toward the Westmarch Road.

I know there are some, even among those in my master's family, who believe that the favor Hakatri showed me was merely a bid for attention in a court that loves the new and the unusual. It is true that I was of the Tinukeda'ya race and that my father, Pamon Sur, was a mere groom, although even the Zida'ya had to admit my sire had a skill with horses that no one of the Year-Dancing Clan could match. Long before I was born he had achieved a good name among the masters of the Homeward City. But I swear it is also true that it was my own diligence, as well as the aptitudes I had from my father's bloodline, that led to Hakatri noticing me toiling in the stables as a child. He said many times that when I first caught his eye, he did not know I was the son of Pamon Sur, but only admired my hard work and my calm way with the horses. My master was never known to lie—and why would he, in any case, about such a small thing? I was far from the only young Tinukeda'ya working in the stables in those days. That is what my people do: we make ourselves useful to the Zida'ya. Whether we sail the ships of our masters or build their houses or take care of their children, we Ocean Children do what we are given to do and do it well.

What is beyond doubt is that Hakatri did notice me. When he saw that I had my father's skill with animals he made me his personal groom, and when he was disappointed by the young Zida'ya offered to him for training as armigers he decided to do a strange and unprecedented thing in choosing me—the first among my kind—to become his squire and right hand. Soon I was not merely tending his horses but accompanying him on his hunts and other journeys. I learned to take care of his weapons and more than a little of how to use them as well, though Lord Hakatri's own friends mocked him for having a changeling armiger and made it clear in more subtle ways that they did not think much of me or my kind.

"Do not heed them, Pamon," he always told me. "The good name you will gain will far outlast even the cruelest jests."

I was not certain even then that he was right, but I know Lord Hakatri believed it, so I tried to believe it too. I tell it now as a mark of how my master thought and how honorably he treated me. Indeed, in many ways he was kinder to me than my own father had been, who had little patience with anyone less painstaking and single-minded than he was. My father made me diligent. My lord Hakatri made me believe I could be something more than just my father's son.

As I grew, I learned the skills of war and conflict, taught both by Hakatri himself and other instructors of Year-Dancing House. I practiced these lessons beside many young Zida'ya nobles, some also training to be armigers, some to become lords-errant in their own right. For a time my lord's younger brother Ineluki trained with us too, and for the first time in my life I felt myself to be almost an equal of the Zida'ya themselves. It was a heady feeling, and also a perilous one, because it soon became clear to me in whispers and glances from my fellow students that many of them did not like to see one of the Tinukeda'ya risen so far above the usual limits on my kind.

Soon enough, though, I realized I would never be much of a warrior. I had a long reach and was quick to learn that which required thought and understanding, but I was not as fast, nimble, or strong as any of the young Zida'ya lords. Still, I worked hard to master the glaive and the swiftsword as best I could, and to learn the Warrior's Way, so that I might at least watch my master with the eye of experience. And though the young lords of Year-Dancing had previously resented my presence, when it became clear I would never threaten their prowess as warriors they softened a little toward me. They never made me feel like one of them, but they at least came to accept my presence, although much of that was due, I think, to the high esteem in which my master was held.

It was true then, and still is, that Lord Hakatri, eldest son of Asu'a's Protector and Sa'onsera, was held in great esteem not just by me, but by all his people. Even the young lords-errant of his generation who sought to rival him could not help but admire him, and that is no surprise, because he was altogether admirable. I never heard my master tell a lie or even consider it—in this he was truly his mother's child—and I never saw him turn his back upon anyone who needed his help. His younger brother often scolded him for this, since Ineluki perceived it as a weakness. "If you are a friend to all," he would say, "then you are no better a friend to those closest to you than to those you barely know."

But Hakatri would only shake his head at these complaints. "And if I decided whom to help simply by their closeness in blood or friendship, I would not be a lord-errant at all but a paymaster, tallying up the figures before deciding how much assistance to give to others."

In those days of general peace among the tribes of the Lost Garden, no role was prized more highly among the young Zida'ya nobles than that of lord-errant, which meant one who used his good name, good sense, and skill to help those who were in need, whether they be farmers beset by giants or settlements plagued by banditry. My master was so well known that even mortals came to Asu'a from leagues and leagues away to ask his help. Ineluki once spoke to me of it, and it was hard to tell whether he found it more amusing or infuriating.

"Your master is like a god to the mortals," he told me. "They leave offerings for him at the gates of Asu'a as if it were one of their shrines."

"He has helped many of them, my lord," I pointed out.

Ineluki gave me a long look that I did not entirely understand. "Yes," he said at last. "And his fondness for strays will cost him someday, I fear, though I pray that I am wrong."

Such a strange pair, my master and his brother. Hakatri was dark and tall, solid as a standing stone, cheerful and talkative when the mood was on him, but more often quiet and thoughtful, even when others were at their most carefree. Ineluki was almost as tall as his elder brother but far more slender, and all the Zida'ya agreed that he had the fairer face. Where Hakatri preferred to read or talk with a friend or two, Ineluki loved to be in a crowd, jesting and singing. But just as the younger brother's good humor could set a room alight, so when he was angry could he empty a festive gathering in a short time. From the hour of his birth, it has been said, Ineluki burned more brightly—and with greater heat—than any of his people.

But despite these differences, the love between the brothers was deep and strong. They fought sometimes as brothers do, of course, especially because Ineluki felt that his elder brother often treated him more like a child than an equal, giving him advice and holding him back from one rash urge or another. Still, in most ways they seemed almost like a single soul with two bodies, and it was rare to see one without finding the other somewhere close by.

Hakatri and his hunting party had soon left the rest of us far, far behind. We were following a much-traveled road, and because it was not easy to know whether our masters might have turned to follow a sideways track, the other armigers and I proceeded at a very deliberate pace through the steep, forested hills of the Protector's Chase. After many hours of riding, we came down onto the Westmarch Road and made our way across the ford at the Little Redwash River. We did not stop with nightfall—the Zida'ya can ride for days without sleeping—and it was all I could do to remain safely in the saddle until dawn at last lit the eastern skies.

Toward midday we crossed the bridge over Great Redwash itself and descended into Kestrel Gap, the flatlands between the river and the White-wake Heights, the hill country south of the Sunstep Mountains. The Zi-da'ya may seldom need sleep, but their mounts need to rest and eat, even the astonishingly hardy horses of the Asu'a stables. We rode until the stars were bright in the sky, then stopped to feed and water our mounts. After tending to Frostmane, I gratefully stole a few hours of sleep. Two days had passed, and we still had seen no sign of Hakatri and his comrades.

The land around us on the third day was unexceptionable and largely flat as we crossed Kestrel Gap, but the meadows were alive with cowslip, bluebell, and red campion. Again we rode well past the fall of darkness, but near midnight we reached the Silver Way in the marshy lands along the outer edge of the fells, and it became too dangerous to ride even for my sharp-sighted fellow armigers. We stopped and built a fire. Large, fierce wolves roamed the Kestrel Gap in those days, and it had been a long, hungry winter in those mostly empty lands, so even the Zida'ya were not disposed to be careless.

As the stars of Lu'yasa's Staff rose into the southwestern sky the other armigers sat around the fire and sang songs of the Garden. I found it a little strange not that they should know so much about those vanished lands none of us had ever seen, but that I should know so little, since both our peoples called it the land of their birth.

"You never sing, Pamon," Yohe said to me that night. It was one of the first times she had spoken to me since we had left Asu'a. "Do your kind never honor the Lost Home?"

"Do not despise my silence—I would honor it if I knew how," I told her. "But the songs you sing were never taught to me."

"How could that be?"

The reason was that my father had never been the sort to sing to his child, and my mother Enla had been carried away by a fever when I was but four summers old. The only thing I remembered her telling me about our Tinukeda'ya heritage was about the Dreaming Sea. She told me it was part of me and always would be, though I never knew quite what that meant. After she died, I asked my father why she had said the Dreaming Sea was in my blood. The question made him angry.

"Do not ever let our masters hear you talk that way," he told me. *"If you speak of such things, our lords will think us ungrateful and superstitious."*

"But what is the Dreaming Sea?"

"An old and foolish story about the Lost Garden. Your mother should not have told you such a thing."

And that was the last my father Pamon Sur would ever speak about it. I was hurt by his refusal—the Dreaming Sea was something of my mother's that I was being denied—but I did not bring it up again, not even with the other Tinukeda'ya I knew, and the memory began to fade. Then, as I grew older, I came to understand that my people kept silent about many such things for fear of displeasing our Zida'ya masters.

"Pamon, are you listening?"

I realized I had been lost in memory. "I ask your pardon, Yohe."

She looked at me longer than felt comfortable. "It must be strange not to know your own story," she said at last.

But I do know my own story, I thought. After all, I was not merely another Tinukeda'ya servant: I was Pamon Kes, armiger and great Lord Hakatri's right hand. Few of my people, I felt certain, had ever been raised higher. But of course I said none of this.

In the late morning of the next day we heard loud hoofbeats as we rode, as of many folk riding behind us up the Silver Way. The other armigers and I turned, prepared to fight if necessary, not certain whether these might be messengers from Asu'a demanding us to turn back or a pack of the mortal bandits that were said to make their home in the dark heights beyond the Gap, though I had never heard of mortals attacking a group of armed Zida'ya. Instead of either of those, though, a company of men appeared from the east and we saw by their banners that they were the same western mortals who had come to Asu'a to ask for the Protector's help.

The one called Cormach reined up as they reached us. "We heard that a company of your people were ahead of us, and we have run our horses almost to death trying to catch you," he said. "But look! Your mounts are not even breathing hard."

I smiled a little. "The horses of Asu'a's stables travel swiftly without much effort, though we were not hurrying."

"I am surprised to find your company so small, though," said the prince. "Did your folk not believe us when we told them about the monster we face?"

Ineluki's armiger Yohe (who always assumed the role of leader in our company of squires, since my master might have been firstborn, but I was not Zida'ya) told him, "Our lords race ahead of us, mortal, but they will wait for us when they reach their destination. Still, there is no certainty they plan to hunt the dragon that has so badly frightened your folk."

Cormach gave her a sour look. I could not help being impressed by this young mortal, who clearly set himself as high as nearly any Zida'ya. "You say that as though only mortals would be afraid, Armiger. Wait until you see the worm and hear its rasping breath. Then we will see what you fairy-folk are made from."

His words seemed to anger Yohe, but Ineluki's squire was not as capricious as her master; she only shook her head, saying, "Nobody knows what they think of the dark until the sun sets."

After a little more talk it was decided that we would all travel together until we either caught up to the hunting party or our roads diverged. It was just as well we did not waste time arguing, because by early evening, when we had made our way a good distance along the lower edge of the White-wake Heights, we at last came upon my master and his company. They were gathered by the Silver Way where it passed the mouth of a steep, narrow valley. I was relieved beyond words to see not only my own master Hakatri but his brother Ineluki too, although it was clear that the two of them were deep in disagreement. Hakatri was so angry he barely acknowledged me, and when Yohe went to greet her own lord-errant, Ineluki waved her back with a hard swipe of his hand.

"You talk to no purpose, brother," I heard Ineluki say, curling his lip. "I came out only to see this creature for myself. If it is as small as I guess it to be, I thought I might also dispatch it and end the threat to the mortals who live here. Surely even our father could not object to such kind stewardship." He smiled, but that flash of white put me in mind of a skin of bright ice hiding the black, cold waters of a winter lake, and I wondered at the depths of Ineluki's unhappiness and anger. Still, his moods changed swiftly, and I hoped a more sensible one would overtake him soon.

"You have been foolish," Hakatri told his brother in a low voice. "You have caused much worry for many."

In the meanwhile, the rest of my master's hunting party were waiting out the brothers' argument. We learned that the company had been halted here at the entrance to the valley since the middle of the day, Hakatri wanting to take Ineluki back but his brother steadfastly refusing.

"I do not mean to interfere in your dispute, great lords," said the mortal prince Cormach, "but as you know, this is the entrance to Serpent's Vale, where the worm has his lair. He is not often seen in daylight, but he emerges by night to take sheep and cattle and even people from the meadows all up and down these hills. It does not seem a good place to continue your argument, especially if you do not think it will be hastily resolved."

It was plain to see that the Hernsmen, as the mortals called themselves, did not like the place, and I confess I felt more than a little uneasy myself. The hills were high and rocky on either side of the gorge, and with the sun all but set and darkness spreading along the grassy slopes, it was a gloomy spot. I heard no birds at all, only a few crickets singing in the long grass to mark the coming of night. And I was not the only one to feel this apprehension: several of my master's own folk watched the mouth of the valley with troubled faces.

"We will not stay," Hakatri told the mortal prince. "We are returning to Asu'a—all of us. As it is, our father will be uncommonly angry, and even our mother will find herself out of patience, but we may yet repair what you have damaged by your willfulness."

"Willfulness?" Ineluki closed his eyes as though his patience was being unfairly tested. "These mortals came to Asu'a with tales of a deadly dragon, so I rode out to see it for myself. Now we stand on the creature's very doorstep and you would turn back? What good is that to these people?" He gestured toward Cormach and his bearded followers. "What lesson will that teach them? That the House of Year-Dancing is empty of brave hearts?"

"We did not come to be taught any lessons, my lord," said Cormach, and now he seemed angry with Ineluki as well. "We came to ask for your help."

"There—do you see?" said Ineluki. "All that is wanted is a little bravery, brother."

"This has nothing to do with bravery and everything to do with the will of the Protector and the Sa'onsera," my master replied. "You left before our parents had made their decision, like a child bored with his lessons who runs out to play in the sun."

For a moment it seemed that Ineluki's anger would overmaster him. He stared at his brother with such fury that I thought he might simply ride away again. Then his face changed once more, his fury either cooled or hidden. "Your argument comes too late, brother," he said in a gentler tone. "Perhaps I *was* heedless. Perhaps I was at fault—the Garden knows, sometimes I lose patience with our parents' excessive caution. But we are here now! At the very least, we must track the beast and learn something of its true size and nature so that we may plan how to deal with this unwanted creature."

The argument between the brothers continued, though they took themselves a little way apart from the rest of us. Cormach and his mortals finally built a fire—it was much larger than the one the Zida'ya and I had made the night before—and we all waited for my master and Ineluki to resolve themselves on what we should do next.

It was well past middle-night when Hakatri came to the fire. "In the morning, we shall make our way into the valley a short way to learn what we can of the worm the mortals say abides there," he told me quietly. "I will ride Frostmane in case we meet trouble."

So my master's younger brother had won the argument. I was not surprised—Ineluki, as his father often said, had the stubbornness of a badger defending its burrow. I was sorry to hear we would be traveling into that grim valley, because I did not like what I had already seen of the place. I spent much of the remaining night making certain my master's spearhead and sword blade were sharp as an icy wind.

If I had disliked the entrance to the gorge, I cared even less for the valley itself. Lord Ineluki and my master rode first, with Yohe and myself just behind them, followed by the rest of the lords-errant and their squires, and then Prince Cormach with his own men. We needed no guide, since the valley was narrow and the walls were high. The mouth of the gorge was strewn with broken or felled trees. I saw my master and his brother exchange a look, with Ineluki unable to hold his brother's stern gaze for long.

The bottom of the valley was crisscrossed with coursing rivulets, so that the ground was everywhere a swamp, with bits of trees and rocks standing out here and there to make the going even more treacherous. Perhaps because of the steepness of the valley's sides, the cloudy sky seemed to hang closely overhead, hemming us in from a third direction. It felt as if we were prisoners being led to some place of execution.

For all the water and mud and new-sprouted grass, the valley seemed curiously lifeless. The birds I had not heard the evening before were still absent today, and the crickets had fallen silent. The only noises other than those we made were the occasional jeers of crows or the hissing of mountain cicadas, oblivious to everything except their own short time in the sun.

Though the sun kept rising through the cloudy sky, I never felt warm. The small streams that ran through the valley had flowed together in spots to make great brackish ponds, with the branches of half-submerged trees reaching up through the murky water like the arms of drowning swimmers. The steep hillsides were covered with thick growth, so that what little sound we made did not echo back to us. I could not help feeling like one who trespasses in another's house by night, hoping only to achieve whatever they came to do and escape before the house's owner awakes.

Suddenly Ineluki raised a hand. His brother, Yohe, and I all reined up and waited silently. Ineluki extended a finger, pointing to a place some distance ahead of us through the muddy, swampy vale, where two large alders grew on either side of the track of higher ground we were following. At first I could make nothing of his gesture—what was before us looked no different to me than what was behind—but now my master also saw what his brother had seen, and I could tell by his face not to speak. Hakatri climbed down from Frostmane, and I took the charger's reins from him. Ineluki dismounted too, giving Bronze to Yohe.

"We should have brought hounds," Ineluki whispered to his brother.

"We are not our cold Hikeda'ya kin," my master said quietly. "We do not send animals or slaves where we fear to go ourselves."

As I watched, the two of them made their way forward, crouching low to the ground. Neither one had drawn a weapon, which puzzled me, but as I swung down from my saddle so I could better keep both of my master's horses calm, I finally saw what Ineluki had spotted. What I had thought only another large tree root or fallen log—a dark, cylindrical shape lying across the earthen track ahead of us—suddenly moved, and I realized it was no root at all but a tail.

The tail was of good size, that was beyond doubt. It certainly belonged to a drake of some kind, or an unusually large swamp-serpent—but from where I sat it appeared nowhere near as massive as I had feared from the stories the mortals told, and though my heart was beating very fast I felt a little relief. Without being asked, I untied my master's boar-spear so that it would be ready for him. I followed, still holding Frostmane's reins, leaving Seafoam waiting, but my master and Ineluki moved more swiftly. They were now some dozen paces ahead of me, creeping slowly but steadily toward the long, dark thing that lay motionless across the track.

As I stood with Frostmane's reins in one hand and the heavy hunting spear in the other, the moment seemed to hang in the air and burn away in silence like a handful of lit straw. The black tail slid forward until it was almost out of sight: my master and his brother stayed close to it, trying to catch a glimpse of its owner. The rest of the company was strung out behind us along the high track. Then a great rattling sound passed all the way down the row of trees beside us and I heard a sudden shout behind me—a shout of terror. I turned in time to see a dark shape plunge out of the leaning trees and knock one of the Zida'ya hunters to the ground, along with his shrieking horse. The attack happened far faster than I can describe it, and it took me a moment to realize that what had struck the rider down was not just a large beast, a bear or angry boar, but a monstrous head on the end of a monstrously long neck. The rest of the beast still lay hidden behind the tangled trees that lined the path.

My master Hakatri and the others had also turned back at that single, terrible cry. The crashing, rattling sound grew louder as more of the dragon's serpentine body emerged onto the higher ground of the trackway behind us. The tail had not been overly large, but that was because we had seen only its very tip. The rest of the worm had been lying in the swampy wrack, stretched parallel to the high ground and hidden by the thick brush and trees. We had passed right by its watching head.

The horses reared in terror as the immense black dragon slithered toward them, then they scattered before it like mice, leaping away in all directions. Some of the startled horses immediately charged into the brackish water and foundered; others reared in panic and flung their riders out of their saddles. The worm's front legs were short and bowed like those of a southern cockindrill, but it moved with surprising speed. The head on the long neck writhed from side to side, striking at everything it could reach like a furious adder. I only saw it in full for a moment, but that first sight of the monster will never leave my memory. The Blackworm had an armored head with a blunt, jagged beak like a turtle's, though no turtle was ever so huge. Its eyes, what little I could see of them as the head swept by, were golden rings at the center of staring black orbs, and its lusterless black armor ran in parallel rings down the length of its body so that it rippled like an earthworm as it moved.

The moment of stillness had given way to a din I hope never to hear again, shrieks of pain from horses and riders alike, the crash and splinter of falling trees, and the dull, hideous crunch of the monster's heavy jaws as it bit through armor, flesh, and bone.

From the corner of my eye I saw my master and heard him shout, "My spear! Pamon, my spear!" Although I scarcely knew what I was doing, I pitched it toward him, but I was shouting, "No, my lord! The beast is too big!" even as I threw it. Hakatri did not listen to my warning, but instead ran past me with the spear clutched in both hands and plunged it into the cold-drake's side. The spearhead sank into the contorting black body, punching in all the way up to the spear's bronze-bound lugs, but the creature hardly seemed to notice; a moment later a sideways contortion of its long body sent Hakatri flying into the trees.

"Master!" I cried, forgetting even my overwhelming terror of the worm in my fear for him. I dropped Frostmane's reins and struggled through the broken trees and floating logs, quickly sinking into muddy water up to my hips as I left the track. Behind me rose the cries of the hunting party, but the worm itself remained oddly silent. I took one look back and saw the great, blunt head rise high into the air, shaking into little pieces someone who had once had a name and a history, showering the track with a drizzle of blood, then I turned away in staggering horror, still searching for my master.

I found Hakatri at last, half sunk in a backwater pool, tangled in broken branches. His face was out of the water and he was breathing, but though

I shook him I could not summon any movement or sign of life. The noises from behind me were terrible, the ragged screams of the hunting party and the noise of splintering spear hafts and shattering tree trunks combined into a skull-scraping din beyond my ability to describe. I got my arms around Hakatri and pulled him onto a higher bit of land, then slapped and tugged at him in a panicked effort to bring him back to his senses. At last his eyes opened.

"Get up!" I cried. "Get up, Master! The thing will kill us all!"

"My spear," he said, trying to fix his eyes on me. "I have lost it. Where is my spear . . . ?"

No spear was going to stop that dreadful thing—a score of spears would not have availed—but I did not waste time arguing. Instead, I dragged Hakatri toward higher ground as quickly as I could, though it seemed that every branch and root in our path caught at him and pulled against me. One of the horses came stumbling past me toward the reeds and I grabbed at its harness. It was Frostmane, his rolling eyes showing white at the edges, though I saw no wounds on him. I called for help, but could hear no other voices now, only the dragon's thrashing movements, so I had to heave my master up into the saddle by myself, which was almost beyond my strength. Hakatri did what he could to help me, and when he was at last mounted he reached down a hand and lifted me up behind him.

"Where is Ineluki?" he said, his words slurred as though he was still dazed. "Where is my brother?"

"I do not know, my lord. All have scattered before the worm's attack." The cracking and snapping of tree-trunks grew louder and suddenly the war-horse leaped forward beneath us, driven by terror of the approaching beast. In a moment Frostmane had found firm ground, and then no amount of pulling on the reins would slow the maddened horse. Even Hakatri could do no more than hang on, and I held on to him, as Frostmane sprang from hummock to hummock through the swampy valley until he had doubled back around the place where the worm had attacked us. Some of the others were already there, racing up the track toward the mouth of the valley, as heedless of our fate as we had been unknowing of theirs. Ineluki was one of them, covered in mud and bloody scratches but otherwise whole, and I thought I saw Seafoam too, her belly strap broken, dragging her saddle along the ground. My master did not even hold the reins tightly but let Frostmane follow the other survivors out of Serpent's Vale.

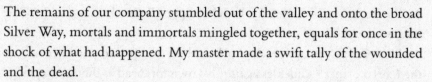

The remains of our company stumbled out of the valley and onto the broad Silver Way, mortals and immortals mingled together, equals for once in the shock of what had happened. My master made a swift tally of the wounded and the dead.

"Where is Tariki?" Hakatri's voice was ragged at the edges. "Has anyone seen him?"

"He and several others are still missing," one of the other Zida'ya announced.

"I pray he lives, but many are dead." Ineluki's eyes were dry but his face was slack and haunted. "My faithful Yohe is one of them. My beloved friend and companion has been snatched from this life. And we cannot even bury her." Ineluki turned to his brother. I have never seen one of the Zida'ya look so lost. "I watched her die under the cold-drake's claws. How can it be true? She has been with me since she was a child. How did this happen to her?" He laid both hands over his breast as though to keep his heart pent inside him.

Yohe's death struck me like a blow, too. She and I had not been anything like friends, but I had known her all my life and had never imagined she might not survive the day. In less than an hour, the whole world seemed to have tipped and fallen over.

"I also mourn Yohe," Hakatri said. "And Lilumo the Poet is dead as well, his songs all ended. Tariki and several more that I love are missing. I want to scream at the sky, brother, believe me. But we must save our strength to care for the living. Many have been badly hurt."

"I see Lord Tariki!" one of the armigers cried. "He is leading a horse with two bodies across the saddle."

"Praise the Grove!" said Hakatri. "Help him, you who are closest. Help those he brings, if they are not beyond it."

Ineluki seemed fixed on something quite different. "Where is the mortal prince?" he suddenly demanded, looking around, his eyes wild with grief. "Where is the one called Cormach?"

"I am here, Lord Ineluki." Cormach was kneeling over one of his Hernsmen; when he sat up, he had blood on both hands.

Ineluki walked toward the mortal prince, and even in the midst of so much mourning, those around watched in fear. Even my master Hakatri, though he could barely stand, lurched after his brother, ready to intervene. As Cormach watched uneasily, Ineluki stopped before him and said, "Give me your hand."

Mystified, Cormach reached out. Ineluki dropped to one knee and set the mortal prince's knuckles against his own forehead as though to pledge fealty—something I doubt had ever been seen before between Zida'ya and mortals. Cormach's hand left a daub of blood on Ineluki's brow. "I was a fool, mortal," said my master's brother, "and both mortals and Zida'ya have died because of it. I was wrong to mock you. There can be no doubt that creature truly is Hidohebhi, one of the Great Worms."

"I take no pride in being right, my lord, especially when so many have fallen, your folk and mine." Cormach seemed confused by Ineluki's un-expected gesture. "As I said, I had seen the beast, and before that followed its tracks for many days."

Ineluki released the mortal's hand. "Still, if I had not been so stub-bornly, cursedly certain of what I did not know, my beloved Yohe might still be with me. I will live with that shame until my last day alive." I had never seen his expression so devastated, so confused and hopeless. It verged, I thought, on real madness.

Tariki Clearsight and those sent to help him now reached the road. "I have two more wounded, Lord Hakatri," Tariki called as the armigers lifted the two limp figures from his saddle. "Rukiyo and Uaye. Both are sorely hurt with many broken bones, and Uaye has lost much blood."

"Ah!" said my master, groaning. "By the Garden this has been a terri-ble day. Yohe and Lilumo dead, so many others sorely hurt." For a moment he fell silent, overwhelmed. Then his head came up, as though he heard some distant horn sounding, and his expression hardened. "We must hasten back to Asu'a as swiftly as we can. Uaye and the other wounded need heal-ers, and the Protector and Sa'onsera must know of the monster we found as soon as we can reach them, but my Witness is lost somewhere in that foul swamp." Without his speaking-glass made from a dragon's scale, we could only send a mounted messenger, which would take days.

"Do as you wish," said Ineluki. "But I will not return to Asu'a."

Hakatri gave him a strange look, half anger, half concern. "It is necessary, brother, but do not fear—Yohe and the rest will be avenged, I promise you. We will come back with a larger company to destroy that evil creature."

"Still," said Ineluki, but nothing more. I could make no sense of that.

Tariki limped over to join my master. "It is a long journey back to Asu'a, Hakatri. Two full days at least, but likely more, because we have lost several horses and those who were badly hurt must be carried."

Hakatri did not answer, but I could read the misery on his face. "It will be as it will be," he said at last. "But we can wait no longer."

"Perhaps we should take the wounded to Silverhome instead," suggested Tariki. "It is closer than Asu'a, and Lord Enazashi will have many healers."

Ineluki was pacing beside his horse. "Talk, talk, and more talk. Yohe is dead! And as we waste time on this useless talk, more folk will suffer and die!"

"There is always time to make a good choice instead of a bad one," my master said.

Ineluki climbed back into his saddle, glowering. "Then make a choice, brother," he said. "My failure is terrible enough even if all the wounded can be healed. I cannot stand to see any more deaths—I fear I will go mad if I do."

"Your pardon, my lords," said Cormach, coming to join them, "but I remind you that Enazashi of Silverhome told us he wanted nothing to do with any hunt for the dragon."

"The worm had not killed any Zida'ya then," said Tariki. "And surely in any case he would not deny help to poor Uaye and the rest of our wounded."

"Even so," Hakatri said, "it will be too long and too hard a ride up into the mountains, I think." I had seldom seen my master appear so defeated. "And you have many injured men of your own, Prince Cormach, do you not? Lord Enazashi is moody at the best of times and does not like mortals. He might refuse to help you." He shook his head. "We could go to Dunyadi, who is a strong friend of Year-Dancing Clan. His house on Birch Hill is only a few hours away from here. I know he would welcome us, and quite possibly the mortals too, but his household is small and I think he may only have one healer."

"What about Skyglass Lake?" Cormach asked.

Hakatri looked up, as startled as if he had been slapped. "Of course! It is only a few short hours farther from here than Dunyadi's house. But will your people be welcome there?"

Cormach nodded. "We often trade with the Sithi of Skyglass Lake."

I was confused. "I do not know that name. Who are these *Sithi*?"

"That is only our own Hernsman word for your master's Zida'ya folk," Cormach told me. "Lady Vinadarta rules over a Zida'ya settlement in the foothills beside Silverhome Mountain. We often trade with them."

"Do they have enough healers?" Tariki asked.

"Yes, and I do not doubt they will help my wounded men as well as yours. We consider Vinadarta a friend."

"Your idea is a good one, Prince Cormach." Some of my master's resolve had returned. "We will ride east, to Skyglass Lake."

We gathered up the fallen we had been able to carry out of Serpent's Vale, mortal and immortal, wounded and dead, and did our best to make those who still lived, comfortable for the journey. More bodies still lay back in that terrible swamp, but we could do nothing for them while the monster lived.

As we rode away, I prayed to the Garden that my master's people would be able to recover all the dead someday and give them an honorable burial. But I also hoped that I, myself, would never have to return to that place.

The land between the Silver Way and Skyglass Lake wound through hills but was not too steep, with open, level track in many places. Our horses made good time despite their unusually heavy burdens. As I rode, I looked around at the trees bursting with new green leaves and wondered that the world could still seem so vital and full of promise on a day so drenched in horror.

The sun, which had not reached noon when we staggered out of Serpent's Vale, was sliding down behind the mountains by the time we passed between two high, craggy hills and into a long valley being swiftly overrun by twilight. Ineluki had fallen back to ride by himself, but my master and Tariki and the mortal prince led the company on at great speed. Slender Skyglass Lake, its silvery waters now gone dark with day's end, stretched for almost a league along the base of the Sunstep Mountains. Soon we saw the settlement, and even by twilight it surprised me. It did not look like any Zida'ya city I had yet seen: the homes and other structures were not made from stone or even wood, but out of colorful fabric stretched between trees, with nothing more solid than pickets of bundled reeds to be seen anywhere. The walls of these unsolid constructions waved and fluttered in every breeze, so that the place seemed more a garden of giant flowers than a place where anyone would live.

"Why does it look as though they have just arrived?" I asked.

"Make no mistake, Vinadarta's folk have lived here by the lake for many Great Years," my master told me. "But they make their homes the way all our folk did when the Eight Ships first arrived in these lands, so that an entire city might be carried on the backs of its citizens."

As we drew closer to the settlement, Tariki called out that he could see a group of riders coming to meet us. I could not see them through the lengthening shadows, but soon enough Tariki was proved right: some two dozen Zida'ya were hastening toward us. Lord Hakatri raised his hand and our company reined up to wait for them.

The leader was female, and though she looked young, she seemed to control both her horse and her followers with ease. She halted them with a gesture but continued forward by herself.

"Surely that is not Vinadarta," said Tariki.

"That is Vinaju, her daughter, my lord," Cormach told him. "But I have seldom seen her so serious or warlike." He lifted his hands high so the approaching rider could see them. Vinaju wore a chestplate of witchwood and carried a spear in her hand. "Lady Vinaju, hail!" he called. "It is Cormach of Hernsland, and several of your own folk are with me!"

"This is an unexpected sight," said Vinaju as she reined up a few paces away from my master and the others, smiling broadly. "Lord Hakatri? Is that truly you, riding with the Hernsmen?"

"It is," he said. "And this is my comrade, Tariki Clearsight. My brother Ineluki is with us, too. We were attacked by a monstrous worm and have lost several of our number. We bring wounded with us, too, some of them very badly hurt."

Vinaju's smile was gone in an instant. "Then let us waste no time. Follow me." She turned and we spurred after her.

Within a very short time we passed in among the rippling cloth walls of the Skyglass settlement. The inhabitants came out to meet us with greetings that quickly turned to cries of sorrow when they saw the state of our company. The wounded were hurried off to the houses of healers and the dead were reverently carried elsewhere.

To be truthful, I remember little more of that evening. When all who needed swift care had been dealt with, Vinaju led the rest of us to a great, billowing hall to meet with her mother, Lady Vinadarta. The white-haired mistress of Skyglass Lake was tall and spoke in a low, strong voice, but I was seated too far away to hear what she said. I was so exhausted and sore that I remember little of what I ate or drank, or how my master and the others told the story of what had happened in that cursed valley. At last, my master Hakatri noticed me nodding in weariness and bade me go sleep.

One of Vinadarta's household led me to a pallet in the tentlike room where my master would stay. Once I lay down I quickly fell into a deep slumber. I was too tired to dream and that was a blessing.

"I told you, I am not going back to Asu'a, brother." Ineluki shook his head, his face as stiffly inexpressive as a festival mask. I had seen him smolder into anger or leap into joy many times, but this occasion seemed different. "If you want to carry the grim news to our parents, you may do so. I swore in front of all our people to kill the worm. I cannot return home until the beast is dead."

Ineluki and the other survivors of our company had gathered in Haka-tri's tentlike chamber, where the morning light made the walls glow with color. My master had proposed we ride home that day, leaving the wounded here at Skyglass Lake until they were well enough to return on their own, but Ineluki's words surprised everyone.

"What madness is this?" Hakatri demanded. "You saw Hidohebhi with your own eyes, brother. This creature is the spawn of Khaerukama'o the Great, who killed thousands! Three score of mounted warriors might be enough to give the Blackworm a moment's pause, but only a dozen of us remain fit to fight—our armigers included in that number. We cannot hope to attack it again without help. In any case, this news must get back to Asu'a to tell the families of the fallen what happened here."

"Go then and tell them." Ineluki did not even look at him. "I cannot. I will not. We all know it was my pride, my headstrong foolishness, that caused this disaster." He paused, then lifted his right hand in the sign for *a pledge*. "Heed me, all of you. I swear by my ancestors and by the Garden itself that I will not return to Asu'a until the Blackworm is dead."

A stunned hush fell over the gathered Zida'ya. I felt a clutch of icy despair.

"Ill thought, and worse spoken aloud," Hakatri told his brother. "I wish you had never said such a thing."

"But I did," Ineluki replied. "Still, it is my oath, not yours, brother. You may do as you think best."

My master shook his head. "Such oaths often turn to curses," was all he said, but I could see that he was worried, even fearful.

Tariki and the others begged Ineluki to take back his pledge, but he would not be moved. I had seen this obstinate streak in him before, but never in such terrible circumstances. Hakatri, too, tried to persuade him, but even his most heartfelt plea could not change his brother's mind, though it did finally drive him from Hakatri's chamber.

When Ineluki had gone, my master was bleak. "I cannot leave him here alone. He is too full of shame over the deaths of our kin. Soon enough his thoughts will turn to redeeming his mistake, and he will go back to try to kill the Great Worm—by himself if no one else is with him. Then he will meet his death." He turned to me. "I should have listened more carefully to Briseyu's fears. I too have been a fool."

"But no matter anyone's fault, you were right in what you told your brother," Tariki protested. "We are too few. If we hunt the worm, we all will die."

"Go back to Asu'a, old friend," Hakatri told him. "Tell my father to send warriors to help us."

Tariki gave him a doubting look. "And while I try to convince them, leave you behind to follow Ineluki into the swamp? Because you know when this mood is on him he will go wherever his temper leads."

"If only we could find a company nearby that would be large enough to have a chance against Hidohebhi," said Hakatri.

"Remember, Lord Dunyadi's house is close by," said Shuda, my master's niece, who was one of his newer hunting comrades. "We could look for help there."

"Dunyadi's household is small." Hakatri stood. "But there are many of our folk here at Spyglass Lake, and Lady Vinadarta is wise. I will speak to her."

The mistress of the Skyglass Lake settlement was taking her morning meal, but graciously invited my master and Tariki to join her. I was not specifically mentioned, but I stayed with my master and one of Vinadarta's folk set out a plate for me as well. I ate bread and sweet butter while my master described his dilemma.

"So you wish to mount a battle company without returning to Asu'a?" She frowned. "I have only just dispatched a large number of our warriors to the east three days past—large by our standards, that is, not by Asu'a's. Giants are in the Limberlight."

"We know," said my master. "That is where we were also bound before my brother took it into his head to seek out the Blackworm."

"The company I sent was less than a dozen strong, in any case," she said. "Not enough to kill such a dread creature as your worm, even if they were still here." Vinadarta seemed genuinely regretful. "I cannot help you, I fear, Hakatri. Not until they return, which will not be until the moon changes, I think."

Hakatri closed his eyes for a moment as if his very thoughts pained him, then suddenly opened them again. "Enazashi!" he said. "The lord of Silverhome has more than enough warriors."

Vinadarta's long, thin face showed doubt. "But would he help you? He has little love for your parents or Asu'a, and Prince Cormach tells me he already refused the mortals when they asked for his aid against the worm."

"But we are not mortals—we are his kin," said my master. "It will do no harm to ask. And in any case, it will keep my brother's mind occupied for a little while. I will go and tell him. We can reach Mezutu'a's Southern Gate by tomorrow evening."

"If you are determined to go, there is a swifter way," said Vinadarta. "I will have my daughter lead you by a hidden passage to Silverhome's Eastern Gate instead." She sent one of her folk to fetch Vinaju.

The young Zida'ya soon appeared in her mother's chamber. She had taken the war-braids out of her hair, which now fell like a veil across her shoulders. Her armor put away, she now wore the same rough clothing as the other Skyglass Zida'ya. "Yes, Mother?"

"Please lead Lord Hakatri to Silverhome's Eastern Gate. You know the way."

"As you wish," her daughter said. "Shall we go now?"

Hakatri rose and bowed to Vinadarta. "I thank you for all your kindnesses, Mistress, but first I must convince my brother to accompany us." He turned to Vinaju. "We will be ready to leave at mid-morning."

"I will be waiting," Vinaju told him with a confident smile. Seeing it, I thought, *Here is one who craves a little adventure.*

When the sun had risen above the eastern hills, we set out—on foot, this time. My master, his grim-faced brother, and I followed blue-haired Vinaju along rough and often hidden paths at the base of the high hills that edged one side of Skyglass Lake. We kept close to the water's edge until we approached the end of the lake. I did not understand how this could be a swifter way to Mezutu'a, and even my master looked puzzled, but Vinadarta's blue-haired daughter led us along the lake's marshy rim until we had reached its eastern end.

The noon sun was above us when we halted at last in a loud place. Here the lake ended in a roiling pool where twin rivers crashed down from the heights and joined to form a single cataract that fed Skyglass Lake. Vinaju led us to a small wharf in a backwater just beyond the churning white waters. The rounded, shallow-drafted boats tied there looked strange to me: instead of being open to the sky, even the smallest of the crafts had curved roofs of lacquered bark held up by slender wooden posts.

Ineluki pointed at the covered boats. "Do we look as though we fear the sun, lakechild?"

Vinaju grinned at him. "Your words tell me you have never traveled the Fernlight Passage before, my lord." She gestured to one of the smaller craft. "Come aboard, please, Lord Ineluki, Lord Hakatri. You too, Armiger."

When we were all in the boat, my master asked if he and his brother should help row. Vinaju shook her head. "I thank you, but I fear despite all your wisdom and skill you would do more harm than good. Wait and see what I do, then you will understand. Do not let your pride be hurt, I beg you."

My master smiled, saying, "It is not, and I see no reason it should be." But I thought Ineluki did not look so certain.

To my surprise, Vinaju did not use a paddle at all, but picked up a long pole from the bottom of the boat and pushed us away from the landing through a thickening cloud of mist and spume, directly toward the roaring cataract. This seemed almost fatally foolhardy to me, but my master looked unworried, so I did my best to match him. Our small craft bobbed and rolled in the seething waters, but Vinadarta's daughter used the long pole to keep it from ever rolling too far.

I quickly saw why Vinaju had kept the task of steering for herself. As we drew nearer to the thundering wall of water, she began to use the staff like a long arm, guiding us between one hidden stone, then another, all invisible beneath the turbulent foam as we bobbed ever closer to the waterfall. The morning sun was high now, and rainbows floated in the spray, making me think of the Third Garden Poet who called such things *"Light singing itself into different hues."* Just as it seemed we must founder beneath the downrushing waters, Vinaju dropped into a crouch, found the bottom of the river below the surface with the end of her pole, then bent her back and with one graceful push sent us into the cataract itself.

The sound of water crashing on the boat's frail roof was deafening, and I was certain any moment it would break and smash down on us, or the sheer force of the water would plunge us down into the swirling maelstrom. Instead, before my heart had beat a dozen times, the thunder in our ears diminished, then an instant later the boat stopped wallowing and began to float as gently as a leaf. We had passed through the waterfall and into a cavern that lay hidden behind it.

When I looked at my masters, Ineluki was grinning, though Hakatri was still impassive. Turning around in the bow, I saw that we had floated through not just a cavern, but a high, dark crevice carved into the rocky base of the mountain, its rough walls illuminated only by sunlight seeping through the waterfall behind us. We were on a river that flowed much more gently than the pair that crashed down the mountainside and joined to form the cataract that blocked the inlet from view. This hidden inlet flowed into Skyglass Lake so gently that no one would ever guess it lurked behind the violent, falling waters.

"Now you will see the Fernlight Passage," said Vinaju.

As we moved away from the opening, the light grew less and less until we traveled in almost complete darkness, though somehow Vinaju never ran aground. For a long time I could see and hear nothing, but just when I began to feel truly ill-at-ease, wondering what kinds of creatures might be clinging to the rocks above me or swimming just beneath the surface of this isolated watercourse, the passage began to lighten again, and with that glow came the noise of splashing water.

"The first garden of the passage," Vinaju announced. Daylight now beamed down through gaps in the stone above. Water flowed through many of those gaps, some in mere trickles, others in arching streams. These sluices of water seemed only slightly quieter than the great cataract, because we had traveled so long in near-silence. Now that light had returned, I could see the huge, nodding ferns and other leafy green things that grew all along the river's edges. Vines grew among them, climbing the walls and sometimes even covering the entire ceiling of the passage.

We skimmed on against the sluggish current, passing through several more of these sunlit gardens and through other narrow places where curtains of water descended from above. At first Ineluki was much taken by the beauty of these unexpected gardens, and, admiring them, sang snatches of old songs. After a while he fell as silent as my master Hakatri, but with the air—or at least so I thought—of one who now wanted the journey to be over.

With Vinaju guiding our little boat, we emerged from the passage at last into a great underground cavern filled by a vast black lake. Here no light leaked down from the sky—we were deep beneath the mountain— but the water was illuminated in spots by a few of Vinaju's people in small boats like ours, each with a lantern in the bow; far across the black lake a strange, glowing archway seemed to hover above the gently rippling waters, washing the cavern's rough walls with a warm glow.

"This is Lake Starless," Vinaju announced. "And the bright arch you see in the distance is the Old Gate. My grandfather once told me it is part of the hull of the Great Ship that founded Mezutu'a."

So saying, she put down her pole at last and took up a paddle. The water was so calm that after only a few dips of the blade we slid away from the Fernlight Passage; soon after, we reached the glowing arch in the massive wall.

The wall itself was high and smooth, slanting upward and away in a very gentle curve until it disappeared far above our heads. I was stunned to think that I was seeing the remains of one of the Great Ships of legend. The huge, smooth structure seemed not merely to rest upon, but to grow out of the very stone of an island, although even with the glow from the archway it was hard to see where that island ended, and whether more of the lake lay beyond it. The Old Gate, as Vinaju named it, was marked out in crystal tiles that glowed rose-pink and warm amber. At the center of the arch stood a gate many times our height, made of what looked to be witchwood with hinges of metal.

Vinaju left us there, accepting my master's thanks with a smile and a bow. However, it was not my master Hakatri she looked at longest as she turned to paddle back across the lake, but Ineluki, who stood staring up at the giant portal, unaware of her gaze. It was something I have often seen. Ineluki's elegance and beauty have captured many hearts and will doubtless capture many more.

By the time we had walked up the stony beach to the great Old Gate, a smaller door opened and a company of Silverhome warriors came out to meet us. My masters were recognized and treated with all due honor, although with a little obvious discomfort at their unexpected arrival. These guards led us up into the city proper, sending messengers ahead. We rode through Mezutu'a's broad, cobbled streets, which were lit at every crossing with rose and amber crystals like those around the gate, so that the entire city gleamed softly, like a dawn sky, though we were deep in the bowels of the stony earth. We saw many Silverhome Clan-folk in the streets. Most gave us courteous greeting, though some were too busy with singing or conversation to notice us. We were led to the Site of Witness and ushered quietly through the doors, then we stopped to wait in the shadowy outer reaches of the great circular chamber. The walls of the Site of Witness are covered in intricate carvings, sweeping, stylized sculptures that portray Mezutu'a's long history. Hundreds of stone benches ring the center of the chamber, but when I first entered all I could make out was the Master Witness itself, a great irregular spike of shining crystal called the Shard. Its clouded, milky glow painted the faces of those at the center of the wide, bowl-shaped chamber. Roughly a score of these Zida'ya nobles were gathered around a stone chair and the one seated upon it, who could only be Enazashi. The Lord of Silverhome was tall and solemn as an eagle on a branch, his face lean and coldly stern. He was one of the oldest of my master's people. Only deathless Utuk'ku, Amerasu Ship-Born, and a handful of others had seen more years of life than he had.

One other figure sat at the center of the Site of Witness with Enazashi, on a bench only a few paces behind his stone chair. To my surprise and confusion, I could see that this small, hunched person was not Zida'ya but one of my own Tinukeda'ya folk. Those of our changeling people who have been longest among the Zida'ya look much like them, as I do, and as this bent figure did, though I never saw any Zida'ya look so fragile and so defeated.

"Who is that?" I whispered to my master.

"Kai-Unyu, Silverhome's other ruler," he told me. "But be silent now, Pamon. I fear this will not be a happy audience for any of us."

Enazashi's celebrant-herald called for my master and his brother to come forward into the light of the Shard. Hakatri and Ineluki began the Six Songs of Respectful Request, Ineluki with his shoulders squared and head thrown back, my master in a more ordinary posture, but Enazashi curtly gestured them to silence. The Tinukeda'ya Kai-Unyu barely seemed to be listening, his eyes fixed on his own clasped hands. If this unprepossessing figure was truly Enazashi's co-ruler, he seemed content to let the Zida'ya lord lead the dance.

"I will not ask you what brings you here." Enazashi's voice sounded more sour than courtesy would usually dictate. "I think I know. Vinadarta and her lake folk have no doubt complained to the House of Year-Dancing about something I have done so you have been sent here to chide me as though I were an errant child instead of a master in my own house."

"Not at all, *S'hue* Enazashi," my master said quickly. "Mortal men from M'yin Azoshai came to Asu'a because a dragon has killed many of their animals and some of their people as well. Yesterday it attacked those of us who came from Asu'a to look on it, killing several of our company and wounding more."

Enazashi might have been expected to show surprise or utter some words of comfort or sorrow. He did not. "So you come not on behalf of your parents, but as advocates for mortal men? I suppose that is no surprise. Shall I tell you what those mortals said when they first came to me with their demands?"

Hakatri looked surprised at the abruptness of this but only nodded his head. "Of course, Lord Enazashi."

"When my messenger told them I would not send an army of our folk to face this swamp-worm, they replied to my servant, 'Then we will go to Asu'a and hope to find a kinder reception from the king and queen of your folk.'" Enazashi leaned toward my master, eyes bright and shoulders hunched so that he looked more than ever like a bird of prey. "Is that how your parents style themselves now, young Hakatri? As king and queen of the Zida'ya?"

"You know that is not so, my lord. It is merely a misunderstanding between the mortal tongue and our own—nothing to do with Asu'a or my sires."

Enazashi straightened, pressing his back against the stone chair. "So, then, what brings you to me if it is not to demand I bend my knee to Asu'a and its rulers?"

"We came seeking your help, my lord. My brother—" Hakatri hesitated for a moment. "My brother and I rode to Serpent's Vale with a small company of hunters, not to fight the worm but merely to see it and learn more about it. But it set upon us by surprise in the marshy valley. Now we know beyond doubt that this creature is truly one of the Great Worms, deadly Hidohebhi, too huge and fierce for our small hunting party. We hope, with your help, to prevent it from taking more lives." He wove his fingers together in a ritual gesture of kinship I had not often seen.

"Taking more lives? It has not harmed any of my Silverhome people." Enazashi spoke calmly, but I could hear anger in his voice. "They are all safe here within the mountain. We have other ways in and out beside the Silver Way—you came by one yourselves, I am told—so we have no fear of this baleworm or anything else."

"Then you are a rare leader indeed, my lord," Ineluki said sharply. "To be so certain of his subjects and their safety that he does not mind having a dragon in his dooryard."

Hakatri gave his brother a swift warning glance before turning back to the master of Mezutu'a. "A Great Worm is an enemy to all living things, Lord Enazashi," he said. "Surely we can find common cause in destroying a creature that cares nothing about clans—or even whether its victims are mortal or immortal."

Enazashi's face now seemed to become, if anything, colder and more remote. "Common cause. A noble sentiment." He turned suddenly to the silent Tinukeda'ya on the stone bench. "Do you hear, Lord Kai? What do you think of that?"

For a moment Kai-Unyu raised his eyes to Enazashi's, then looked down again, waving his hand in a gesture I did not recognize.

"Lord Kai agrees with me," Enazashi says. "Yes, your 'common cause' is a very noble sentiment indeed—if sparing in how it has been applied in the past by the House of Year-Dancing."

"Insults," muttered Ineluki. "That is all this ancient tyrant will give us. We are wasting our time, brother."

"I do not understand you, my lord," Hakatri said quickly and loudly, perhaps to distract from his younger brother's whispering. "How have the rulers of Asu'a failed you? When has any call for aid from Silverhome ever gone unanswered?"

Enazashi gripped both arms of his chair as if to keep himself from leaping up. "When? Why, when the lands of M'yin Azoshai were given to the very mortals you came here to assist. Of course the creatures called 'men' went to Asu'a to beg help. Because it was your own grandsires who made them a present of those lands in the first place—lands which rightfully belonged to the Silverhome Clan."

At last I understood, though I am certain my master already knew the source of Lord Enazashi's bitterness. Long, long before I was born, one of the first and greatest of the Zida'ya, Lady Azosha, had made her home on the hill Enazashi apparently coveted. She was of Enazashi's clan, but there had never been much love between them; when the Great Ship came to rest in the place where Mezutu'a would later be built, she had left the rest of her kinsfolk behind to make her own way in the new world. Perhaps because of this, when she reached her final days, Azosha bequeathed her lands to the mortal folk of Hern the Hunter. When the Silverhome Clan disputed her right to do so, the matter came at last to my master's grandmother Senditu, who was the Sa'onsera in Asu'a at that time, to make the decision. Senditu held that because Azosha had made her home there before Silverhome was built atop the bones of the Great Ship that had brought them all, Enazashi's clan had no right to claim Azosha's land.

This dispute was already centuries old and I felt sure there was nothing my master or his brother could do to soothe Enazashi's bitterness. But a moment later a happier thought came to me. It would be useless for us to try to kill the Great Worm with so small a company, as my master himself had said. Since Enazashi clearly would not help, we would have no choice but to return to Asu'a.

One of the other Zida'ya near the lord's chair was speaking now. He was young, at least by the standards of the Zida'ya, but he spoke strongly. "Father, surely this old feud should not be allowed to affect a situation of real need. The worm is an enemy to all of us—"

"Silence, Yizashi," said his sire. "You are not the lord of this place yet, and if you would be so craven as to give up your birthright for nothing, you may never be lord of anything. I have made up my mind. We will treat these visitors from Asu'a with courtesy—our shared blood demands it—but I will not risk a single warrior in the pursuit of this monster. If it threatens the mortals who have usurped our lands, Lord Hakatri, then let those mortals help you warriors of Clan Sa'onserei to kill it." And with that he flattened his hands before him, signaling that the audience was over.

"What about Lord Kai?" my master asked. "He has not spoken."

The look Enazashi gave him was bitter, but a smile played across his lips. "Ah, of course. Jenjiyana's blessed legacy—my co-ruler." He turned to Kai-Unyu, who seemed to shrink before his gaze like a piece of meat on hot stone. "Do you agree, Lord Kai? Does my decision meet with your satisfaction?"

For a long moment the Tinukeda'ya did not look up or meet his eye. At last, in a voice so quiet that only those of us near the Shard could hear him, he said, "Yes, Lord Enazashi." His words might have been the rustle of blowing leaves.

"There. Are you satisfied now, young Hakatri?" Enazashi demanded. "All has been done just as your ancestors of Year-Dancing House intended. The rulers of Mezutu'a are in perfect harmony." He rose then, and though he swayed a little at first, he waved away his son's help. "I still have a few Great Years left in me," he said. "I do not need to be propped up, nor do I need to take lessons from my own child." Enazashi clutched his robes around him and made his way slowly across the Site of Witness, his courtiers following behind him. His long legs and halting gait made me think of a shore bird stepping through the surf. The lord of Mezutu'a held his proud head high until he had passed out of the great chamber and we could see him no longer. A few moments later two Zida'ya guards mounted the daïs and led the one called Kai-Unyu out of the Site of Witness as well. With a guard holding each elbow, I thought he looked more like a prisoner than a monarch.

"What was the meaning of all that?" I asked my master later. "I understand that Enazashi is angry with your parents over the mortals, but who is Kai-Unyu?"

"I wish you would not ask me, Pamon," he said. "It shames me to have to talk about it. And we are awaited at the table." Hakatri and his brother were being hosted in one of the great houses of Silverhome for the night— not all the nobles of that city were as sour toward the Year-Dancing Clan as their lord. The master of this particular house, Lord Gondo, had sent splendid suits of clothes for my master and Ineluki, though not for me.

At another time I might have given way to my lord's reluctance, but the strange spectacle I had seen take place before the Shard had confused and disturbed me. "Please, master. Explain to me."

He sighed. "You know of the Parting, where Utuk'ku's Hikeda'ya and our Zida'ya separated themselves from each other."

"Of course, my lord," I said, although as with many bits of Zida'ya history, I knew it because of what others had said, not because I had studied it myself.

"At that time Jenjiyana, my great-great-grandmother, gave your Tinukeda'ya people mastery over three of the Nine Cities—"

My astonishment was so great that I actually interrupted him. "My people, my lord? The Nightingale herself gave the rule to my folk?" I had never heard this, had never even dreamed that my people might have once been set so high in the world.

Hakatri nodded. "Yes. It was agreed at the Parting that they would rule over Mezutu'a, Hikehikayo in the north, and the island city of Jhiná-T'seneí. But Jenjiyana's decree—well, things did not go as she had hoped."

Jhiná-T'seneí, the City of the Column, had vanished beneath the southern seas long before I was born, thrown down in the great earth-shake that had also demolished fabled Kementari, but the other two cities still existed—we were in one of them. "What happened, Master?"

He was clearly reluctant to go on. "It is a sad and, to me, shameful story, Pamon. In Hikehikayo the Tinukeda'ya were opposed from the first by Hikeda'ya loyal to Utuk'ku, already styling herself a queen. Their attempt to throw down the Tinukeda'ya leaders failed—barely—and most of the Hikeda'ya left for Nakkiga, Utuk'ku's throne city. Today there are only a few of our folk left there, and the city is much diminished from its heights."

"But the other two?"

"Jhiná-T'seneí did better, and the Tinukeda'ya there ruled with the cooperation and help of both the Hikeda'ya and Zida'ya. Then the great calamity befell them and the city was lost."

"You have not told of Mezutu'a yet," I said.

"Because that is the hardest, most unpleasant tale," he said. "To put it as simply as possible, the Zida'ya here in Silverhome never fully accepted Jenjiyana's ruling, and when Enazashi inherited rule of his clan from his father, he seized power back from the Tinukeda'ya."

Again, I was shocked. "Against Jenjiyana's wishes?"

"The Nightingale's spirit had gone back to the Garden by then, and though my foreparents made clear they did not support Enazashi's seizure of power, their only true resort would have been to take up arms against him—against their own kind."

I fell silent. The unfairness of it seemed beyond understanding. "You are saying Asu'a did nothing to stop this?"

I heard a little heat in my master's voice. "They did not ignore it, Pamon. Their protests forced Enazashi to set up the former Tinukeda'ya ruler as a second monarch, but that was no more than a sop—Enazashi does not share his rule. Mezutu'a's Tinukeda'ya wield no power and are scarcely consulted."

I recalled the sad, defeated look of Kai-Unyu, and I understood: Worse even than being powerless was having it proved again and again in front of all Silverhome. I was silent as I helped my master dress himself in the finery Lord Gondo had sent.

Any other night, I think, I would have been quite willing to sit and watch the gathering of Mezutu'a's nobility, but that evening I was restless and angry, though I did not entirely know why, and even gossip of outstanding quality did not much tempt me.

My restlessness grew, and at last, when the banquet had all but ended, I went to my master's side and quietly asked his permission to go out walking in the city.

"Of course, Pamon," he said. "Remember that we will leave again early in the morning." He paused for a long moment then said, "But I caution you not to go into the part of the city nearest the mines, where the Tinukeda'ya live."

"Why, my lord? Have you forgotten that I am Tinukeda'ya too?" It was an extraordinary thing for me to speak that way to my master, but I was troubled in a way I had never been before.

"Of course not," he said. "But it can be dangerous sometimes."

I had certainly never heard of a part of our home in Asu'a or any other great city called dangerous before. On any other night I would have stayed far away, but in that strange, unsettled mood I felt almost defiant. I found out where the mines were from one of the other servants—a youth of my own folk, who also warned me to stay away—and then deliberately set out in that direction.

I was so wrapped up in my frustration with what I had heard about Enazashi and the onetime Tinukeda'ya rulers of Silverhome that I hardly noticed my surroundings as I walked through the high-ceilinged thoroughfares of the underground city. I later learned that, to add to the shamefulness of Kai-Unyu's treatment, Mezutu'a had been almost entirely built by the first generation of my own people who reached this new land.

Many Zida'ya of lesser rank were out on the wide boulevards, but they seemed little different to me than the nobles at the banquet I had left behind, full of merriment as they crowded the drinking-places and public squares beneath the stone-lights. Few of them seemed to notice me, which deepened my bleak mood. I did not know much about my master's

ancestors beyond their names, but I knew Amerasu and Iyu'unigato as well
as I knew my own parents: it hurt my heart to think they would allow
such a crime against my folk to go unpunished. I had always known them
to be kind and honorable, especially Lady Amerasu, and I knew my master
to be the same, but that did not excuse the injustice I had seen. No matter
how I turned it over and over in my mind, I could not find a satisfying explanation.

So caught up was I in these thoughts that I did not notice at first that
the stone-lights were becoming farther and farther apart, though here and
there a torch burned in a sconce at the place where two streets came together. Even the taverns had different signs, marked not with the Zida'ya
runes I could read but in symbols I did not recognize. As I stood in the street
before one of these shadowy inns, looking absently at a handful of young
Tinukeda'ya males who huddled outside the door, I felt someone tug at my
sleeve.

Suddenly aware of my own obliviousness, I looked down to see a young
girl of my own race with a dirt-smudged face looking back at me. She said
something, but I could not understand her and said so.

"Don't go there," she said in clumsy Zida'ya speech.

I looked at the tavern. "I wasn't going to. Why?"

"They hurt you."

She was staring at the clutch of young Tinukeda'ya outside the tavern,
so I asked, "Do you mean those fellows? Why would they hurt me? I am
Tinukeda'ya too."

She shook her head. "Not those clothes."

"What do my clothes have to do with anything?"

"Stand-up clothes," she said, tugging at my sleeve again. "Tall Folk clothes.
You go now."

And as she said it, the group of male Tinukeda'ya began to make their
way across the street toward us. It was much darker here than near Lord
Gondo's great house, but even by the light of the single torch I could see
that they all looked strange, hunched and crooked, many of them bent so
badly their backs might have been broken.

"Go," she said even more urgently. "Get hurt if you stay."

The look on the young males' faces quickly told me that she was correct, though I still couldn't understand why. I turned and walked hastily back into the center of Silverhome and the safety of Gondo's palatial house.

As I waited for my master there, I began to understand what had happened. My clothes, the girl had said—"tall folk" clothes. She meant that I was dressed like the Zida'ya nobles, which seemed ridiculous to me, since I was still wearing the tattered garb I had worn trudging through mud and tangling undergrowth after Vinaju. But to the little girl—and the mob of young males—I was dressed like one of the masters, not like the bent and broken underlings who had doubtless become that way working in the mines of Mezutu'a.

My own people had seen me as an enemy, I now understood. Only the kindness of a child had saved me from a beating or worse.

When my master at last left the banquet hall he found me waiting outside, but though I rose to go with him, I stayed silent as we made our way to our night's lodgings in the uppermost floors of our host's high stone house. I could not sleep for some time after I was abed.

Hakatri must have found a Witness to use in Lord Gondo's house, for he told me the next day that he had spoken with his mother, Lady Amerasu. I did not learn what she had said—it was not my place to ask—but the look on my master's face suggested it had not been a happy conversation. He would have told her about those who fell in Serpent's Vale, of course, which must have been hard for both of them. He did not know, of course, that worse news was to come soon.

When the next day dawned in the world outside, marked in Mezutu'a by the tolling of the famous Gathering Bell, we made our way back down to the Old Gate and across the underground lake. It was not pretty Vinaju who ferried us back through the Fernlight Passage this time, but a male youth of the Skyglass Clan. On our return, we shared a meal in Lady Vinadarta's dwelling with Tariki Clearsight and the other survivors of Serpent's Vale, then my master and his brother rose to say farewells, because Tariki and the rest were setting out for Asu'a. Lady Vinadarta came out with many of her clansfolk to bid them a good journey.

Tariki took my master aside as the rest of the party mounted for home, his usually sunny face clouded with worry. "I beg you once more, my friend," he said, "leave Ineluki here while this stubborn idea overwhelms his thoughts. The lake-folk will look after him, and later we can bring back enough warriors from Asu'a to be sure we can kill the cold-drake."

Hakatri shook his head. "You do not know my brother as I do. When he is in a mind like this, he is liable to do anything. Do you recall the time in his youth that he swore he would fight Lord Kuroyi over some innocent japery Ineluki took as an insult? I will always be grateful that the tall rider would not raise his blade against one so inexperienced, because I do not doubt my brother would have been badly hurt at Kuroyi's hand. No, Vinadarta and all her folk would not be able to restrain him in one of his fell moods. I must stay while this dark oath hangs over him—over all of us—to keep him from some fatal foolishness. Because of this, I beg you, old friend, to assure my wife that I now take her forebodings very seriously, and that I will be careful."

"I do not think Lady Briseyu wishes to hear such important words from me instead of yourself."

"That cannot be helped."

Tariki sighed, a rare open show of unhappiness. "So nothing can change either Ineluki's mind to remain, or yours to stay with him."

Hakatri shook his head. "I have not yet seen any way to solve this puzzle my brother has set for me, old friend. But I have not given up hope."

Tariki made the gesture *regretful parting* before vaulting into his saddle. "Then I pray that the Garden that waits for us all is not greedy for the company of Year-Dancing House's two young masters, dear comrade. Farewell!"

Prince Cormach had satisfied himself that his wounded Hernsmen were recovering with the help of the Skyglass Lake healers, and now he, too, was making ready to leave the rippling walls of Vinadarta's settlement. For a moment, as he looked at Hakatri, Cormach's face changed in the swift way that mortals have, expressions coming and going like the wind setting ripples onto water. "You came to help us when you did not need to do so, Lord Hakatri," he said, "—and Lord Ineluki too, of course. We Hernsmen will not forget that. I wish you luck, though I fear you will need more than that."

Lady Vinadarta stepped forward. "You know I am troubled by this dangerous oath of Ineluki's that somehow commands you both, Hakatri of the Year-Dancing." She saw the younger brother scowl. "I can only speak honestly, young lord, whether it troubles you or no—but I beg you not to scorn my counsel. I wish no harm to come to either of you, for the sake of your parents and our people. If you are truly determined to face the Great Worm again without waiting for assistance from Asu'a, then I beg you go and speak to Lord Xaniko of Ravensperch. He is one of the few living folk who know about the killing of dragons."

"Xaniko of the Hikeda'ya?" Ineluki was not happy with this suggestion. "The one called 'the Exile'? What use could he be, that we should go to him like beggars? He crudely insulted our father once. In truth, he insulted the entire court of Asu'a during a single audience and was driven out, never to return."

"He has insulted many more than that, I am told," said Lady Vinadarta with a wintry near-smile. "And not just those of our clans, but also his own Hikeda'ya folk, many times over—even Queen Utuk'ku herself. That is why he is called Exile and can never return to Nakkiga."

"Your pardon, Lady, but I think this advice is foolish." Ineluki waved a dismissive hand and walked away.

The mistress of Skyglass Lake shook her head. "It is up to you, then, Lord Hakatri, to decide whether my idea is worthwhile. Xaniko makes his home in the northern end of these very mountains, in his high fortress on a peak named the Beacon. My own people know the place and avoid it— we do not trouble him and he does not trouble us."

"We Hernsmen have taken much the same path with him, my lady," said Prince Cormach.

"And that is wise," she said. "But you, Lord Hakatri, may wish to risk the Exile's anger. If anyone can offer you wisdom about dragons, it will be Xaniko. There is no one alive who knows more about the ways of worms and the killing of them."

"Thank you for this counsel, Lady." My master bowed. "I promise I will give it much thought."

"Then good fortune to you both." Vinadarta left us then, her people falling in behind her.

"I mourn your losses as much as my own," Cormach told Hakatri. "My gratitude again for your aid."

His words clearly discomforted my master. "Do not credit me with anything more than looking out for my headstrong brother, young prince. So far, we have done nothing to solve the problem that brought you to us."

"That is more than a problem," said Cormach. "That is a dragon. One of the old and fatal ones, too. But perhaps a day will come when we will be able to hunt it together again, with better success."

"Perhaps that day will come sooner than you think," said Hakatri. "If so, I will come to you at M'yin Azoshai."

"We call our country Hernsland now." Cormach reached out and clasped my master's arm, surprising Hakatri a little: no other mortal man had been so easy and open with my master or his folk, at least during my time. "And as long as I live, you and your brother will always be welcome there."

My master thought Lady Vinadarta's advice good, but Ineluki did not, though he could suggest no plan of his own. Because of this uncertainty we rode only a short distance that day, as far as the crossing where the road to Skyglass Lake met the Westwood Track that followed the line of mountains, then stopped to settle on the direction for our journey from there—north toward Xaniko's high castle, or south toward the Silver Way and Serpent's Vale.

Ordinarily nothing would have been more important to me than this debate between the brothers, but I was troubled that day by many things. The scene at the Site of Witness had bothered me deeply, like a sliver that had worked its way under my skin and could not be forced out again. Then, only that afternoon, Lady Vinadarta had wished the two brothers good fortune without mentioning or even looking at me, as though I were no more than a beast, a horse or hound. Enazashi was one thing, a sour old tyrant, but Vinadarta was known as a wise, kind ruler. Was I invisible? Had I unwittingly done something to offend her? Or was I simply not worth acknowledging?

No matter how I turned these questions over in my mind I could make nothing useful of them, so I did my best to push them away. But turning my attention to the brothers' conversation did not bring me much cheer, either.

Hakatri was still begging Ineluki to take back his ill-conceived oath, though he and I both knew that such a thing would never happen. When he could not convince his brother to forswear himself, my master insisted they should seek out the Hikeda'ya exile Xaniko, as Vinadarta had suggested.

"What good could such a one do us?" Ineluki demanded. "No one has seen the Exile since he left Nakkiga in a fury. Everyone says that he is half mad, that he wants nothing to do with any of the folk of the Garden, Hamakha *or* Sa'onserei."

"I care little what everyone says," Hakatri replied. "I care only about what Xaniko *knows*. He was the last of our kind to kill a worm with his own hands. If you are so determined to honor this hasty pledge of yours—a rope that will drag at least me along with you, if not many others—then we must learn what we can about a worm this large and deadly. As long as your stubbornness and your ill-advised oath keeps you from returning home—and my own duty prevents me from leaving you—we have no choice but to seek for a way to destroy the Blackworm."

"Do not shame me with talk about your duty," said Ineluki bitterly. "If you insist on making my oath your own, how can you fault me? And in any case, what secret knowledge can there be to killing a worm that no one knows except a minor Hikeda'ya noble who was driven out of Nakkiga?"

"The trick of staying alive, for one thing," Hakatri said, his fury only a little less than his brother's, though he spoke in a more restrained tone. "You saw it, I saw it—that creature in the vale is so long it could not dip all of itself at once in the Pool of Three Depths. But you refuse to return to Asu'a, where the memories of our people, both living and dead, could be searched for answers, where we could find others to help us hunt the beast. What choice do we have but to ask the Exile?"

"I do not need—"

My master did not let him finish. "*You* do not need. *You* do not want. Do you know any other words, brother?" I have seldom seen Hakatri so angry. "Why do you think we are here at all? Why does your beloved Yohe—and a half-dozen more of our folk—lie unburied in a foul swamp? Because you thought only of yourself—of *your* anger, *your* pride."

"Do not chide me with their deaths, brother." In that rage-filled voice I also heard a despair more agonizing than I had guessed. "Make no mistake—I know whose fault this is. I know why those good folk are dead. What do you think drove me to that oath if not the knowledge of

my own terrible fault? But no one else needs to suffer because of my shameful, careless decision to seek the worm—not you, not Tariki Clearsight and
your other friends, none of you. This burden is mine alone. And I do not
need one of the Hikeda'ya to advise me, either."

"Then you are a fool," Hakatri said bitterly.

"That is fair enough," his brother said with a crooked smile that made
me turn away, so painful was it to see. "I have often lived as one, as you
yourself have many times pointed out. It seems only proper that I should
die one as well."

Their quarreling went so long that I fell asleep, then woke again in the
darkest hours of the night in time to hear the resolution: Ineluki still
would not take back his oath, but Hakatri won the argument about asking
help from the renegade Xaniko. This reassured me a little: I had often seen
their disagreements resolve this way. In fact, I think Ineluki often preferred his brother to be the one to decide what actions they should take so
that he was free to argue for whatever brave, vengeful, or foolish thing he
wanted, knowing that it would be Hakatri's more cautious approach that
would win in the end. But as they both knew that night—and I knew, too—
it was still Ineluki's angry, poorly considered pledge that would drive us on
to whatever fate awaited us.

In the morning's light the three of us set off, riding north. We followed
the Westwood Track as it wound along the foothills of the Sunstep Mountains, which loomed over us like a great thunderstorm frozen against the sky.
We were headed for the northernmost peak of the range, called the Beacon.
Though the season of renewal had begun, it had not quite reached this part
of the world yet. The skies were gray, full of brief but cold rain showers, and
the wind could not seem to make up its mind which direction to blow. No
matter how I adjusted my cloak, I always felt a chill.

We stopped the first night in a glen that reminded me of Serpent's Vale,
though the main likeness was in the lonely silence that hung over the spot.
Even the reassuring stars were hidden by the all-shrouding mist. Ineluki's
oath and what might come from it weighed heavily on all of us. The brothers scarcely spoke after we stopped for the night but sat staring into the fire
long after I finally dropped into fitful sleep.

We rode several more days, usually in silence, the stark shapes of the mountains looming always at our left, until we reached the farthest end of the range.

The northern heights of the Sunstep Mountains are rocky and steep, and except for the endless fields of heather and moss and bracken that cloak them are mostly bare but for a few trees on the highest slopes. Fogs rise out of the ground, but not far, hanging close to the slopes. We often rode through murk so thick I could see nothing beyond the brothers' horses in front of me. As we reached the last cluster of peaks, the Beacon tallest among them, we turned onto a smaller road that wound steeply uphill. Our horses had to tread carefully to avoid the deep ruts left by wagon wheels.

My master told me that watch-towers with great signal fires had once stood at the top of the mountain, raised by the first Zida'ya to travel into those empty lands. These earliest settlers had built their guard-posts at the time the first mortal men began to cross over from the unknown west, but their early redoubts had long since crumbled away. After a long absence, a succession of both Zida'ya and Hikeda'ya nobles had rediscovered the spot and made homes for themselves near the peak, even as mortal men spread across the moors below. Most of these immortals did not care much for company, I suppose, although not always for such obvious reasons as the Beacon's current master. Still, despite the dreariness of its weather and its great isolation, this part of the world has a strange, raw beauty that has never quite let go of me since that first journey.

I did not know much about Xaniko sey-Hamakha, the infamous Hikeda'ya noble we were on our way to see, except that he was a distant relative of Queen Utuk'ku. (She has lived so very, very long after the death of her only child that all of her living relatives are distant.) But I learned more about him later on. Xaniko was infamous among his own people for something they called the "Exile's Letter," a long and complex poem he had written before he left Nakkiga. It was forbidden to Utuk'ku's subjects to possess that poem, to read it, or even to mention it, but that had not prevented it becoming known by many among both Keida'ya tribes, Hikeda'ya and Zida'ya—especially my master's folk, who did not have to fear execution for acknowledging its existence. Xaniko's poem spoke of living in a corrupt court under a ruler who had once been fair and good, but who had descended into vengefulness, and cruelty. Although this ruler was never named in the poem and the setting was clearly fanciful (perhaps because Xaniko still felt some small sympathy toward his Clan Hamakha kin) no one doubted who was being denounced, and the Exile escaped the stony fastness of Nakkiga only a short hour ahead of the Queen's Teeth guards sent to arrest him. After wandering for many years and being rejected by my master's people as well, Xaniko at last settled atop the Beacon, rebuilding an ancient castle now known as Ravensperch. He had married, too, a matter of much talk and gossip among my master's folk, though as we rode up the winding way into the heights I did not know why his choice of a bride so fascinated the Zida'ya.

As we climbed higher and higher up the mountain I had trouble filling my lungs, though Seafoam, as always, seemed tireless. We passed a few farms perched on terraces along the mountainside and saw animals pastured in many of the high meadows, but no sign of the mortal owners, as if visitors were not just a rarity in that high country but something to be feared. The gloomy sky and the mists that clung to the hillside muted all the colors, and it was hard not to feel we rode through an alien world that did not care for us.

Ravensperch Castle stood, square and spare, on a high promontory where the earliest tower and its warning beacon had once stood. The castle's empty black windows looked out over the somber meadowlands that blanketed the mountain's foot; its slate roof tiles gleamed with rain even in the dimness of late afternoon. I only realized later that the castle seemed positioned to watch especially for enemies from Nakkiga in the north, Xaniko's old home. But Ravensperch seemed to fear not just enemies but any visitors at all, hiding itself from the world with only a single main tower standing above its featureless walls of dark stone, like a suspicious face peering over a gate. A few armored guards stood atop those walls, the first creatures like ourselves that we had seen in some time, watching us in silence as we rode toward the gates.

To my surprise, the soldiers who stepped out of the gatehouse were mortals. After the brothers presented themselves, they made us wait for no little time, then the portcullis was raised and we were allowed in. The gateyard was narrow and as unornamented as the walls; the tall, stone-faced tower of the keep looked no more inviting.

A small troop of soldiers conducted us to the door of the great hall.

When it opened, we were greeted by what I first thought must be a noble-woman of the Zida'ya. It was only as I drew close to her that I saw the color of her skin, a much paler gold than Hakatri's or Ineluki's, and realized she was not of either clan but was instead one of my own Tinukeda'ya folk. Her gown was modest homespun, but she carried herself like a great lady; I could not take my eyes off her. Something about her even reminded me of my master's mother, Lady Amerasu—not the woman's features so much as her calm self-possession.

"Enter, Lord Hakatri and Lord Ineluki," she said. "Be welcome, guests. I am Sa-Ruyan Ona, mistress of this house. My husband will come down to you soon." She smiled—it almost seemed as though she directed that smile at me, though I knew I must be mistaken—then gestured for us to follow her into the dark, modest hall. When we were seated, she sent servants to fetch us refreshment. After we had been served with food and wine she told us she had pressing tasks to see to, but that her husband would join us very soon. Then, to my surprise, she looked straight at me and said, "You, too, are most welcome here, fellow Child of the Garden. *Din so-nosa beya Vao-ya ulluru.*"

I had no idea what those last words meant. I could only stare in con-fusion as she walked away.

Ineluki turned to my master, saying, "I had heard the Exile took one of the Ocean Children for a bride, but I thought it only another fanciful tale. Still, she is pretty enough. I would not chase her from my bedchamber."

Hakatri frowned. "We are guests, brother."

Before Ineluki could reply a very tall figure appeared in the inner door-way of the hall, accompanied by several soldiers. Ineluki jumped up—he might even have closed his fingers around the hilt of his sword—but Haka-tri put a hand on his arm.

"Greetings, Lord Xaniko," my master said, rising and bowing. "My brother and I thank you for your hospitality and your time."

"All I have offered you so far is bread and salt," the newcomer said in a deep, slow voice. "Whether I give you anything else depends on what you have to say."

Xaniko was one of the tallest people I have ever seen. The top of his white-haired head loomed a full handspan above those of my master and his brother, who were considered of good size among their own people.

Xaniko wore only black, and he had the deathly pale skin of all his Hike-da'ya clansmen. His snowy flesh looked so thin as to be almost translucent, suggesting advanced age, but his bearing was surprisingly youthful, his movements precise but graceful. He gestured for Hakatri and Ineluki to sit, but he remained standing. "So," he said. "Speak. Have you come to re-dress some wrong you think I have done your house?"

Ineluki made a sound that almost sounded like a laugh, but Hakatri ignored him, saying, "We have no interest in old slights and old griev-ances, my lord. We come to you because we were told you might be able to help us."

Xaniko looked at him as if with no real interest. "I doubt it, and I certainly have no desire to help any of the Sa'onserei, in any case."

"But this is not a matter of clans or houses," said my master. "This is a matter of concern for all living things. We seek your wisdom, Xaniko sey-Hamakha, because a Great Worm has come down into the lands south of here and has already taken many lives, mortals and Keida'ya alike."

Xaniko's lip curled. "It is amusing, in a way, how it is only when one clan wants something from the other that the old word *Keida'ya* is brought out and dusted off. But your folk and mine are not one people anymore, as you know, and I have no allegiance to either clan."

"So we have heard." Ineluki's tone made his brother squeeze his arm again, but Ineluki ignored him. "They say you call yourself the Exile and want nothing to do with either our clan *or* your own."

"What of it?" asked Xaniko, cold as his windy mountaintop. "I do not dwell in their lands or in yours, unless Year-Dancing House and its med-dling master and mistress have now declared this place to be their fiefdom. If we have already run out of things to discuss, you Zida'ya princelings should be on your way as swiftly as possible."

The way he said this made me look anxiously toward the soldiers still standing in the doorway. They too were mortals, which seemed strange to me, but they looked well-armed and strong and not afraid of even two Dawn Children as famed as my master and Ineluki.

"I beg pardon for my brother's unconsidered words—" began Hakatri.

"Do not apologize for me!"

My master went on as if Ineluki had not spoken. "—but as I said, we did not come here to air old grievances, Lord Xaniko. Hidohebhi has come down out of the north, and Lady Vinadarta of Skyglass Lake told us that you of all living folk would be most able to advise us how to deal with this beast."

"Not by brave charges or stirring songs," said Xaniko. "No, I have nothing to offer you Sa'onserei. Still, you may spend the night. The road down is too steep and treacherous even to walk upon at night."

"Thank you, Lord Xaniko. Go and see to the arrangements, Pamon," Hakatri told me.

The lady of the house was waiting in the chamber outside. I bowed to her and asked where I should put my master's things. She only looked at me for a long time, until I became dismayed.

"Yanum dok sin ro danna bir?" she said at last.

It was complete nonsense to me. "I beg your pardon, my lady, but I don't understand."

"I'm sorry," she said, but I found her expression odd and unsettling. "I asked, what is your name?"

"I am called Pamon, my lady."

"Not your family's name—*your* name."

I was surprised. Not even my master addressed me by anything other than my family name. "Kes, my lady."

"I apologize for staring at you, it has just been so long since I saw a male of my own kind. That was my people's tongue I spoke—your people's, too, since we are of the same kind."

"I confess I did not recognize it."

"But that is strange . . . Kes. Are you and the lords you serve not from Asu'a?"

"To put a finer edge on it, my lady, I serve Hakatri, the elder brother. But yes, Asu'a is our home."

"And do none of our people there still use the old tongue we Tinuke-da'ya brought from the Garden?"

I shrugged. "I do not doubt some do, Mistress. Certainly many Tinukeda'ya live there, but they do not speak much about old days and old things. As for me, I never learned any such things, and my parents, if they knew, did not teach me." I was uncomfortable and suddenly a bit ashamed by something that was no fault of my own. "I take it from what you said earlier that Tinukeda'ya are rare in this part of the world."

"In this particular part, yes. As you have seen, all our servants and guards are mortals—Sunset Children."

I was curious about that, so I did something rare for me: I asked her a question that a mere servant should not ask a noblewoman. "Was that by your choice, my lady?"

She shook her head. "No, that was my husband's doing. I think he did it for me, however. He thought I would not want to see my people forced to serve."

"And do you feel more comfortable with mortal servants?"

She made a gesture I did not recognize, though it stirred a dim memory. "There is no easy answer to that. And what of you, Kes? Are you happy in service to the Dawn Children—to the Zida'ya?"

I told her very firmly that my master had always treated me very well.

"That does not answer my question, but I do not wish to be rude," she said. "Let me ask it another way. Are you happy in your life?"

I found this astonishing. "Of course! I told you, I have been lucky beyond almost any of my kind—of *our* kind, my lady. As have you, it seems, if you will pardon me for speaking when it is not my place."

"Your place?" She laughed, which I did not understand. "Yes, I suppose I have done well for myself in this world—I have found a mate who does not despise my heritage. The rest of his kind are not so forgiving, though, which is why we live in this out-of-the-way spot."

"I am told that the Cloud Children banished your husband from Nakkiga."

"Yes, but your Zida'ya masters would not have us either, Kes. The people of my husband's clan and of your master's once could live together, but it was never truly accepted that either of them might marry one of *our* kind."

I did not know what to say. I had never considered such things, and until that moment I could not have imagined it. Why would one of the immortals want to marry one of my race instead of one of their own? "I know nothing about such things, my lady," was all I said.

"I have discomforted you, I fear." Her smile looked sad. "Still, I wish to ask you one more discomforting question—why do you serve Lord Hakatri and his brother?"

"Because they are good to me," I said, then amended it to, "Lord Hakatri has always been good to me." I do not know why I qualified my response. Ineluki had always treated me well enough—as well as he treated any of his inferiors, whether Zida'ya or Tinukeda'ya.

"Yes, but why do you *serve* him? Why is Hakatri the master and you the minion?"

Again, I did not understand her question. "Because we Ocean Children have always served the Dawn Children, since back in the Garden."

"Ah." She nodded. "And your master's Dawn Children revere the memory of the Garden. They celebrate the Garden even long after they left it behind." She leaned closer, a strangely intent look on her face. "But our people *were* the Garden."

Before I could even try to make sense of this, her husband Xaniko emerged from the great hall of the keep with my master and Ineluki. They seemed to be arguing.

"I owe nothing to anyone, but I owe less than nothing to the House of Year-Dancing," Xaniko said with a face full of bitterness. "In any hap, my days of struggling against the great worms are over."

"Have you lost your courage, then?" Ineluki's handsome face was flushed with anger, the gold of his cheeks suffused with a mild bloom of sunset red.

"Brother, I bid you be silent," said Hakatri in a voice soft but sharp. "Do not insult our host." It seemed that Ineluki would say something more, but a look passed between the two of them and the younger brother turned away. "Lord Xaniko," my master said, "forgive us. We have been discourteous, I fear. We do not ask you to join us. We want only your advice, your wisdom. You are known for your brave deeds, and the songs of your fight against the fire-drake called Snareworm say that you faced it by yourself and killed the terrible creature with only a witchwood spear. What can we learn from you?"

Xaniko looked at my master for a long, silent moment, then at Ineluki, who stood regarding a wall tapestry of birds and branches as though it were the most engaging sight he had encountered in a long time.

"Come with me," he said at last.

Hakatri signaled me to accompany them. Xaniko's wife bowed and went out.

We followed The Exile out of the keep and toward the stables where our horses were stabled with those of the household. For a moment I thought Xaniko would order us to take our mounts and go, but instead he pointed up toward the stable's high, slanted ceiling. In the rafters hung a great witchwood spear, as big around as my master's strong forearm and more than twice his height in length.

"Do you see the black stains along the shaft?" Xaniko asked. "Those are from the Snareworm's blood. I trow that if you handled the spear now, even after so many years, that dried blood would burn your flesh. That is why it is hung there, out of reach. And do you see how heavy the spear is, how thick?"

My master and his brother stared up at the long, dark thing. "It looks a mighty weapon," Hakatri said at last.

"It had to be. And even so, it was almost not strong enough. It bent like an archer's bow while I held it braced against the earth until the beast was close enough to spew its foul stench into my face before it died. I am only here because the Snareworm had no fire left to belch. But that did not keep it from burning me." He pulled off one of his gauntlets and held up his hand. It was misshapen, the white skin covered with ropy red flesh and the two smallest fingers melted together like candle wax. "A few drops of the dragon's blood did that—scorched through my mailed gauntlet as though it were the thinnest parchment. Witchwood will not burn at the touch of dragon blood, but all else will—including you."

"But still, you killed it," said Ineluki, looking at Xaniko's hand with more fascination than horror. "Surely that is all that matters. You killed the Snareworm. And if you help us, we will kill the Blackworm."

Xaniko shook his head. "The Snareworm was young and only ten paces or so in length. Even the great Hamakho Wormslayer himself could not kill Hidohebhi, golden Khaerukama'o's deadly progeny, with only a witchwood spear."

Ineluki, always full of feeling, cried, "But you yourself say you killed dragons with a spear! Surely Hamakho was greater than you!"

Now Xaniko again grew cold and calm. "Yes, I do not doubt it. But the Wormslayer was aware of many things which you are not, young Master of All Truth—and so am I."

Hakatri interposed himself between his brother and their host. "Then tell us what you know, please! Our people are in danger. Many around Silverhome and in the north have been killed by this beast . . . and not only our own kind. Many mortals like those who serve you here have suffered and died in this monster's jaws."

For the first time I saw the hardness in Xaniko's face soften, if only slightly, though his voice was still harsh. "Mortals? You would concern yourself with mere mortals?"

Ineluki made a noise of disgust.

"I would not stand by and see them destroyed by such a foul beast," said my master. "They are not our kind, but they have a right to live."

Xaniko looked at him so long I wondered if he would ever speak again. "Very well," he said at last. "I will tell you what I know. And the first and most important is this: What Hamakho and the other wormslayers back in the Garden knew, and what I know, is that when a worm is young the places between its scales are still tender. A sharp spear can pierce those places, especially if the beast itself drives against the spear with all its weight and strength. But as they grow, the dragons' hides become harder and harder until their armor is like bronze even between the scales." He gestured up toward the ceiling of the stable again. "Hamakho himself might have wielded that spear, but against a worm who has lived as many years as ill-famed Hidohebhi, it would have snapped like a dry twig and even the Wormslayer would have been worm food. So that is why all this talk is bootless. There is not a spear you could lift that would be strong enough to pierce its flesh."

With that, he turned and led us out of the stables and back toward the keep.

My master's people hardly sleep, although when they choose to do so—or are forced to it by some great exhaustion—they may sleep for a long time. But I am not of their kind: I sleep nearly every night. So, it was strange for me on that first night in Ravensperch to find myself so utterly unable to find rest. No single idea beset me, but rather many ideas—the murderous worm, Kai-Unyu shamed and mocked by Enazashi, the angry faces of the

bent and crooked Tinukeda'ya who had wished to harm me only because
I was dressed like my Zida'ya masters. Woven through all these memories,
like thread of a single but noteworthy color, was Lady Ona speaking to me
in a tongue I did not understand but which she said was my own. Each
time I drifted down into something like sleep, it was only a short while
before I again bobbed up into wakefulness in the small chamber.

After hours of such frustrations, I finally rose from the bed. I peered
into my master's chamber and saw that he was awake, reading from a pile
of scrolls that Lord Xaniko had given him. He looked up. "Pamon, have
you seen my brother?"

"No, my lord."

His eyes strayed back to the scroll. "If you see him, ask him to come to
me tomorrow in the morning. There are things he and I must discuss."

"I will, my lord."

Since my master had already returned to his reading and did not look
likely to need me for anything else, I went quietly away from the apart-
ments. Wrapping myself in my cloak, I climbed up the stairs past nodding
mortal sentries, headed for the top of the keep because I badly wanted to
stand beneath the sky and let my head clear. But as I neared the landing of
the uppermost floor I almost stumbled into two shadowy figures standing
so close that I feared at first I had disturbed a pair of lovers.

The larger figure turned toward me; I recognized Ineluki. A moment
later the smaller figure tried to slip away, but Ineluki moved to prevent it,
keeping himself between me and what I now took to be a female in an
embroidered cloak and hood—possibly Lady Ona herself. I was stunned
and alarmed by this thought and at first could not imagine what I should
do; but as I stared at her my master's brother moved again to keep her where
she had been. I was seized with the need to do something.

"My lord," I said loudly.

"What is it, Pamon?" Ineluki's words were flat and harsh. He looked
at me as he might look at a stain on his garment.

I did something I had never done before and have never done since: I
told a deliberate lie to one of my master's family. "Your brother urgently
desires to speak with you."

"Now? Truly?"

I could barely meet his gaze and had only the courage to nod.

Ineluki flicked his fingers in a gesture of annoyance, then turned away from the hooded figure and went past me down the stairs without a backward glance. When I turned, the female figure was already moving swiftly away down the hallway. She opened a creaking door and shut it behind her.

Not quite certain what I had interrupted, and sick with worry about what would happen when my master's brother learned of my deception, I made my way up to the roof of the keep.

The wind outside was fresh and strong. It had blown away the mists so that the stars shone fiercely. As I sometimes did, I wondered what the stars of the Lost Garden had been like. I knew many of their names, of course: my master's people talk about them almost as much as they do the stars under which we live now, in the way that the names of relatives both living and dead are mixed together in conversations about old family gatherings. I wondered if the Garden-star named Light of Joy had been truly as brilliant as the oldest Zida'ya claimed, or if fond memory had colored their recall in the same way my own memories of childhood were warmed and made into something sacred because it was now lost to me.

Something large and dark swept through the sky above me then, blotting out the stars where it passed and startling me so that I took several steps back from the tower rampart. It was not a winged dragon, as my weary, strained imagination had thought in that fearful moment, but only a large raven flying close above me. It landed a few paces away and strutted in a wide circle making disapproving sounds, then spread its broad wings, shook them, and flew across the tower top to one of the parapets at the far side. I could not see where it landed in the darkness, but I heard several other croaking voices and guessed it had joined others of its kind there.

I stood for a while listening to them until they had quieted, and then an even longer time enjoying the silence. The night air cooled my face and seemed to cool my unsettled thoughts as well, and my heart had just found its proper pace again when someone behind me spoke, surprising me so much that I jumped.

"Armiger Pamon. There you are."

My master's people can be as silent as shadows when they wish. Like a guilty child caught with a piece of stolen fruit, I was terrified to meet Ineluki's eye, but I forced myself to turn. "Yes, my lord?"

"Did my brother truly send you for me?"

"I thought so, my lord. If I was wrong, I can only beg your pardon—"

"He told me he wanted to see me tomorrow morn. Not tonight."

He did not sound as angry as I had feared. Something else seemed to have distracted him since we spoke on the stairs. "I can only offer my apologies, my lord. I must have misunderstood."

"No doubt, no doubt." His tone suggested he was not convinced. "But bide here awhile, Pamon."

After that, he remained silent for a long, worrisome time, so that I quailed inside at what might be coming. Ineluki seldom addressed me at all unless it was to give me an order or ask me a question about something Hakatri wanted or had said, so I could think of no reason he would keep me except to punish me for my interference.

"My brother . . ." he began at last, sounding oddly reluctant. "My brother cannot . . . Pamon, if you care for him, you must convince him to return to Asu'a."

I was astonished by this, that instead of raging at my interference on the stairs he should instead set me such an impossible task. "Me, my lord? That is not my place. You can speak to him that way, but me—?"

"No, I cannot speak to him that way," said Ineluki bitterly. "Do you doubt that I have tried? He will not heed me. He is determined to protect me from my own prideful foolishness."

"He loves you."

"That is not a reason for him to die."

I was shocked, chilled. I had never heard my master's brother speak in this familiar way, as if I were one of his own family, and it seemed an ill omen. "Pray do not even say such a thing, my lord!"

"There is no help for it—I can think of nothing else. Since I made that cursed oath, I have felt doom hanging over us."

"Then take it back, Lord Ineluki."

He laughed. It was not a pleasant sound. "It is nothing so simple. When you declare yourself to the powers that watch over our world—over all worlds—you cannot simply turn around again and say, 'I did not mean it. Forget my words.' Fate, or whatever name you choose to give those powers, has already heard you. Like a great millstone driven by a rushing river, the engines that force our actions have begun to grind and they cannot so easily be stopped again."

"But why do you fear for him—for my master? Have you walked the Dream Road and seen evil signs?"

By starlight, I could just make out Ineluki slowly shaking his head. "I do not need the Road of Dreams to see the signs—they are all around us. Look at this place! It is like the hall of Death itself beyond the veil. Black birds of ill-omen all around us, and this empty, blighted land—!" For a moment I thought I heard something like utter despair. "And as if to remind himself of the ultimate fate of all our kind, the master of this house has even surrounded himself with the mortals who will take our land from us one day."

"I do not understand you, my lord. The mortals?"

He turned to me, as if only just remembering that I was present in the flesh, not merely a voice in the darkness. "Yes, the mortals, Armiger Pamon. The creatures that will one day own this entire world for themselves. Surely you can see that as clearly as I can." He laughed harshly then. "After all, the elders say your race is rich in foresight."

"Perhaps so, but that gift has not been given to me." His words had turned my worry for myself into something sharper, colder. "And your brother may have gifted me with attention far beyond what I could have hoped for, but he would not listen to me if I told him to desert you. You know him, my lord. Once he has set his mind on something, that is that." *Like you, Lord Ineluki,* I thought, *though Hakatri does not come to such a place so easily . . . or so foolishly.* Still, at that moment, though I fiercely resented what Ineluki had done to my beloved master, I could not be angry with him: his regret over what he had set in motion was too clear. "Can you truly not take back your oath?"

Again Ineluki fell silent. "Go now," he said at last. "It was a mistake thinking you might understand." He made a curt gesture of dismissal.

As I turned back toward the stairwell, the ravens in their stony refuge croaked in sleepy voices.

A feeling like the thick-headedness of a fever rolled over me as I made my way down from the tower roof. If Ineluki himself could not change the course that fate would take, what had he expected of me? I wondered if he had spoken to me, not because he thought I could truly persuade his brother to turn his back and return home, but because in some way I would now share the blame for whatever happened. I made a prayer to our Garden then, sacred because it is both a place and an idea.

Watch over my master. Do not let him lose his life in this terrible, needless pursuit because of a single vain, dangerous oath. Do not let Hakatri die!

I often wondered in later days whether my prayer might have been to blame for what happened.

I had become a little lost in the dark keep, uncertain which floor housed my master's chamber, when I heard soft footsteps. Turning a corner, I found myself face-to-face with a small, slight figure in a hooded robe—the same I had seen before in the stairwell. Her pale face was only partly visible. Still thinking it must be the mistress of the castle, I dropped to one knee.

"Forgive me, my lady," I said. "I did not mean to intrude on you earlier. I was on my way to the roof."

"Ah, see!" she said. "It is my lord-errant returned!" It was not the voice of Sa-Ruyan Ona. "I thank you for saving me from a difficult position, sir."

As I stared at this stranger in surprise, I heard more footfalls behind me and turned to see Lady Ona herself approaching, dressed for bed but also wearing a heavy cloak—Ravensperch was a cold place at night. "So, I am not the only one who cannot sleep," she said. "Is this why you are so slow with your errand, Sholi?"

"I was hurrying back, my lady," said the other woman. "Then this fellow appeared out of nowhere and dropped down to his knees in front of me. He is quite the young gallant."

I realized I was still kneeling and rose. "My apologies, Lady Ona," I said. "I lost myself coming back from walking in the night air. Then I mistook this lady for you."

"Do you see, Sholi?" said Ona. "A perfectly reasonable explanation. Now, did you bring me some wine as I asked?"

"Yes, my lady," the other woman said. "The very last of the good red, I fear."

"We shall send for more when the next wagons come. Until then, we can make do with less noble vintages." She turned to me. "Will you take a cup, Pamon Kes? Sholi here will be with us—you need not fear for your honor or good name."

I was still shaken by my talk with Ineluki, but I could not easily think of a reason to turn down this kinswoman of mine, although in truth our first encounter had made me a bit fearful of her. That no doubt sounds strange, since she had said nothing to me that should have disturbed me much. Perhaps it was the sense that, since we had left Asu'a to seek Ineluki, things normally hidden—and sensibly so—had risen too close to the surface to be safely ignored.

I followed Lady Ona and Sholi down the hall to a retiring room. Ona lit the lamps with her own hand, then lowered the hood of her thick cloak to reveal her long silvery hair, let down for the night. Sholi vanished into the next chamber, but soon returned with three cups and an earthenware jug on a tray, which she set down on a small table. Then she shrugged off her own cloak to reveal a mass of loose, fair tresses. She was dressed in a thick sleeping robe with what looked like a fine nightdress showing its hem beneath it.

"As you have likely noticed," Ona said, "when it is the Hare's Moon here on the Beacon, it feels more like the Wolf Moon. My husband chose this place for its isolation, not its comforts."

"The cold has not troubled me," I told her—my second untruth of the hour. In fact, I had shivered through much of my conversation with Lord Ineluki, though not entirely because of the chilly air.

Lady Ona poured the wine and passed the first cup to me, the next to the young woman. I had a chance to observe this Sholi more closely now, and though I did my best not to make it obvious, it was hard not to stare at her. Where Lady Ona's features were fine, her nose prominent, her cheekbones and jaw so precisely defined she might have been of my master's people, Sholi was quite different. She had round cheeks, flushed from the first sips of wine (or perhaps from escaping the cold corridor) and her nose turned up a little at the end, which gave her a mischievous appearance. But at the same time, something in her wide-set eyes and pale golden complexion, not to mention her long, slender fingers wrapped around the cup, made me certain that this Sholi was Tinukeda'ya, just like Lady Ona. And just like me.

"You are correct," said Ona, as if she could hear my unspoken thoughts. "My lady-in-waiting is also one of the Ocean Children, like us. She is of the Tur Clan."

"Not precisely like you, my lady," Sholi said easily. She was a good deal younger than Lady Ona, that was clear from her skin and her speech, but she seemed to treat Ona as an equal. "My family are *Sha*-Vao."

I did not know the word. Ona saw my confusion, smiled, and gently said, "Our new friend Kes does not speak the old tongue, Sholi."

"Truly?" The surprised look she gave me made me freshly ashamed. "Forgive me, then. My people are of the Sea Watchers."

"Niskies?" I was more startled by this than she had been at my ignorance. This Sholi did not show the signs I was familiar with from the Sea Watchers I knew: her arms seemed no longer than mine or Lady Ona's, and I saw none of the usual roughness on her skin. "Are you from the south?"

Sholi laughed. "No, and glad not to be. Our people along the southern coasts are strange and inbred. My family is among the last of its kind still in the north. I come from the town of *Da-Yoshoga*—Goblin Rock."

I had heard of it, a good-sized settlement along the coast west of the Sunstep Mountains. In recent years, both the Zida'ya and Tinukeda'ya have largely been replaced there by mortal Hernsmen, and Da-Yoshoga has become a busy port town. The mortals call it *Crannhyr*, a name whose meaning I do not know, but it has always been a strange place where many sorts of folk came together and many kinds of trade took place—some less wholesome than others.

I felt out of my depth at first, to be sitting with these two, members of my own race though they might be. Of course, I was a resident of the great court at Asu'a, so I assumed that was the reason for their interest.

Instead, though, the two women seemed fixed on me. "Armiger Pamon rescued me from a bad moment," Sholi announced. "He spoke up to one of his masters who was paying me uncomfortable attention, which gave me a chance to escape." She turned to me. "It was not what it seemed, though. Lord Ineluki was asking questions about my lady's husband Lord Xaniko, and I did not think I should answer them. Your arrival was still most appreciated."

"Ineluki is not my master but my master's brother," I said. "In any case, though, you give me too much credit, my lady." I turned to Ona. "I merely gave Ineluki a message from Lord Hakatri."

"Yes, I think I heard them talking about it as I passed your master's room," said Lady Ona, smiling. "Hakatri was saying that the message was wrong, that he was not intending to speak to Ineluki this night."

"There!" said Sholi. "I was right. This Pamon is a true lord-errant, rescuing the innocent."

I was still so bothered by deceiving my master's brother that I could not much enjoy their banter. "Lord Ineluki can be heedless and contrary, but I am sure he meant nothing ill, Lady Sholi."

The mistress of Ravensperch turned to me. "Are you one of those who sees only good in others, Kes? That can be a kind of blindness that endangers you more than those you defend."

"I think you see altogether more things in me, Lady Ona—for good and for bad—than a life like mine warrants."

"So you did not try to help Sholi?"

I was uncomfortable. "Are you asking me to speak ill of my master's brother, my lady?"

She stared for a moment, her yellow eyes fierce even by candlelight. At last, she reached out and patted my hand. "Of course not. But on Sholi's behalf, I still thank you."

A little flustered by so much attention, I let the mistress of Ravensperch turn the subject to less complicated things, questions about Asu'a and its leading family.

"I have always wanted to meet the Sa'onsera, Lady Amerasu," Ona said. "I hear that even those who are not of her own Year-Dancing Clan call her First Grandmother."

"Was she truly born on one of the Great Ships?" asked Sholi.

"So it is said, and so I believe."

"And is she as wise as all the tales of her say?"

I smiled. "Here I will have no trouble speaking. I have never met anyone like her. Amerasu's patience, her wisdom, her love for her people—for all her kind, even Utuk'ku's Hikeda'ya folk—are all remarkable. To me, she is like the dawn itself. If you had never seen it, you would think the tales of its magnificence were exaggerated. But the first time you saw the night retreat and the sun rise, you would know you had not understood the truth until that moment."

Sholi laughed and clapped her hands. "My lord-errant is also a poet!"

Ona was again looking at me intently. "And is she as good to the Tinukeda'ya of Asu'a as she is to her own folk?"

"She has never treated me with anything but kindness and dignity," I said quickly.

"And your fellow Tinukeda'ya? How is she to them?"

I hesitated, since my first reply had been warmer than I might have wished. I thought carefully about what I had seen of Lady Amerasu's dealings with my own folk. "From what I have seen, she is as good to us as to her own kind. She was gracious with the mortal visitors as well—the mortals whose pleas for help started us on this journey."

"Ah, yes. Tell us more about that," said Ona. "My husband has barely spoken to me since you came, so what brings you here is still much a mystery. I know only that it has to do with a dragon."

Lady Sholi wrapped her cloak tighter. "I am not sure I want to hear about dragons—not in the middle of the night."

I begged her pardon, then did my best to relate what had happened since we left Asu'a, but I did not dwell too long or too deeply on the death and mayhem our company had suffered in Serpent's Vale. "That is why we came to your husband, the famous dragon-slayer," I finished. "My masters want to end the menace of the Blackworm."

"I cannot even hear that name without shuddering," said Sholi.

Ona patted her hand. "Then let us change the conversation. Tell us more about Asu'a, Kes. As you know, we do not hear much news in our mountain retreat."

I told them a few more stories about Asu'a and other places I had seen in my master's company but did not say much about the disaster in Serpent's Vale or Ineluki's pledge. The two women gave me the courtesy of listening attentively, and I even made Sholi laugh a few times, which was quite a charming thing to hear, a flurry of silvery notes like the splashing of a mountain stream. Once she laughed so hard that she had to reach out and clutch my arm for support. I found myself responding, both in my flesh and in my feelings, and could have happily remained longer in such pleasant company, but then I remembered my duties. I drank off the last of my cup, stood, and bowed. "Lady Ona, Lady Sholi, I thank you for your hospitality. My master usually rises early. If I do not sleep a little, I will be small use to him."

"Of course," Ona said. "Sholi, will you walk our new friend Kes to the door?"

"Certainly, my lady." She rose to accompany me. *A Niskie,* I thought as I watched her. *Does she think often of the sea? Long for it? Or is she like me, content with where she is and the life she has been given?*

As we reached the door of the retiring room, Sholi smiled and said, "My thanks again for your gallantry. I hope we will see more of you, Armiger."

I bowed once more and took my leave, though I was too enlivened by both the wine and the company to sleep for some time afterward.

We stayed at Ravensperch for several days. My master spent a great deal of time deep in conversation with Lord Xaniko. They even made drawings, as though working out the plan of a battle—which, I suppose, was exactly what they were doing.

Ineluki, as was often the case even at home in Asu'a, seemed to lose interest in the planning before too long and took his horse Bronze to ride the mountain paths instead. By the third day we spent on the Beacon he would be out from early morning until almost dark. Ineluki always had that streak of impatience. I think if he had been with anyone other than his brother, he would have insisted we leave, though it was his own ill-starred oath that had brought us to this isolated castle. But even in his strange mood he remained deferential to Hakatri.

As for me, I spent many hours over that span talking with kind Lady Ona and clever Lady Sholi. I could not guess what they liked about my company, but I was happy to provide it to them, since my master required little from me while we remained atop the Beacon.

"You must forgive me taking up so much of your time," the mistress of the house told me one day. "I love and honor my husband very much, but still pine for company. I knew Xaniko was of a solitary temperament even when I first met him, and I knew it even better by the time we wed, but I confess the solitude began to wear on me. In truth, it was Xaniko himself who suggested I invite Sholi to be my companion."

"Invite? I was all but kidnapped," Sholi said with a smile to show she jested. "But the Garden is my witness when I say I found life rather dull in my father's house and did not resist much."

I enjoyed my time with the two ladies very much, but there were still moments I felt myself to be at a disadvantage. I was never certain whether they actually enjoyed conversing with me or if I was an object of interest because Ona was fascinated—or frustrated—with my ignorance of our shared heritage. At first we spoke mostly of the simple things of everyday life at Ravensperch—trying to find a sunny spot for Lady Ona's garden, or Sholi's pampered cat Lambkin and his life-and-death battles against aggressive ravens. But sometimes Ona gave me little lessons about our Tinukeda'ya people and their long history, a history usually hidden beneath the shadows of our Keida'ya masters, both Hakatri's people and Xaniko's death-pale folk. Of course, my father had told me almost none of this, if he had even known it.

One day, as I told them of the way the Tinukeda'ya co-ruler was treated in Mezutu'a, I saw Ona's face grow somber.

"That is not the worst thing that has been done to our folk," she said, "but it truly is one of the most shameless. Enazashi could not simply push the Tinukeda'ya out, for many reasons—our people are too necessary to the mines and other things Silverhome needs—but Enazashi has made certain they have no power." The spark in her eyes looked dangerous. "You saw Kai-Unyu—that poor, gelded creature. He and his wife were once the leaders of our folk in Mezutu'a, but now they are nothing but Enazashi's puppets. Mark my words, a struggle will come one day, and I fear it will be a bloody one. You cannot hold a people down forever."

This kind of talk unsettled me, of course, and not least because I feared for the Tinukeda'ya of Silverhome. If such a struggle happened: Enazashi, I felt sure, would be remorseless in his dealings with any threat to his rule. But I also wondered what would happen if such unrest spread to Asu'a and other Zida'ya settlements. I did not think Tinukeda'ya were anywhere near strong enough to overthrow their masters, but I feared what such a struggle might do to the long bond between my folk and my lord's.

And what of me? I thought. *Surely I would have to side with my master's people if Hakatri and his kin were in danger. But against my own race?*

These thoughts disturbed me, and kind Sholi seemed to sense it. "Let us talk of something else," she said brightly. "It is a fine day. It seems a shame to waste it on such sad things. We could walk on the battlements."

Lady Ona waved her hand. "You go, dear Sholi. Take our new friend Kes out and let him breathe the air. I am tired, but I will join you later."

As I look back now, it seems clear that the two women were conducting a careful campaign, but as has, sadly, often been the case, I was slow to grasp the truth. In any case, Sholi and I were about to be alone together for the first time.

The day was bright, but the wind was still brisk, and our cloaks billowed as we walked along the walls. Below us lay the forested skirts of the Beacon, and beyond them the hilly meadowlands spread in all directions, lush with the greenery of Renewal.

"You look gloomy, Kes," Sholi said. "Are you downhearted about your master and his brother?"

I was still unused to being addressed by my own name, and it seemed even stranger from the lips of someone I considered above me in station. "I fear for them both, of course, Lady Sholi—and myself too, I suppose, since I am bound to my Lord Hakatri wherever he goes."

"Why?"

For a moment I could not understand the reason for her question, since the answer seemed so obvious. "Why?" I said at last. "Because I am sworn to him, of course. I am bound for life to his household. He chose me for a great honor."

"Being his servant."

"His Armiger." I felt a need to defend myself. "The first of our race ever to be given that privilege—to be treated almost like one of the Zida'ya themselves. I can never forget that." I was nettled she could not understand it. "And you? Could you leave Lady Ona?"

She gave me a hurt look, as though I had changed the rules of a game without warning. "She would be alone here if I did, with no one of her own kind to share her exile. Xaniko is a good husband in most ways, but he is also full of brooding silences that can last for whole seasons."

"So perhaps our loyalties are not so different," I said, and in that instant I still believed we were talking only about obligations to our benefactors.

Then, as we stood in the swirling breeze in that high place, she asked me, "So you owe your master everything, Kes—even your chance for some happiness of your own?"

Surprised by her tone, I looked at her and suddenly realized what I should have seen long before: Sholi was not merely interested in me because I was from Asu'a, a guest to their backwater castle who could tell stories of the great court.

A surge of feelings washed through me then, but they were as mixed as the convergence of several streams, some muddy, some clear. In the past, I had known a few women of my own race to look on me with favor, but always, I assumed, because of my rarefied position as Hakatri's squire. This seemed different. I was flattered and moved by Sholi's interest in me, of course, but also saddened, because I had told her the truth: I could not leave my master without betraying my honor.

Of course, callow as I was, I saw the contradiction even then. *The same sort of "honor" has thrown Ineluki and my master into terrible straits,* I reminded myself. *The same honor may kill all three of us in the end, and who knows how many more? And Sholi is bound by honor too, though of a slightly different kind.* But I only said to her, "The Garden does not always give us what we want in life, Lady Sholi."

After that we fell silent, both of us lost in our thoughts, both brooding over things that could not easily or happily be spoken aloud. Lady Ona did not come to join us, and at last we went down out of the wind.

"Are you learning much from Lord Xaniko?" I asked my master on the third night atop the Beacon. As might be guessed, I was hungry for distraction.

"Yes, I am, Pamon—about many things. He has a thousand stories to tell of the Hikeda'ya court, some that amuse, many that horrify."

"I was under the impression," I said carefully, "that we came here to learn about killing one of the Great Worms."

Hakatri smiled. "Oh, we have spoken much of that, do not doubt. In truth, I have learned what I need. I expect we will ride out tomorrow, so be ready before the sun drives the Heart from the sky. We will have a long ride back to M'yin—" he checked himself, "back to Hernsland."

"So we are going back there," I said, trying to hide my apprehension. "I will go to the castle kitchens, then, and see what I can get from them for our journey and afterward. How long will we stay among the mortals?"

"Long enough to kill a dragon, I hope." But though his voice was light, his statement hung in the air between us.

I could think of nothing to say at first, so great was my unease at the idea of hunting the worm of Serpent's Vale or even approaching that deadly spot again. "May the Garden keep you and your brother safe," was what I finally summoned. The past few days of rest and comfort had allowed me to pretend that we were only on another journey, another hunt, but my master and I both knew that was not the truth.

As I was finishing the last of my arrangements for our departure, I encountered Lady Ona—by accident, as it seemed. She was sewing in the antechamber outside the castle's main hall, and she rose as I passed through it. "Armiger Pamon Kes," she said. "I hear that you and the two Sa'onserei lords are leaving us."

I bowed. "So it seems, my lady."

"We have enjoyed meeting you." The "we" she spoke of must mean herself and Sholi, I guessed, since I doubted Xaniko would even remember me. "Perhaps we may hope to see you back at Ravensperch again one day." She tipped her head a little at that, as if looking to see something confirmed that she had only heard about.

I bowed, suddenly weary with my muddle of feelings. "If my master's service brings me back here, it would make me very happy, Lady Ona." This was not mere courtliness on my part. It had been a rare and pleasurable thing to be sought for my own company, not just because of my master's high name.

In the last hours of dark, one of Lord Xaniko's guardsmen brought my master an earthenware jar, handling it with exaggerated care, as though it contained some dangerous living creature. Hakatri put it in a leather sack and hung it on his saddle. He and his brother were both more silent than usual, as though neither had spent a restful night. A short time later we rode out into the dawning light, the evergreen trees of the mountaintop gleaming around us in the early sun like icicles turned upside down.

As we rode back along the edge of the mountains the brothers did not speak much, either to me or each other. I suspected they had fought again over Ineluki's oath. When we struck the wide Silver Way, we turned and followed it northwest. At the end of the day we reached the road that led to Snowdrift, Lord Dunyadi's house on Birch Hill, where a small group of my master's people had settled near the confluence of two important rivers, the Great Redwash and the Mountain's Milk. To our surprise, we found someone waiting there on horseback.

"It is my wife's sister, Nidreyu!" said Hakatri when he was close enough to see the rider's face, although at that distance she was still little more than a blur in a gray cloak to me. I could hear anxiousness in his voice and understood it immediately—he feared something had happened to his family back in Asu'a. Ineluki looked no happier to see her, although he and Lady Nidreyu had always been so close that many thought they would marry one day, though many who knew Ineluki's ways did not think that day would come soon. As Hakatri spurred ahead, his brother hung back, as if he knew already what Nidreyu wanted and was in no hurry to hear it.

"Greetings, Lady," Hakatri called as he reached her. "I hope you do not bring us bad news."

"No, no, you can ease your heart on that account," she told him, smiling—though I have seen happier smiles. "Your wife is well and so are your daughter and your parents."

"Thank the Garden for that. And your own father, Lord Ja'aro?"

"Well, too, though he complains often about the way the world spins," she said, "—not to mention the flaws of everyone born since ice took Tumet'ai." The father of Nidreyu and my master's wife Briseyu had been known in younger days as Ja'aro the Silent, but if the name had once been appropriate, he had long ago outlived it: as Nidreyu had suggested, Ja'aro had a word to say about everything, and most of those words were unfavorable.

"May I ask, then, what brings you so far from Asu'a?"

"Must I have a reason to visit good Lord Dunyadi and his clan?" she asked. "Although I confess I also brought a message to him from the Protector and Lady Amerasu." Her expression grew more guarded as she said this, giving a hint of the complicated feelings hidden beneath. Nidreyu was not an arresting beauty like her sister Briseyu, but she was handsome and graceful and extremely clever. She might have been young by the reckoning of the Zida'ya, but her witty tongue made her seem older, and I was not the only one in Asu'a who thought highly of her.

She looked up as Ineluki approached. He had not hurried. "And see!" she said. "Here is the very fellow who has been the subject of so much conversation in Asu'a of late." She smiled at him, but he did not look mollified. "Greetings, my lord. It is good to see you hale and hearty."

"It is good to see you, too, Lady," said Ineluki. "But I do not think I will like the message you bring."

"I am sure you will not. But let us not stand in the road like peddlers. Dunyadi sent me out to tell you that you are most welcome at Snowdrift, and that he would consider it an honor to shelter you for one night or many."

"Of course we will stop," said Hakatri, though his brother was shaking his head.

"One night, if we must." Ineluki could scarcely look at Nidreyu, which seemed strange to me. The last time I had seen them together, only a short time past, they had been constantly in each other's company, flirtatiously jesting and teasing like true lovers. Now a curtain seemed to have fallen between them. Nidreyu felt it too, I am certain, but she was not the sort to show her disappointment.

As we made our way toward Dunyadi's house in the hills, Nidreyu rode closer to me. "Well met, young Pamon," she said. "I hope you are well. I warrant you are half a hand taller since the last time I saw you."

I smiled. "I think you exaggerate, Lady Nidreyu—that or your memory is failing with your advanced age." She truly was older than me, but I was only teasing. Where her sister Briseyu was kind to me but never less than formal, Nidreyu had chosen early on to treat me more like a younger brother than a servant, which I had always enjoyed, even if it sometimes confused me as to how I should behave in return. But over the years of knowing her I had come to realize that she did not merely permit me to tease her in return, but actually seemed to enjoy it. I felt freer around her than I did with any other member of the Sa'onserei household, and I was relieved to see that even if Ineluki was treating her oddly, things had not changed between Nidreyu and myself.

Lord Dunyadi was the leader of the Birchwood Clan. He was related to the Sa'onserei, as were almost all the Zida'ya, though his connections were more distant than some, at least in blood. He and Lord Iyu'unigato had fought together against the giants in the days of the wars against those creatures, and he was considered both Asu'a's firm friend and an important ally, though his clan was small; in fact, Dunyadi's kindness and cautious wisdom were well regarded by all the Dawn Children. His house, Snowdrift, was a low compound with a single tall tower, set atop an eminence called Birch Hill. The house and hill took their names from the dense stand of tall white trees that surrounded it, which in leafless winter made it look as though the house's tower sat atop an immense pile of snow. The view from any of Snowdrift's windows is of white-barked trunks standing sentinel around the house. In autumn all the leaves turn bright yellow, so that it seems as if the last bits of the fading sun had stuck there to quiver in every breeze.

Once we had left our horses in the stable, we went to greet our host, and we found him seated in his spacious hall. It seemed to have more windows than wall, vast openings covered by the most finely woven netting I had ever seen, the crossing strands so slender that nothing but air seemed to stand between those inside and the swaying birches that surrounded the house.

Dunyadi the Ram waited on a raised platform covered with beautiful rugs. His daughter Himuna, the Birchwood Clan's high celebrant, sat by him, and they were surrounded by the Zida'ya nobles of Dunyadi's small court. Snowdrift's master was not as tall as most of his people, but countless stories told about how clever and deceptively gifted in the fighting arts he had been in his prime. In fact, there had been a time when many had thought him the chief swordsman of all the Zida'ya, although Dunyadi was the first to laugh and protest that even if it might once have been true, those days were long past. He also had that curious feature seldom seen among the Dawn Children since they left the Garden—a beard upon his chin. It made him look like something out of an ancient rendering, like Ekimeniso Blackstaff of the Hikeda'ya, Utuk'ku's long-dead husband. The Ram's beard was not full and shaggy like the whiskers of mortal men, only a wispy tail of hair at the end of his chin, but it made him different from almost all his kind.

"My lords Hakatri and Ineluki!" he cried merrily when he saw us, as if our visit were a complete surprise, which it could not have been if Nidreyu had been out waiting for us by the main road. "Come and be seated. Welcome to Snowdrift!"

"Yes, friends, welcome to our house," his daughter Himuna echoed with a graceful flutter of her hands—*doves alighting*, an ancient gesture of greeting. "It has been too long since you have guested with us, good lords."

My master and Ineluki made all the proper signs of respect, and then, along with Nidreyu, seated themselves cross-legged around the low table. I stood with Dunyadi's servers, though I do not doubt that the liberal master of Snowdrift would have allowed me a place nearer my master if I had wished. For a little while all seemed cheerful and ordinary, as Dunyadi told of recent happenings—an incursion by a giant, the struggles of a particularly harsh winter. The brothers shared tales of their own travels, although even a stranger might have noticed that they spoke about the things they had seen without ever mentioning why they were so far from home. Dunyadi was particularly interested in their stories of Enazashi, and of Xaniko the Exile and his castle atop the Beacon.

"I have wondered many times whether to send him an invitation," Dunyadi said after Hakatri finished describing Ravensperch.

"I would not worry much on that account," said Ineluki. "He would not come. He has turned his back on his own kind, but he shows even less interest in ours."

My master's face was placid, but I sensed a little annoyance in the way he clasped his hands together in his lap. "My brother might have seen more kindness in Lord Xaniko if he had spent more time in his presence. But I fear I must agree with him on one thing—I doubt very much that The Exile would accept an invitation or extend one in return."

"Too bad, too bad," said Dunyadi. "There is much to be learned from him, and I for one am eager to know more about what goes on among Utuk'ku's folk in Nakkiga these days." He took a sip of the sweet wine his servers had poured for all the guests—even I had a cup—and shook his head. "But I am sorry to hear you had a trying time with Enazashi. I do not know why he still bears such ill will toward Year-Dancing House. With all the Sunstep Mountains as his fiefdom, I think he attaches too much importance to M'yin Azoshai. After all, Lady Azosha was never part of his household, and her claim to those lands was never contested during her life."

"Perhaps that is why," Hakatri suggested. "I think it might be that he is still angry that Azosha made her own way and did it right beneath his nose."

"You may be right," said Dunyadi. "Did you meet his son, the one they call Little Grayspear? Unlike his temperamental father, I have heard only good things of him."

"Yizashi? He was there, but we did not get the chance to speak privily." I thought I could hear some impatience in my master's tone. "Lord Dunyadi, we thank you for your hospitality, but you must know we are here for a reason."

"Everyone knows," said Nidreyu, who had been largely silent.

The master of the house nodded solemnly. "I do, Lord Hakatri. But I saw no reason to ruin our happy reunion by stepping directly onto ground that is not, as you know, the firmest or most reassuring."

"The great worm Hidohebhi is only a few dozen leagues from your own doorstep," said Ineluki suddenly and with heat. "You must have known. You must have already pondered what to do if it came onto your lands."

Dunyadi made a vague gesture. "Of course. But we are a small settlement here on Birch Hill. We do not have the means to go looking for trouble."

Hakatri frowned. "But trouble is here, my lord. We have seen the beast and it is no hedgeworm or young drake that could be dispatched by a dozen well-armed warriors, or even a score. It is Hidohebhi of the old tales, huge and covered in armor black as night. This hall could not contain it."

Dunyadi considered, letting his eyes rove across the screened windows and the long beams of the roof. "A most terrifying creature, I have no doubt," he finally said. "All the tales about it are dreadful. And as you say yourself, it is not something that might be dispatched by even a score of well-armed fighters. So what do the two of you intend to do by yourselves?"

"Find others to help us," said Hakatri promptly. "Nor will we try to defeat the monster with main strength. Xaniko taught me a few things that may give us a chance against the worm. But we will still need help." My master paused, as if he had now come to the difficult part. "We will also need a witchwood tree."

Dunyadi's eyebrows rose. I think this was the first thing he had heard that had truly been new to him. "And will you return to Asu'a, then, to the sacred witchwood groves there?"

"Do not pretend," said Ineluki. "You have no doubt heard that I cannot go back there."

"Rather that you will not." The strong, cold undercurrent in Lady Nidreyu's voice could have swept an unwary person to his death. "Your pride will not let you."

Ineluki would not meet her eye. "There are worse things than pride."

"Said every proud creature about to meet a foolish death." She stared at him as if daring him to look back at her. He still would not.

"Please, my friends, no more of this strife." Dunyadi rubbed his hands together in the sign for *we seek accord*. "Things are difficult enough. If we talk only of our disagreements this will fall out badly. The lessons of the Lost Garden are always before us."

"Then tell us, Lord Dunyadi," said Hakatri, "what we can do to agree. Because we," he flicked a glance at his brother, "have sworn to destroy this beast before it kills more of our folk or the mortal men of M'yin Azoshai. Can you help us?"

Dunyadi shook his hand. "You know better, I think, young Lord Hakatri. There is no witchwood grove at Birch Hill nor has there ever been one. And your father Iyu'unigato has made it known that if I let you take any of my retainers it will damage or even destroy the old friendship he and I share. What would you have me do?"

"Stand up to him!" said Ineluki, and I thought he sounded more despairing than angry. "Our father is not a king like the mortals have, or even a self-professed monarch like that ancient witch Utuk'ku. I have always been told you were one of the bravest of our folk."

"This is not a question of bravery." Dunyadi did his best to keep his voice even. "This is a question of intruding between parents and children. It is not up to me to decide whether Protector Iyu'unigato is right or wrong." Now he spoke directly to my master. "I beg you to hear the wisdom in what I say. A war between a son and his sire can have no winner. Go back to your father and mother. Your argument is with them, not me."

"The only argument here is between Lord Ineluki and his own stubbornness," said Nidreyu.

At that, Ineluki abruptly stood. He made only the shadow of a bow then left the hall. Within moments we could see him passing between the white trunks of the trees outside, walking alone. He did not look back at the great house.

"Forgive my brother, Lord Dunyadi," said Hakatri. "He knows as well as the rest of us that he has trapped himself with this terrible oath, but he does not know a way to step back from it."

"Simple," said Nidreyu. "He can say, 'I renounce my oath' and have done with it. Then the lords of the Zida'ya can meet and decide what is to be done about the Blackworm."

"As always, Lady Nidreyu goes to the heart of the matter." Dunyadi trailed his fingers through the hairs on his chin. "Neither as carefully nor as kindly as some of us might prefer, but that does not lessen the truth of what she says."

My master looked down as though an answer might be found in the pattern of the rugs on which he sat. "Nidreyu is right, but it changes nothing. My brother cannot take back his oath."

"Will not, you mean," she said.

"Can you not understand, Lady Nidreyu?" Hakatri's words sounded almost like a plea. "You of all people should know—for Ineluki, there is no difference. That has always been his curse."

Silence fell over the gathering. At last, the talk turned to new things, haltingly at first but then with better cheer as my master, Dunyadi, and Nidreyu spoke of other people and other places. But although I saw him walking all around the hilltop on which Snowdrift sat, Ineluki did not return to the hall for a long time.

"We cannot go back to Asu'a, so the witchwood groves there are beyond our reach," my master said to his brother as they shared a cup of wine in the chambers they had been given. "And Xaniko's advice is useless without witchwood. We might consider trying to destroy the beast with spears and arrows had we a hundred stout fighters, but I fear that even then we would fail."

"Why do you tell me this?" Ineluki's anger was gone, or at least better hidden, but it seemed to have been replaced once more by despair. "What you mean is, *I* cannot go to Asu'a, because of my oath—the one that you keep moaning about—and you do not trust me alone, as though I were a child. But Asu'a does not have the only witchwood grove. If I must, I will ride to Nakkiga and plead with Queen Silvermask herself for a tree."

Hakatri shook his head. "And even if Utuk'ku granted you permission, then what? Ride back a hundred leagues across the dangerous Snowfields, dragging a huge witchwood trunk behind you? We need a full-grown tree. Do you think the queen of the Hamakha has so much love for our house that she will give you not just an entire precious witchwood, but also a train of wagons to carry it away and a company of her Sacrifice soldiers to guard it?"

"I see all the difficulties as well as you." Ineluki's hidden anger now burst into flame again. "And I know you fear that my stiff neck will get us both killed. Go back, then, brother!" he cried. "Go back to your wife and daughter and our parents' house. There is nothing in this doomed quest for you in any case. It is my fate that is at chance here, and mine alone."

"Now you truly are speaking foolishly," Hakatri said. "I could no more leave you to fight this terrible beast alone than I could leave our mother, my wife, or my child to the same fate. You are my brother, closest of my blood. I love you."

All of Ineluki's fury seemed to melt away then, leaving him hollowed out, as a stream undermines a riverbank until, without warning, it falls into the rushing water. For an instant or two I thought he might even weep, something I had never seen him do and which I doubt had happened since he was a child. As for me, I wanted nothing more than to be somewhere else; Ineluki's pain was so clear and strong that it threatened to make my own heart break. "Why do I do these things, brother?" he asked at last. "What deadly spirit haunts me?"

"No more of that talk." Hakatri clasped his brother's hand so tightly his knuckles paled. "No spirit haunts you but your own swift temper."

"But that isn't true, *Haká-sho*." That was the first time in years I had heard him use his brother's childhood name. "I try—always!—to be like you, to make our parents proud, to make all our people proud. But sometimes I feel as though I shall fly apart like a dropped jug. Other days, when I am happy, the sun seems to shine on everything—all is brightness and color, like the winged attendants of the Yásira. But when I am angry or mournful again, it seems as if I walk in a dark gorge like the dragon's swamp, but it is a place I can never leave."

"You have a poet's spirit, that is all." Hakatri lowered his voice. "Ease yourself. Somehow, we will solve this puzzle. And we will do it together— that I promise."

I will not claim I knew that disaster was waiting for us, but something about my master's soothing words to his brother gave me a superstitious chill.

We guested that night at Snowdrift, though the visit had become less comfortable after Lord Dunyadi's regretful but firm refusal to assist the brothers. As twilight crept over the hills, I saw Ineluki and Lady Nidreyu walking together through the birchwood. I do not know what they spoke of, but I could guess at least a little, and the look of emptiness on both their faces seemed to confirm what I suspected: she could not forgive, and he could not—or would not—give in.

Dunyadi's rustic court was quiet and somber that evening. The shent boards had been put away, and even simpler games like Gatherer's Questions could not enliven things. At last the master of Snowdrift called for Nidreyu to sing.

"I do not think I have the voice for it tonight, my lord," she said. "Ask your daughter Himuna—her voice is far sweeter."

But Dunyadi would not let her excuse herself. "Nonsense, child. You always give the old songs—the best songs—a fine touch. It reminds me of my childhood. Please do not disappoint me, *Nidi-sa.*"

She remained reluctant. "I have only sad songs in my thoughts, Lord Dunyadi," she said. "Surely someone else could better give you a tune that would lift everyone's spirits."

"I do not care whether my spirits are lifted or not," declared the master of the hall. "If tonight's spirit is mournful, so be it. But even sad old songs can remind us that bad times pass and are remembered in later, better days."

Nidreyu bowed her head. "Very well." She turned toward Ineluki and waited until he at last raised his eyes to meet hers, then she said, "I will sing the Moon-Woman's Lament."

Dunyadi gestured and the lights in the chamber grew dim. His eldest son picked up a harp and began to pluck out the familiar, ancient melody.

Nidreyu closed her eyes again and began to sing in her deep, tuneful voice. I thought I detected a ripple of unease pass through the folk in Dunyadi's hall.

> *Where is my husband?*
> *I have a bitter taste in my mouth. I do not know what to do to make*
>   *him come back*
> *I do not miss him*
> *But this house is lonely.*
> *I take off my house slippers, then I put them on again.*
> *The moon is a cold place,*

A place of silver ice and white stone.
My heart is cold too.

Even I knew the old, old Zida'ya tale of the moon-woman Mezumiiru, who fell out with her husband Isiki, the lord of all birds. Mezumiiru gave her name to the Net, the great froth of stars that stretches across the night-time sky from south to north. For my master's folk, she is the mother of all their kind.

My own Tinukeda'ya people have different stories of the First Days, or so I understand, though I do not know them. My parents never taught them to me. I think they might have been ashamed.

Nidreyu's voice rose and fell in haunting phrases that faded at the end of each verse like a woodlark's wistful song. All in Snowdrift's hall knew the story intimately, but the gathered company still listened with solemn attention. Only Ineluki seemed unmoved, his head back, eyes fixed on the ceiling, and hands clenched in his lap, as though he listened to some other song, one only he could hear.

I am not beautiful enough to keep him.
But I do not want him.
But I do not want to be alone.

Her voice changed then, the sad but sweet tone now more discordant, as though she was becoming abandoned Mezumiiru in truth.

Where are my children?
Why can I not hold them?
Seven he took to the Land of Birds beyond the Garden.
They will not know me.
They will never know me.

The pain in Nidreyu's voice was hard to hear. It seemed to me, at least, that she was not merely singing of the moon-woman's pain and fury, but her own—not about Mezumiiru's stolen children but children of her own, children she had imagined but now could no longer believe in. Perhaps I was being too fanciful, but I would have sworn by the Garden on

that night that I heard Nidreyu mourning for children she would never
have.

> *Two I have hidden. If he comes not to my side, they will not know him.*
> *I will take them from him.*
> *I will curse his name to their ears and make that name foul in their hearts.*
> *Why does he not come?*
> *Does he think himself so far above me?*
> *I am the daughter of the sky-lord*
> *My mother is the mistress of all growing things,*
> *My husband, he is but a winged thief.*
> *He has stolen my honor*
> *He has stolen my happiness . . .*

Though middle-night had not yet arrived, when Nidreyu finished
singing all the Zida'ya in Dunyadi's hall began to drift away, talking quietly among themselves. When I looked around Ineluki was gone and my
master wore a grave expression. I could tell he did not want to speak to
anyone, not even me, so I made my way to my bed and dreamed of a
clutch of eggs covered by shifting silver sands.

We left Snowdrift in the hour before dawn, the slender birch trunks
swaying in the night breeze like hungry spirits. Nidreyu did not come out
to say farewell, and Dunyadi only embraced the brothers silently before
returning to his hall.

Part
Two

The Silver Tree

Hakatri and his brother did not speak as we rode down from Birch Hill and back to the wide Silver Way. When we reached it in morning's light it felt as though we had reached a crossing of more than one kind. I had not dared to ask which way we would turn when we reached the road, though of course a desperate, foolish part of me prayed that Ineluki would see sense, and we would turn toward Asu'a, our home. But the silence remained unbroken, and when we finally reached the great road, Ineluki headed Bronze west toward the mountains without even looking back. Hakatri followed him, and I, of course, followed my master.

The lands of the west, which of late we seemed to be crossing back and forth like a weaver's shuttle, were almost empty. The dwellings of my master's people, like Lord Dunyadi's Snowdrift, were few and far between, and so were the rougher settlements of mortal men. Most of the settlements we passed were little more than farmsteads or small villages. Only in the distant south did the mortals build cities and live together in large numbers, though at that time I had not yet seen such a thing and could not picture how an entire city of mortals might look. In my imagination they were only larger versions of the settlements we passed, with town walls of trimmed logs and houses of mud and thatch. It was not until I journeyed to Nabban that I discovered mortal men also built with stone, and that some of their creations rivaled Asu'a or lost Tumet'ai in size and grandeur.

In fact, as we followed the winding Silver Way in a beating rain, splashing through the ruts made by previous travelers, I saw more than a few crumbling piles of ancient stone almost completely covered over by grass and trees. These looked more like ruins than natural outcroppings, and I wondered whether this place could have been occupied even before my master's people and mine had come from the Garden. At one point, with the rain pouring down and my heart full of sadness, I asked Hakatri who had first built here.

"Only animals and birds lived in these lands before our Eight Ships came," he told me. "That is why we made landing here—or so the stories tell."

"But your mother, Lady Amerasu, was alive then!" I said. "She must know."

"I tell you the stories she told me, Pamon. But mortal men came soon after, at least the first of them, traveling from the unknown west."

"Did they come in ships like ours?" I asked.

"No. Or if they did, they had left them behind before they reached this land. My mother and those of her generation saw the mortals arrive first as wandering groups and marveled to encounter thinking creatures so different from themselves. Soon they realized how short the lives of these mortals were, how close to animals they seemed in some ways, and then the disagreements began among our folk."

I nodded—that part of the story I knew well. Those disagreements over what should be done about the interloping men led at last to the fabled Parting, when the Hikeda'ya separated themselves from my master's Zida'ya folk, the greatest number of them led by their mistress Utuk'ku, departing to make their home in the great sleeping fire-mountain Ur-Nakkiga. Only a few Hikeda'ya now live outside that far country, and only in a few of the cities.

Since my master seemed willing to talk for the first time since we had left Dunyadi's house, I asked him, "Where are we going now, my lord? Back to that valley, where Hidohebhi waits?" I tried to keep the fear from my voice, but I do not think I succeeded.

"Not yet," he said. "I think even my brother knows we can accomplish nothing against the dragon by ourselves except to die. No, we are going to M'yin Azoshai—Hernsland, as the mortals now call it—to find warriors to help us."

This made me only a little less fearful than the idea of returning to Serpent's Vale. Prince Cormach and his men had seemed fairly civilized, but I wondered if their fellow mortals would be as respectful to my master and his brother, let alone to me, a mere changeling (as they often called the Tinukeda'ya). Every child of Asu'a knew the story of Nenais'u, Jenjiyana's beautiful daughter, and how she had died at the hands of mortal hunters.

When I cautiously shared this worry, Hakatri dismissed it. "That was long ago, Pamon, and what happened to Nenais'u was mischance, terrible as its result was."

"The tale says that the mortals took her for a swan," I said.

"Errant nonsense!" said Ineluki. He had been silent all morning, so his sudden words surprised me. "Nenais'u was famously beautiful, like her mother. I have no doubt the mortals tried to capture her. She fled them and they killed her."

"You sound like one of Utuk'ku's minions," Hakatri told him. "Do you also disbelieve that Drukhi killed himself? Did the mortals murder him too, as the Hikeda'ya claim?"

"It seems likely to me, yes," said his brother. "Why do you defend them?"

"I defend no one. How could I claim to know one way or another about something that happened before we were born—something that our people have argued about ever since? *Nobody* knows the truth. Nobody will ever know. Those who were present are all dead."

"Perhaps. But somebody should speak for those dead." I was surprised by the heat in Ineluki's voice. "The mortals breed like rats. They spread farther over our lands every day." He swept his arm across the expanse of rain-soaked hills. "In the end, all this will be theirs, and we will not even be a memory."

Hakatri rode awhile without speaking. "Strange, then, since with your agreement we are riding to the mortals' village to ask their help."

"I do not say they are all murderers, brother. I do not doubt that many of them are honorable—in their way—and I have no complaint with Cormach and his men. No, I speak of what will happen whether they hate us or love us. Already there is scarcely a place in our old lands between Kementari and Hikehikayo that the mortals have not reached, and the southern lands are now completely theirs. Everywhere they go, they stay and grow in numbers. Can you not see that our doom is already written?"

"You are too grim for me, brother," said Hakatri. "And too sour. Nobody knows the future. Not even the so-called Queen Utuk'ku, who was old before the Great Ships left the Garden, can see what the years ahead will bring."

There had been enough contending between the two of them in the past few days that I did not want any more of it, so I asked my master a question in the hope it might distract them from their disagreement. "Is Utuk'ku truly so old, then? I thought it might only be a story."

"The story is true," he said. "She was a great-granddaughter of Hamakho Wormslayer himself. She is the oldest of all who still live, and not by a small span."

"Is that why she wears a mask?" I asked. "Is she so aged that, as they say of mortals when they grow old, she is withered and hideous underneath it?"

"Watch your words, changeling," said Ineluki. "It is not your place to speak so of our eldest relative."

"I am very sorry, my lord," I said hurriedly. "I meant no offense. I only wondered."

Hakatri looked troubled by his brother's words, but to me he said only, "No one knows why Utuk'ku wears the mask. They say many of her closest counselors and most trusted nobles have taken to wearing them also. Our mother says it is vanity, but she also says Utuk'ku is not vain of her looks, though back in her youth in the Lost Garden she was known for her beauty."

"I do not understand, Master. Vanity, but not for her looks?"

Hakatri actually smiled. "When next we see Amerasu you have my permission to ask her to explain. The Sa'onsera likes you, Pamon. I do not think she would be insulted by your question—although Utuk'ku herself might be."

I felt a clutch at my heart at the mere thought of meeting that ancient and infamous figure. "I would never dare ask Utuk'ku anything."

"Nor would I." He laughed, and a little of the strain went out of his voice and posture. I was happy with myself for distracting him, but Ineluki still looked dark and distant.

We rode all that day and late into the evening before stopping in the foothills to rest and feed our mounts. The horses seemed in good health when I looked them over. The worst of the rains had passed, and the trees gleamed in the last of the twilight. As we made our way upward, the sound of dripping water from their branches was all we heard. When we finally halted for the night the country around us was so quiet we seemed to have entered some other world. Hakatri and Ineluki did not speak but sat beside the fire I built from what dry wood I could find. My master and his brother did not feel the cold as I did, but there is something reassuring about a fire that even the Zida'ya appreciate. We sat together until the star called Night-Heart reached its highest point, then I finally rolled myself in my cloak to snatch some sleep.

The next morning found us riding through the uplands that had once been called Azosha's Garden but which I supposed had been given a new name by its mortal inheritors, Cormach's Hernsmen. We began to pass mortal farms and other smallholdings, and to see sheep, pigs, and even an occasional cow grazing on the hillsides. As we drew closer to what had been M'yin Azoshai we passed by a number of small settlements. Almost all the mortal men and women stopped what they were doing to watch us pass. They did not look hostile, but neither did they seem particularly welcoming, and though a few made signs of respect as we passed—the brothers' witch-wood armor must have made it clear we were no ordinary travelers—most of the mortals watched us with decidedly cautious expressions.

We sighted the Hernsmen's settlement well before we reached it. In late morning we approached its outer walls, a palisade of tall, sharpened posts. The gate was large, more than twice my height and built of sturdy oak with massive metal hinges. Racks of antlers had been mounted along the top of it, all taken from what looked to have been uncommonly large deer, and the banner that fluttered above the gate displayed a white stag on a field of bright green. The guards at the gate, shaggy men wearing matching cloaks of the same grassy hue as their flag, seemed uncertain at first what to do with us. My master conferred with them for a short while—the leader of the guards spoke a little of our tongue—and after a runner was sent up to what the guard leader called "the House" and quickly returned, we were allowed in. A small company of gate guards escorted us up the winding track toward the inner walls, but already we were passing clustered dwellings and a few larger wood and stone buildings I took for temples. I do not know much of the gods the mortals worship, but I know there are many of them.

The city's inner wall was made of great chunks of stone held together by mortar, which was nothing unusual, but as we were led through the second gate my master stopped me. "See, Pamon," he said, pointing. "It looks like the mortals pulled down Azosha's house to make their fortification." When I looked closer, I saw that the chunks of stone in the walls were no ordinary rocks, that their surfaces were smooth, almost polished, and many were covered in fine carvings. Hakatri shook his head. "It is a shame what they have done to your people's work."

At the time, I thought he meant only the hard labor of erecting the stones, and I merely nodded. "A pity."

"Someday we will be gone and all the world will be like this," Ineluki said, but with less heat than I would have expected. "Mortal men living in the ruins of what we built, as a snake slithers into an abandoned burrow."

"If you begin talking about abandoned burrows when we are in the mortal court," Hakatri said sourly, "I will walk out and leave you there."

"Turn a blind eye if you wish," said Ineluki. "At least the snake waits until the badger is dead before stealing its home."

"Both badgers and snakes still share the world, if not a single burrow," his brother said. "And in any case, the Hernsmen did not make their dwelling here until after Lady Azosha gave it to them."

The city, small as it was, was named Hern's Horn, perhaps because of its antler-festooned gates. I would guess that something like two thousand mortals lived there, although I do not pretend to know. As we mounted the highest hill we reached the final stone wall and saw within its circuit a sprawling structure of wood—the House. It was larger than Dunyadi's Snowdrift, though not by much. Just as I was thinking we would have to wait all over again at the tall front doors, a familiar figure appeared.

"Lord Hakatri, Lord Ineluki, you are most welcome!" cried Prince

Cormach. "You do our household a great honor. Will you come and meet my grandfather, the king?"

"May we wash ourselves first?" my master asked. "We have been on the road many days."

"Of course, of course," Cormach said. "Come and we will give you hot water and dry clothes. You have likely heard that mortals hate bathing. I cannot speak for those Nabban-men in the south or the troll-folk of the far north, but we Hernsmen are a clean people, like you."

Hakatri smiled, though Ineluki looked a little offended. "I am glad to hear it. Thank you."

I used my master's tub after he had finished. It was good to get the mud of the road off me and soak the chill out of my bones. When I was out, I helped Hakatri dress in the colorful but coarse-woven clothing that the Hernsmen provided, undergarments of linen and outerwear made from the dyed wool of sheep.

When we were ready, Cormach returned and led us into the main hall of the House. There we found at least a score of mortals waiting to see us, mostly thick-bearded males dressed in furs and heavy wool cloaks, so that we seemed surrounded by animal-men. Some of them, I do not doubt, had never seen a Zida'ya. (They may not have seen my kind either, but it was the brothers they had come to stare at in wonder.) The roof was high, and a great fire burned in a stone fireplace at one end of the room, but the house itself was built entirely of oakwood, and I wondered what these mortals would do if it ever caught fire. I discovered later that the wooden houses of the mortals often caught fire. I still do not understand why they would build that way when stony mountains ripe for quarrying surround them.

"Come, my good lords, and meet my grandfather and my father." Cormach led us across the long, high hall amid the wondering stares of his fellow Hernsmen.

I had never before been in the house of a mortal, let alone a mortal king, and I wish now that I had paid more attention to my surroundings. I do remember that many wooden carvings hung on the walls, animals and birds and vaguely manlike shapes. But if I did not look around as carefully as I should have, it was because I was staring at the oldest creature I had ever seen. Rather, I should say the oldest-*looking* since, as is the way of the Zida'ya, both Hakatri's parents appeared little older than their children or grandchildren.

"My grandfather, King Gorlach ubh-Grainh," said Cormach. "And my father, Rian, Prince of the Coastlands."

I hope my astonishment was not too obvious or too impolite, but I had never seen a truly old mortal before. Those who came on embassies to Asu'a were usually in the prime of their lives, however short those mortal lives might be. But King Gorlach was ancient by the standards of his folk, his hair so thin his scalp showed through even on the sides, his beard so straggly that it looked like white tree-moss. His wrinkled face, to my eyes, was just as much a ruin as any tumbled stone wall of an abandoned dwelling. King Gorlach's limbs were so thin, age-spotted, and knotted with veins that he might have been made out of animal hide that had been left in the sun for years; and his head bent so low it almost seemed to spring directly from his breastbone. I was so taken by this wreckage of what had doubtless once been a tall, strong mortal man that I did not for some moments look to Gorlach's son, Cormach's father. When I did, I received another surprise.

Prince Rian was a cripple. That was obvious immediately, and not merely because of the withered arm that he held cradled against his chest like a sleeping child. Rian was handsome for a mortal, like his son, but his head trembled and nodded, and even his good hand quivered when he lifted it to greet us. I could not tell for certain because of the thick clothing he wore, but I thought from the way he sat that one of his legs might also be shrunken and lame as well.

"It is rare to s-s-see the immortals among us." Rian's use of the Zida'ya tongue was creditable, though he had no little trouble speaking because of his palsy. "Have you come to rid us of this noxious worm? If so, you will have all our g-g-gr—" he paused to compose himself, "our gratitude," he finished.

The old king said something in the Hernsland tongue, which to me sounded more of throat-clearing than proper speech.

"My grandfather thinks you have come from Nabban," said Cormach. "He is a trifle confused today. He has days that are good and days that are bad." Cormach replied to his grandfather in the Hernsland tongue and the king leaned far forward to listen. When Cormach had finished, Gorlach sat back, though he appeared to view us with a good deal more suspicion than before.

"Fear not, Fair Folk," said Cormach's father Rian. "You are w-welcome here in our house and our lands."

I understood in an instant why such a confused old man as Gorlach should still sit on the throne. If Rian was the king's only son, as seemed likely, the Hernsmen would be reluctant to put a cripple on the throne unless it was absolutely necessary.

Beside Rian on the bench sat a woman I took to be his wife, Cormach's mother. The lady was covered head to foot, including a cowl over her head, so that only her face showed. Her otherwise pleasant features were set in lines of what I guessed was weariness.

The strange audience did not last long, and then Prince Cormach led us out again, back to the part of the large compound that seemed to be his, where we were offered food and drink.

"I apologize for my grandfather's misunderstanding," he said when we had been served, but my master waved it away.

"Many responsibilities must fall to you, Prince Cormach," Hakatri said.

"Can you not simply take the crown for yourself?" Ineluki asked. "Is that not what your people want instead of a sickly king and a sickly heir?"

I thought I saw Cormach wince, and my own master clearly had to suppress a bark of annoyance at his brother's indiscretion, but the prince replied courteously.

"We do not do things so, Lord Ineluki. Nor do your own folk, from what I know."

"Such a situation does not arise among our folk," said Ineluki, but now my master interrupted.

"We can discuss such things another time," he said. "But now, Prince Cormach, we must tell you what we have learned about dragons—especially the terrible Blackworm that preys upon your people."

The tale of our trip to Ravensperch and our days with Xaniko was a long one, made longer because the mortal prince had many questions. Like us, he had heard of the Exile but never seen him and was struck with wonder by nearly every detail of the castle atop the Beacon.

"But for all his helpful advice," Hakatri finished, "Xaniko could not help us with the most important part. To make a great witchwood spear to use against Hidohebhi requires a tall witchwood tree, and there are few left in the world in these diminished days. Of all the witchwood groves that once grew in the cities of our people, only those in our home and in distant Nakkiga still thrive."

"Could you not find a suitable witchwood in Asu'a?" Cormach asked.

"Our father sent word that the groves of our home are forbidden to us unless Ineluki renounces his oath and returns to Asu'a. That does not seem likely to happen."

Ineluki shook his head, his face grim. "It will not."

After an uncomfortable pause, the talk moved on to other things—the worm was still snatching livestock from the hills and dales around Serpent's Vale, and more than a few Hernslanders had vanished as well, thought to have been taken by the beast. As we spoke, drinking the sour honey-wine that Cormach's servants brought us, one old retainer came to his master and whispered in his ear. I thought perhaps the prince was being called away, but Cormach only nodded when the old man had finished, saying, "I had quite forgotten, good Dermod, but I too have heard that story. Tell our guests."

The old man, who though bald and bent and wrinkled looked as though he could have beaten King Gorlach in a race even while carrying Prince Rian on his back, looked at us in blushing confusion. "Go on," Cormach urged him.

"It is just, do you see," said the old man in a far more uncertain way than he had whispered into his lord's ear, "that I am remembering, I am." His Zida'ya speech was a bit strange but understandable, and I was reminded that once, most mortals in this part of the western world had grown up knowing it.

"Do not be afraid," said the prince. "These lords of the Zida'ya want to hear what you have to say."

"Just that I was remembering a tale I heard from my old gran when I was small," Dermod said, his face still red across the cheekbones. "About the Lady's Grove—the woods that was once Lady 'Zosha's."

"I know nothing of this," said Hakatri. "Was it a witchwood grove?"

"That I couldn't say, good master," the old servant replied. "But the tale I heard was that it was a magical place forbidden to all, full of what we call graywood trees, like what Hern's famous spear was made from."

"Does it still exist?" my master asked. "Is it somewhere near?"

The man shook his head. "Not near here, no. Up in the highest crags of Old Whitecap is where it lies. But when Lady 'Zosha died, the fairy-king Enazashi claimed it for his own." He shrugged. "I know naught of what happened to the graywood trees afterward, though, begging your lords' pardon. When I was young we used to look for the grove but never found it. They say it is close-guarded by the Old Ones." The color, which had finally begun to drain from his cheeks, came rushing back. "Beg pardon, Lord Hakatri, I mean by your folk."

My master and his brother looked at each other. "A witchwood grove on the mountain?" Hakatri turned to Cormach. "If it is anything more than an old story, perhaps there is yet something we can do about this murderous drake."

I will not detail all that came afterward. It is enough to say that when only a few more suns had set and risen we left the house of King Gorlach, but not alone: Prince Cormach now traveled with us, leading several of his closest companions and almost two score other retainers and men of his household. Our horses were rested and, like us, had been well fed and well kept—the Hernsmen learned much of their horsecraft from my master's people back in the old days—and so it should have been a light-hearted party setting out. But though my master and the mortal prince seemed in fair temper, Lord Ineluki was still sunk in a mire of brooding silence, and the prince's men, though Cormach assured us they were among the bravest Hernsland had to offer, were also quiet and barely spoke, even among themselves.

It was not hard to understand. The Zida'ya lord Enazashi whose witchwood grove we aimed to find and plunder had been master of the mountains and the hidden city of Silverhome since long, long before even Hernsland's old King Gorlach had been born; in fact, Enazashi was almost as dire a figure of myth to the mortal Hernsmen as Queen Utuk'ku was to my own folk. Further, in the servant Dermod's old stories about the Lady's Grove, Enazashi had promised that any mortals found there would be put to death without mercy, so Cormach's men, though loyal to their prince, were clearly fearful what the days ahead might hold.

"I have heard much talk of late about Lady Azosha," I said to Lord Hakatri. "But I know little about her beyond what I have heard on this journey. Why did one of your people give her land to the mortals?"

"Nobody knows all the story," my master told me. "But Azosha was always thought strange, even by her own kin. She came to these lands, as did Enazashi and his clan, on one of the Eight Ships. But Azosha did not want to be ruled by her shipmates simply because they outnumbered her, so she left the landing place in the earliest days, before the city of Silver-home had been built around the ship. With her servants and retainers—for she had been an important noble in the Garden—she built her own house on the high hill that was afterward called by her name, *M'yin Azoshai*. There she lived as she pleased, and many of the most learned—or most unusual—of our people came to visit her. Many never left, preferring her settlement even above Tumet'ai, the first great city of our folk. Her house became famous for the artists and philosophers who were her guests."

My master paused as his horse made its way over a fallen tree, and as he did, Cormach spoke up. "Our stories say that she was a great sorceress, though not a wicked one."

"I am sure she seemed so," said Hakatri, smiling. "And it could be that Azosha and her friends dabbled in practices that others considered strange and perilous, but for the large part, the stories I have heard describe her mostly as one who went her own way and did not pretend to care what others thought."

"But still, why would she give her land to the Hernsmen?" I asked. "It seems strange that a Zida'ya noble should do such a thing."

"That is the question no one can answer," Hakatri said. "Though many have tried, and there have been as many ideas as there are birds in the sky."

"Among our people," said Prince Cormach, "it is told that she fell in love with Hern the Hunter, who was a mighty man."

Again my master smiled. "Perhaps. All that is known beyond doubt is that in her last years—because Azosha, like Utuk'ku of the Hamakha, was already old when our people fled the dying Garden—she wrote a testament in her own hand that gifted her lands to the descendants of Hern. Being mortal, Hern had not lived to know of the gift, but her legacy was affirmed to his heirs by the Sa'onsera Senditu, my grandmother. This was much to Lord Enazashi's disgust, as you heard from his own mouth, Pamon. Hern's descendants, like the prince here, have lived on those lands ever since."

"Lady Azosha must have been very strong-minded," I said, but for some reason I was thinking of Ona of Ravensperch, The Exile's wife. The odd things Lady Ona had said to me had been in my mind ever since we left the Beacon. An idea could be like a seed, I was discovering, small to begin with but quick to grow. A person might die or be left behind, but an idea might live on and on.

"Our race has never been short of strong-minded females," Hakatri said, and though he laughed as he said it, he also sounded proud. "But all would agree that Azosha was one of a kind. She wrote poetry, but also studied the philosophy of nature and loved to talk about it. A bard of her court once called her 'the Mistress of Uncomfortable Questions,' and some of her ideas still spark arguments among our wisest elders to this day."

This too struck home for me. What had Lady Ona asked me about my Zida'ya master? *"Why do you serve him? Why is he the master and you the minion?"* It was easy to imagine Azosha asking such questions, easy to imagine the discomfort they would have caused.

As we continued up into the heights, Hakatri asked the prince, "Was your grandfather surprised to find that the Zida'ya had come to help?"

"The king does not know," Cormach said. "He was confused. He thought you had come from the Imperator of Nabban."

"But your grandfather was the one who sent you to Asu'a for help in the first place, was he not?"

"I will tell you something, Lord Hakatri, and trust your wisdom and kindness not to share it with others. These days, the king of Hernsland understands very little. You have seen how his age has overtaken him." Cormach shook his head. "Make no mistake, my grandfather once was a great king indeed, which is why Hernsland has grown under his rule. But he is past four score summers now and his wits are all but gone. It was my father and I who decided that I should go to Asu'a."

"Then why is your father not the king?" asked Ineluki.

"You saw his frailties, my lord." Cormach looked as if he did not like the question much. "The chieftains would not accept my father as king. Many say the gods have cursed him with his illness. If he took the throne, many of the chieftains, especially the most powerful, would likely turn their backs on the throne and our family. There are others in our western lands who fancy themselves kings, even if they do not use the title. Some of them are highborn chieftains, but some are mere *prehan* as we call them—crows—warlords little better than bandits. If they knew how utterly my grandfather's wits have wandered, or if my father accepted the crown in his place, they would think the throne weakened and descend like the carrion birds whose name we give them, plucking the kingdom to pieces, each taking a bit for himself. Things would soon be as they were before Hern the Great—worse, even, because many of these chieftains have prospered under our leadership and have built fortified cities and powerful war bands for themselves."

"Then, if I may ask," said my master, "why do you not take the throne yourself, Cormach? Surely your father would see the sense in that."

"He likely would, but I would not do it while my grandfather lives. Bad enough my father must suffer the scorn of the ignorant, who treat him like a witling though his mind is strong and he is as full of wisdom as any in his line before him." The bitterness Cormach felt had become apparent on his face and in his voice. "I will not see him passed over that way. When my grandfather dies, my father will take the crown but announce he is too unwell to rule and pass it along to me. I cannot take that dignity away from him."

I thought Cormach very noble for a mortal but could not help wondering if his determination might be wrong-headed. Surely everyone in Hernsland must already know that the old king was unfit. Such a thing was not completely unheard of even among my master's people, though it was rare. My master once told me that Soniso, the first lord of Kementari, was known to have become very morose in his age and eventually descended into a kind of madness, but it was so uncommon that the few others to suffer that way were said to have "become Soniso."

We climbed the steep, winding track up Old Whitecap in the cold rain. The farther we climbed, the harder it was even to make out the path, and eventually it vanished entirely, overrun by forest. But we knew the Lady's Grove was near the top, and if there was any direction that was easy to discern on those steep slopes it was upward, so we made our way slowly higher as gnarled oaks and ash-trees were gradually supplanted by dark evergreens. We wound around the upper reaches of the mountain until we could see most of the western side of the Sunstep range before us, and even caught an occasional glimpse of the Silver Sea beyond, burning like molten bronze as the sun sank into the horizon.

At last, as twilight spread across the sky, we found another track through the dripping trees, an ancient one, much overgrown. Soon we could see a place just above us where a circle of tall pines stood against the darkening sky; I thought I could make out a deeper darkness within that circle, a dim, almost invisible core that swayed silently in the evening wind. Before this shadowy grove lay a stretch of open land, and in the midst of that clearing stood a large, upright stone. Unguessable years of wind and rain had worn much of its surface away, but as we approached my master said, "Those are our people's old runes. There is not enough left to read, but I think we can guess what they say." He turned to Cormach. "Your men must not pass this boundary marker. I do not doubt we have found the entrance to the Lady's Grove. Take them a little way back down the mountain and make camp to wait for us."

Cormach turned and called to his men in their own tongue. At his words I saw relief on all their faces, which had been very somber.

"I will come with you, my lords," the prince said as he watched his Hernsmen turn and begin moving back down the track.

"I thank you, Cormach," said my master, "but you will not. This is for my brother and myself to do. Any blame must fall on us alone. Lord Enazashi would never dare to execute two of the Sa'onserei—not for mere trespass—but I doubt anything would restrain him from revenging himself on you and your folk."

Cormach objected to this, but after some quiet argument my master won out. "I pray for your success, Lord Hakatri and Lord Ineluki," the prince said at last, then turned and rode after his men.

"He knew you would not let him come with us," said Ineluki. "I think the mortal's bravery was only for show."

"Perhaps," Hakatri said. "Or perhaps you judge him too narrowly. But if you truly wish to discover the Hernsmen's mettle, there will be ample chance later when we return to Serpent's Vale."

I wondered for a moment whether the protection my master expected for himself and his brother as Sa'onserei would serve for me as well, but dismissed the thought as unworthy: I felt sure Hakatri would not let anything happen to me.

As we passed the ancient standing stone and entered the ring-grove of trees, I began to notice a new odor, as strong as the sharp, cool scent of the surrounding pines, but different. It had a spicy sweetness to it, but also something darker beneath, a whiff of wet moss combined with a tang that I can only described as earthy or mineral, like the scent of stony ground after the rains have come and gone. My master's folk name this odor of living witchwood *A't'si*—"earthblood." The poet Tuya had called it "one of the greatest good things," but I had never noticed it in the finished witchwood of blades or armor, which was the only sort I had encountered. It was overwhelming, climbing straight from my nose into my very thoughts.

As we passed through the outer ring the air seemed to grow damper and warmer. The noise of the wind had become entirely muted among the tall trees, and the light of the moon and stars was strained through the crowding leaves until I could barely see my own hands holding Seafoam's reins.

My eyes are not as sharp as those of my master and his people, but not so poor as a mortal's either. As I grew more accustomed to the darkness, I could make out a little more of the center of the grove—not only the shapes of the witchwood trunks, which were thicker and more widely rooted than the tall pines, but also the pale strands of creeper that hung everywhere in the grove, twining up the twisted pillars, dangling from branches, and stretching between trees as if someone had haphazardly tried to bind the trunks together. The creepers were whiteweave—*yedu-ame*—and I am told they grow only on witchwood.

The stillness and the heavy, wet air pressed on me until I found it difficult to breathe, though my master and his brother did not seem bothered. They were already examining the trees in the central ring, which surrounded an empty space that showed where the first witchwoods had been planted. I heard Hakatri and Ineluki talking quietly to each other and the magnitude of what we were doing suddenly struck me. For the first time in my life I was in a holy witchwood grove, but we had come as thieves, not lawful gatherers. A sudden chill ran through me. I wanted to call out to my master to hurry, but the quiet of the place pressed me to silence. My concerns seemed petty, almost meaningless set against the age and solemnity of the grove, but a part of me felt as if we were about to rob a sacred tomb.

Until my master and Ineluki selected a tree, I had not considered the practical issues of felling one of the large witchwoods and then carrying it out of the grove. I could not see the top of the one they chose, but it was no sapling: I could not have reached my arms all the way around its trunk. While I watched over the horses, who seemed curiously calm (certainly more so than I was) the brothers drew out their swords, Ineluki's Gleaming and my master's fabled Thunderstroke—*Indreju* in the Zida'ya tongue.

My master once told me that it was a pity I did not know more about the making of a witchwood blade, since my own people had always been the masters of shaping the sacred wood. That idea was new to me—one of many things about my own folk I had not known. I learned later that the tree's core must be pressed, hammered, and suffused with various compounds until it is flexible as well as hard, as strong as any metal. But even that night, as my master and Ineluki labored in that silent grove, I knew that shaped witchwood was stronger than the raw wood of the tree, which is why after a great deal of work—hours of it—the two brothers were able to cut through the trunk far enough to fell the witchwood they had chosen.

"What now, brother?" Ineluki asked as they walked up and down the length of the trunk. "Will we trim it before we—"

"Halt, thieves!" cried a voice from the darkness in the Zida'ya tongue. "Take another step and our next flight will find your flesh."

We stopped, of course.

"We discovered your allies down the mountain," the voice continued. "They do not even know we have found their camp, though our archers surround them. Now, step out—and no tricks! We can see you far better than you can see us."

"We do not fear you!" cried Ineluki.

Hakatri, as always the less combative of the two, called back, "We can see you perfectly well, kinsmen. We are no mortals, though our companions on the mountainside are. Hold back your swift arrows and we will step forward." And as he spoke, he set down his sword and spread his hands so the hidden enemy—hidden from my sight, anyway—could see them.

"By the Garden!" said the voice from the darkness in astonishment as my master stepped out into the moonlight. "It is Hakatri of Asu'a!"

"It is. Who stands before me?" asked my master.

Then, like one of the spirits of the dead in an old story, a figure appeared from the shadows, taking on shape by starlight until I could recognize an armored Zida'ya holding a long war bow, his black hair worn in a horse-tail.

"I know your face," my master said. "I saw you at the Site of Witness. You are Yizashi, son of Lord Enazashi."

The black-haired one made a gesture of respectful greeting, but his face was stony. "And you are trespassing in my father's lands. Worse, you have stolen a tree from his grove."

"Your father has no right to this grove!" cried Ineluki. "This was Lady Azosha's."

Yizashi gave him a hard look. "Strange to hear the scions of Asu'a so concerned about the rights of one long dead. And stranger still to find them stealing a witchwood tree instead of asking permission. I cannot imagine you would deal kindly with us if our Silverhome folk had come to Asu'a's sacred grove and tried to take a tree by stealth."

"Are you calling us thieves?" Ineluki demanded.

"I can think of no better word to describe what I see here."

"I beg you," said my master, "let us sit and speak of this without threats—" he turned to his brother, "—or angry posturing. After all, we came from the same Garden, we share the same Exile. When you hear what we are doing here, Yizashi, you may feel differently."

Yizashi stayed silent. Ineluki said, "But—!"

My master did not give his brother a chance to argue further, silencing him with a single harsh whisper. When he turned back to the heir of Silverhome, Hakatri asked, "Can we speak peacefully, as kinsmen? Let us leave the felled tree here and go a little apart. Perhaps we can even make a fire—I think Pamon, my armiger, is feeling the cold."

I almost told him he was wrong. I may not be as hardy as my master's folk, but neither are we Tinukeda'ya as helpless as mortals. But I realized before I spoke that the reason for a fire was not important to Hakatri. He was not truly worrying about my comfort but trying to change the nature of conversation from an armed deadlock to something more like a negotiation between respectful foes, or even between allies.

Yizashi considered for a moment, then signaled his men to lower their bows and move back. My master and his brother—and I, of course—then went to him, leaving the fallen witchwood behind.

Hakatri said, "And the mortals you have surrounded are innocent. They did not enter the grove. They accompanied us up the mountain but did not know what we planned—or what we intend to do next."

Yizashi gave him an odd look, then turned and summoned one of his archers and spoke briefly. The archer slipped away. "So, then," Yizashi said. "We will make a fire and talk."

Yizashi's company built a fire near the standing stone. The worst of the rains had passed, and only a few tattered clouds obscured the stars wheeling across the sky. My master and his brother explained what had brought them in search of a witchwood. Yizashi, as with others we had met, was full of questions about the exile Xaniko.

"Did he tell you to come to my father's grove for a tree to make this great spear?" he demanded.

Hakatri shook his head. "No. He said it must be witchwood, that is all." But instead of revealing the Hernsmen's stories about the grove, he only said, "We learned about your father's claiming of Azosha's witchwood trees from old tales."

Yizashi was silent a long time when my master had finished. "If you saw me at my father's side, you will remember that I did not want to turn you away, or to ignore the peril of our neighbors, even if they are only mortals."

My master nodded. "I remember."

"But you have put me in a hard situation." The firelight showed me Yizashi's face clearly for the first time, and I was struck by how youthful he looked—younger than either my master or Ineluki. "It is one thing for me to disagree with my father—the Garden knows it is not the first time, nor will it be the last. But it would be quite another thing for me to let you take one of his trees, especially when he was already made aware that there were strangers on the mountain."

"But they are not his trees!" said Ineluki, then turned to Hakatri. "Brother, this is another bootless argument."

My master did not take his eyes off Yizashi. "In times of great need, no one of good heart can remain indifferent. Remember, I have seen this dragon, Yizashi, and it is truly a fearful thing. It may be mortals who are most threatened by it now, but ultimately we of the Dawn Children will be in terrible danger as well. All you need to do to help us fight this scourge is to turn a blind eye."

Yizashi laughed, but it sounded sour. "Turn a blind eye? My father does not turn a blind eye to anything that belongs to him. He will ask me what I discovered here on the mountain. I will not lie to him."

"Bootless," muttered Ineluki.

"But my father is not as cold and pitiless as you might think him from our audience," Yizashi continued. "It is just that the arrival of the mortal Hernsmen turned his mind to old grievances. He is not always so hard-minded."

"I do not doubt it," said Hakatri. "Still, here we sit in middle-night, waiting for your decision." I could see that my master's temper was strained, caught as he was between his brother and Enazashi's son. There seemed no common ground to be found. But instead of arguing, Hakatri only lifted a stick and poked at the fire until sparks leaped up and swirled away into the night.

"It is not as though the tree can be re-planted, now that it has been felled." Yizashi spoke slowly, as though listening to how his own words sounded. "Neither can I imagine trying to drag the scions of Year-Dancing House back to Silverhome in chains."

"You could not," said Ineluki. "It would be a crime against the Garden itself—"

"I beg you to be quiet and listen, brother. Speak on, Yizashi."

"The Balance Beam is overhead," he said at last. "The constellation of mercy. In this confusing hour, I will let the sky advise me." He extended his hands in the sign of *judgment*. "The witchwood has been felled. That cannot be undone. But in my father's eyes, it is a crime that cannot be ignored." He lifted a hand as a call for silence, though my master did not seem as though he meant to speak—perhaps Yizashi meant to forestall more angry words from Ineluki. "Therefore, I release the tree to you, to be used against the dire beast Hidohebhi. But afterward, whatever may happen, I charge you to come back to my father's court and tell him what you told me."

"And what if your father declares it a crime?" demanded Ineluki.

"He is no more likely than me to strike a blow at Year-Dancing House, I think," said Yizashi carefully. "But nothing can be certain. That is my judgment, and only with that provision can I let you walk away from the grove tonight."

Hakatri gave his brother a warning look, then said, "We agree, and I thank you for your generosity and forbearance. You have my word we will return to ask your father's forgiveness."

Yizashi seemed amused. "If you expect forgiveness, I think you may be disappointed. My father is seldom that way disposed. But I salute your courage in risking your lives for the good of others."

Hakatri made a gesture of gratitude. "We will not forget this."

"Then go and summon your mortal helpers, because I do not think you will be able to carry the tree down the mountain without them." Yizashi stood. "My company and I will leave now, both because I do not want to linger long enough to regret my decision and because I must prepare for the unenviable task that you two have shirked—telling my lord and father what happened here, and what I decided."

Yizashi led his men away. When only my master, his brother, and myself remained, Hakatri stood. "Let us get to work. There is much to do."

As the night turned toward morning the two brothers hacked away the largest of the witchwood tree's limbs with their swords until little was left but the great trunk, then they respectfully burned the unneeded limbs, which would quickly lose their potency now that they had been removed. The smell of the smoke was so strange and so strong that it made me feel as if I had stumbled onto the Dream Road.

When my master and Ineluki had finished, the trunk was still almost ten paces long and very heavy. We harnessed the horses and began to drag it out of the grove, past the standing stone and down the mountain. Along the way we met scouts from Prince Cormach's company, who then hurried back down to fetch the rest of their comrades. With their help we made a cradle of ropes that allowed a score of the prince's men to lift the tree and carry it much more easily down the forested mountainside than we could have dragged it.

Many of the prince's Hernsmen, though ignorant of how close they had been to death during the dark hours, were nevertheless so pleased at leaving the vicinity of the grove that they began to sing as we made our way down from Old Whitecap's heights.

I confess that as we hauled the massive witchwood trunk down the mountain I was already fearful about returning to Serpent's Vale. The memory of that grim spot, its broken trees, treacherous muddy pools, and most of all, the terrible beast that hid there, worked on my thoughts like an unending cold downpour, but I felt a superstitious reluctance to ask my master about it. For a long time he stayed silent, deep in thought, but because I rode near him he finally looked up and must have seen the discomfort in my expression.

"What troubles you, Squire Pamon?"

"I confess, Master," I told him, "that I am afraid of going back to that valley."

"In the end, we can do nothing else." He looked around for Ineluki, who was riding Bronze a little ahead of the rest of us, lost in thoughts of his own. "My brother has pledged his honor that he will not return to our home while the worm lives. However rash that may have been, he will hold to it even if it kills him. And more and more I despise the idea of leaving the mortals to fend for themselves against such a monster. Do we not carry the blood of the Dragonslayer in the same quantity as the Hike-da'ya? Our forefather Hamakho risked his life again and again to keep our people safe from the great worms."

The Dragonslayer had led the killing of many of the dragons that threatened the Garden in the days before its destruction. Though Utuk'ku's people claimed him as their own—the queen's clan called itself "the Hamakha"—my master's Zida'ya people were Hamakho's descendants as well, though his wife Sa'onsera had parted from him before my master's people fled their ancient home.

"Why did Lord Hamakho stay behind when everyone else left the Garden, my lord?" The thought of what lay ahead still oppressed me and I selfishly wished to distract myself when I should have let my master plan his strategy.

"Because he was dead," Hakatri said with a grim look and a shake of his head. "Killed by his own Dragonslayers as the scourge of Unbeing swept over the Garden."

I was startled. "I have never heard this! Great Hamakho murdered by his own kind? How could such a thing come to be?"

"It is a long tale, full of shame and sorrow," my master said. "It is also much disputed, especially between Zida'ya and Hikeda'ya."

"I would still like to hear it."

He looked less than pleased. "Why, Pamon? Why should you care? It is a terrible story, and it is not even a tale of your own people."

This shocked and hurt me, and for the first time that I can remember I felt as though Lord Hakatri did not understand me. I had been raised among the Zida'ya all my life. Asu'a was my only home, and though my own Tinukeda'ya people lived there too in great numbers, I had spent far more time among my master's kind than among my own. Utuk'ku and a few other Zida'ya immortals might still remember the Garden, but none of my own folk did except through stories and prayers. What other people did I truly have but my master's?

I did not say any of this, of course. Many concerns must have troubled Hakatri at that moment, and all of us feared what might happen in Serpent's Vale. He did not need me to add to his worries.

But as I rode silently beside him, he took a little pity on me, saying, "In any case, if you are frightened of what is to come, remember that you will not have to face the worm yourself. That is a task only for Ineluki and for me."

After his earlier words, this felt like a blow to my chest. Did Hakatri truly think I was only concerned for my own safety? "But it is you I fear for, Master, not myself. You and your brother."

"Ah." For a little while he was silent again. The trees of the lower mountain paraded past us as we descended, most covered with a green pelt of moss after Renewal's early rains. The stone banks that jutted out from the slope were as dark as peat. It was a striking landscape, wilder than the lands around Asu'a, but that only added to my feeling of unease. After years of reassuring routine, though so much sameness had sometimes frustrated me, I could no longer guess what might happen next.

"The Hikeda'ya tell of Hamakho's death as a betrayal," my master said abruptly, as though the tale now forced its way out of him. "They say that

Rinno, the leader of his hunters, was a son of Clan Kaura, which was more closely connected with the Sa'onserei clans than most of Hamakho's partisans. They say that in the Garden's final hours, Rinno and the others tried to force Hamakho to board the last ship, but the Great Protector refused until he could be certain all of his people had been found and brought onboard. At last they tried to carry him away by force, but Hamakho defended himself so fiercely that he killed three of his own dragonslayers before being struck down by their arrows. Even after this, Hamakho was still so revered that his kinsman carried his body to the clan's tomb before they fled the dying Garden."

I said nothing. My master's face was full of disgust, though whether over the deed itself or the version of the tale he had just related I could not tell.

"The Hamakha Clan held a tribunal on the Great Ship *Singing Fire* as they fled the Garden," he continued after a short pause. "As Hamakho's acknowledged favorite, Utuk'ku made that tribunal one of her first moments of forceful rule over her clansfolk. Under her direction, Rinno and the other surviving dragonslayers were judged guilty of Hamakho's murder. I do not know what happened to them—some say they were cast over the side of *Singing Fire* into the Ocean Indefinite and Eternal. None of them reached these lands. But when they were being judged, Hamakho's killers told a different story, though Utuk'ku and her nobles did their best afterward to suppress it.

"You see, even then, not all the Hamakha—the Hikeda'ya-to-be— were comfortable with Utuk'ku's seizure of power. These quiet renegades whispered that Rinno had spoken with great regret of how Hamakho had gone mad in the end, that when they tried to get him to board the waiting ship, he struck and killed the messenger who had been sent to him, and when the rest of his dragonslayers came—many of them his own kinsmen, who had braved and suffered much at his side defending the city of Tzo and our people—he attacked them as well, killing more of them. At last, terrified by his strength and growing madness—Hamakho was the mightiest of all the Garden's warriors—they loosed their arrows and cut him down before he could take more lives."

"But which is true?" I asked.

"We will never know for certain. Like Hamakho, Rinno é-Kaura and the others never reached this land, so they had no chance to tell their stories to more sympathetic ears than those of Utuk'ku and her followers." He shook his head. "I had not meant to tell you this story. It is particularly sad for our family, because Rinno was a cousin of my grandmother Senditu, and she never forgave the Hamakha for executing him without any of his clansfolk present."

"I am sorry, Master."

"No fault of yours, good Pamon." He looked at me for a searching moment. "Are you still fearing Serpent's Vale?"

"I confess I am, Master."

"If it brings you any peace to hear it, we will not go there soon. We have much to do before we enter that waste again. For one thing, we must prepare this witchwood trunk for our use, and since we do not have proper woodcrafting tools, that will not be a swift undertaking."

"So we do not go first to the swamp?"

"No. We will camp somewhere close enough that we need not travel far when our spear is finished, but we do not want Hidohebhi taking us unaware either, so a little distance is called for. Also, I still have much planning to do with my brother before the day comes. We will choose a spot at a safe distance from Serpent's Vale."

This relieved the worst of my fears, though I knew it was to be only a respite. The day would come sooner than I would like when we would have to ride into the vale again to face the beast. But the knowledge that it would not be this particular day was enough to lighten my thoughts.

After searching for a few hours at the bottom of the mountain, we found a wide, grassy dale that suited our needs. The Hernsmen told us it was named "Sithmead" because the river that flowed through it originated in the heights at Skyglass Lake, home to Vinadarta's Zida'ya folk since before the mortals arrived. If Cormach and his Hernsmen saw anything curious in it now becoming the camp of actual fairies (as they thought of my master and his people) they did not tell us. In fact, unless they were working directly with Lord Hakatri or Lord Ineluki, all of the mortals except the prince and his closest companions largely avoided us, setting their camp a goodly distance away from where my master laid his own fire.

I did not mind. The presence of all those mortals was strange and often disconcerting to me. Few of them spoke the Zida'ya tongue, so they talked among themselves in their own speech, which I thought sounded like the barking of dogs, full of harsh sounds and—I must reluctantly say—truly unpleasant scraping noises made at the back of the throat. Neither would most of the prince's followers look directly at my master or his brother when they spoke to them. Cormach explained that many of them feared the fairy-glamour, as they called it, convinced that gazing too long into the eyes of one of the *Sithi* (as they called even me!) would put them under some kind of spell. It was not worth disputing this ridiculous idea, but the mortals' mistrust of us added to the strain we all felt as we prepared to face a deadly foe. Of the mortals, only Prince Cormach seemed utterly un-afraid, and as the days passed in Sithmead I began to believe that if the Hernsmen lost him before he became king it would be disastrous, not only for Cormach's own folk but for my master's folk as well, making it much more difficult for the Zida'ya to maintain a healthy peace with the mortals. But the prince would not let himself be treated differently than his men. He shouldered the same burdens and assayed the same wearying, painful tasks of preparing the great witchwood trunk for use.

"Could we not use *kei-vishaa* on the end of the spear?" Cormach asked my master as they planned the work. "I have heard that in the old days the poisonous dust brought down some of the most terrible worms. Is that what you have in the jar Xaniko the Exile gave you?"

Kei-vishaa is made from the pollen of the witchwood tree's luminous white flowers and is well known among healers. It is rare, which is likely a good thing; in small amounts it can bring pain-ease, along with strange dreams. But too much of it, breathed or swallowed, could easily kill a mortal or one of the Zida'ya.

My master shook his head. "Xaniko's jar is something else, as you will learn. No, I fear that even if we could go to all the cities of my folk and gather enough of the precious dust, it still would work too slowly. A beast as large as Hidohebhi might take an hour or more to fall under its spell, and in that time it could still destroy many lives. Worse still, the madness *kei-vishaa* can cause might goad it to even greater rage. Better to try to kill the monster with a single stroke to the heart. At least we will know quickly whether we have succeeded or failed."

By the end of the first day in the valley we had finished setting up our camp beside the stream—a sort of guild-yard, with our only roof the naked sky. A few of the prince's Hernsmen became sentries, watching the valley from its outer hills so that the worm might not come upon us unawares. The Blackworm was always on our minds, and we all knew that the mortals and Zida'ya killed in our first encounter with it still lay in the marshy valley only a short distance away in Serpent's Vale, unsung and unburied.

Those of Cormach's men not standing sentry helped to roll and move the great tree trunk so that Hakatri and Ineluki might trim the stubby remaining limbs from the trunk and smooth its surface so that it would pierce instead of catch. They did this work with the only suitable tools we had, the brothers' swords *Indreju* and *Kimeku* and a witchwood hand-ax from my master's saddlebag.

My task was to sharpen whichever of those implements was not currently being used. I had much experience with Zida'ya whetstones but was surprised and pleased when the Hernsmen brought me a sort of mushroom that grew on birch trees; dried, it finished the edge of even one of those fabled Zida'ya blades as well as could be asked for. In truth, the woodcraft of the mortals proved to be very useful, as they knew the trees and plants that grew in Sithmead and the surrounding hills far better than we did.

As my masters and some of the men trimmed the trunk, other Hernsmen selected and felled sturdy oaks to make buckets for hauling water from the stream, and also used that strong wood to build huge racks on which the trunk would be lifted off the ground for hardening by hammer and fire. When I saw some of them working on the rope harness that had carried the witchwood trunk down from the grove, I thought at first they were making nets for fishing, although the spaces seemed much too wide to catch and hold any fish smaller than the largest pike or catfish. When I asked about this, Prince Cormach was amused. "We are making a stronger harness for the witchwood spear," he explained. "Your master said we must be able to lift it quickly when the time comes."

I nodded as if I understood, but I could not form a picture in my mind of what Hakatri planned. All our lives were at risk if the plan did not work, but I had spent most of my life trusting his wisdom, so I put my questions aside and went back to sharpening my master's sword.

When one end of the tree had been carefully trimmed and sharpened to a point, we were ready to finish the huge spear. The surface of the witchwood trunk had been scraped until it was very smooth, and the fire we had built had burnt down to coals, so the Hernsmen used their rope harness to lift the trunk up onto the heavy oak racks with its pointed end above the flames. Then several of the mortals took up wooden hammers and began to pound on it. At the same time, the embers beneath the sharpened tip were fanned back into life so that the witchwood could be hardened. As the Hernsmen pounded away, my master sang a quiet song he called the "*Dalala*," which he said came from my ancestors and helped to soothe the wood as it was being shaped. I could not understand the words, but I thought I recognized some of the sounds, though I could not say whether that was because of the times Lady Ona had tried to speak to me in our people's tongue or because of things I had heard from the other Tinukeda'ya in Asu'a. In any case, just hearing Hakatri sing those words made my skin prickle.

The coals were only allowed to smolder under the spear tip for a short while, the men turning the long wooden post the whole time, then the coals were raked away. The hammering continued through the day, Cormach's men pounding the witchwood until it was almost as hard as the finished strength of my master's sword.

"We have done very well with what we have," Ineluki said as the men completed their tasks.

"Yes," Hakatri said. "We have all done well. We will have a celebration tonight."

And we did. Three full casks of mead from Hernsland and a large jug of wine from Snowdrift were opened and emptied. Many, including my master, raised their voices to the skies in laughter and more old songs. For that moment, anyway, there was something like true accord between my master's folk and Cormach's men.

Surely, I thought then and still believe, this world has never seen anything quite like that night at Sithmead when the great witchwood spear was finished—a night when mortals and Zida'ya drank and ate and sang together, perhaps for the first time ever, and possibly also the last.

With our tree-sized spear now finished, the Hernsmen rolled it onto the huge rope sling so it could be carried to the battleground. I say battleground, but the place we had picked was only a pond just across the Silver Way from Sithmead, a short distance into Serpent's Vale. My master had chosen it because the muddy water was deep enough to hide the whole length of the spear, and because the end of the pond opposite where the dragon lurked was an insloping, angled wall of granite. Using other stones as tools—this was no work for a precious witchwood sword—we chipped away for hours at that slab of granite until we had made a notch just below the waterline which was big enough to hold the butt-end of the shaped witchwood trunk.

"It is possible the tree might shatter," my master said, "but it will not slip. It is held fast against the stone like a lord-errant clutching a lance."

Heavy ropes had been tied to the edges of the spear's harness. With the stonework finished, the cookfires lit, and the sentries sent out to keep watch, my master gathered us all around him and explained the plan that he and Xaniko the Exile had worked out.

"We must lead the worm onto the spear," he said. "Even a hundred of us would not be strong enough to thrust it between the scales of his breast, but if we brace its back end against the stone, as a hunter digs the butt of his boar-spear into the earth, we can hope that the beast's own strength and haste will do the work for us."

"*Skei, Sudhodaya!*" Ineluki snapped at a pair of weary Hernsmen who were whispering to each other. "Stop chewing your beards and listen, mortals. All our lives may depend on it."

The scolded Hernsmen fell into shamed silence at Ineluki's harsh words, but I saw several of their comrades share disgruntled looks.

"With the new, longer ropes on the spear's cradle," my master continued, "you men will only have to stand before the great beast for a few moments. See how the ground slopes up on both sides of the water." He gestured toward the rim of the pond, which had the granite shelf at one end, but was otherwise surrounded only by dirt and stony scree. "The moment I call out, you must pull the ropes at the front of the spear. That way it will rise up from the water with the sharp end higher and the other end socketed against the stone. If luck is with us, the worm's headlong rush will bring it onto the killing point. When it is impaled, let go of the ropes and run as far and fast as you wish to keep safe from its tail, which will lash and flail mightily, as Xaniko the Exile warned me."

"But, if I may ask something, Lord Hakatri," said Prince Cormach, "I see the wisdom of the plan, but how will we convince the worm to come toward us and to move swiftly enough to drive itself onto the spear? If we send men with sticks and torches to beat it out of the wrack as we drive boars out of a thick wood, will it not merely attack them instead?"

The question set the Hernsmen to murmuring again, and I thought that my master would be annoyed with the prince, but a moment later I realized that Cormach and Hakatri had planned this aforetime, because my master answered quickly and without rancor.

"A very apt question, Prince Cormach. No, we will not send beaters into the swamp, especially after dark, which will be the best time to effect our strategy, since the spear will be even harder to see then. Lord Xaniko gave me something to draw out the worm." He patted the wax-sealed jug which had come from Ravensperch and had sat for so long in my master's saddlebag. "These worms mark their territories just as bears and wolves do, with scent. Before he fought the deadly Snareworm, Lord Xaniko followed it for some time to learn its ways, and he collected some of the branches and grasses that the Snareworm had marked. That is what is in this jar."

"How does it smell?" one of the Hernsmen asked.

"Worse than you can imagine," said my master with a bit of a smile. "But trust me—by the end of this, we will *all* know the stink of it better than we'd like."

"Why would the *Drochnathair* come to the scent of another dragon?" a second man asked.

"To fight a rival, of course," Hakatri said. "The Blackworm cannot know that Xaniko killed the dragon that made this noisome stuff a long time ago. It will smell its own kind and come to defend its lair. At least that is what we hope."

The talk went on for some time—the Hernsmen, as anyone can understand, had many questions. At last the sentries were changed and the rest of the mortals took their rest while their prince, my master, and Lord Ineluki sat up to finish with their plans.

"It is not enough that Hidohebhi come to investigate this stranger's reek," Hakatri told us. "The great worm must be angry. It must be in haste to drive out the intruder. We need it to come running pell-mell into this little valley, and to do so without the ordinary caution even a large and dangerous beast maintains."

"And that is where your brother and myself come into things," said Cormach, pale and determined.

Ineluki sighed. "Brother, my oath hangs on me like an awful weight of chains." He had a fevered look in his eye. "Let me be the one to steady the great spear instead of you. The risk should be mine."

Hakatri shook his head. "No, brother. You are the more nimble rider, while I have better knowledge of the spear and its harness. You must be the one to lead the creature down on us—you and Prince Cormach."

They argued, but Hakatri would not budge. Ineluki gave in at last, but he did not look pleased. "Then I will take my own spear," he said, "so at least I can strike the first blow."

"As you wish," my master told him. "But if you fail to lead the beast down into this pool all will be for naught, and many of us may die. Do not let your honor cause you to forget that."

Ineluki gave him a strange look, half shame, half anger. "Do not treat me like one of the mortals, brother—like someone whose courage you doubt. You and I have fought side by side against giants and other fell creatures. You know my quality."

"I do, which is why I gave you the most important role of all. Prince Cormach will entice the great worm out of his swamp, but it is you who must convince him to chase you to the spear."

"I will not fail," said Ineluki firmly. He spoke the truth, as it proved, but in the end it was not enough.

Hakatri nodded. "Then we all know our parts."

"Except me, my lord," I said. "You have given me nothing to do."

"You will be my second, Armiger Pamon. You will stand with me. If something happens to me, you will act in my stead to make certain Cormach's men do what they must."

It sounded as if he was trying to protect me, to keep me from harm as he might protect a child, but a moment's reflection suggested that if Hakatri truly did not want me in danger, there were many places more wholesome he could have chosen than standing beside him as an angry dragon rushed down on us. My pride was soothed, but at the same time the sheer magnitude of what we would do the next day swept over me like a thunderous ocean wave, making me gasp a little and shiver, although I think none of the others noticed.

In the middle-night, as the Hernsland mortals slept, something huge crawled past our camp in the darkness. The sentries sent one of their number to let us know, but we had heard it already. Hakatri ordered the guards to move back into the camp, then he, Ineluki, and Prince Cormach waited together, listening for any sign that the creature might approach us. I was at my master's side, of course, and again I heard that ghastly rattling as the great worm's armored body scraped against trees and over stones, and the snapping, loud as war-drums, as smaller trunks broke under its great weight. As we crouched, listening, I could not help thinking of the horror of the first encounter, of Yohe and Lilumo and the others who had been killed by that dreadful beast. I trembled in all my limbs, but even terror would not force me from Hakatri's side.

In the dim starlight I watched him for signs of the same fear, but my master's people do not easily show their inner thoughts, and I could see nothing but calm attention in his face as he listened. That helped me a little, but what aided me the most was how the sounds gradually diminished in the distance. We did not hear the great beast again that night, so it must have returned to its hiding-place by another way. Either the sheer number of men on the meadow had led it to pass us by, or it already had its stomach set on some easier prey, but the cold-drake never came close enough to threaten us. Still, I could not forget that even if we survived the night, the next day would bring us face-to-face with the creature. When the dawn finally came, I felt almost as exhausted as if we had fought it.

"Now, while the sun is bright," my master announced that morning, "we must make everything ready. Into the valley!"

Ineluki rode ahead with Prince Cormach to search out the best path from the dragon's lair to the waiting spear. As the two of them rode off, talking quietly, I realized I had never before seen my master's brother speak to a mortal as though to an equal. It was an arresting sight, and I confess to a pang of envy or something like it, because Ineluki had never treated me as anything but a servant.

The plan was simple enough: our pond and the witchwood spear were on the western side of a rise at one edge of the swampy vale. Prince Cormach was to ride farther into the valley, then draw the worm's attention and induce it to follow him. He would then ride up the slope of the rising ground, leading it toward the place at the top where Ineluki waited. It was then up to Ineluki to become the quarry in place of the mortal prince, and to lead the terrible creature down the slope to the place where Hakatri and the Hernsmen waited at the pond. At the last moment, before the great worm could turn away, the mortals would heave the sharpened end of the stone-braced spear up out of the water so that the dragon's own weight and headlong rush would bring it onto the hardened point.

Prince Cormach's men made their way down to the edge of the pond and took the harness ropes in hand. Returned from his scouting expedition, Cormach rode up on Seafoam. Hakatri had decided that the sure-footed mare would be a better choice for him than Cormach's own horse.

"Remember, this mare needs only the lightest touch to guide her this way or that," my master told the prince. "She knows your thoughts almost before you do." He then passed Xaniko's jar up to the prince, who began to remove the wax seal, but Hakatri quickly raised his hand.

"Do not open it yet, I pray you—not until you are much closer to the worm's lair. We do not want to bring it down on us until all is ready. Also, you have not sampled its astonishing scent yet, but I have . . . and I am still trying to forget it. Trust me, good Cormach, and wear this over your nose and mouth or you will be choking from the moment you unstop that jar." He handed the prince a scarf of fine weave. When Cormach had tied the cloth across his face below his eyes, he took the jar and a little hand-broom made of twigs and set off up the slope of the dell cradling the pond. The prince carried no weapon except his sheathed sword, since he would need both hands to carry out his task.

Ineluki appeared then, balancing a long war-spear on his shoulder. He had donned his witchwood armor, as had my master, and I thought I could see their great forebears in them, heroic wormsbanes like the Garden's

Hamakho and Aisoga of Hikehikayo. But many of those noble Zida'ya
came to ignoble ends, I realized with a foreboding I did my best to ignore.

Ineluki looked over the swampy hollow one last time, making certain
of the landmarks, measuring out the path he would take to lead the great
beast down on us. "Whatever happens next, brother," he called, "this will
be a deed that will be sung long after we are gone."

"Let us hope that we live to enjoy at least a few of the songs," Hakatri
called back. "Ride swiftly, *Inka-sho*. I beg you, do nothing foolish."

Ineluki laughed, though I thought it had a wild edge. "Foolish? Me?"

"I know our parents will never forgive me if harm comes to you," my
master said. "Your bravery is well known. Take no risks."

"That is a strange thing to say to someone going to seek out a Great
Worm and beg it to chase him—but I hear you, brother."

"Then you and the prince, fare you both well."

Ineluki lowered the visor of his helmet and raised his spear in salute
before riding over the crest of the rise that separated the pond in its shallow dell from the rest of marshy Serpent's Vale to the east. Within a few
moments he had disappeared from sight.

"And now you, Pamon." My master pointed up the sloping wall of
stone where the butt-end of the spear was lodged. "I want you at the top,
there."

"But you said I would be beside you!"

"As I told you, if something happens to me you must take my part and
finish it. If you are standing close beside me and I fall, you will likely fall
too. Also, someone must watch from a high place to tell me and these
mortals what is happening before Hidohebhi comes into our view."

I climbed to the spot he had indicated, trying not to show reluctance.
What he said seemed wise, but in those long-ago days I feared being
thought a coward by my master's folk more than I feared for my own life.
At least that is how I remember it. Memory, though, is not always the most
trustworthy historian.

From the top of the stony slope above the pond I could see far beyond
the rise where Ineluki now rode back and forth on lithe, proud Bronze,
the war-ribbons on his spear fluttering like a flag as he waited to do his
part. Beyond him, and much smaller, I could just make out Cormach
mounted on my lord's pale horse, Seafoam. The mortal prince had opened

The Exile's jar and dipped in the twig-broom, and as he rode deeper into the swampy valley he waved it in the air, spreading the scent. After a few more moments Cormach vanished behind a row of leaning, broken trees, and I could not see him anymore.

It was not too much longer, though, before the breeze brought me my first smell of the dragon-spoor from Xaniko's jar. I saw my master wrinkle his nose and turn his back to the wind. A moment later it struck me too—a dreadful stench, even at such a distance. It smelled not just of foul old urine, which attacked the nose with stinging vapors, but also putrefaction and a thick, beastly musk—a cursed marriage of strong and dreadful scents. The Hernsmen holding the ropes on either side of the pond began to groan and protest, some gagging, as the first invisible wave of it swept over us but my master barked at them to keep their wits about them, and they fell silent, though they continued to wag their heads and scowl in disgust. I could not help feeling sorry for Prince Cormach, who must have felt as though he rode through a storm of that foul, foul stink.

Cormach's tiny, mounted figure rode back and forth at the edge of the trees as he flicked his broom like a celebrant sprinkling the waters of the Garden over a crowd of supplicants. At first it seemed to have no effect. What felt like an hour crept by, and even I, wound as tight as the string of a harp, began to think that the worm-spoor had failed, that we would have to try to lure the creature out of its nest by more direct methods.

The sun had set a short while earlier, and though the hills and watery dales were still lit by the white twilight sky, evening was close at hand and distant objects were becoming harder and harder to see. Because of that, I did not notice for a span of several heartbeats that something had swayed up out of the swamp beyond Prince Cormach. Even when I finally saw it, it seemed nothing more at first than another tree trunk bending in the freshening evening breeze, but its motions were different than the other trees, which bent as one thing in the wind. Cormach was still doggedly riding back and forth at the edge of the deepest part of the swamp as I realized the truth.

"Master!" I cried. "It comes! The worm has roused!"

At my sudden call, cries of alarm came from the Hernsmen below me, though I doubt most of them understood my Zida'ya words. Some of the mortals, who had let go of their ropes, now floundered and splashed in the muddy shallows as they tried to find them once more. I could not say with certainty that Cormach heard my cry of alarm, but just as I shouted, he turned and saw the great head on its long neck, watching him as intently as a viper that has spotted a rabbit. To my surprise, though, the prince did not immediately turn and ride away, but continued to canter back and forth, waving his worm-bepissed broom in the air. I faintly heard him shout, *"Ha! You darksome thing! Are you afraid of Men of the West? Come out, you stinking snake with legs!"*

Now the great dark head swayed again, following his movements. A heartbeat later the beast abruptly began to move out of the wrack where it had been hidden, its long neck dropping down as it wound toward the mortal prince through the broken trees and undergrowth, its dreadful, bony head seeming almost to float in the air. Cormach was brave but he was no fool, and it had become clear in an instant that the worm, despite its great size, could move almost as swiftly as a running horse. Cormach turned Seafoam and dug in his heels, then they sprinted away over the marshy ground, sending up gouts of muddy water each time Seafoam's hooves touched down.

"Cormach is coming!" I shouted. "The worm follows!"

"Where is my brother?" Hakatri moved in beside the mortal men to steady them. If their hearts had suddenly grown faint, I did not blame them. On top of my stony rise, I was the safest of all, yet I was terrified.

"He is waiting, my lord!" I shouted. "Ineluki sees the prince coming and he waits!"

"Pray to the Garden he does not wait too long!" Hakatri called. "Tell me when he starts toward us."

The evening light had now turned blue and subdued. Things silhouetted against the sky seemed clear and distinct but details closer to the ground were murky. Prince Cormach guided nimble Seafoam up the rise, dodging from one high, dry place to another, and in that moment I was glad beyond telling that the brave mortal rode my master's swift, clever steed. The dragon's short but powerful legs drove it across the swampy ground with frightening speed, and its size meant that even the deepest pools and muddiest bogs did not slow it. Indeed, the weight of its massive body and long, dragging tail emptied even the largest ponds as it wallowed through them, splashing up great peacock-tails of dirty water. I remember the immense, jagged jaws hanging open, and a tongue the color of slate. I also remember its black and gold eyes seemed to glow like lanterns, though that may have just been a moment's reflection of the fading western sky— all I have is memory, after all.

As Cormach neared the place where Ineluki waited on his stallion Bronze, the last of the dragon's immense body became visible as it clambered out onto open ground. Its size was even more astonishing than I had realized when we first saw it, a nightmare out of another time, another world. It was as long from head to tail-end as an ocean-going ship, forty cubits of powerful sinew, plated black armor, and murderous jaws. I confess that in that moment, I lost hope. I could not imagine anything even slowing such an abomination, let alone killing it, and it took every bit of bravery I had to stay where I was, though my master was the one in the greatest danger.

"'Ware, my lord!" I cried. "It has almost reached the top of the rise!"

"Is Ineluki riding?" he called.

"Not yet," I cried. "He is lifting his spear!"

"Spirits of the Garden, what is he thinking?" I heard true despair in Hakatri's voice, something I had never heard from him before. "Do not stay, you fool!" he shouted to his brother. "Ride to us! *Ride!*"

Ineluki rose then, standing in his stirrups as the worm came scraping up the rise toward him, its great claws tearing up and flinging aside dirt and large stones as if they were dandelion fluff. As Prince Cormach reached Ineluki and rode past him, the creature was only a few dozen paces behind. Ineluki drew back his arm and flung his spear with all the force he could muster. It flew, straight and true, and struck the monster just below its eye, which was set in a ring of bony armor like a sacred jewel in a temple wall. He missed the eye by a handsbreadth only, but so mighty was Ineluki's cast that his spear pierced the plate of the dragon's cheek, sank in, and stuck there, quivering. The great worm did not slow even a step. Ineluki yanked hard at Bronze's reins and they turned and leaped up the slope with the monster close behind them.

Each moment thereafter seemed to happen as if I were dreaming: I could see all but do nothing.

The worm still did not roar or even growl as it charged after Ineluki but made a dreadful hissing noise like water thrown on hot embers. His spearcast may not have wounded it badly, but it had fixed the monster's attention and its anger on him. Prince Cormach crested the rise first, then headed Seafoam to one side as he and my master had planned, while the creature followed Ineluki on Bronze as the horse dug his way up the last part of the slope. None of the waiting Hernsmen had yet seen the monster, so when Cormach appeared they cheered to see him safe. An instant later Ineluki appeared behind him, crouched low in the saddle. Then the worm's great head topped the rise on its swaying, serpentine neck, and the mortals below me shouted out in horror.

I realized that the one thing my master had not been able to do was prepare the Hernsmen for the first sight of the cold-drake Hidohebhi. He had tried, telling them again and again that the creature was dreadful to see, that they must at all costs not run, and that if fear overtook them, they should close their eyes, since they only needed to hear his command to raise the spear. And to their credit, though a few of them staggered back in horror and dropped their ropes, my master's angry commands drove them back to their stations.

As Cormach urged Seafoam out of the worm's path, Ineluki sped down the slope toward the pond. The dragon was fifty paces away from us, then forty, moving with horrifying speed, but Ineluki seemed safely ahead. Already, at Hakatri's command, the ropes had tightened and the sharpened tip of the huge witchwood spear was beginning to rise from the murky pond. Then everything went terribly wrong. Even as the dragon lurched over the top of the ridge and began its half-crawling, half-slithering rush down the slope, Seafoam stepped into a hole.

As I have said, I watched it all but could do nothing. As terrifying as it might have been, everything was still unfolding as my master and the others had planned, but then Seafoam abruptly pitched forward and crashed to the ground, rolling and skidding in a tangle of long, pale legs, her head bent back in agony. Prince Cormach was thrown over her neck and into the path of the oncoming worm. Hidohebhi was fixed entirely on retreating Ineluki, who was already threading his way across bits of solid ground as the worm sped after him in a hissing rage. As the Hernsmen below me screamed in terror at their prince's helplessness, the worm's great clawed front foot landed with awful force. It just missed the limp and motionless prince, but as the massive foot lifted again, by pure chance it caught up Cormach and flung him aside. He flew through the air, limp as a rag, and bounced and slid over the top of the rise and out of sight.

At the sight, the Hernsmen pulling on the ropes to lift the spear lost their wits. At least half of them simply dropped their ropes and fled the dragon's path, scattering to either side, but many ran toward where their prince had fallen. We will never know whether the remaining Hernsmen might have been able to lift the great witchwood trunk by themselves. As it was, they saw their fellows flee, then looked up to see the great worm still chasing Ineluki toward them, and they despaired. All the remaining Hernsmen dropped their ropes and floundered out of the water, all thought gone but to get out of the way of the enraged, hissing monster.

Ineluki was already riding through the pond and did not see what had happened to Cormach, but as he made his way past the witchwood spear he must have seen that all the mortals had fled. He could not stop Bronze, though—the stallion's speed was too great and the ground too slippery. Their breakneck pace carried both horse and Ineluki past the pond and past his brother as my master watched the collapse of the hunt with a face frozen in dismay. Because he could not stop Bronze's headlong flight, Ineluki pulled hard on the reins and the horse leaped up onto the granite rock face below me.

"Master!" I shouted to Hakatri in desperation. "Get out!" I started to scramble down toward him, but my feet slipped on wet stone and went out from under me. I hit the back of my head and for a terribly long moment could only lay stunned on the stony, sloping bank, staring up at the darkening sky.

Ineluki had finally pulled Bronze to a halt and turned him, but the horse caught sight of the worm and reared, forelegs kicking, and Ineluki fell from his saddle. As he and I struggled back to our feet, we lost the moment. Instead of fleeing as the mortals had done, Hakatri plunged into the muddy water and began trying to lift the huge, sharpened trunk by himself. The worm reached the edge of the pond and came at him in a tumult of brackish water and broken trees, hissing like a bellows, its bony, snapping jaws foremost, like the prow of a ship.

"No!" Ineluki shouted. "Hakatri, no!"

I still do not know how my master managed it. In those last instants, he came up beneath a log that a dozen mortal men had struggled to carry in its sling, his teeth bared in a mirthless grin of exertion, the veins beneath his golden skin bulging on his forehead and neck as he lifted the punishing weight of the witchwood. I heard him cry out in pain and desperation—the worst sound, I think, that I have ever heard, and one I will never forget.

As his brother and I watched in helpless horror, my master was able to heave the terrible weight upward until the sharpened tip rose above the pond's surface. The dragon came down on him like a vast boulder tumbling down a hillside, and for a moment, as the monster came down on him, everything disappeared in the froth. Then the spouting, splashing water turned black, and though the hissing continued, I saw that it came now not from the monster, but from a fountain of black blood splashing out over the pond and the bank. Where it struck, the water boiled, sending up billowing clouds of steam like a bronzesmith quenching a red-hot bar in a bucket. Moments later, as the billows thinned, I saw the bulk of the worm sprawled in twitching coils, half in and half out of the pond, the spatters and gobs of its shiny black blood sizzling where they touched moisture. Then Hakatri began to scream.

I scrambled down the slope and began flailing in the water, blinded by steam, reaching toward my master's terrible cries as I waded deeper. I had to step over the worm's gigantic tail. I should have looked first to make certain the beast was truly dead before turning my back on it, but at that moment all I could think of was Hakatri. His cries were terrible beyond describing. There were no words in them, only the raw sound of agony. I found him before I could see him, my hands closing on his arm. Then, as I began to drag him toward the edge of the pond, I felt a fierce burning pain from the smears of dragon's blood scorching through my gloves. I shucked them and threw them away, then wriggled out of my cloak and wrapped it around Hakatri's arm. Thus protected for the moment, I was able to ignore the pain of my own burns long enough to drag him toward the shore of the pond. His terrible cries did not abate.

A few moments later Ineluki reached me, and together we pulled Lord Hakatri up the bank so that only his feet were in the water. He was still screaming. Muddy water and black blood covered his face, so I used the cloak to wipe it away, but my master was insensible of anything except the pain. I splashed water on him in a frantic effort to wash off the worst of the worm's blood—I could see it steaming in spots, as though my master himself had become red-hot metal—but it did not seem to do any good.

"His armor!" Ineluki said, then shoved me roughly to one side and began to cut away the thick leather straps of my master's witchwood breastplate. In a few moments he was able to pull it away, then we rolled Hakatri off the back plate and into the pond once more, scrubbing him with gobs of mud and my cloak, which was already falling apart simply from touching the dragon's caustic essence. Doing my best to ignore my master's dreadful cries, though my eyes were so full of tears I could scarcely see, I helped Ineluki strip his brother naked as we raced to wipe all the scorching blood from his skin. Everywhere we cleaned we found terrible welts, red and rupturing, so that I despaired of my master living out the hour. My own hands, though barely touched by the black blood, hurt so badly I could not even imagine my master's suffering.

At last Hakatri fell into limp silence. I spread the last clean corner of my cloak across his chest, then laid my head against his scorched and streaming flesh.

"His heart still beats," I said.

"We must find healers," cried Ineluki. "Snowdrift—that is the closest house." Beneath the horror that was plain on his face and in his voice, I heard something else: an unimaginable anger, although in that moment I took little notice. I was still lost in a dream—a terrible, almost unbelievable dream—and I could barely keep my thoughts in order from one instant to the next.

There was no time to make a litter or anything else to carry Hakatri. When we had washed all the black blood away, Ineluki heaved his brother's burned, naked body up onto his saddle and clambered up behind him; then, without another word to me, he spurred away toward Birch Hill.

Numb, feeling as blackly dazzled as if I had been struck by a thunderbolt out of a bright and cloudless sky, I watched him ride off at tremendous speed, Bronze's hooves barely touching the ground. Realizing an instant later that I had been left by myself, the mortals and my Zida'ya masters all gone, I had a fearful thought and turned to see if Hidohebhi was truly dead.

Even though it lay before me in a pile of massive coils, dark tongue lolling and gold-shot eyes already filming, it was hard to believe that such a creature had truly lived. The Blackworm had been pierced through its

breast by the tree-spear just a little to one side of center. My master had
managed an astounding feat, and I could only pray he would not pay for
it with his life. Later, though, I had cause to wonder whether it might have
been better if he had not survived.

The dragon's head was almost as long as I was tall, a great, blunt thing
so thickly armored it looked as though it had been carved out of black
stone. I spat on it, then turned away.

My hands still stung me bitterly, but I had been fortunate, and though
I felt the pain of those burns a long time after, I did not suffer a hundredth
of what my master did. For long moments after silence fell, I could only
stare at the ruination of our plans—the discarded, torn rope harness, the
great, scraping tracks of the monster's approach, and the crushed, lifeless
body of poor Seafoam. With no one else to help me, I could not even
make a grave for my master's horse. Though the fault was not hers, and
though she bravely did her rider's bidding to the end, I had to leave her
body for the wolves and other scavenging creatures.

This hurt me more than my scorched hands did. I had tended the swift
mare for years, and now I had to leave her where she lay, like a discarded
apple core or a broken wheel. But the dragon was dead. Who could I hate?

At last, still feeling as though I had awakened to find the world empty
of everyone but myself, I gathered up my master's belongings. His clothes
were ruined, but his armor, though stained and burned in spots, was still an
ancient family treasure. I found his sword *Indreju* still in its scabbard, the belt
burned through in the first moments of the dragon's thrashing death, and I
took that too. I wrapped them all in my tattered, wet cape, then climbed
onto the saddle of Hakatri's war horse, wincing as I took the reins. Frostmane started a little as I mounted, though I had cared for him for years.

"I know," I said, as he paced in a restive circle. "The world has turned
upside-down." I pointed his nose toward Birch Hill, then took one last
look at the place where everything had changed so suddenly and so dread-
fully. The evening light was almost completely gone; the great, sprawling
corpse of the dragon might have been a pile of rocks or a huge fallen tree.
I turned away from the scene of devastation and gave Frostmane my heels.
The world was growing dark around me. It did not feel as though the sun
would ever rise again.

Part
Three

The White Walls

We did not learn of it for some time, but the mortal prince Cormach survived that dreadful day. He was badly hurt, with broken legs and other injuries, but he lived on to a good old age and led his people well, although after Serpent's Vale he always walked with a limp.

Ineluki carried the mortally injured Hakatri as swiftly as he could out of Serpent's Vale and back to Birch Hill, the closest settlement of my master's people.

Lord Dunyadi's house Snowdrift did not have the array of healers that lived in Asu'a, but it would have taken days of riding to reach them. As luck would have it, though, one very wise healer lived at Snowdrift. His name was Geniki, and he was old enough to have treated the terrible burns caused by dragon's blood before—although, as he himself admitted upon seeing my master, never with such dreadful injuries. By the time I arrived Geniki had already put Hakatri to sleep with a powerful draught of *kei-vishaa* and called for some of Dunyadi's retainers to make their way into the mountain heights nearby in search of snow. Frantic and unable to do anything else to help his brother, Ineluki rode with them, and by nightfall they had brought back several washing tubs packed with the year's last snow. Lord Dunyadi gave up his own bath so that my master could lie in it while the healer packed the snow around him. Lord Hakatri still breathed, but I could guess nothing else about his condition.

I sat with him that way for two days. I could not even hold his hand or touch him, though I ached to, because even the lightest brush of fingers on his skin—even those places that showed no mark of being burned— made him moan and writhe. He did not speak, except for once when he suddenly awakened, tried to sit up but could not, and said very clearly, *"Again and again she peers behind the veil. The cold ones outside are taking notice."* He mumbled a few more words after that but I could make nothing of them, then he lapsed back into insensibility again.

I have never wept so much, not even when I was a child. I was certain it was only a matter of hours, days at the most, before my master died.

On the third day after Hakatri had been put into his snow-bath, Lord Dunyadi's daughter Himuna came to my master's bedside. Her manner was calm and her words measured, but her sadness at Hakatri's suffering was evident. "How fares your lord today, Armiger Pamon?" she asked me.

"I wish I could tell you he seemed better, my lady, but I see no improvement," I admitted. Himuna was Birch Hill's chief celebrant—not the sort who wanted foolish optimism. "He cries out in his sleep betimes, as though he dreamed the worm's attack again, but he says many other things that make no sense at all."

"None of us can guess what your master might be seeing," she told me. "The touch of dragon's blood brings the Dream Road close, but that road is always full of phantoms." Himuna shook her head. "In any case, it is not Lord Hakatri I have come for, but you."

"Me?" I was more than surprised. "Why, *S'huesa?*"

"Because Lady Amerasu wishes to speak with you."

I leaped up, startled but also relieved. Surely Amerasu would know what to do. Surely the Sa'onsera would put things to right—or at least as much as could be put right after such a terrible tragedy. "First Grandmother is here?"

"No, no. I have spoken to her through a Witness. Now she wishes to have words with you."

"But why?"

"That is not for me to say, Armiger. But you should not keep her waiting. Follow me."

I had scarcely left my master's side since we had come to Snowdrift, terrified that his last moments might occur while I was away. Still, I could not imagine turning down Amerasu, even were she not the oldest and greatest of my master's folk. Above all else, she was Hakatri's mother, and I knew her heart must be aching. When I was young, I was felled with a wasting illness and my mother Enla did not leave my side, even when the fever took her as well. I lived. My mother did not. My father barely spoke for months afterward and was never the same. From the day she was buried on the headland he all but made the stables his home, and because of that, I did too.

I followed Himuna through the bright hallways, blind to the beauty of Snowdrift's decoration as I was blind to everything but my master's suffering. She led me into Lord Dunyadi's residence. His wife Uzu'una had died many years before, but none of her things had been removed: a delicate robe the color of a summer sky still hung on a peg on the wall, as if she might return at any moment and wish to put it on. A polished, intricately carved table still held Uzu'una's jewel box and mirror, and for a moment I thought the mirror might be the Witness that Himuna had mentioned— it was very old, and its frame was beautifully ornamented—but she led me through the apartment without pausing, then slid aside a panel to reveal another room.

Much of the center of the room belonged to a living birch tree, which stood in an open space in the middle of the floor, rooted directly into the hill beneath Snowdrift. The roof was open just like the floor, and though the tree's branches did not reach past the ceiling, nothing stood between them and the sky, sun, and rainclouds.

"This ancient birch came from the Lost Garden as a seed," Himuna told me. "While others hoarded witchwood to bring to the new lands, my forebears wanted something that spoke to them of their old home." It was a beautiful tree, resplendent in that moment with green spring leaves, the bark so white that it looked as though it had been washed and polished within the last hour. (Perhaps it had been. I never asked.)

Beneath the tree and set on an otherwise empty table stood an upright mirror. It was the size of my two palms side by side and its frame was almost the opposite of Lady Uzu'una's dressing mirror, an undecorated black oval with a stand to hold it upright.

"I will leave you alone," said Himuna, showing me a deference that confused me: I was nobody. Was she honoring the mere fact that Amerasu wished to speak with me?

"I have never used a Witness, my lady. I have seen my master use one, but it is mysterious to me."

"All you need to do is sit before it—here." She took a stool from against one wall of the room. "If the Sa'onsera wishes to speak to you—and she said that she did—she will do the rest. Just sit and look at your reflection."

The celebrant went out then, leaving me alone beneath the tree and the patch of open sky. A cloud passed over the house, momentarily darkening the room, and a fine mist of rain floated down onto the leaves and my face and hands as I sat looking at my reflection. It was not an edifying sight, nor an entirely familiar one. It has never been my practice to stare at myself in a glass, though of course I knew how I looked, and the face that gazed back at me seemed even less interesting than usual. Back in Asu'a there were always many other Tinukeda'ya to see, but except for the two ladies of Ravensperch, I had been in the company of only mortals and my master's folk for more than a moon's waxing and waning; it was hard to believe the unexceptional being looking dully back at me had lived through so much in such a short time.

As one of the Ocean Children, I do not have the shaggy animality of the mortals—for which I am very grateful—but neither do I have the gem-like, near-perfection of the Zida'ya, who even in great age retain all their grace and most of their youthful beauty. Instead, I was then—and remain— something in between, neither one nor the other, and I felt it sorely. We Tinukeda'ya, at least those of us who still live among the Zida'ya, have something of their slenderness, something of their fine features, but to my own eye I seemed a poor imitation of my master's kind: shapeless, impre-cise, a copy made by a less competent artist. My hands are long like those of the Zida'ya, but my fingers are wider and flatter, and though my eyes do not have the muddy color of most mortal eyes—and they are certainly not the near-black of the Hikeda'ya—they do not have the compelling golden hue of the Zida'ya either. As if arranged by compromise, mine are merely yellow, the eyes of some dumb beast like a goat or a fowl of the air.

As I stared in dissatisfaction, the image of my own features seemed to shimmer, as if the mirror's polished surface was water rippled by a passing breeze. Then I felt her, and although her presence was calm and even warm, the strength of it—the sheer force of her thoughts—shocked me, like reaching out in the dark and finding a wall where an opening was expected.

Pamon Kes, greetings. Her words were in my head, not my ears, as plain to me as if I rehearsed something that I wished to say before saying it.

"*S'huesa!*" I said, then realized I had clumsily spoken the word aloud. I tried again, trying to keep my mouth closed and my tongue stilled as I dutifully began the Six Songs of Respectful Request: *Lady Amerasu, revered Sa'onsera, I give you my most humble greetings and pray that I find you hale in heart and hale in body—*

Even at a less fearful time, you need not stand on ceremony with me, young one, she said, silencing my greeting. I was astonished at her lack of formality. I was her eldest son's squire, of course, and thus had spoken to her many times, but only to answer questions that she asked, almost always about Hakatri when she wished to know something of his plans. In fact, though she had never been anything other than correct and even kind with me, I was more than a little frightened of her. And if the power of her immense age and wisdom had been daunting in those other circumstances, how much more so when I could sense her power not just reaching out to me but surrounding me and all my thoughts? I felt like an infant held by a gentle giant.

You are too generous, my lady.

Let us not waste time debating my generosity, she told me, and for the first time I sensed a current of fear beneath the strength. *My eldest son is terribly wounded. My other son will not speak to me. Dunyadi has told me what he knows, but he was not present when Hakatri fell. Tell me. Tell me what happened to my son—to both my sons.*

My heart was beating fast. Out of pure selfishness, I did not want to be the one to tell her the whole story of what had happened in Serpent's Vale. Already I had spent long stretches of the vigil beside my wounded master pondering what had gone wrong there and why. Unhappy thoughts will overwhelm an idle body, and my mind had turned back again and again to the tragedy. But some of what I saw as mistakes were things that my beloved master and his brother had chosen to do. I could not imagine myself blaming them to Lady Amerasu, not just because she was the Sa'onsera, the most revered of all the Zida'ya, but because she was their mother.

Why do you hesitate? she asked me. *Please, do not make me wait to know more.*

Only to put the thoughts in my head into some kind of order, I told her, though our connection through the Witness seemed so intimate that I felt sure she could guess I was not telling her the entire truth.

First tell me of my eldest son. I have had Dunyadi's account, but I want to hear from you. Does Hakatri suffer? Is he in pain?

That question at least I could answer honestly. *He does not show it, Lady Amerasu, but I think that is because he is deep in the fog of the* kei-vishaa. *He moves a little, and sometimes he speaks, but mostly only in single words, and I cannot often make sense of even those.*

Will he live? she asked.

I am not the one who could tell you that, Lady. I know that he is strong. I know that the healer Geniki has done all he can. But I fear what will happen when my lord is no longer pressed down into slumber by the witchwood powder.

Then Hakatri must come back to Asu'a, she told me. *Geniki has done well, and I would trust him with my own life as I have trusted him with my son's, but I doubt he can do all that is needed.*

I had a moment of hope. *Are there healers at Asu'a who can cure my lord?*

Cure him? I felt rather than heard the tremor in her thoughts. *There is no cure that I have heard of for the bane of dragon's blood. But there are other ways to ease his pain, ways that even Geniki does not know. Hakatri must come back to Asu'a. He must come back to us.* For a moment her fear and sorrow were plain even to me. *I beg of you, Pamon Kes, use whatever persuasion you can to convince my sons to return to their home.*

I will try, *S'huesa* Amerasu. *Of course I will.* My world was shaken. Amerasu had always been a respected and even beloved figure, but always remote, at least from my humble vantage. Now she was pleading with me—with me, a Tinukeda'ya servant!—to help her get her children home.

The day after Amerasu spoke to me through the Witness, my master awoke. He had been taken from his bath of ice and moved to Dunyadi's own bedchamber, where he lay on the softest, smoothest bedding that could be found. I was sitting beside him, of course, which was where I spent most of my hours, reading to him from a book of poems written by Benhaya-Shonó of Kementari, one of the greatest bards of my master's people. I did not always understand these old, old poems—they held subtleties that I guessed only other Zida'ya could appreciate, references to famous tales from the Garden that I did not know and to people of the Great Exile who had died long before my time—but Benhaya—an invented name of the poet's own choosing that meant "Sparrow"—had also created passages so sublime that I sometimes forgot the one who made them was not of my race, that he had been writing not for me but his own folk.

As I read, a murmuring noise from the bed made me look up to see that Hakatri's eyes were open and that he appeared to be trying to say something. I moistened his lips with water, then lifted the cup to his mouth so he could drink.

"It hurts so, Pamon," were his first words.

I was so full of joy that he recognized me that it was all I could do not to grab his hand and kiss it. "Master, it is good to hear your voice!"

He groaned, and when he spoke it was in a nearly breathless whisper. "I wish I could say . . . that it is good to be alive. But there is fire burning all through me, Pamon. In my body, all the way down into my bones. By the Garden, it would have been better if I had died."

Even the mere daub of watered wormsblood that had briefly touched my own hands was still causing me great pain, as if I had held them in a flame: I could not doubt he was in terrible agony, but I could think of nothing to do but reassure him, however baselessly. "No, Master! What is wrong may be remedied. There is no remedy for death."

But Hakatri was no longer listening. His moment of wakefulness had taken all his strength, and he had lapsed back into insensibility once more.

In the days that followed my lord was awake more and more. Though his pain was always present, and he spoke about it in the wondering tone of a child who has discovered something utterly new, at times he seemed nearly himself. He asked if the dragon was dead, and of course for news of Ineluki. I assured him that the worm had died but Ineluki had not, that by luck his brother had avoided all injury. That was not entirely true: Ineluki might have avoided wounds of the flesh, but his spirit seemed sorely injured. I heard many tales of his bitter anger at the mortals who had fled before the dragon, and I also heard he spent most of his time walking alone among the trees of Birch Hill with a face like stone, so that nobody dared approach him.

Reassured about his brother, Hakatri asked me about Cormach and his Hernsmen. I had not yet heard the news of the prince's survival, so I could tell him only what I had seen in Serpent's Vale. In all ways but his suffering, my master seemed so like his ordinary self—if he had not, I might have kept silent about the hatred Ineluki seemed to have conceived for the mortals. But I spoke, and though Hakatri was disturbed by Ineluki's fixation with the Hernsmen's supposed crimes, not mere failures, my master himself seemed to feel no anger toward them.

"They feared for their prince," he told me through cracked lips. "We none of us know precisely what we will do in such a moment. Whatever my brother's feelings, I hope Cormach survived. He was one of the best mortals I have met."

And that was my master, summed up. Do you wonder that I loved him? To suffer such a terrible thing and yet to feel pity for lesser creatures?

With Hakatri's wits apparently restored, I was finally able to tell him of his mother's words to me. By the time I finished, his pain had once more grown too great for him to talk, so I hastened in search of old Geniki who brought more *kei-vishaa* and gave it to my master in a cup of wine. Then, before Hakatri sank down into sleep once more, he told me, "I will go back to Asu'a as soon as it can be arranged—I will have to be carried, I fear. I cannot even stand yet, let alone sit a horse. But I do not know what my brother will say. I worry for him. When I am awake again, I will . . . I will . . ." Then the witchwood powder pulled him back into slumber.

"When our *kei-vishaa* is gone, Pamon, his suffering will be fearful," the healer Geniki warned me in the passage outside my master's room.

"That cannot happen!" I said, suddenly terrified. "As it is, he can barely live with the pain!"

"I have sent to other healers I know in nearby settlements, asking them to share some of their own store, but none of them have much by the end of a Great Year. And even Asu'a's deep groves, where the witchwood trees still stand in large numbers, may not provide enough blossoms to keep his pain forever at bay. We would use up every bloom the seasons give us. Witchwood trees take a long time to flower and renew themselves."

"What are you saying, Master Geniki? That we will not be able to stifle his pain at all? That my poor master will have to live with agony that he already says is killing him despite being given *kei-vishaa* every day?"

The healer's long face was mournful. "I fear that is exactly what I am saying, Armiger." He put a hand on my arm, a rare intimate gesture between one of the Zida'ya and one of my own people. "I can tell you are devoted to him. I tell you this sad truth so you can consider your own path."

"Path?" I was confused. "My path is my master's path. I will stay with him no matter what may happen."

"Even so," the healer said. "Heed me carefully. I have been told that Lord Ineluki's unfortunate oath led to this disastrous state of affairs. I would suggest you take that lesson to heart. Do not make promises you may regret in the fullness of time."

I could not understand what he meant then. I see it differently now, and I am grateful for what Geniki tried to tell me. I was too caught up in the moment, in my master's suffering and my own sense of what I owed him, but if I saw the healer again I would thank him. He tried to think of what was right for the servant as well as the master—a rare thing among any of the world's people.

A few days later, Hakatri i-Sa'onserei was carried from Birch Hill on a litter by a foursome of Lord Dunyadi's retainers. A small company of other young Zida'ya traveled with us to protect my helpless master. The bearers remained silent through most of the long journey, as though they carried a corpse instead of a live body. At times they would sing quietly, though whether to cheer themselves or Hakatri I do not know. I made certain to talk to my master whenever possible, though he seldom responded with more than a glance or a shadow of a smile. His face was scarred by the dragon's blood, but not as badly as his arms, chest, and belly, where the burning black stuff had been trapped against his skin by his witchwood armor.

Traveling must have been dreadful for him. I can only guess at the agony he endured for days of being trundled over hills and down dales, despite the care his bearers took with him. I certainly did not begrudge him either his waking silences or his long bouts of murmuring, sometimes whimpering slumber: the suffering on his face when he was awake made me grateful that he could sleep at all.

We went by barge up the Redwash to the Moonpath Bridge, where the keepers—Zida'ya all—stood at mournful attention as we carried Hakatri ashore, then watched for a long time as we continued on toward Asu'a. Lord Ineluki was with us, but even more silent than the bearers: I do not think I had more than a few curt words from him during the journey, until we finally sighted the pinnacle of Nightingale Tower on the sixth day of our sad passage. The statue of Jenjiyana looking toward the Lost Garden glinted red-gold like burnished copper as it threw back the setting sun.

"It is always good to catch the first glimpse of home," I said to Hakatri, who had awakened a short while earlier but was keeping his eyes closed. "All those who love you must be waiting anxiously to see you."

"To see his wounds," said Ineluki from behind me. The abruptness of his speech and the bitterness in his voice surprised me. "To see what I have done to my own brother. To curse me."

I turned. The younger brother's fair face was set in lines of deep misery: he looked as though he were being led to execution. "Surely, my lord," I said, "they will be as glad to see you whole and hale as they will be to see my master returning."

He stared at me then, the first time he had truly engaged with me since we left Dunyadi's house. "You think so, do you? You are a servant, Pamon, and not even one of my people. What do you know of their long memories? They have still not forgiven Nerudade of the Hamakha, who died even before we left the Garden. Do you think they will welcome me back? I all but killed their darling—their favorite." For a moment I saw something deeper beneath Ineluki's sour expression, something frightening—a spiteful emptiness in his golden-eyed stare that was ordinarily hidden, I suspect, and with good reason. That look of icy rage quite transformed him, and for the first time ever in my life I feared my master's brother.

I could not bear to meet Ineluki's gaze any longer; I turned back to my master and offered him a drink. He tried to lift a hand to take it himself, but it was too painful, so he let the arm drop again and waited for me to bring the cup to his lips.

"Brother," Ineluki said, "this was my fault, but I swear that I will—"

"*No!*" Hakatri's speech was slurred but we had no trouble understanding him. He opened his eyes and stared at his brother. "No oaths. Swear nothing . . ." He tried to lift his arm again and this time managed to raise it high enough to make the sign that signified *peace upon you.* "Anger . . . breeds anger."

"The mortals deserted you—ran like rabbits at the moment of our greatest need!" Ineluki was struggling with himself, I could see, fighting to keep his words measured. "How can I not hate them almost as much as I hate myself?"

"Anger . . . breeds . . . anger." That was all my master could manage, then his eyelids sagged again and he spoke no more that evening.

I cannot imagine a world without Asu'a the Eastward-Looking, or a time in which that great city no longer exists, but I could not have imagined a world without Lord Hakatri in it either. The chief lesson fate can teach us, I think, is to trust no certainties.

I have approached great Asu'a from many directions over the years as I traveled at my master's side, from a boat on the Ocean Road as we slipped from the river into wide green Landfall Bay, and through the flowering meadows of the north, while the wide-winged cranes flew over the palace roofs and wheeled about the tallest towers like leaves caught by the wind. But the time I will always remember above all others is that journey back from Birch Hill, when we brought my wounded, suffering master home to the city's white walls.

Colorful pennants of many clans flew from Asu'a's high places, the cloud-tall spike of Nightingale Tower, the huge but gracefully curving walls of Thousand Leaves Hall, and the walls of glinting island-marble, white as new-fallen snow. When I think of Asu'a even now, it is the Asu'a I saw that day that looms first in my memory. May it always stand on the headlands above the bay as a beacon to those of good heart.

From the number of Zida'ya and Tinukeda'ya and even dark-garbed Hikeda'ya waiting to see us as we entered the city gates, an observer might have thought we had returned in glory from war. We *had* defeated our foe, though at great cost, but the folk of Asu'a had barely heard of the worm before Hakatri fell: this was not so much a triumphant return as a mournful one. My master was much loved and talk of his terrible wounds had swept through the city. The crowds were mostly silent as we carried him past on the litter. A few sang songs—old, proud tunes like "Senayana's Ode," or the touching strains of "Garden of Memory," which spoke of the deaths of Drukhi and Nenais'u. This last upset me, and I wanted to shout at the ones singing it, "My master is not dead! He will live! He will do great things!" But I stayed silent, as usual.

Amerasu and Iyu'unigato themselves, dressed in everyday robes as though to emphasize that this was no celebration, met us at the base of the Tan'ja Stairs. They accompanied our sad procession as we mounted to the upper floors of the palace, Hakatri still carried in his litter. He was breathing faintly, but otherwise insensible. Once my master's mother reached to touch him, then seemed to remember his terrible burns and stopped short. I thought I saw a tear glinting on her cheek as she withdrew her hands and let her long sleeves fall over them once more, but I could not be certain. I had never seen any of the highest Zida'ya weep.

When Lord Hakatri was carried into his bedchamber the healers were already there waiting for him, almost a dozen all told. As Ineluki and I and a few others lifted him carefully from the litter—despite all our caution my master still gasped in agony at being handled—the healers watched closely. Most of their faces were golden, but I saw a few white-skinned Hikeda'ya among them. When Hakatri was lying on his own bed for the first time in two moons or more they all gathered over him like a flock of gulls fighting over a fish. I nearly wept.

And just like that, I was pushed from my master's side. He belonged to the healers now. Pamon Kes was no longer useful.

The Moon of the Dove soon gave way to the moons of the Nightingale, Otter, and Fox. Day after day, as his wife Briseyu sat helplessly by, the healers plied my master with potent syrups and rubbed his skin with soothing unguents. I stood outside the door of his chamber and listened, but his cries of pain were often too much for me to bear. I visited him whenever I could, and as the Season of Growing set in and the weather grew warm, he seemed to recover a little of himself, though his agony only eased for short stretches. Other than Briseyu and my master's mother, the Sa'onsera, who both sat for hours at his bedside, his most constant companions were Lady Athuke of the Gentle Hands, Asu'a's most renowned healer, and Magister Jikkyo of the Hikeda'ya Order of Song, who had been sent by Queen Utuk'ku herself to attend Hakatri. One or both of these skilled healers were almost always at my master's side, although Athuke did not seem overly fond of the Singer, as those of Jikkyo's order called themselves.

Jikkyo was blind, his eyes clouded so that they were as white as his skin. Since he also affected white garments and his hair was of the same hue, I found him a ghostly and unsettling presence. He spoke softly, which was all to the good in a suffering lord's chamber, but many times when I came in to see my master I would find Jikkyo there, talking urgently to Hakatri in a low voice, but the Hikeda'ya mage would stop when he heard me enter. The suddenness with which he would fall silent disturbed me. What could he be saying to one such as my master that he thought should be hidden from a mere servant like me?

Perhaps because of his blindness, Jikkyo always had an acolyte beside him. This female Hikeda'ya was quite unexceptional of feature and indeterminate in age, but she seemed as odd to me as the Magister of Song himself. She never spoke, and when she was not helping Jikkyo in some way, she sat and stared at nothing, appearing as blind as her master, though she was not. But every once in a great while she would turn those dark, dark eyes on me, and at such times it was all I could do not to shudder, because I saw nothing that I recognized in that stare. She was flesh and blood, but when I met her gaze she might have been a child's doll, her eyes only shiny paint. Athuke told me the acolyte's name was Ommu.

But I have told the story as though I was in Asu'a with my master every moment, and that leaves out the errand I undertook for the Protector and the Sa'onsera.

During the Nightingale Moon, when we had been back in Asu'a for some time, Hakatri's parents summoned me to their chambers. Lord Iyu'unigato was obviously distraught: he stood at the window, staring down onto the waters of Landfall Bay, but Lady Amerasu greeted me with gracious kindness and served me a cup of wine with her own hands.

"Sit down, Armiger Pamon," she said. "We thank you for coming to us."

"Ask him about our son," Iyu'unigato said from the window, but did not turn to look at me. The Protector was tall and usually straight-backed, but he clutched the windowsill as if he might fall without it. "Ask him."

"I beg pardon, my lord and lady," I said, "but surely you have had the entire tale by now. What can a mere servant tell you about your son's injuries or our battle with the worm that you have not heard a dozen times already from Lord Ineluki?"

Amerasu gently shook her head. "We do not want to ask you about Hakatri, faithful Pamon. I have spent much time with him, and when he was able to talk, he has told me all he remembers. It is our younger son whose thoughts concern us. We know of Ineluki's oath, of course, and what came from it. But since returning he scarcely speaks to us, or to his close friend, Lady Nidreyu. We cannot but wonder whether something else happened during this fateful journey that we have not been told. Why should our younger son treat us like strangers?" She spread her hands in a gesture of honest helplessness and my heart flew toward her. She must have felt that she had lost two sons at once.

"I do not pretend to understand Lord Ineluki," I said slowly. "But since it is you who ask me, *S'hue* and *S'huesa*, I will tell you what I think." I took a breath. "He is weighed down by his shame. He regretted his oath the moment it was spoken, but could not let himself unmake it—"

"Could not?" Iyu'unigato turned from the window, his handsome, spare features made almost unrecognizable by unhappiness and confusion. "Would not. And now all of Year-Dancing Clan will suffer for it."

I had never seen the Protector so out of temper, and I was startled into silence.

Amerasu looked at her husband with sympathy before turning back to me. "Do not think of us as anything but a mother and a father, frightened for their children, Armiger Pamon. We understand that Ineluki is furious with himself as well as ashamed, but we sense an even greater unhappiness in him, one that threatens to consume him. Do you know anything of that? Did he speak of it to you?"

"Ineluki has conceived a hatred for the Hernsmen, my lady—that may be what you sense. He blames the mortals for failing his brother, for fleeing when the dragon came down on us."

"Mortals," said Iyu'unigato, and his voice had a strange, despairing sound. "Always it comes back to the mortals!"

I did not understand what he meant and so I stayed silent.

"It is true that the Sunset Children seem to be woven through many of our most fateful times in this land, husband," Amerasu said carefully. "Whether that is because of the mortals themselves or what they bring out in us remains to be seen. But Utuk'ku and the Hikeda'ya have already made up their minds that mortal men are our enemies. I can see nothing good coming from that in days ahead."

I was disturbed to be given such an intimate view of the masters of Asu'a, and still uncertain about where the boundaries lay in this odd new world, but Amerasu's words had brought something to my mind. "Forgive me if I speak out of my place, my lord and lady," I said, "but something has been troubling me, and this seems like the time to speak of it. The Hikeda'ya healer Jikkyo is much with my master, often whispering in his ear, yet he always falls silent when I enter the room."

"It is good of you to tell us," said Amerasu, "but do not fear. Hakatri is too wise to give much credence to the words of Utuk'ku's conjuror, whatever those words might be."

She was right, as it turned out, but what was true for one of her sons was not so true for the other.

One more surprise awaited me. It seemed the audience had ended, so I bowed as if to leave, but Iyu'unigato said, "Hold. There is another reason we called you here, Armiger."

"Yes, my lord?"

"We have heard about our sons' visit to Xaniko, the Exile of Nakkiga, and the part his advice played in the killing of Hidohebhi. We have heard that The Exile too was burned by the Snareworm when he destroyed that menace many Great Years ago."

"Yes, Protector. One of Xaniko's hands is badly damaged."

"Go back to him. Give him this from me." Iyu'unigato took one of his rings from his finger, a polished circle of witchwood carved to look like a twining rosebush, each thorn a shining chip of garnet. "This ring once belonged to Initri, Jenjiyana's mate. Tell Lord Xaniko I send it as a gift, and ask him to come to us in Asu'a, where he will be received with all honor. Tell him of our son's suffering. Ask him to come and tell us all that he knows about dragon's blood."

I took the ring, awed and more than a little worried to have been entrusted with such a hallowed thing. Initri, husband of Jenjiyana the Nightingale, had been the Protector of Tumet'ai when that was still the first city of my master's people, before the ice took it.

"I will do as you ask, my lord," I said. "But I fear the Exile will not come. He struck me as a very stubborn—"

"Enough. It is not your place to make predictions." Iyu'unigato sounded weary and impatient. He did not even look at me but stared at his own empty hands. "If you love your master as truly as you claim, convince Xaniko to come to us. The Exile has long been unwelcome in the cities of both his people and our own. Tell him that if he will come to aid us, those days are ended and he will be welcomed among the Zida'ya for the rest of his life."

I confess I was taken aback by the Protector seeming to question my feelings for my master, a love and loyalty that had been the center of my life nearly as long as I could remember. It must have showed on my face, because Amerasu spoke up.

"Do as the Protector bids you, faithful Pamon," she said. "It can do no harm and might do much good."

Except to me, I thought fretfully. *I will be separated from my master at a time when he is most in danger.* But I only bowed again—what else could I do?— and said that I would go at once. I made my way from their chambers even more distraught than I had entered it, and barely heard Amerasu's kind words of parting.

When I went to my master's chamber to say farewell, Hakatri was deeply asleep and did not know I was present. Pale, blind Jikkyo was there, as he so often was, and his acolyte Ommu held a steaming cup with the remains of the sleeping draught they had just given him.

"Do not worry, little changeling," the Singer told me in a voice like a cracked flute. "We will take excellent care of your master—you may rely on that."

The silent, unblinking figure beside him nodded.

My master, of course, could not ride any of his horses after the battle against the dragon, so I decided that I would take his charger Frostmane to Ravensperch. As I put the saddle on him, I had a moment of sadness remembering poor Seafoam, whose bones still moldered in Serpent's Vale. Amerasu and Iyu'unigato had sent a company to the valley to recover the bodies of the Zida'ya like Yohe, who had been killed by the dragon in our first encounter, but they were not bringing back Seafoam or the other horses, which saddened me. I also mourned for the mare in a smaller, more selfish way: Frostmane was a proud and difficult steed, and never behaved as well for me as he did for my master.

I rode for many days until I again reached the northern end of the Sunstep range and the looming shadow of the Beacon, then guided Frostmane onto the steeply climbing track once more. It had been only the turning of a few moons since I had been there, but so much had changed that my first visit seemed almost a dream.

When I reached high Ravensperch the mortal guards came out to survey me with the same slightly mystified air as on the first visit, but they opened the gates and admitted me.

Lady Ona met me in the dark entrance hall. Only a few torches burned, and there were more shadows than patches of light. After having spent time back in Asu'a I could not help being struck by the gloominess of the place. Lord Xaniko was Hikeda'ya, of course, and needed little in the way of illumination, so I wondered whether the darkness of their great house was meant to soothe his homesickness for the stony deeps of Nakkiga.

Ona smiled to see me, and I was truly glad to see her face. "Welcome back, Armiger," she said as I bowed. "We did not expect to see you again so soon, but it is a pleasure to have you here."

"You are kind, my lady. I hope you and your husband are well—and Lady Sholi, too, of course. I bring a message for Xaniko from the lady and lord of Asu'a themselves."

She nodded. "We shall make certain to tell him. In the meantime, let us give you something to drink and eat after your long ride."

We sat together at the long refectory table in the hall, side by side and alone except for the silent guards by the door. As I ate bread and cheese and cold meat, Lady Ona sipped on a cup of mead. "I have never become entirely used to the taste of this," she said, "but it is a comfort on cold nights, and it is hard to get good wine up the mountain. We are always running out. I miss the ease of the old days."

"Where were you raised, my lady?"

"In Da-Yoshoga, by the sea, just like my dear Sholi." She patted my arm. "That is where I met Lord Xaniko, too, but that is a very long story.

I will tell it to you some other time if you wish, but not when you have just arrived and must be weary."

Other than a few silent mortal servants moving through the shadows like phantoms, we seemed to be the only people in the castle. "Will his lordship join us?"

"Not tonight," she said. "He is in one of his deep moods."

I asked the question that had been in my mind since long before I had seen the castle's walls again. "And Lady Sholi? Is she still staying with you?"

She smiled as if she had been expecting my question. "She is, Kes. She has already gone to bed for the night, but she sent her greetings. You will see her tomorrow." Lady Ona gave me a long, searching look that made me a little uncomfortable. "Have you considered the things we spoke about?"

"Which things, my lady?" I asked, though I thought I knew perfectly well what she meant. "We conversed on many subjects when my master and his brother were guests here."

"Ah, yes, your poor master." She shook her head. "We do not receive much in the way of goods, but we do get the odd bit of news. I was so very sorry to hear what happened."

What happened seemed utterly inadequate to describe that dreadful day, a day I will remember until my last breath. "He lives," I said. "But he still suffers. In truth, that is why I am here—to ask your husband's help."

Her face was troubled. "As I guessed. Although I had half-hoped you had come back just to see Sholi and me. As I told you, we do not have many guests, especially of my own people—*our* people."

And there it hung, the very subject I had hoped to avoid, not because it was meaningless or offensive to me, but because I simply did not know how to respond. "I remember, Lady Ona. And I remember the things you said. I still feel shame that I cannot speak the language of our people and that I do not know more about their history."

"You say it as if your own ancestors were something foreign to you, Kes, lost along with the Garden, but the Dreaming Sea is still as much a part of you as your blood and your bones, and is for all of us Tinukeda'ya."

Her words set a flame alight inside me, small at first but soon to grow. When I was small, my mother had spoken of the Dreaming Sea, though I could not remember all her words. After she died, I asked my father what this memory meant, but he had forbidden me to speak of it.

"What does that mean, my lady, when you say this Dreaming Sea is a part of me? Because this is not the first time I have heard of it, though I remember almost nothing."

She looked at me in honest surprise. "It is where we came from, Kes. Why do you think your masters call us Ocean Children? Our kind were born from that sea, back in the Garden."

Born from the sea? I was confused. Had my mother believed this too? "But I was not raised to know any of this, my lady. The truth is, I was taught almost nothing about those . . . about our people, except that we came from the Garden on the Eight Ships, and service is our honor and duty."

"Service to our Zida'ya—and Hikeda'ya—masters, you mean."

I shrugged. "That is the world into which I was born, my lady. It is the world in which I still live—and will always live. And my master has treated me well."

She swirled a little of her drink around in her mouth. "I love honey," she said abruptly. "Why is it that mead always tastes somewhat strange?" She swallowed the last of it and set down her cup. "Now that you've had food, would you like me to show you to your room?"

I would have thought a servant would do that, and perhaps my surprise showed on my face. "You are very kind, my lady."

She waved a negligent hand. "It is a real gift to have visitors, Kes, believe me. As I have said before, I chose my husband and this life willingly and would not undo it, but it can be hard. Before Sholi came to stay with me I would often wander this house feeling like a ghost." She smiled at her own lugubrious words. "Do not worry—I will not keep you up talking."

When she brought me to the doorway of my room, she said something strange. "When you see my husband, please try to be kind, Kes. This has all been very hard for him."

I took the lamp from her and went in, but even after I sank into the comfort of a clean bed, I spent no little time trying to puzzle out her words before I finally fell asleep.

Lady Sholi came down for the morning meal wearing a beautifully embroidered wool robe and slippers made of rabbit fur. I confess that I was amused by the informality of the household—I could not imagine seeing the Sa'onsera or her husband Iyu'unigato in their nightwear—but was very pleased to see Sholi. Her fair hair was lifted and gathered atop her head and held by silver pins, though a few curls had already escaped to dangle beside her cheeks.

"Armiger, it is good to see you again," she said as I bowed.

"And I can truly say the same, Lady Sholi." I had thought of her often in the days since we had first met, especially during the ride from Asu'a. I felt I might be looking at her more than I should, so I turned quickly to Lady Ona. "Will your husband join us?"

She shook her head. "No, my friend—he is still occupied. But he will see you later and hear your embassy. Until then, I fear you must make do with only the two of us for company."

She jested, of course. The two of them were excellent companions, and for a little while, as we ate bread and honey and some splendid berries I had not tasted before, I almost forgot the sad errand that had brought me. Sholi told funny stories about the proud Niskie families of Goblin Rock, and Lady Ona asked me questions about life in Asu'a and about its rulers.

"They say that there is no more beautiful city in all the world than Asu'a the Eastward-Looking," she said. "I wish I could see it for myself."

"It is the most beautiful place that *I* have ever seen. That I can truly say, my lady. And you would be a welcome guest there, I feel sure. The masters of Asu'a have promised to honor your husband if he helps Lord Hakatri."

Again her smile had more sorrow than joy in it. "I do not think that likely, Kes, but it is a lovely thought."

After we had eaten, Lady Ona led us out to the balcony. The sun was shining and the mountainside below us was carpeted with new grass and bursting with wildflowers. The foothills around the mountain's base glimmered with blossoming hawthorn, the pale flowers like a sprinkling of unseasonable snow. Grazing sheep wandered everywhere, like clouds that had settled to earth. Ona called one of her mortal servants to bring more honey-mead and we three drank together, watching the shadows of clouds slide across the meadows.

"It is very peaceful here," I said. For the first time in longer than I could remember the drumbeat of duty had quieted a little inside me, and I felt a small contentment.

"Peaceful, yes," said the lady of the house. "But it is cold in the winter, and with so few in the household I sometimes feel lonely, as you have already heard me say."

"Lonely? With me here to amuse you?" said Sholi in mock annoyance. "Some people are never satisfied."

Ona laughed and embraced her. "You are the best of all companions, my dear one. But you know what I mean."

Sholi gave her friend a last squeeze. "Yes, of course." She turned to me, bright eyes flashing. "We often talk about how nice it would be to receive more visitors."

I wondered again if I might be nothing more than a diversion; if they would have been just as friendly and forthcoming to any visitor. That struck me as an unworthy thought, so I did my best to push it away and enjoy the sunshine and the company instead. It almost seemed, though, that my fleeting worry had somehow changed the balance of the day, because Lady Ona suddenly grew more serious.

"It is sad there are so few of our folk around," she said. "I mean those of *our* kind, who can think and act for themselves. Nakkiga is full of the other kind, the ones who were shaped for their labor, bred to be little more than animals."

"Shaped?" I asked in surprise. "What does that mean?"

"Remember," she said, "we are children of the Dreaming Sea, Kes. Our nature is change. Even back in the Garden, the Keida'ya masters had begun using our own nature to breed us into beasts of burden or living tools, like the Delvers."

"The Delvers?" This was new and astonishing. "You mean the famous builders, the creatures who could shape solid rock as if it were wet clay? *They* were also Tinukeda'ya once?"

"Yes, but no matter what was done to them, they are all still Tinukeda'ya, still *Vao*—that is our own name for our kind—just as you and I and Sholi are. Change was forced upon their bodies, but not their minds and spirits, although some of their less fortunate kin like the carry-men had even their knowledge of themselves taken from them to make them more useful servants. And it was not only Utuk'ku's Hikeda'ya who used our folk that way." Her expression had become stern, even angry. "All the Nine Cities in these lands were built by our kind, and they brought far more to making those monuments than just strong backs. The Vao were the guiding spirits that created the shining walls and towers of Asu'a, your home. Your masters seem to have cheated you of this knowledge, Kes."

"I cannot believe that. My master Hakatri has never lied to me."

"There is a difference between telling a lie and avoiding a truth."

I turned to Sholi, almost as if I hoped she would contradict Lady Ona, but instead she was watching me with what looked like keen interest.

"I do not mean to insult your Lord Hakatri," Ona went on. "I do not doubt his kindness to you, but even the most honorable Zida'ya never lifted their voices against the terrible treatment of our folk. Hakatri's silence may come mostly from shame."

I could only shake my head. "This is much to take in, Lady Ona."

"I know, Kes. But few of us who still remember these things will speak of them. You are a favorite of one of the most powerful Zida'ya lords. I would rather burden you with knowledge than leave you happily—and dangerously—ignorant."

Dangerously? I was very quiet after that, which should be no surprise, and the two ladies shifted their conversation toward more ordinary things—the mortal servants, the weather, the few guests who had come to Ravensperch between my two visits. But Ona's words would not leave my thoughts.

"The more we speak together, the more I realize how little I know, my lady," I said to her at last. "May I ask you about something else that has puzzled me? You told me when we first met that your name was Sa-Ruyan Ona. Is the name of Ruyan common among the Vao?"

"No, Kes," she said. "My name means I am of that line, just as yours means you are of the Pamon clan."

"But my clan name is merely that of my family, Lady. Ruyan the Navigator is famous the world over! Are you truly of his blood?"

"So I was always told and so I believe. Perhaps that is why I care so much about our people's past—and our future." But before I could ask her anything else, Lady Ona abruptly rose from the bench. "Come, Sholi," she said. "The time has come for our friend Kes to take his message to His Lordship. You and I must also put on more acceptable garb. Look! It is almost noon and we are still wearing our night clothes."

Sholi yawned and stretched, which does not sound charming but was, even in my troubled state. "I am tired after all that wine and talk," she said. "I think I might go back to bed."

"You will do nothing of the sort." Ona pretended to be strict. "We have the week's accounts to do, and the cook has demanded I go through the larder with her so she may plan for the next trip down to market. First, though, lead our friend to Lord Xaniko's retiring room."

"Is His Lordship expecting me?" I asked, still a bit befuddled by the swift change in the conversation.

"He asked us to send you to him at midday," said Ona. "That hour has come. Sholi will take you. If my husband does not answer at first, knock again. On days like this he is often far away—in his thoughts, I mean."

I supposed from the significant looks that passed between Ona and her friend that Sholi was also meant to give me some message, but she stayed silent as she led me through the castle to the tower, then up the steps. When we reached the heavy oak door she paused to look at me, and I prepared myself for some whispered revelation. But Sholi only nodded—not so much to me as to herself. "We hope we will see you again before you depart, Pamon Kes," she said quietly, then left me there on the doorstep. Puzzled, but with the purpose of my journey now at hand, I knocked. I was prepared to knock again, but Xaniko's voice bade me enter.

Inside the tower room the windows were all covered; a single candle burned in a dish on a small table. Lord Xaniko sat in a high-backed chair beside the table, wearing his usual dark clothing, his head low and shoulders hunched, so that my first impression was of a raven, or even a bat. His long white hair was braided in back but hung down on either side of his face like curtains. The room itself must have been his library, with books and parchment scrolls stacked high on shelves along the walls.

"So. Armiger Pamon from Asu'a." Xaniko did not sound particularly pleased by my entrance, but neither did he seem angry. In fact, he seemed like one who cared little about such mundane things as visitors and conversations of any sort. I had the clear feeling that I was disturbing him at a time when he would rather have been alone, so I bowed and greeted him with all the trappings of proper respect, then told him of the invitation from Protector Iyu'unigato and Lady Amerasu, and I set Initri's rose ring on the table before him as proof of what I said.

"Tell them I will not come," he said when I had finished, then pushed the ring away with the tip of his forefinger, as though he did not much want to touch it.

Surprised, I stood silent for a long moment after this abrupt refusal. "Is there anything else I can tell them, my lord?" I finally asked. "Is there some medicament you know of that might give my master relief from pain? After all, you told us that you had been burned by dragon's blood as well. You showed us your hand."

For the first time Lord Xaniko really looked at me, as though he had forgotten that day until I spoke of it. "It is useless," he said. "There is nothing to be done."

"I do not understand, Lord."

"I cannot imagine why—can it be made any clearer?" He pulled the glove off his crippled hand and lifted the burnt flesh toward me. "There are times when the pain of this is almost beyond bearing. It was spattered with the Snareworm's blood more than three Great Years ago—long, long before you were born—yet there are days it still pains me as badly as it did when it happened. Your master's wounds are worse." He shook his head. "But that is not the whole of the story. Worm's blood . . . it has power, terrible power. It fills your head with thoughts and infects your dreams as well. Does your master talk about his dreams?"

"Yes. But dreams are common with fevers—"

"Not this kind. Not dreams that show you other places—other worlds, even. Not dreams that tell you what others are thinking, or what the future will bring."

"Do . . . do you have such dreams, my lord?"

"Not every day. But I do have them. It is like a sort of fit. I do not know when it will come until it is upon me. Sometimes it is an ecstasy, like casting off the chains of life and stepping out to bathe in the sea of stars. Other times it seizes me with such dreadful visions that my heart feels like it will burst. But the pain, the burning feeling in the flesh—that never goes away for long. And I fear it will be the same for your master, or even worse, because his injuries are greater than mine."

My own pain from touching the dragon's blood had largely faded, and I suppose I had half-hoped something like that would one day be true for my master as well, so Xaniko's words felt like a blow to my body; I may even have taken a staggering step backward. "Are you saying that my master will never recover?"

"I am saying exactly that, Armiger, and I am also saying that in some ways, the master you knew is gone, just as if he had died in Serpent's Vale or whatever the wretched place is named. He will never be the same. The worm's black blood is in him now. There is no remedy, or I would know of it."

I could barely draw breath. "And his terrible pain will never cease?"

Xaniko lifted his gloved hand in a gesture. "Oh, the pain, that is the least of it. That comes and goes, though it never entirely recedes. There may be things that the healers of Asu'a can do to ease it a little."

I must have stared at him in a way that was unbecoming, but at that moment I could barely even think. "You put a dire weight upon me, my lord," I said at last, and picked up the witchwood ring the masters of Asu'a had sent. "You will not come to Asu'a, and the only message you send is that all is hopeless for Lord Hakatri."

He laughed harshly. "What did you expect? That because I had suffered something like, I could come to Asu'a and anoint him with a secret healing oil and all would be well again?" The Exile got up and walked to the window, as though he could look right through the heavy draperies that covered it. "Putting aside the distaste I have for your master's kin, who never offered me kindness or even civility until now, I tell you in truth that there is nothing I can say or do that will help. I cannot be clearer than that."

"So that is the whole of your reply?"

"It must be."

"And you have never found anything to ease the pain of your own wound?"

He lifted his hands. It was hard not to stare at the red and ruined fingers. "Nothing. Witchwood is too much like the dragon's blood. Any medicine like *kei-vishaa* that is made from it will eventually fail. Your master's caretakers will find that as time passes it does less and less to ease his suffering."

I was in such despair that I almost did not hear what he had said, but after a moment it struck me. "What do you mean, Lord Xaniko, that witchwood is like dragon's blood?"

"So my studies tell me." He waved his crippled hand at the shelves lining the walls. "Since I was wounded, I have read every book I could discover that speaks of wormsblood, and I have corresponded with healers of many kinds and many races. I have learned much about the horrifying pain it causes and the bond it creates between the blood-burnt and the Dream Road."

"I still do not understand. How can the blood of a creature like the Blackworm also be like witchwood?"

"Because they both come from the living heart of the Garden—from the Dreaming Sea." As I sat, struck by hearing those words again so soon after Ona had used them, Xaniko sat down once more as if suddenly weary. "Your own people likely understand it better than I ever could—some even say your kind were born from that lost ocean. But even the Tinukeda'ya healers who have shared their knowledge with me have not found a way to counter the effects of such burns, though they admit the connection is real."

"Connection?" I was overwhelmed by so many new ideas, but even more by Xaniko's refusal to help my master.

"Between the dragons we unknowingly brought to this land and the witchwood we carried here because we had built our lives in the Garden around it." He pulled the glove back over his scarred fingers. "I am weary now of talking. Go back to Asu'a, Armiger. Tell them what I told you. Assure the high lord and lady that I am not lying or withholding anything that might aid their wounded son. I have no aid to give because I cannot even aid myself."

Though I was reeling inside, I bowed and made my farewells as courteously as I could manage, then let myself out. The last I saw of Xaniko the Exile he was staring at his wounded hand as though it did not belong to him.

I spent that evening with Lady Ona and Lady Sholi, but I was so stunned by my audience with Xaniko that I am sure I did not make a very satisfying companion. I shared a little of what he had told me, but otherwise found it hard to make conversation, even in such agreeable company. All I could think of was my master, whose terrible suffering I had hoped would at least diminish over time, whether Xaniko could help or not.

Now I would have to tell him that there was no relief to be found at Ravensperch, or perhaps anywhere.

I went to bed early, apologizing to the ladies, who were disappointed but gracious.

In the morning I made ready to ride. My heart was heavy, and as I tightened Frostmane's saddle straps in the stable, I heard someone call my name. When I looked up, I saw Sholi standing outside the doorway of the stable.

I washed my hands in a bucket and went to her. Her presence lightened my spirit a little, which was heavier than it had been since we had brought my master home. Seeing her bathed in morning sunlight as I left the dark stable was like coming upon a hidden stream in dry hills.

"I heard you are leaving," she said. "I came to see you off."

"I would have come to give thanks and make my farewells in person."

"My lady is not feeling well today. And Lord Xaniko is still in his tower room." She smiled. "The only one to whom you must bid farewell is me, and here I am."

I was sad about the news I had to take to my master, very sad, and the thought that I might never again meet this pretty, clever, and kind young woman only added to my misery. "It was good to see you, Lady Sholi. It gives me a little heart to know such kind folk as you and your mistress are in this world."

"Your own folk."

"My own folk. Yes. In Asu'a, the other Tinukeda'ya are less like me than my masters are, if I can say that without sounding conceited. In a strange way I feel at home here, and it is hard to leave."

"It is also difficult to see you go, Kes," she said, then drew a letter from her sleeve. It was sealed with wax. "My lady sent this for you. She bade me give you her kindest regards and her wishes for a safe journey. As do I."

She seemed to be waiting for me to say or do something else, but I could think of nothing appropriate, so I took the letter and bowed. "Farewell, Lady Sholi," I said. "I shall always remember my time here at Ravensperch with fondness, but I must bear the news I have been given by Lord Xaniko back to my master."

Sholi stared at me and flushed with what looked like anger, as if she

would denounce me or even curse me. A moment later she forced herself
to a more ordinary expression. "You are a bit of a fool, Pamon Kes," she
said evenly. "But it is not all your fault, and I will miss your company."
Then she turned and walked away across the courtyard, leaving me to
stare after her in wonder and sadness.

Having failed to bring back Xaniko, I did not hurry my return to Asu'a.
As I rode down the mountain from Ravensperch I read Lady Ona's message.

> *To the Honorable Armiger Pamon Kes,*
>
> *I am sorry I was not able to see you off this morning. I was unwell and
> I beg your pardon for sending only this letter instead.*
>
> *I must confess that I never believed you would be able to convince my
> husband to accompany you. It would take far more than a sudden invitation
> from the lord and lady of Asu'a to lure him from this place. He chose Ra-
> vensperch and its remoteness for a reason. He is as unlikely to leave it as any
> animal that feels threatened is loath to leave its burrow.*
>
> *But that does not help you in your quest to aid your master, I know,
> and so I wish to share a suggestion with you.*
>
> *I understand that your master's health is your first responsibility. If Lord
> Hakatri continues to search for a cure for his suffering, I suggest he should
> not scorn the possibility of help from our own Tinukeda'ya folk—your folk,
> Kes. My husband has consulted those he knows, but there are more than a
> few Vao healers in the wide world. Many of them live among our Niskie kin
> in the mortal city of Nabban. Just as they differ from your master's kind in
> other ways, some of the Sea Watcher healers may have knowledge about his
> dreadful condition that his own people do not, since the dragons are said to
> have first come from the Dreaming Sea, back in the Lost Garden—as we of
> the Vao also did, according to our oldest stories. Also, it is not impossible
> that the mortals themselves may have found new healing arts that the im-
> mortals do not know. If your master is truly desperate for help, there are
> worse places he could go than south, to the lands that now belong to men.*
>
> *I wish you luck, and I wish it for your unhappy master as well. I know
> he means much to you. I hope you will come back and see us again before
> too long. We enjoy your company very much.*

She signed it, *Your friend, Ona, Lady of Ravensperch.*

As had been true after my first meeting with the residents of Xaniko's tiny fiefdom, I was left puzzled. Ona's letter said, "We enjoy your company very much," but Sholi had called me a fool to my face. I admired Sholi, and she seemed to enjoy my company as well, but it seemed arrogant to believe she thought of me as anything other than a pleasant diversion in a lonely place. And even if she did feel real affection toward me, the sort that might grow into something deeper, had we not both agreed during our first meeting that I could not leave Lord Hakatri and she could not leave Lady Ona? So how could there be a purpose to anything between us beyond friendship?

I had promised my life and service to my lord. Perhaps that was foolish, as Sholi had said, and perhaps Lady Ona was right when she suggested that my master's folk had misused my people—but even that did not release me from the bonds of love and honor that held me.

That night, in my camp beside the road, my mother came to me in a dream, dressed in mourning white and wearing a blindfold of linen across her eyes. *"My child,"* this beloved phantom said, *"I will always be a part of you, just like the Dreaming Sea."* When I awoke, I thought it was only a sort of fever-dream created from Ona's words. But as I think back now, after all that happened, I believe it was true memory, and I am grateful for it.

I did not get back to Asu'a until the Otter Moon had appeared. I reached the city walls at the same time as a sad procession returned from Serpent's Vale. As I waited at the gates, the wagons bearing the covered bodies of Yohe and the others Hidohebhi had slain passed into the city. A crowd waited on the Court of Gathering to honor the return of the city's dead. Those who retrieved them had also brought back a trophy of sorts, the Blackworm's skull, which had a wagon to itself at the end of the procession. The people of the city watched it pass, not with cries of loathing, but with sad faces and silence. Many of them wore mourning masks of ash painted across the eyes, their golden stares gleaming out of the darkness like treasures in an ancient cave.

As soon as I had given Frostmane to a groom, I hurried to my master's chamber, but when I reached his door I was kept from entering by several Zida'ya servants. This unnerved me, and I argued with them, but they would not let me in, nor would they tell me why I was being kept out. As I begged to be let in to see him, the door opened and a tall figure emerged from my master's bedchamber. It was Hakatri's wife, Lady Briseyu, and seeing her my heart sank even lower; I feared something terrible had happened.

"Pamon Kes," she said in a soft but stern voice, "why do you make such noise here?" Her expression should have lifted my spirits—I saw no sign of mourning or deep sorrow—but the feelings of my master's folk are often beyond my ability to recognize.

"How is my lord Hakatri? I have only just returned. Why can I not go in to him? Please tell me, my lady."

She held up her long fingers in a gesture for quiet, then opened the door and stepped aside so I could see.

My master lay stretched on his bed. His eyes were closed, and I could make out nothing of his condition. A figure dressed all in white sat on a stool beside him, but it looked too slender to be the Nakkiga Song-lord, Jikkyo. For a moment my dream about my mother's shade came back to me, filling me with dread. Then I saw that the pale shape sitting beside my master was not my long-dead mother but Hakatri's living one, Lady Amerasu. The Sa'onsera held her spread hands above his chest, and I could hear a low murmur of song. I could feel something else, too, a heaviness to the air inside the chamber, as though I breathed something more tangible than what usually filled my chest. Then Briseyu of the Silver Braids pulled the door closed once more.

"As you see, his mother is with him. She does what she can to ease his suffering, which is why you were kept out. You need not worry so, Armiger."

"I did not know that Amerasu was also a healer," I said, struggling to calm myself.

Briseyu smiled, but she looked very weary. "She is the Sa'onsera, Armiger. She can do many things. She has been often with him in recent days, trying to help him. Just now she has sung one of her most powerful songs, invoking a Word of Preservation to give him some protection against his pain."

"Did his suffering increase while I was gone?"

Her smile disappeared. "Somewhat. But let us see what Lady Amerasu can do for him."

I waited in the hallway as an hour or more passed. At last the singing behind the door stopped and the Sa'onsera left my master's bedside. Amerasu's drawn face and uneven steps as she came out to us showed how much strength that Word of Preservation had taken from her. As Briseyu took her arm to help her back to her own chambers, Amerasu's golden eyes briefly met mine, but she did not greet me or even seem to recognize me. She looked like someone who had barely won a hard-fought battle and knew the war would eventually be lost.

When Briseyu and the Sa'onsera had gone, I rushed in to see my master. The chamber still had a strange feel to it, like the air after a sudden summer storm, and also an odd, lingering scent, acrid but also sweet, like a mixture of rose petals and the ashes of Peja'ura cedar wood. Hakatri seemed to be sleeping peacefully, but I could not forget the look of defeat I had seen on his mother's face, and I ached at the thought that I still had to return the ring and relate the Protector of Xaniko's refusal.

"I worried for you all the time I was traveling," I told my master when he was awake again. "Has the Sa'onsera's song helped to lessen your pain?"

"As terrible as it is, my pain is still only a thing of the body." In truth, he looked a bit stronger than he had before I left, but his expression was troubled. "My mother's song has helped some, but the other part of my malady is beyond even the Sa'onsera's powers. The worm's blood has changed me, Pamon, in many strange ways. I feel as though I have grown another set of eyes and ears. I see things I never saw before, hear things that I was deaf to before the dragon's blood burned me. And it becomes even more uncanny when I sleep and dream. The whole world seems to roll beneath me, showing me everything, but the visions are so vast, so powerful, that I often cannot understand them."

"It sounds like you still have fever, my lord."

He shook his head. "It is nothing so simple. From what you told me, Xaniko would understand it better than most. It is a pity he will not come. I could learn much from him."

"Perhaps, my lord, but he holds many grudges. I do not know Xaniko's history except what you and his kin have told me, but he strikes me as the sort who does not forget any injury done to him."

My master gave a bitter little laugh, then winced at the pain it caused. "Yes, I know someone like that. All too well."

"In any case," I said, "I am happy and grateful to see you more like yourself, my lord. I did not want to leave you, but the errand was for your sake, and it came from your father and mother."

He nodded. "You have nothing with which to fault yourself, faithful Pamon. And good may come from your journey after all. I read the letter Lady Ona gave you."

"She seems sincere in wanting to help, my lord."

"But to seek among the mortals—!" He laughed again, though his teeth stayed clenched in discomfort. "It will confirm everything my brother fears." It was good to see him jest, but it pointed up the changes his misfortune had worked on him. Hakatri, once the very soul of steadiness, now seemed as changeable as a horse beset by flies, laughing one moment, then suddenly gasping or twitching, his face creasing as the agony of his burns escaped his ability to suppress it. It tugged at my heart to see him still suffering so badly, even after his mother's intervention, but I also wondered what other changes the dragon's blood had wrought.

"And will you take Lady Ona's advice?" I asked.

"Not yet, Pamon. There are more healers of my own kind I should seek out first. Asu'a may be the first city of our people, and the learned folk here have done everything they could, but who is to say that in Hike-hikayo or even Nakkiga itself we could not find scholars who know more than anyone in my parents' court?"

"You would go to Nakkiga, my lord?" I said in astonishment. "To Utuk'ku Silvermask's court?" I could not help wondering whether Jikkyo the Singer had put this idea in my master's head.

"To Nakkiga? That is a foolish question." He fixed me with a hard look, but I saw something deeper and more frightened moving beneath it, and for the first time I understood how terribly hard he was laboring simply to keep up the illusion of what he had been. I remembered Xaniko's warning that I might never again see the Hakatri I had known so well, my master and my hero; that the dragon's blood might have changed him beyond all recovery. "I would go anywhere if I could find something that would make me myself again," he said. "Anywhere."

So it was that after being back in Asu'a for only a short time, I prepared for yet another journey, feeling a little like the Harcha sunbird, which is said to have no legs and only stops flying when it dies. But I could not let Hakatri go out into the world without me, so I hid my weariness and made ready.

To my surprise, Ineluki insisted on accompanying us to Nakkiga. Much as he loved Hakatri, I suspected that joining us had more to do with how unhappy Ineluki was within the walls of Asu'a, where many blamed him for his brother's terrible injuries—though never to his face. Ineluki was always thin-skinned, at least compared to my master.

We set out a little after Midsummer, at the beginning of the Fox Moon, when the northern weather would be kindest to travelers, though my master would have preferred to go in the depths of winter. "Despite my mother's efforts, even the merest touch of the sun makes the burning worse, Pamon," he confided to me after the first time he tried to leave his bedchamber. "It feels as if I have set my flesh in living flame."

He did not exaggerate. On our journey to Nakkiga, Hakatri spent nearly all the daylight hours, even early morning or twilight, in a closed litter. Sometimes he was borne on a wagon, but other times, when the going became too difficult, servants took up the litter and carried my master on foot. On the worst days, Hakatri could not bear even the touch of his feather-light robes. I had to undress him so he could lie naked on his pallet in the litter, and even when the robes had been removed he moaned as if we had wrapped him in thorns instead of silk.

The roads we followed on this long, harrowing journey were ancient ones, scarcely used these days because so few travel between Asu'a and the lands of the Hikeda'ya. Where the roads still connected Zida'ya settlements they had been maintained, but in many stretches across the wide, empty Snowfields the roads all but disappeared. Some mortal men still hung on in these dreary, gray lands, but we saw few of them, since they mostly kept their distance from my master's people.

The great mountain became visible long before our journey ended, watching over the last days of our travel. Some of my master's people say that Ur-Nakkiga was once a fire-mountain like S'un Hinakta, ancient curse of the southern islands. When the Eight Ships first came from the Garden, Ur-Nakkiga still belched flame and smoke and made the earth around it shake, but it has long since fallen asleep. Even silent, though, the great mountain stares down over the small, bashful hills that surround it, ominous as an angry elder.

We reached the outer city at last and rode along the Royal Way toward the entrance. There was no hint of ceremony for our arrival, though I guessed it had been a very long time indeed since any of Clan Sa'onserei had come to Nakkiga. White-skinned faces peered out at us from doorways and windows, but the watchers did not leave their houses, as if my master's terrible malady might be dangerous to others. We approached Nakkiga's massive gates through a vast field lined with weather-worn stone statues. The gates stood ten times my height, made of witchwood so ancient it was almost black, with massive bronze hinges aged to the green of dying grass.

Lord Hikhi, the queen's High Celebrant, wore a mask that covered all of his face but his dark eyes, as many of Utuk'ku's closest minions did and still do. He met us in the massive entry hall beyond the gate. As it turned out, he was the highest official we ever saw; neither Queen Utuk'ku nor any of her closest advisors seemed interested in us—or so I thought. Later I learned differently. But we had nothing to complain about in High Celebrant Hikhi's greeting, which was respectful and welcoming.

We had just finished a very long journey across the barren Snowfields and the colder, mountainous uplands called Cruel Winds and I was quite weary. I stared at the strange buildings and statue-haunted crossings as we made our way through the open spaces of Nakkiga's main level, but I could not summon much interest. The streets were dark and wide, and a somber image of Drukhi the White Prince, Utuk'ku's dead son, seemed to watch us wherever we went. The roaring waters of the gigantic Tearfall, which plummeted down from somewhere high in the mountain and filled half of Nakkiga with spray, could be heard in all parts of that ground level except behind the thickest walls. And I glimpsed other sights just as astounding—park gardens of ghostly white fungus, massive temples as dark inside as the bottom of a well even when crowded with Nakkiga-folk—but all of them seemed like shadows to me. Now I mourn all that I failed to study or even notice, since I doubt I will ever see that strange, secretive city again, and it is unlike any other.

I was, of course, mostly worried about my master. He had taken a turn for the worse as we approached the mountain, his dreams becoming ever more florid, and his intervals of sense more widely separated. As we trudged through the steaming mists that seemed to choke every street and public place in the Hikeda'ya stronghold, Hakatri moaned and cried out in his litter. I always found it hard to comfort him at such times because I could not touch him: when he was suffering badly even the lightest stroke against his skin felt to my master like the burn of a red-hot iron.

Distracted by his misery, I remember little of our long, slow passage up the massive ceremonial stairs to the upper levels, where High Celebrant Hikhi led us to the house that had been provided for us, a nearly window-less block of stone from the outside, a shadowy labyrinth inside.

In the days that followed I scarcely left Lord Hakatri's side as he was visited by healers and even a few of the Nakkiga nobles. If I had been largely ignored by the important folk of Silverhome and Skyglass Lake, I had at least been treated with courtesy as a valued servant. Utuk'ku's courtiers did not even seem to see me. But I had not expected anything different—I knew the Hikeda'ya thought of my folk only as slaves—and I was there for my master, not myself. I did my best within the strictures of my duty to ignore them as thoroughly as they ignored me.

In truth, even if I had been well treated, I would have been unhappy in Nakkiga. The weight of the queen's rule kept her subjects abject and largely mute, and the few of my own Tinukeda'ya people I encountered were all slaves. Unlike most other places I have visited, even in the mortal lands, the endless, shadowy streets did not make me want to explore them. The darkness in which the Hikeda'ya lived seemed not merely an absence of light, but the actual manifested spirit of the hidden city.

The healers who came to our lodgings minutely examined my master, staring, poking, and asking questions, sometimes with such aggressive inter-est that they persisted even after he had fallen asleep—sleep he always badly needed, since it was one of his only ways to escape the pain of his wounds. But with my master's sleep came dreams, and the Nakkiga-folk seemed fascinated by these as well. Chief of these observers was one Lord Yedade, who I learned was the son of Nerudade, one of the Hikeda'ya's chief philosophers when the Garden was still our home—the one, in fact, that some claimed had loosed Unbeing and thereby caused his own death and the Garden's destruction. Despite this, Yedade was apparently as prized for his learning by the queen's Hamakha Clan as his father had once been, and he certainly showed no signs of shame over what his sire might have done.

Yedade had the most colorless skin of any Hikeda'ya I had ever seen, not merely white but almost transparent. At certain angles it seemed I could see all the way down to his veins and the workings of his muscles and bones, which moved like ornamental fish swimming in a cloudy pond. Yedade was also achingly thin, but his dark eyes were very large and frighteningly intent, as though every single thing he saw was an object of surpassing interest, with scant distinction between the living and the unliving.

In the days after our arrival, Lord Yedade and his fellow philosophers spent a great deal of time clustered around my master's bed, but unlike the healers, they seemed far more interested in the malady than in the sufferer. They even scraped at his burn scars and took the bits away in folded squares of parchment. Neither could I make any sense of many of the things they asked him. "When the fit is on you, do you see a wall or curtain of deep red?" Yedade would ask, as if something useful could be gleaned from the visions of a fever dream. "Do you hear voices? What language are they speaking?" Sometimes one or two of the Lords of Song—Utuk'ku's order of high mages—joined Yedade at my master's bedside. I particularly remember one named Karkkaraji because he was extremely old and had long, yellow fingernails that curved like claws. I never heard him speak. He communicated with his fellow Singers only in gestures, the secret language of signs his order use among themselves.

The more ordinary Hikeda'ya healers who attended Hakatri were not as obtrusive as the mages, but neither did they bring my master any true relief, despite all their pastes and salves and the many unpleasant liquids they made him swallow.

We stayed in Nakkiga for most of the Lynx Moon. During that time I saw little of my master's brother Lord Ineluki, but was told by one of the healers that he alone of our company had been invited to the royal palace, the *Omeiy'o Hamakh*, to meet with Queen Utuk'ku. Ineluki came to visit his brother after this meeting, but I was sent from the room and do not know what passed between them. My master Hakatri was in agony at the time, almost insensible with pain, so I doubt he had much to say, or in fact heard much of what Ineluki told him.

It was not a comfortable visit and not a comfortable place. During our stay in Utuk'ku's underground city I felt currents, heard whispers, and saw shadows around me that I could not fully understand, as though the people of that city were all engaged in some secret conversation about a subject I did not understand. The misty streets, what little I saw of them, seemed haunted, and not just by the ever-present effigies of Drukhi, the queen's son, whose memorials were everywhere. From the conversations I did hear, people of that strange city seemed to care only about things that had happened in the past, seemed to believe the present era was little more than an illusion—something to be endured while worshipping things and places and people now lost beyond hope.

In the end, it became clear that Nakkiga's healers could not help my master. I was not sorry when we decided to leave that place.

We had planned next to travel west to Hikehikayo, the other great mountain city. But Lord Ineluki insisted that a journey there would be useless. "The queen says that the few healers left in that city are far behind what can be done here in Nakkiga."

"Which was nothing." Hakatri's face was pale and damp with perspiration after one of his bouts of intense suffering.

"All the more reason not to risk journeying a long way across the freezing north," Ineluki told him. "The queen says that nothing like what happened to you has ever happened before, and she is the oldest of us all by many, many Great Years. She says we would learn nothing new in Hikehikayo."

"Queen Utuk'ku seems to have shown you much favor, my lord," I said.

"I am not one of those who hate her, Armiger." His tone was hard, grudging. I think if Hakatri had not been there, his brother might have spoken to me much more sharply. "She has her own people to protect, her own lands to defend."

My master roused himself a little. "Remember, her people *are* our people, brother."

But that was all he found the strength to say, and we did not travel on to Hikehikayo.

Halfway through our journey back across the seemingly endless Snowfields we had to stop for two full days because my master's suffering became so terrible that he could not bear even to have his litter carried. In the middle of the second night, with only myself and one of our Asu'a healers present, Hakatri sat up, gasping in pain, and cried out, *"She is behind the veil, too! Her tracks are everywhere!"* He grabbed my hand with such desperate strength that I could not use it without pain for the rest of the day, but those were the only words he spoke that I could understand. Afterward he fell into a fit, thrashing and moaning until my heart nearly broke.

When Hakatri could be carried again we continued back across the Snowfields, but when we reached Great Redwash he came up from his swoon like a deep-diving swimmer and declared that we would not go home but instead turn southwest toward the city of Mezutu'a. I protested, but he said, "I promised Enazashi's heir that I would come to Silverhome to make my apology for taking the witchwood tree from his grove. Who knows if I will ever be well enough again? Honor demands I take this opportunity."

A part of me shuddered—after all, "honor" had led us to this terrible situation in the first place, though it had been Ineluki's honor, not my master's. Still, I no longer had much faith in its value at all. When I said this to the healer who had accompanied us from Asu'a, though, she looked at me as though I had suddenly begun to speak a foreign tongue: she simply could not grasp what I was saying. "I do not like your master's choice, of course," she said. "I am running out of what I need to make the salve that helps him, so I wish we could return directly to Asu'a. But we cannot take away from him the little he has left."

"Do you mean his life?" I said, trying to keep my anger down but not entirely succeeding. "Because the more he travels, the more I fear for his survival."

She only shook her head. Like the other healers, she was kind and compassionate, but it was one of the times I felt I did not understand my master's people at all.

This time, because of my master's frailty, we did not enter Mezutu'a from Skyglass Lake and the Fernlight Passage but followed the ancient Silver Way up into the mountains to the city's proud Southern Gate, with my master still in his curtained litter. Word of our return had spread, and after we were admitted to Silverhome the streets of the underground city filled with citizens eager to see us. Ineluki seemed to enjoy the attention and the crowds, but my master barely opened the curtains on his litter. He was in dreadful pain, I could tell, but determined to do what he had promised.

We carried Hakatri at last to the Site of Witness, where Enazashi was holding court in the shimmering glow of the Shard; I saw no sign of Kai-Unyu, his supposed co-ruler. The lord of Mezutu'a's narrow features were set in hard, unhappy lines as he watched Hakatri's litter being carried down the steps toward the center of the vast chamber. His heir Yizashi watched too, features carefully empty of emotion, although it was not difficult to guess that what he had allowed Hakatri and Ineluki to do in Enazashi's witchwood grove had been the subject of many hard words between father and son.

"So, Lord Hakatri, you return to us at last," Enazashi said when the litter had been set down at the foot of the daïs. "I told you I would give you no assistance in trying to kill the worm. You took what you wanted anyway. Do you come now to beg forgiveness, or to boast about your great deed?"

I could see the angry flush on Ineluki's face even by the Shard's inconstant, glimmering light. "You said you would give us no soldiers to help us, Enazashi," he said, and did not hide the bitterness he felt. "We took no soldiers. We took a tree—a single tree."

"You took a sacred tree of the Garden Root from my grove—stole it! And worse, you made my son your accomplice. For that alone I should banish you from the Silverhome lands forever, yet here you sit, unashamed. Your brother will not even show me his face, though I am told he was the leader of the company."

"How do you dare—!" Ineluki cried, and a rustle of dismay went through the room. I saw several Silverhome guards reach for their weapons.

"Stop," called Hakatri from inside the curtained litter, and though he did not speak loudly—could not, at that time—Ineluki was startled into silence. Even Enazashi seemed to pause, as if waiting to see what would happen next. The curtain trembled, then slowly drew back. My master clambered out of the litter to stand swaying beside it, his robes rumpled and damp with perspiration.

"Lord Enazashi is right," he said.

All around the great chamber the members of the Silverhome Clan stared in wide-eyed surprise. It was not my master's obvious frailty that startled them so much as his visible wounds, I think, those ghastly burns on his neck and arms that were still bright and red even after the change of many moons. It was also clear by his panting breaths and quivering limbs that he had expended a huge amount of strength simply to leave the litter, but even the most observant of the Mezutu'ans would not have guessed from his stolid face the agony in which he spent each day. His brother knew. The other servants and I knew, too, and we were all amazed that Hakatri was standing at all.

"My lord," he said to Enazashi, "I have done wrong to you, and I admit it. I did not plunder your grove for my own gain, but I still regret the necessity that made me a thief and made you a victim."

His brother Ineluki clearly did not agree. Ineluki's pride was also his curse, I had heard some of his fellows say, and at that moment I could see him struggling with it. His better nature, or at least his more cautious nature, won out: he stayed silent.

"That is all well and good," said Enazashi. "But the story does not change. You came into my grove and took one of the sacred witchwood trees without permission, in darkness and secrecy. And you made my son your accomplice. If this were Nakkiga, that would bring a judgment of death."

Ineluki's eyes bulged at this, but Hakatri stared at him and his younger brother somehow remained silent.

"Your son was given a difficult, even desperate choice to make, *S'hue* Enazashi," said my master. "He let his conscience guide him, as did I. And as you will."

"What does that mean?" The master of Mezutu'a narrowed his eyes.

Hakatri began to walk toward the daïs. Each step was slow and difficult, and everyone present could see the perspiration beginning to bead on
his face as he struggled forward. Ineluki turned away, whether in shame
or sympathy I could not tell, as Hakatri at last reached the first step of the
daïs, a short distance from Lord Enazashi's feet. He swayed as if he would
fall then, and Yizashi reached toward him, but my master waved him
away.

Hakatri bent first one knee, then the other, gasping with pain at every
movement, though he tried his best to hide it. Sweat was dripping down
his cheeks as he lowered himself to the step. It was a terrible spectacle, like
watching some great beast pierced by many arrows finally giving up its
life. With a final, muffled groan, Lord Hakatri dropped to his knees before
Enazashi. When he spoke, his obvious suffering made it hard to understand him. "I . . . am yours, Lord Enazashi. We are all of . . . of the Garden, and that means we must honor all that we share. I have . . . wronged
you. If you would take my . . . life for my crime . . . against you, it . . . is
yours."

I was so horrified by my master's agony that I did not notice for long
moments that Enazashi was staring down at him, and that the lord of Mezutu'a's eyes were red as if with welling tears.

"Someone help Lord Hakatri back into his seat." Enazashi's voice
sounded nearly as unsteady as my master's. "By the Garden that birthed us
all, you are forgiven, son of Year-Dancing House. You are forgiven."

Part
Four

The Gray Lands

"Only a few moons ago, it was your brother who refused to go back to Asu'a," I said to Hakatri, "and you called him stubborn. Now Ineluki is returning, but you will not." I had never spoken to my master in such a way, but I was frightened for him. "I do not understand this, my lord."

"You think I should return home?" he demanded. "Return to what? A life that is barely a life? I cry out in my tormented sleep until no one else in my house can rest. I cannot hold my wife in my arms because the pain is too great, and my child—" I had never seen Hakatri so despairing. "Do you know what Briseyu said when we spoke through the Witness last night? That our daughter Likimeya wants to know when her true father will finally come back. My own daughter no longer recognizes me, I am so altered by this dragon-curse, and you want me to return to Asu'a!" His teeth were clenched against the agony of his wounds, but he was angry, too. "Will you now also turn away from me, Pamon?"

I was shocked that he had shared the private words of his wife, something I could never have imagined, and even more wounded that he should question my loyalty, but I knew it was only his suffering that made him chide me. "I will never turn away from you, my lord. You chose me and raised me up when no one else of your folk would have given me a second look. But that does not mean I will stay silent when I fear you are making a dreadful mistake." But in truth, it was only in this strange new world in which we found ourselves that I dared to question him. Some things *had* changed, it could not be argued.

Lord Ineluki was leaving Silverhome to ride back to Asu'a, along with several of those who had accompanied us this far. I did not blame him for departing, since he could do nothing to make Hakatri better, and it must have been particularly terrible for him as the maker of that terrible, fateful oath, to watch his brother's continual suffering. The two brothers saying their farewells was one of the saddest things I have ever witnessed: they had so much love for each other, and yet could not embrace. As Ineluki struggled for words, Hakatri stopped him.

"Do not fear for me, brother," my master said. "If Unbeing itself could not destroy our people, a few spatters of worm's blood will not take my life away. We will see each other again." So saying, he raised his hand in parting.

Ineluki bowed his head and kept his face expressionless as he mounted Bronze. As he rode away, he did not look back.

Hakatri and I, along with a half-dozen retainers and guards to carry my master's litter, made a slow journey out of the mountains that hid Mezutu'a and down to the coast, coming at last to the harbor town of Da-Yoshoga, Lady Ona's and Sholi's former home. It was inhabited by many Zida'ya, a few pale-skinned Hikeda'ya, and a surprising number of mortal men and women—those folk, however, called the place "Crannhyr." Tinukeda'ya lived there too, of course, as they still do in most port towns, north or south, and as I had gathered from the women at Ravensperch, the old Niskie families of Da-Yoshoga, though they were fewer than in the past, were proud of their heritage and took a leading role in the trade that was the town's main activity.

But though the port was a busy one, few Zida'ya ships called there, so we bought passage on a merchant ship out of the kingdom of Nabban. Despite the uneasiness of its mortal crew at our presence, we voyaged with them south along the coast to the broad, rocky island of Kementari, which had been one of the greatest residences of my master's folk. The famous city of the same name was only ruins now—it had been thrown down by the same shaking earth that had destroyed Jhiná-T'seneí. As we made our way inland from the largely derelict harbor, we could see the disheveled remains of wide ceremonial roads and the tumbled stones of what had once been proud walls. Their legendary facing of striped sardonyx—which had once made the city walls gleam so brightly that the approach to Kementari had been called "the Dazzling Way"—had long since been plundered.

This once proud, now gutted metropolis was not one of the cities given to the Tinukeda'ya to rule by Jenjiyana, but when Hakatri and I came there, the remnant of my folk and of my master's folk were still living together in relative harmony. The Hikeda'ya who had lived beside them during Kementari's greatest days were gone, though. They had fled soon after its walls and palaces fell, heeding Utuk'ku's demand for all her clansfolk to join her in Nakkiga. The Zida'ya and Tinukeda'ya who still remained in Kementari's ruins spoke bitterly of how the Hikeda'ya had claimed the city's Master Witness, an object called the Breathing Harp, and carried it away with them to their new home. This outrage had taken place many Great Years in the past, but as we sat with Kementari's leaders in the empty stone shell of what had been the Temple of Witness, those who remained mourned as though it had just happened.

It hurt me to see these sad remains of what had been one of the famously beautiful Nine Cities, and I know it hurt my master too. Where once a great population had lived, trading up and down the mainland coast in their swift ships, now only a thousand or so hung on, more than a few of them recent mortal settlers. Kementari and its citizens had once thrived because of the spices and beautiful fabrics that passed through its port; now they survived only because of the goats and sheep that grazed the hills at the center of the island and the farm steadings that grew grain and root vegetables. Despite this, the Zida'ya of Kementari were still so proud of their ancient heritage that though my master desperately wished to help them, he could not do it openly. He made instead a secret gift to the governors of the island—a sizable part of the gold we had brought so we could trade in the mortal lands. We left it behind in their plundered Temple of Witness so it would not be discovered until we were gone. I hope that it helped them, especially my own Tinukeda'ya folk, most of whom eked out a meager living netting fish from their small boats or quarrying the rocky island's bones. As we made our way back down the broken and disrupted stones of the road that led to the port, I heard the calls of fisher-folk, both my own people and mortal men, and could not help remembering Ineluki's warning that soon the mortals would replace my master's folk everywhere.

From Kementari we took ship again and made our way south, and on a warm morning early in the Tortoise Moon we arrived in the busy port of Nabban itself, the heart of the great mortal kingdom.

As I observed the teeming life of the broad harbor, big ships floating at anchor like sleeping ducks as hundreds of smaller boats darted in and out among them like water-striders, I was astounded by Nabban's size and the nearly impossible task before us. I had never seen mortals in such numbers, never realized that so many mortals existed in all of the world, let alone squeezed into one city spread over a few hills. There might indeed be healers capable of helping us in such a vast place, but how would we find them?

Lord Hakatri was one of the most widely known of his folk, so more than a few Nabbanai dignitaries waited to greet us when we landed. The general style of their dress was not greatly different from the Hernsmen and other northern mortals, but they wore tailored capes instead of rough cloaks, and the cloth of their garments looked much richer and more colorful. Many also wore hats of shaped and dyed wool, some in forms I found quite puzzling, since they offered no protection against sun or rain and instead seemed created purely to amuse.

The nobles who greeted us at the dock told my master he was invited to the Sancellan for an audience with the Imperator—their strange word for king, I assumed—but though Hakatri thanked them with all ceremony, he told them he was too unwell at present and would have to put the honor off until he had recovered, and that he had come to Nabban in search of a cure for his wounds.

The dignitaries who welcomed us obviously spread the word of my master's poor health, because within a day of our arrival our place of lodging near the port was all but overrun with dozens upon dozens of Nabban-folk offering to help Lord Hakatri. A few were mortal philosophers and practical healers, and these my master bade me bring to him, but most of those who appeared before our doors each morning were either novelty-seekers only interested in meeting an actual Zida'ya lord, or fraudulent healers offering concoctions of common herbs, animal blood, graveyard dirt, and even less savory ingredients, foolish nostrums far more likely to kill an infirm person than to help. I put in hours before noon each day ferreting out the one or two individuals worth taking to my master from the army of frauds and simpletons who clamored to see him. In the end, though, even the most gifted thinkers of the greatest mortal city had nothing new to offer him.

Being Hakatri's gatekeeper was not all my duty in Nabban, nor even half. With Ineluki returned to Asu'a and just a few servants now remaining to take care of my master's most basic needs, I was the only one left who could soothe him when his agonies were at their worst, and we spent many nights sitting up together when the pain would not let him sleep. Sometimes we talked, but other times my master could not even do that, and then I read to him from his favorite poets, Tuya and Benhaya-Shonó, or from Diritu's *Chronicles of History in the New Land* as he lay on his bed, shivering.

Unimpressed by what I was seeing of Nabban's mortal healers, I was determined to find healers of my own race for my master, as Lady Ona had suggested. Even Hakatri agreed that with their connection to the Dreaming Sea and the Garden, the Tinukeda'ya might offer our best chance against the curse of dragon's blood. But now, for the first time since the mistress of Ravensperch had shamed me on my first night in her home, I truly regretted not speaking my ancestors' Vao tongue, because few of the local Niskies spoke anything but a mixture of Vao and the local mortal speech. This made my search almost maddeningly slow and full of misunderstandings, but I persevered, leaving Lord Hakatri's side for hours each afternoon—hours that I begrudged, because I did not trust the rest of his retainers to tend him properly. Accompanied by one of my master's Zida'ya guards, I went hunting through the markets and taverns and Sea Watcher guildhalls for anyone who might be able to help us.

In the end, though I walked until my feet were sore and asked questions up and down the Nabban waterfront until my throat was hoarse, what I had been seeking came to us instead. We had been in Nabban for no short while—the Tortoise Moon and Rooster Moon had both passed—when a young male Niskie came to our inn.

"I am Fen Hasha," he told me. "I hear you and your master are looking for a true healer."

"And that is you?"

He shook his head, grinning. "No. But my aunt is the greatest healer in all the South."

We Tinukeda'ya are sometimes called "changelings" in mockery, or even as an insult, but the name is not without reason, since it is our nature as a race to grow like the things that surround us. Those of us who live in far northern lands tend to become paler and better able to survive the cold. Those who live near the ocean, like the Niskie-folk, become more like sea creatures. It sounds strange but it is true. And those like me, born among the Zida'ya, have always looked more like those immortals than do the rest of our kind. But this Fen Hasha who came to our door had been born into Nabban's Sea Watcher community, and he had all the telltale signs. His eyes were large and heavily lidded, his arms were long, and he had the telltale Niskie roughness of skin—I might even say *scaliness*—especially around his neck. I was not immediately ready to trust this stranger, though Fen Hasha assured me that his aunt, Fen Yona, was a healer of great renown who had cured many folk, rich and poor, mortal and otherwise. He did not ask for any payment in advance, which relieved some of my suspicions, and when I asked for the names of those who could vouch for his aunt's skills, he gave me several, which also raised him in my eyes. Most of the false healers who had milled at our door would not even explain the details of what they would do for my master, cloaking their methods in secrecy, which is one of the chief weapons of all swindlers.

Many of the people Fen Hasha named were trading captains who had been troubled by strange maladies caught in the southern islands— maladies of both body and spirit, the Niskie told me—but they were all at sea during that time of the year and could not be questioned. But a wealthy mortal woman spoke glowingly of Fen Yona's skills and told me my master would not regret employing her.

I think at any other time both my master and I would have wanted more proof of this healer's abilities, but Hakatri had been suffering grievously again in the most recent days and seemed willing to try almost anything, so we hired a boat to take us to this Fen Yona's home. The craft was not in the most reassuring condition, but Fen Hasha assured me its captain was a relative of his and was giving us a very good price, so the next morning we left Nabban and set out across the bay for Tapu, the tiny island where the healer lived.

I shall not spend long describing the journey, or about meeting Fen Hasha's aunt in her round hut near the shore, for reasons you will soon discover. The old Tinukeda'ya woman was pleasant enough, but she was vague about what she could actually do to heal my master. She first per-formed a ceremony that, as far as I could see, consisted mostly of spreading incense smoke as thickly as possible while members of her family played a tuneless sort of music on flutes and drums, then she pronounced that my master's condition was unusual and could only be helped by someone she called "the Lady of the Star of the Sea," which would require another short voyage by boat. Having come so far already, we agreed, and we soon found ourselves aboard a small craft braving the rough swells, this time by night.

After perhaps two hours' journey we reached a spot a long distance from shore. It looked no different to me than any other part of the open sea, but the healer Fen Yona bade the captain drop anchor, then once more she began to chant and disperse smoke from an incense burner, but this time she added loud prayers addressed to the Lady she had mentioned. I was beginning to doubt that anything at all would happen, and that we had spent our gold for nothing, but as she sang and waved her arms, I did finally notice a change in our surroundings.

My master, who could barely sit upright, likely saw nothing but the odd dance that Fen Yona was doing, but I could make out a faint light beginning to glow in the water beside the boat. At first I thought it only the shining tide that is sometimes seen on the nighttime ocean, but it grew brighter and brighter until I could make it out quite clearly. It was not a formless cloud like a shining tide, but a single spot of glaring green light. The astonishing thing, though, was that the green glow came from deep beneath the ocean's surface.

When I announced this, Fen Yona increased the violence of her dancing and chanting, crying, "The Lady comes! The Star of the Sea is kindled!"

My master did not take heed of any of this but swayed back and forth with the motion of the small boat, his eyes tightly shut, struggling with agonies the rest of us could only imagine. Then, as the woman's song or prayer neared what sounded like some sort of loud peak, she stooped near my master to set down her incense burner and I saw something flash in her hand. I thought it was a knife, so I flung myself between the Niskie-woman and Hakatri. She was startled and complained angrily about my intrusion. I demanded to see what was in her curled fingers, still fearing some kind of murderous attack, though I could imagine no reason for it—our gold had been left safe on shore with my master's Zida'ya guards. The healer's nephew Fen Hasha tried to pull me away from her. I may have not the strength of my master's folk, but I had trained with the young warriors of Asu'a, and now I was grappling with one of my own kind, protecting my master. As we struggled, I managed to get my foot behind Fen Hasha's ankle and pushed him overboard. Instantly his aunt began shrieking that the kilpa would take him, that I must help him climb back onto the boat. At the time I thought she exaggerated, but I was told later that kilpa did swim around boats that dared the ocean by night and would sometimes even snatch an unwary sailor off the deck and into the sea.

I refused to help the Niskie woman's nephew until she showed me what was in her hand. She called to her Tinukeda'ya relative whose boat we had hired, but he was struggling with his oars, trying to turn the craft against the push of the waves and back toward floundering Fen Hasha. The woman finally spread her fingers to show me what was nestled in her palm—a shard of broken mirror. I understood everything then, and knew I dared not leave Hakatri's side, so I stood over him and left the boat's owner to drag Fen Hasha back onboard by himself.

After much arguing and many threats, both mine and theirs, the Niskies at last carried us back to Tapu, which we reached as the first warm light of dawn was climbing into the eastern sky. We found another boat there and paid its owner to take us back to the Nabban mainland, since I no longer trusted Fen Hasha and his aunt or any of their numerous relatives. I was ashamed that our first visit to a Tinukeda'ya healer had turned out so woefully, but my master was overwhelmed with his own suffering and hardly noticed anything but the fact that he had not been healed.

"They were frauds, my lord," I told him when we were safely back on the mainland. "Cozeners, tricksters, whatever you like. The green light—the 'star of the sea' as the Niskie-woman called it—must have been the sunken glow from the fabled Green Column, the Master Witness of Jhiná T'seneí, gone down beneath the ocean so long ago with the rest of the island city. We must have been floating just above the city's ruins."

"No," Hakatri said. "The city and its island sank far from where we were. But who knows? Perhaps Mezumiiru's tides have rolled the pieces of the Witness a great distance along the sea floor. But you said it began to glow in the deeps only after we reached it, Pamon, as if she had summoned its light. If they were only tricksters, how could that be?"

"She had a piece of a Witness hidden in her hand, my lord. I doubt she knew how to do anything more with it than to briefly wake the Green Column. But it would be a most effective way to fool mortals and those who are ignorant of history, would it not?"

For a moment he sat silent. "It was not all false, though, Pamon. While we floated there, a new dream came to me—a very strong dream, like no other I have had. Whether they meant to rob us or not, something true was at work. It was much like what I have felt from the Pool of Three Depths in Asu'a and other Master Witnesses."

"All the more reason then, after what happened to you in Serpent's Vale, that you should be kept away from those people and their foolish use of someone else's power. Who can guess what the untutored meddling of a Niskie hedge-witch might have done to you if we had not stopped her?"

"I am not certain we did stop her," Hakatri said. "The dream that came to me on that boat was strong, so strong, and I still feel it. A figure stood before me—slender, pale, and distant. It spoke to me in a woman's voice, saying *'Come to me. I have a message for you.'* It was so strong and strange! It did not feel like any of the other dreams I have had since the worm's blood burned me." He lifted his hands to his face, as if to make certain he was still the same person. "I no longer know what to do, Pamon, what to believe."

Privily, I thought the pale female figure of his dream sounded like the Hikeda'ya queen, Utuk'ku, who was known to walk the Dream Road as easily as others might walk the Silver Way or the Snowfields Road, sending her spirit into dark places where even the wisest of the Zida'ya did not dare to go. Hearing Hakatri's fascination with this vision, I was fearful it might lead us back to dark Nakkiga; but in the end, our travels turned out much differently than I had imagined.

We returned with my master's remaining guards and retainers to the inn on the Nabban waterfront so my master could decide what to do next. I discovered that in my absence a letter from Lady Ona had arrived for me, sent on from Asu'a, along with a letter to my master from his wife. I postponed reading Ona's letter to take Lady Briseyu's message to my master's chamber.

"My eyes ache and they will not fix on anything." Hakatri had scarcely risen from his bed since our return. "Read it to me, Pamon."

I unfolded the delicate silken note, feeling as much an intruder as if I roamed through the lady's chamber, grubbing among her belongings.

My husband,

I read out,

I saw you yesterday in your favorite chair, drinking from a cup of black wine as you often do in the evenings. But it was not you, only your robe, draped over the cushion.

I saw you again today in Thousand Leaves Hall, and even called out to you, but it was only a shadow that for a moment had your shape. When I spoke your name, many turned to look at me in pity.

I seek for you often in sleep these nights, upon the Dream Road, but when I find you, you never turn your face toward me. When I speak to you, it is as though you stand in a high place, the wind fierce in your ears, and cannot hear me.

You are a ghost, Hakatri, and I am a widow, our child an orphan. I feel like a lost pilgrim in a strange land, who kneels beside an ancient, ruined fane, praying to a departed spirit that cannot hear her . . .

"Enough," said my master, his voice full of wretchedness. "I cannot hear this now. Leave it until I may read it with my own eyes." He turned his face toward the wall. I set the letter on the bench and carried away the parchment from Ravensperch, but my heart was sore for my master and his family.

Dear Kes,

my letter read,

I hope this finds you in good health, and that your master Lord Hakatri has found some respite from his suffering. It has been a difficult time here.

During the last moon, my dear Sholi fell ill with a terrible fever,

As I saw those words my heart clutched in my chest—for a moment I could not even breathe. I hardly dared to read further, but after some moments I mustered my courage and continued.

> *and I feared I would lose her. I am glad to say that she has passed through the worst of it now and appears to be on her way back to health, though she is still weak and remains in her bed. But she is eating again, and I can finally say that I feel confident she will recover. She asked me to send you her greetings and her good wishes, and I now do so. I was terrified, of course, not just for Sholi, so young and with so much life still before her, but for myself as well. As you know, I often do not see my husband from one day to the next, and—as I have no doubt made clear before—Ravensperch can be a lonely place. It is terribly selfish to say it, but I do not know what I would do without my beautiful Sholi's company.*
>
> *I hope that when you and your master have returned from your long journey, we may hope to see you again. You were a breath of fresh and welcome air in a house that often seems stale with over-familiarity.*

Since I did not know when I would next have the chance, I wrote back to Ona that evening, hoping I could find a way to send the letter to her. I knew she would be most unhappy when she heard how our fellow Tinuke-da'ya, the criminal Fen clan, had tried to cheat my master, so I related only the bare bones of that misadventure. I also sent my greetings and my sincere wishes for continued recovery to Lady Sholi and suggested that any further letters the ladies wrote to me should be sent to Asu'a, since I felt sure we would be returning there as soon as my master was fit to travel again.

Foolish Kes! Or perhaps not so much foolish as unlucky. How was I to know that almost four seasons would roll past before we saw Asu'a's bright towers again, before I once more stood upon the Tan'ja Stairs? How could anyone have guessed?

As the moons spun slowly through the sky and the Season of Gathering turned to the Season of Withering, we continued to search the Southern lands for healers who might be able to help Lord Hakatri. It is a sign of how desperate we were, and how fierce my master's suffering, that he spent so much time in the lands of mortals. I doubt any other member of his clan had ever traveled so much among them or came to know those short-lived folk so well. Some of the mortal scholars we consulted tried very hard to help us, but most seemed more interested by the chance to meet with a Zida'ya noble from the leading clan. In the end, we did learn a few things here and there, but I cannot say that the search was worth the effort, at least among the mortal philosophers of Nabban.

My master's Zida'ya folk scarcely sleep, but we Tinukeda'ya must, and it was exhausting for me to tumble into weary slumber at the end of each long day only to be awakened before an hour had passed by the sound of my master Hakatri's moans and harsh breathing. It is perhaps surprising for me to say it—and it was far more confounding to me to feel it—but I was beginning to weary of living with my lord's almost constant suffering. This, of course, made me feel like the worst sort of traitor. Hakatri had picked me out as a child and allowed me to take a place in his life that would normally have been reserved for a youth of his own race. He had made me his armiger, an honor never before given to one of my people. And he had always shown me a kindness that went beyond mere condescension. Once, before my father died, Lord Hakatri even dined in our house, praised our poor fare, and complimented my father on raising such a good and helpful son. I am certain that my father must have been overwhelmed with pride to hear that, although it was not his nature to show much emotion, especially in the presence of our Zida'ya masters.

If my father Pamon Sur had been one of the antique sort of Tinukeda'ya, his life devoted utterly to hard work and stolid silences, my mother Enla must have been a different kind. I scarcely remember her—the fatal fever took her when I was only a few summers old—but every memory I had, or tale I heard of her, spoke of someone who loved life in all its forms. She would come to the stables to nurse the sickly foals, even when my father told her they would not survive and she was wasting her time. Sometimes he was right, but just as often she would bring one back from the brink of death with her loving care.

During my long, lonely evenings tending my master, and sometimes during sleepless nights, I thought about my childhood and the mother I had lost. One such night, as my master struggled with his foul dreams, a memory returned to me, as if a door had been opened to the past, and I suddenly recalled what my mother had said about the Dreaming Sea.

That day I had been called a harsh name by one of the Zida'ya children when I tried to join in their play, and I was bitterly sad. My mother took me on her lap and told me, "Do not be ashamed, Kes, by being different than the others. Someday, at a moment you most need it, you will feel the Garden inside you—you will feel the heartbeat of the Dreaming Sea." At the time, I now remembered, my childish imagination had pictured her words as very real, and I had envisioned a great and surging flood that would burst out of me, throbbing with the living essence of the great ocean (though I had never seen the Dreaming Sea, of course, nor any body of water except nearby Landfall Bay). As young as I was then, her words seemed more of a warning than a reassuring promise, and perhaps that is why I gave in so readily when my father later ordered me not to ask or speak about what she said.

Soon after the fever came to both of us. I recovered, but my mother Enla never did. During her last days, as the illness overwhelmed her, she was confined to her bed, but she had me come to her every day for at least a short while. She would ask me to share with her all the things I had seen and heard, then we would pray to the Garden together. When she finally died, I did not know what to do or even what to feel. A part of my child's mind wondered if it had been my fault, since the fever had come to me first, but that unhappiness was one of many things I never shared with anyone else, along with my mother's words about the mysterious sea that was somehow a part of me.

My father Pamon Sur must have been nearly as bereft by losing her as I was, but he had his work in the stables to occupy his thoughts. I had only the silent Tinukeda'ya neighbor-woman who lived beside us and watched over me in his absence. This woman had no children of her own and seemed to know nothing about tending them, nor did she care to learn. My father came home late every night, exhausted and silent. I see now that he was grieving in his own way, but to me it felt as though I had been entirely abandoned. It was in this time, in the seasons after my mother's death, that I began to follow my father to the stables every day, and it was in that place that my master Hakatri first came to know me. It would not be foolish to say that in the Zida'ya lord's kindness I found something I had been desperate for, though I did not know it. It was not only his interest that saved me, but also the fact of who he was. Insignificant little Pamon Kes had been noticed by one of the most important people in all the world. It was this feeling, like a door opening to let sun and air rush into a dark, smoky room, that gave me hope for my life to mean something.

After my master had questioned all the best-known mortal healers and clerics we could find in Nabban, he began to seek for other sorts of wisdom—healing secrets that the city-men had lost or never owned. Hakatri did not scorn all mortal knowledge, so as the moons and seasons fled past we began to explore some of the more distant outposts of mortal men in the Southern lands, the places where the earliest mortal arrivals had settled, far from the wide roads and stone walls the city-folk built later. At last, we began a difficult and agonizing journey into the swampy lands east of Nabban in search of a wise woman whose tale my master had heard from mortal clerics, a woman who supposedly cured even the worst illnesses by secret rites. Legends said that she had been practicing her art in the depths of the swamp for well over two Great Years—more than a century by mortal count—and that gave my master hope.

"She must be something different than an ordinary mortal, Pamon, if the stories are true," Hakatri said one night when his pain was so great he had awakened me to keep him company. His every word was forced out through a grimace; he had to breathe slowly and shallowly to be able to speak at all. "She might be another of your own folk, Pamon, or even one of the Zida'ya or Hikeda'ya who has fled to this backwater."

His decision made, Hakatri sent his remaining guards back to Asu'a with our horses, which would be no good to us in the marshes. The guards also carried letters to his family, so I was able to include my own letter meant for Lady Ona at Ravensperch.

It was only the two of us now. We made our way east to the edge of the immense swamp that mortals called the Wran, but which my master's people had much earlier named the Vastmire. When we at last reached a place called *Kwan-To-Po*, a sprawling, ramshackle settlement that had grown up beside a much-traveled estuary on the edge of the vast wetland, we hired a local guide to carry us in his boat into the depths of the swamp.

After several days in the flat-bottomed craft, sliding through the damp, insect-haunted marshes, we at last reached the wise woman's village. Her name was Hurma, and she was, in spite of my master's hopes, a mortal. She was also tiny, toothless, and extremely kind. She lived in a house made of wood and reeds at the edge of a wide, sluggish river. In our ignorance, my master and I had entered the swamp during the Wolf Moon, the beginning of the rainy season. Hurma kindly let us shelter with her and her sizable family, and we lived in their house through the long season of incessant storms—as cramped and miserable an experience as you might imagine.

From my first sight of it, the swampland felt far too much like Serpent's Vale for me ever to feel comfortable there, but it was a Serpent's Vale writ so large that it seemed an entire world. And the longer we spent in that wet, unpleasant place, the worse I found it, until the rain drumming on the thatched roof—or on my head when I had to leave the healer's hut—threatened to drive me mad. But once the rainy season had begun the rivers all flooded and we could not leave. If Hurma and her family had not sheltered us, I do not think we would have survived.

As it turned out, we lived almost three full moons among those kind people, beneath those tangled trees. Vines that looked like snakes hung on nearly every branch, side by side with deadly snakes that looked like vines. Most nights our only music was the braying of apes and the incessant screeching of birds, and not only the serpents were deadly in that blighted land. In truth, some of the swamp creatures were scarcely less frightening than the worm whose blood had burned my master. Armored cockindrills as long as two-team carriages floated in the muddy water just a stone's throw from Hurma's door, and one day I saw a spotted cat as big as a pony, a sharp-toothed hunter who, the healer warned us, could climb trees and drop down silently on its victims from above.

It was good that I spent most of my time in Hurma's hut, tending my master, because in that swamp, death seemed to wait everywhere. Just during that rainy season one of the healer's sons was nearly taken by some creature in the river—he escaped, but we never found out what had seized him—and one of her numerous grandchildren was snatched by ghants and never seen again. Many say that the earth-goblins of the northern plains are dreadful to see, but they are nothing compared to ghants, which look like huge, nearly man-sized crabs, but can stand on their hind legs like apes and live together in horrid nests made of mud and slime.

But even more disturbing were the changes that overtook my master as we suffered through the long rainy season.

"My dreams, Pamon," he said to me one day. He had not been able to get out of his bed that morning. "Something happened to me that night on the ocean, when we floated above the Green Column, and it seems to grow stranger and stronger each time I sleep."

"Truly, my lord?" I found that hard to believe. Hakatri had told me so many outlandish tales about his wormsblood visions that I could not imagine how they could be any more strange.

"Because now something or someone is calling me," Hakatri told me when I asked. "And it is different from the other dreams, maddening as they are—this one seems more real and far more powerful. Often I see a tall, pale figure, like a woman in a white robe, waiting for me."

My skin crawled. "Ever since you first told me about it, I have thought that your summoner sounds like the queen of the Hikeda'ya."

He shook his head. "I do not think it is Utuk'ku. I see no silver mask in these dreams, and sometimes the figure is no figure at all, but more like a finger held up before me, as if in warning."

"But you said the dream was calling you. How can it also be warning you?"

He fell back, exhausted, though the day had just begun. "I do not know, Pamon. I do not even know whether it is real or just more madness, Sometimes I feel as though the dragon's foul blood has burned all the way through me, even into my waking thoughts—as though it is destroying everything in me that existed before Serpent's Vale."

"Do not say such a thing, Master!" I was truly terrified. "That is only despair speaking. You are still you. If anyone knows it, I do. You are the same person, though you have suffered in a way no person ever should."

His head lolled on his pallet of marsh reeds. "To tell truth, I am no longer certain I can tell what is real and what is imagined. Am I speaking with you now, or with some dream-Pamon, some memory of my old life?"

"My lord, never say such things!" And even though I knew it was cruel, I reached out and took his hand. He grimaced at my touch, but I held on. "This pain is real—but so am I." I was in tears at his agony, but I clung to his fingers until he at last managed to pull away. "I am real, Lord Hakatri. Never doubt that."

"Still, I must find this thing that calls me," he said. "Of all the visions that have plagued me since the dragon's death, only this new dream seems to have a meaning—a point. I must find that tall, pale figure. I sense that it portends more than my own life. When I see it, I feel a great cold emptiness—like a deep hole opening beneath me after I have already taken a step and cannot stop myself." He shivered and sat up. "Help me, my good and trusted servant. Promise you will help me learn what this dream means. I have no more claims on you—"

"No more claims?" It was all I could do not to grab at his hand again. "Master, you have every claim on me, both of loyalty and friendship. I swear I will never desert you—never." Sadly, I had still not learned the lesson that Ineluki's pride had taught us.

Lord Hakatri let out a long, ragged sigh. "North," he said. "It calls me north, Pamon. And I must follow its call." After those words he fell back into restless sleep, leaving me to wonder what it all meant.

The old healer Hurma never found a true cure for my master's afflictions, but she tried many things, and at last managed to concoct a paste from the roots of swamp plants that, when spread on his wounded skin, eased his suffering somewhat. I was grateful, for we had used all our small supply of *kei-vishaa*.

When the rainy season finally ended and we could leave the marshlands, I gathered up our few possessions, which now included a sack full of Hurma's root bulbs. We left the healer a goodly amount of our remaining gold to repay her for her time and hospitality, then slowly made our way back through the jungle along the brackish waterways of the marshlands.

Our journey north started well enough. We returned to Kwan-To-Po and used the last of our gold to buy new horses. The trader, seeing my master's ailing condition, tried to sell us inferior beasts, but after a lifetime in the stables of Asu'a tending the fairest, swiftest horses in the world, I was easily able to tell the useful ones from the hopeless. I forced the trader to sell us mounts that were, if nowhere near the quality of the horses we knew, at least capable of crossing the wide grasslands between us and home. Because I knew we were still overpaying for barely ordinary stock, I used the trader's superstitious fear of my master's kind by hinting at fairy curses if he mistreated us, and thus convinced him to give us a pair of decent saddles and other tackle for the horses as well. It hurt my heart to use the cruel mouth-bit mortals favored, but these animals had never known anything else, and I had neither the time nor any moth harnesses to retrain them.

My master chose the unimaginatively named Gray, while I took Boots, a chestnut with white feet and a white blaze on her nose. They are not long a part of this story, but I name them because they gave surprisingly good service, especially considering the dubious honesty of their former master. In fact, they both seemed quite pleased to leave his stable, and also seemed to enjoy the care I gave them as long as we had them.

Once mounted, Hakatri and I set out north beneath gray skies, across the seemingly endless, grassy plain the Zida'ya called the Whisperwaste. I hoped that we were heading home, but I was to be disappointed, at least for quite some time.

The heaviest storms had passed, but at that time of the year the mists still hung over the grasslands late into the day, only burning off when the sun was high. But the sky seldom lost its blanket of heavy overcast, so that we seemed to ride through a world without color. Occasional rains still swept across the flat plains, turning the meadows to mud and slowing our progress considerably. But nothing could hold back my master's dreams.

"It is hard to rest," Hakatri told me one night as we sat by the fire I had made. We never rode much past twilight because our mounts were not as sure-footed as Zida'ya horses, and we feared one of them might break a leg in the dark. "It is only while we travel north that this feeling of being tugged along subsides a little."

"But we *are* traveling north, my lord."

"Whatever summons me does not cease its call when we stop for the night, Pamon. It pulls at me every moment."

I could only shrug. Now that I was Hakatri's last and only servant, the journey was wearing on me badly. I cared for the horses, made a fire every night when we stopped, foraged for food and prepared a meal for the two of us, then took the roots Hurma had given us and crushed them into a paste to spread on my master's wounds while he recovered from the agony of the day's ride. At the end of each evening I would fall into a helpless, exhausted sleep until the thin light of grassland morning woke me to my duties again.

I did not know then that those were to be the most comfortable days of that journey.

But during the first days crossing the Whisperwaste, things seemed almost hopeful. All around us the approaching Season of Renewal was turning the grasslands a vital green. My master found enough relief in old Hurma's root salve that he could sit in his saddle and ride and could even sleep sometimes without the terrifying dreams that had punished him since he killed the Blackworm. His mother's Word of Preservation doubtless had a part in that as well, and some days it almost seemed as if the old days before Serpent's Vale had returned. I sang songs for my master, ancient ones that I knew he liked, though he laughed and told me that I mangled the old words terribly. I could almost convince myself that things were slowly returning to what they had been, that Lord Hakatri and I would make our way north across the grasslands and be back in Asu'a before Renewal had given way to the Season of Growing.

Then, as we rode deeper into the Whisperwaste, the wise woman's root salve stopped working. It did not happen suddenly, but once it began it was impossible to ignore. The easing of Hakatri's terrible pains no longer lasted as long, nor did the paste soothe the agony as much as it previously had. As the days passed, each one as empty as the flat, grassy landscape around us, we used more and more of the salve, so that I spent at least an hour every night pounding down the next day's supply into something that could be rubbed gently on his scarred flesh. The sack of roots was fast emptying, but even if we had turned then and rode straight for Asu'a, we would have run out long before we got there.

My master even considered a return to the swamps for more of the soothing medicament, but I pointed out to him that with just the two of us and our horses, even if we went back and filled our saddlebags to the top, we would never be able to carry enough to cross all of the Whisperwaste before it ran out again.

"So then, what do you suggest, Armiger Pamon?" he demanded. "That I just lie down here to die?" The anger in his voice and the glint in his eye frightened me: in all our time together, my master had never spoken to me in that way before; for a moment it felt as though I looked at a stranger. "You are always so full of wisdom when I do not need your suggestions," he said. "Where is that wisdom now?" And Hakatri actually lifted his hand as if to strike at me. When I started back with a cry of surprise, he realized what he had done and his face crumpled in horror.

"Forgive me, good Pamon," he cried. "I scarcely know what I am doing or saying sometimes. The pain has returned—I am on fire! It never stops, not even when I sleep, but still that pale figure commands my dreams and calls me onward. I have no other hope now but to follow the summons and pray that it signifies some possibility of salvation."

In truth, Hakatri grew increasingly strange as we crossed the grasslands, even before Hurma's salve stopped working. The scars on my master's chest and belly and arms had lost some of their furious redness, but if the pain had subsided a very small amount, other aspects had grown worse. Several times during our journey I woke from sleep to find him hobbling back and forth across our campsite in darkness, swiping with Thunderstroke, his sharp witchwood sword, muttering and moaning. The first time I thought he might be practicing, using the night hours when we did not travel to keep himself in some kind of fighting trim, and I only rolled farther away and went back to sleep. But when it happened again and I listened to what he was saying, it became clear to me that he was sleepwalking—or, rather, sleep-fighting. This of course frightened me, because even wounded and limping my master was a deadly hand with a blade, and if his dreams caused him to mistake me for an enemy, I knew I would stand little chance. When he finally woke to something like his ordinary mood, I asked him about the dream and he told me he had been fighting Hidohebhi. "I stabbed it and stabbed it," he said, "just as I did in Serpent's Vale, but the monster would not die."

I did not bother to remind him that he had killed the dragon with a great spear made of a witchwood tree.

Another night I woke up when Hakatri violently lifted me off the ground. For a moment, in my confusion and fear, I thought my master would break my back, but it soon became clear he thought I was his brother Ineluki, and that he believed I had been killed by the worm of Serpent's Vale. He cried out so loudly and mournfully that I feared wolves or bandits would come to see what made so much noise in the middle of the empty grassland.

And all through our travel across the grasslands, that mysterious but powerful summoning, the tall, white shape, came to him again and again, generally during his fitful sleeps, but even sometimes when he was awake.

The Whisperwaste is a strange place, and our time crossing those wild lands was strange, too. My master sometimes seemed to have a purpose firmly in mind, but at other moments he would ask me where we were going and why, and seemed distressed when I told him that he was the one leading us, not I.

As we journeyed, we met a few of the mortals who lived on that monstrously empty plain, herding folk for the most part, traveling in family groups. The men let their chin whiskers grow long and rode on small, strong ponies. These folk could draw their bows and loose arrows from horseback better than most mortals could manage while standing on firm ground. They roamed from one side of the wide grasslands to the other according to the season, following their cattle and sheep, and though we did not see many of them, those we saw were generally cautious of us, or outright fearful, but did not offer us harm. A few of these mortals even warned us to be wary of any company of solely male riders, since the grasslands were also a refuge for outlaws, thieves, and murderers.

One day early in Renewal we were beset by bandits in truth, although it was not one of my master's loud nightmares that called them down on us. Nearly a dozen riders spotted us from far away in late afternoon—my master saw them first, of course—and steadily narrowed the distance between us as the sun slipped down the sky. Their first mistake was to attack us as soon as they were close enough, which happened to be just after the sun had set and twilight was fading. I doubt they had ever met any Zida'ya before, and it is likely they did not know how much better my master could see in near-darkness than they could.

Their second mistake was to take my master's slumped posture and obvious discomfort for the signs of an easy target. In fact, when they closed on us in the darkening evening, it was me that they avoided in order to attack him first, which would have made me laugh when I realized it, had I not been so terrified.

These two errors alone were enough to doom them, but they still might have won the day if they had only used their bows while they were still far away from us. My master had his own bow, but they could have overcome him if they had all shot at once. Instead, one or two loosed their shafts, but those seemed meant only to keep us from escaping as they made a thundering rush in our direction, curved swords slashing the air over their heads.

My master killed three of them with arrows in moments, then he unsheathed his sword and spurred toward them. I kicked my heels against my own horse's sides and turned back to fight beside him. I took the hand off one of the whiskered attackers—his look of indignant shock was almost comical, as though I had mistaken some kindness he planned—and saw him tumble out of his saddle, but before I could even reach the next bandit my master had killed one of them and wounded another, wielding Thunderstroke as swiftly and devastatingly as the lightning for which it was named. Within moments, as the bloody mist of the last killing still drifted down through the air, the remaining bandits gave up their attack and veered away. They turned in their saddles as they retreated and loosed arrows toward us, but we were lucky or they were too frightened to aim well: none of their bolts came close to us.

I hurried to my master to thank him—I was very certain that if I had been with any less dangerous warrior, I would have been killed—but had a frightening moment as I caught up with him. He was bent low in Gray's saddle, gasping. It was only as I reached out to him and he violently drew back that I realized he had not been struck by a stray arrow but was overcome entirely by his exertions. It had been a long time since I had seen him so helpless, and as I watched he half-slid, half-tumbled out of the saddle and onto the ground.

I quickly dismounted and pulled the last root paste from my saddlebag. I set a fire and heated a clean stone as quickly as I could. When the stone had begun to crack with the heat, I picked it out of the fire with sticks and dropped it into our cooking pot so the water would boil, then used the hot water to soften the root paste. When it had cooled, I took it to Lord Hakatri. When he finally recognized me, he allowed me to daub the root-salve on his wounds.

The night grew darker as I waited, but my master stayed huddled on the ground. At last, as the moon drifted up into the sky, he stirred and sat up. Even by moonlight, I could see the fear in his eyes.

"I thought that time the wormsblood dream would not end," he told me. "Faithful Pamon, I thank you. I do not know what I would do without your loyalty and help. I owe you more than I can ever repay."

I flinched at that. Such talk turned things upside-down. I did not want to live in a world where my master was so weak, so pitiful. It was against the order of everything I had ever known. "I am your servant," was all I said, but I had become strangely uncertain what serving him truly meant.

One night, deep in the unmapped reaches of the Whisperwaste, I dreamt that I was on fire. But it did not feel like a dream.

I woke up, shrieking and squirming, trying with flapping hands to beat out the flames that I could feel running up my limbs, only to realize that those flames were not real. But they *had* been real, or at least they had truly felt that way. Even as I crouched beneath the stars and the stretching night sky, the pain was still alive in me, an agony like flayed skin, an attack on my wits as terrible as an endless scream. When after a dozen heartbeats or so the torture finally began to ease and I could catch my breath, I saw that my master had sat up and was staring at me with wide eyes.

"What is it, Pamon?"

"I do not know, my lord." I struggled for air. "It felt as if someone threw boiling oil on my skin. It was only a dream, I suppose, but it seemed to continue even after I woke."

"I am so sorry." The look on Hakatri's face was grim, but at that moment I did not understand it. My heart was beating so fast it made my chest ache, and my lungs were still short of air. It was a long time before I dared to let myself fall sleep again.

That was not the last time I seemed to partake of one of my master's dreams. Often in the days that followed I would awaken from fearful visions to discover Lord Hakatri writhing in nightmares of his own, and I became more and more convinced that I was sharing something of his night-torments, though I could not understand how. But it was not only those terrible dreams of burning that plagued me. Sometimes, especially on the edges of sleep, I seemed not to be dreaming at all, but to have slipped past the veil that surrounds all our lives and into something quite different—something eternal and unknowable. It was a fearful thing indeed to sense how little separated our waking selves from unknown gulfs of madness.

I awakened early one morning to find Hakatri up and moving around our camp. He was packing up our possessions in a sort of fever, as though preparing to flee some danger, but he seemed more excited than worried.

"Up, Pamon, up!" he said as I sat rubbing my eyes. "I know our direction at last. I know what the White Phantom is!"

"And will you tell me, my lord?" I asked.

"I will do better—I will show you! To horse! It waits for me."

I dutifully gathered up the remains of my cooking tools and the few other things I had taken from my saddlebags and prepared to ride. I had no sooner climbed into my saddle than Hakatri put heels to his mount and was off, and I had to ride Boots hard to keep my master in sight. The morning mists swirled between us as we rode, and at times I felt as though I rode alone, chasing something far less substantial than a lord of Asu'a.

The sun had almost reached noon and the mist had burned away when Hakatri reached the top of a low hill and reined up, calling back to me, "There, Pamon! Did I not tell you?" His voice was full of joy, so much so that it troubled me. Whatever he had found had been leading us on for many days, and I felt only apprehension as I hurried to catch up, a feeling that increased when I reached his side.

The meadowland stretched before us like a serving platter, but for the first time I could make out the dim shadow of the great Oldheart forest that girdled the grassland's northern edge, and I was surprised by how far we had come in just the last few days' riding. But I was even more astonished by the angular shape that loomed far above the swaying grasses—a slender hillock of rock and earth that did indeed look a little like a figure dressed in pale robes. But no person, giant, or even dragon had ever stood so tall: the tor jutted high into the sky before us, an angular prominence jutting from the earth like the lower half of a column, though its sides and crest were shrouded in grass and thick with trees. It rose out of a shallow lake that surrounded it like a moat, but it was no castle, and no mortal or immortal hands had shaped it. In truth, the hilly spire before us looked more than anything else to me like the blunt end of a massive skeletal finger, and I shuddered to see it.

"What is this place?" I cried.

"Sesuad'ra!" called my master. "The Leavetaking Stone."

I had never seen that hill before, but I knew its story as well as I knew of the Flight from the Garden or the death of Nenais'u. Many, many Great

Years before, the two clans of my master's people, Zida'ya and Hikeda'ya, had met atop the Leavetaking Stone to arrange their separation, a moment known ever since as the Parting. Afterward Utuk'ku had led her people back to Nakkiga to shelter in the mountain's fastness, declaring they would never live with Jenjiyana and her clansfolk again. After Sesuad'ra, nothing had ever been the same for the immortals who came from the Garden.

"But why are we here, Master?" I asked. "Surely the place is empty."

"Of people, yes," he said, spurring his horse down the slope toward the great pillar of stone and earth. "But it was always alive—and it calls to me."

And with that he gave Gray his heels again, forcing me to drive my own horse to a gallop simply to keep him in sight.

Our mounts picked their way through the shallow water at the base of Sesuad'ra with exaggerated caution. It did not take my years of experience in Asu'a's stables to see that these horses reared in mortal lands did not like the Leavetaking Stone: they took every step as though under the eye of a large and lightly sleeping beast of prey. Nor did I think much of the place, either. The tales of the Parting do not speak often of Sesuad'ra itself, but it is unlike any other spot I have visited in my life, huge but deserted, its very size making it seem like something unnatural that had been set down in that empty land and then forgotten.

"I see the remains of the causeway," Hakatri called to me. "This way, Pamon. We can follow it to the stone itself and our horses will barely get their bellies damp." His good humor worried me as much as his bad dreams and pained suffering had in the days before, and I could not help wondering aloud why this place had become so important to him.

"Because I have seen it in so many dreams," he told me. "The very dreams that are part of my affliction."

"But is that not a reason to stay away?" I asked. "We are but a day's ride west from the walls of Enki-e-Shao'saye. We have been in the saddle for almost two moons. You have suffered so much, my lord, and we are both weary. Hungry, too, and the roots Hurma gave us to soothe your wounds are all used up. Let us turn toward home instead, or toward Enki-e-Shao'saye—in the Summer City we can rest and strengthen ourselves. Then if you still wish it, we can come here again on our way back to Asu'a."

Poor, foolish Kes! I still believed at that point that after many moons of travel, we would be home within a few days.

Hakatri only shook his head, as though I failed to understand some elementary fact. "But we are here, Pamon. The Leavetaking Stone has called to me in my cursed dreams for so long—how could I turn away now?"

The spiral track that wound upward around the great stony hill was wide enough for two wagons to pass each other. As we rode, Hakatri told me more of the place. I cannot say it made me any less uneasy.

"This hill itself is a kind of Witness," he said. "There is power here—a power that even the wisest of my people have never entirely understood."

"Do you mean this great rock is a Master Witness? I thought there were only nine of those all told, one for each of the great cities, like the Pool of Three Depths at home in Asu'a." The word "home" was beginning to have an ashy taste on my lips. Many times since we had set out to travel to Nakkiga I had feared my master would never see his family again, that I would have to bear the news of his death back to his mother Amerasu and his wife Briseyu. More recently I had begun to hope that my fears had been wrong, that we might actually find our way back, but now, suddenly, things had changed again.

"You already know there is more than one kind of Witness," Hakatri told me as our horses leaned forward into the steep track. "Those like the one I carry"—he reached into his tunic and produced the mirror he had acquired after losing his first in Serpent's Vale—"and the Master Witnesses you have seen, like Asu'a's Pool or Mezutu'a's Shard, which can command the lesser Witnesses or speak to many Witnesses at once. But another sort of Master Witness also exists, and one of them is here at Sesuad'ra. It is in the stone itself, or perhaps even deep in the earth beneath it. No one knows. Its full strength cannot be mastered even by the adepts of my people, but it enhances the power of other Witnesses, sometimes in ways even the other Master Witnesses cannot match. The thing hidden beneath us is called *Rhao iye-Sama'an*—the Earth-Drake's Eye. Its power is why this place was chosen for the ritual of the Parting, to bind the fateful agreement with Words of Power. All the other Master Witnesses have long been claimed by Zida'ya or Hikeda'ya, but the Witness buried here belongs to no one."

Listening, I struggled with worry and even a little anger. "But that still does not explain why we are here and why you are so determined to ride to the top of this stony hill, my lord. Can you tell me that?"

"No, Pamon, I cannot, because I do not know. But I do know that I was summoned—I was meant to come here." He said it as though that should lay my fears to rest.

But who or what is summoning you? I wondered. I had not believed things could be worse for my master than what he had already suffered, but in that isolated, eerie place, with the wind moaning through the empty grasslands below and rippling the shallow waters around the base of the great stone, I feared for the first time that the worst might be ahead of us.

My master's people have a favored saying, part of a long poem by Benhaya of Kementari.

> *First the ocean, then the island*
> *First the forest, then the tree*
> *First the tree, then the branch, then the nightingale*
> *But in the nightingale's song is everything*

I will tell the truth: I do not well understand what it signifies. The Zida'ya often recite it when they mean to say that some things cannot be understood in part, but only as a piece of a greater whole. But "nightingale" was also the name my master's folk called Jenjiyana, the most beloved of all the Sa'onserei who came to this land after the flight from the Garden, still remembered long after her death for her beauty and goodness. Jenjiyana, or so it is said, was born with hair that was not white, as with the rest of her kind, but black as a starless night, and instead of the warm golden skin most of her people had, Jenjiyana's was a pale, buttery shade like the blossom of a spring primrose. The tallest tower in Asu'a is topped with a statue of her staring back toward the east, some say toward the Garden itself, others say to the city of Tumet'ai, which was swallowed by ice during Jenjiyana's long lifetime. In many ways, that statue is the symbol of the Zida'ya in this land, so I know the nightingale is more than just a bird for my master's people.

I was still pondering Benhaya's poem as we reached the top of the Leavetaking Stone. What had at first seemed merely a huge outcrop in the middle of the grasslands had become a steep, spiraling slope, but as the track broadened at the top and we rode out onto Sesuad'ra's heights, the place appeared to be something else entirely—an island floating in the sky.

The ruins atop the great stone were now revealed to us in all their forgotten splendor. My first impression was of an entire deserted city, with roofless buildings and open stretches of tile that had sunk into the soil in some spots but had been thrown down in others by the vegetation growing up through it. After a few moments of open-mouthed staring, though, I could see that the deserted site was too small to be a true city, but that its buildings were too large to belong to some lesser settlement. The realization settled on me that all this must have been built simply for the great and terrible ceremony of Parting, then abandoned once more.

"Yes, Pamon," my master said, misreading me for once. "Your people labored hard to build all this. No one else could be trusted to do so in a place of such power, but the Garden is strong in the blood of your folk."

I was so busy looking around me that I did not really grasp what he said, but later I wished I had asked him what he meant. Even now, I wonder how many things that are still great mysteries to me are known and barely considered by my master's people?

"I do not much like this place, my lord," I said.

"You can feel it is alive, that is all." His feverish mood seemed to be returning. "Or at least that something is waiting here to be awakened."

"You make me dislike it even more, my lord."

Hakatri was scarcely paying attention to me now. His eyes had lit on the largest building on the promontory, less decrepit than most of the others. It was round as a barrel's lid and a furlong or more across, with an odd, shallow dome.

"That is the *Kosa'ajika*," he said, "the Crossroad, as my ancestors named it."

I stared at the weird structure. "Crossroad? Why should it be called such a thing, my lord? I do not see even one road, let alone a crossing."

"The whole of its name was 'The Crossroad of Time,'" he said. And with that still hanging in the air, he rode toward it. I followed more slowly.

Moss clung to the dome's pearly stone in many places, and grasses and other greenery had crept far up its sides. I thought I could now sense what my master had meant by the place being alive, and it frightened me. I could feel it in the way someone lying in the sun might feel a shadow cross his body, but this shadow fell on me and remained. If Hakatri felt anything like that, though, it did not slow him. He dismounted and passed swiftly through the empty socket where the doors had once stood. I still hesitated just outside the entrance, watching as my master continued to the shadowed center of the low, round central chamber, still holding his Witness. After a moment Hakatri sank to his knees, lifted the mirror in his upturned palms as if he had scooped a drink of water out of a stream, then bent to look into it.

Suddenly full of alarm, I hurried across the uneven tiled floor to his side, but he gestured for me to stay back.

"As I said, I do not know what will happen." He was staring into his Witness, which already seemed alive with shimmering light. "Do not come too close, Pamon, and in no circumstance should you touch me. I do not want you harmed by any of this."

Despite my growing fear, I almost laughed in pained surprise at his words. My lord did not want me harmed! As if his great suffering had not harmed me already, simply because I loved him. And now Hakatri's visions had even begun to spill over into my own dreams, burning me without ever leaving a mark, terrifying me with things I could not understand. It was far too late to save me from harm.

"Why have I been called here?" Hakatri asked as he stared into the Witness. "Who calls me? Do you offer a cure? Or another curse?"

And then, as I looked on, an even more curious thing happened. The distant walls of the domed Crossroad seemed to shrink inward around me. My view grew narrower and narrower, darkness pushing in on all sides, but I guessed I must be seeing with Hakatri's eyes instead of my own, because the gleaming circle of the Witness grew before me until I could make out nothing else. The reflection was like a cloudy sky at midday, full of roiling gray, with beams of light here and there piercing the murk for a moment before disappearing again. Then, suddenly, I fell forward into that whirl of shine and shadow.

A small figure gradually formed out of the chaos, cloaked, hooded, but also tenuous as smoke. I could make out little of the face, but it spoke with what sounded like a woman's voice.

Finally, through all the years, I have found you. I heard her not with my ears but in my thoughts.

Are you the one who called me here? The voiceless reply seemed to come

from me, but the words were my master's, not my own. I could feel Hakatri's pain now as I sometimes did in my dreams. It grew worse by the
moment and made it hard for me to listen and to understand.

No, the voice told him—told us. *Something greater and subtler than I am
has drawn you here. But I have gambled much that you would answer the call. The
hour has come. Not here, not now, and not for you, but for everything else. All is
balanced, but in a mere moment that balance will tip.*

But why have I been summoned? my master asked. *Will you tell me? Is there
some reason for my suffering after all?*

The dim figure made a gesture of negation. *Do not ask questions, I beg
you. Our moment is short. You are the One Who Burns. That is the truth, and it
is beyond me to change it. I cannot bring you surcease of pain, Hakatri i-Sa'onserei,
or even explanation. Suffering simply is. It is what happens despite it that matters.*

Growing dread clawed at my thoughts, or at my master's thoughts—it
was impossible to tell—threatening to tear them into rags. The *Kosa'ajika*
or the Witness or both seemed to be making the pain worse. *That means
nothing! This torment is all I know!*

There is no help for that. Be silent. Please. The female voice balanced both
sorrow and impatience.

I felt my master's sudden despair—we would find no help here for our
suffering. *Speak, then,* he said—I said. *Speak and be cursed.*

That is entirely possible. The pale figure spread its arms and began to
smolder, like a coal blown back into life, and the darkness narrowed
around it. *I bring you no prophecy, but a memory that has not yet come to be.
There will come a moment when only you, Hakatri of the Year-Dancers, stand
between life and darkness. In that moment, you must remember this, and you will
have to choose.*

Choose? What choice do you mean?

*There are no words I can give you to help you understand. The choice has not yet
been offered. It may never be offered. But when it is—and somewhere, sometime, it
must be, it will be—you must remember this moment. Choose carefully. And now
my time is over.*

But wait, I still do not understand! My master's thoughts were desperate,
confused. *Choose what? And who are you?*

Who I am is not important. The smoldering light was beginning to dim.

You will know me when we meet again. If we meet again. The light guttered like a candle in a strong breeze. *When we meet again . . .*

No! Come back! Do not leave me with so little—!

Those are the last words I remember.

I struggled up at last from a deeper blackness than I think I have ever known. I lay sprawled on the Crossroad flagstones, staring at the dome above my head; the cracks between its stones gleamed with sunshine as bright as lightning. For several breathless moments I simply remained there, confused, heart speeding. Then I thought of my master and clambered to my feet.

Hakatri lay stretched on the uneven floor a short distance away from me, face down and motionless. Terrified, I did my best to rouse him, but except for the shallow rise and fall of his chest he seemed lifeless and his skin was cold. His Witness, which had fallen to the tiles, felt no warmer or livelier when I picked it up.

No matter how I tried I could not rouse my master back to wakefulness, and at last I put my arms around his chest and pulled him, his feet dragging, toward the empty doorway and out into the fading afternoon sunlight. I managed, with an effort I did not think myself capable of, to heave him up at last and drape him over the saddle of his restive horse. My own head felt like a drum that had been beaten and beaten until the stretched skin had split, and I could think only of getting Hakatri away from that place.

As I rode down the winding track from the hilltop, leading my master's horse and its insensible burden, I was terrified that those moments in the Crossroad of Time, fearful as they had been for me, might have dealt Hakatri some mortal blow. I needed to find help for him as quickly as possible, but Asu'a was several days' ride away. When our horses' hooves finally touched the waters of the lake around Sesuad'ra's foot, I turned east toward Enki-e-Shao'saye instead, which was only a few hours distant. Evening had now fallen; I would have to ride in the dark. The grassland along the edge of Oldheart was a dangerous place, stalked by wolves, bears, and mortal bandits, and the forest itself was home to other dangers, but I dared not waste time waiting for the safety of sunlight.

I had a dark and uneasy night's ride. I had to stop frequently to push my master back into place so he would not slide off the saddle, and I was no longer riding one of our sure-footed, clear-seeing Zida'ya mounts. Our progress seemed achingly slow, and my only moment of relief happened near middle-night, when I heard my master groan. He did not wake, but at least I knew he still lived.

The short ride seemed to last for days, not hours, but at last the ancient city appeared out of the forest shadows, its walls agleam with lamps. A small company rode out of the gate to meet us, most carrying torches. In those days the Summer City did not receive many visitors, so even in darkness we had been spotted from a great distance. When the riders were upon us I recognized Minasao Redwing as the leader of the welcoming procession—or at least I hoped that was what it was—by his famed helmet with its wide-spread wings, and his hair, dyed the purple of flowering betony. Minasao is the Protector of Enki-e-Shao'saye, child of the city's chief celebrant, Lady Sonayattu, both of whom are among Year-Dancing House's most trusted allies.

"Hail, stranger," he called as we approached. "Are you friend or foe to the Summer City, and who do you carry? Is he dead or wounded?"

"I bring Lord Hakatri of Asu'a. He is alive, but he sorely needs a healer." I spoke more straightforwardly than I might have in other circumstances. Nursing Hakatri for so many moons had made me impatient of polite ceremony, especially when it kept my master from help. As I expected, Minasao and the other riders looked at me with surprise, only realizing at that moment that Hakatri's companion was a Tinukeda'ya servant—and an over-bold servant at that.

"That is Hakatri of the Sa'onserei?" the Protector asked. "Have you two been attacked?"

"You will have heard that my master slew the black dragon Hidohebhi," I said, "and likely that he was badly scalded with the dragon's blood as well. He has been in search of healing and pain-ease ever since. We climbed high Sesuad'ra at my Lord Hakatri's insistence. When he used his Witness in the place he called the Crossroad, some dire force I do not understand struck him down. Helping him was beyond my skills, so I brought him here."

Minasao Redwing showed his good sense immediately: he bade one of his followers mount behind my master and hold him safe in the saddle, then he sent another back to Enki-e-Shao'saye in haste to prepare a bed for my master and to summon healers. "Can he speak?" Minasao asked me.

"He has said nothing at all since Sesuad'ra. He walked the most frightening parts of the Dream Road nearly every night as we crossed the Whisperwaste, and his dreams were always strange and terrible. I do not think he had much strength left even before we climbed to the top of the great stone."

Minasao looked puzzled. "I knew he had left Asu'a some time ago, but has he—have you—truly traveled so far?"

"I could not tell you how far, my lord—our road was long and anything but straight. I have stayed at his side these many moons, doing my best to keep him alive and as comfortable as I could." I leaned closer. "I am weary too, Lord Protector, but I promise that if you wait until we have found my master a place to lie down, I will answer all your questions."

Minasao gave me a strange, shrewd look. "What is your name, servant?"

"Pamon Kes, my lord. I am Hakatri's armiger."

He laughed, more startled than amused. "Of course! I had forgotten about you—Hakatri's Tinukeda'ya squire." Again, the considering look. "Yes, we will speak at greater length, Armiger Pamon—you and I."

Full darkness had fallen as we reached the heart of Enki-e-Shao'saye, so all I could make out of the fabled place were the strange ways that the forest and the Summer City had grown into each other. In many places the largest trees had been made important parts of the city's buildings, great beeches, oaks, and hemlocks festooned with platforms and linked by swaying bridges as nearly invisible in the leafy heights as spiderwebs. Elsewhere, stone buildings had been constructed around natural rocky outcrops in such a way that it was hard to say which parts had been built and which had stood there since the dawn of the world. Everywhere I looked, forest and city seemed to have grown or been woven together into one thing, so that it was nearly impossible to tell what was made by pure nature and what had been crafted by skillful eyes and hands.

Not even the dim, shadow-haunted passages of Nakkiga had seemed as strange to me as Enki-e-Shao'saye did that first evening. While I marveled at the beauty of the place, I was also astonished by how empty it seemed. In the past months I had seen many of the fabled cities of the Zida'ya people—Nakkiga, Mezutu'a, and even ruined, nearly deserted Kementari—but it was only in Enki-e-Shao'saye's leaf-canopied streets and public places that I began to wonder whether Ineluki might be right, that my master's people were losing their mastery over this world that had received us after the Garden's destruction.

Goldenleaf House, the chief residence of Minasao's clan, was built with five massive lightning oaks as its pillars. A wooden roof had been built between their trunks over the main platform, and two more levels stood above that, so that the house's uppermost chambers looked out over the top of the forest.

My master, still insensible, was carried to an empty set of chambers. Even as he was set on the bed, healers surrounded him, though how many came to help and how many simply to stare because of the fame of his person and his battle with the Blackworm, I could not guess. I left him in their care and was conducted to a much more modest chamber. Still, I did not have to share it, nor would I have given much joy to anyone seeking company, since immediately after being relieved of my responsibility, I fell into a deep sleep.

In that slumber I again felt fiery pain, but this time it was not quite as terrible, and once more I could perceive something of the dream beyond the torment—a glimpse behind the veil. I found myself in a place, a strange place, all darkness and wind, with gleams of light that led me one way, then another, but remained elusive as foxfire. I saw figures around me that were dim and distant at first, but when I tried to catch up to them, drawing so close that I should have been able to see them clearly, they never became more than misty, indistinct shapes.

I am dead, I thought. *I am Hakatri,* I thought. *No, I am Kes, the servant.* But in this dream there seemed little difference between those two things: my master suffered and I suffered. I floated helplessly in that place of dark fogs and keening voices as wordless as the cries of birds. Then the pain returned, hot as a killing fever, scalding me mercilessly, and I awoke with a sharp cry, my face dripping with sweat.

A lone and clearly young Zida'ya stood in the doorway, concern written on his face.

"You are Pamon Kes?" he asked.

I nodded my head, but I was still shocked by the dream. "I was when I lay down."

He did not know whether I was making a joke. Neither did I. "Lord Minasao has asked for you," he said.

I felt a sudden chill. "How is my master?"

"A little better—or at least so I have heard. Come with me now."

Relieved, I got up and followed him. I had assumed the young Zida'ya would lead me to Hakatri's side, but instead we descended past the main hall and out into the forest garden that surrounded Goldenleaf House, then past several smaller buildings that lined the curving main road from the city gate. The streets still seemed almost deserted and I wondered why. Was it some ritual of the Goldenleaf Clan to spend the evening away from its public places? Not even Nakkiga had seemed so devoid of residents, though its subjects were imprisoned by countless strictures handed down from Utuk'ku's throne.

At last we reached an extremely large oak standing by itself in a clearing, hung with a succession of ladders leading to its upper reaches. I could not climb them with the swift surety of my young guide, but I followed him as best I could. At the top, on a wide platform under a spread of branches thick with leaves, I learned for the first time that my questioning would not be done by Minasao alone: his mother Sunoyatta no-Sha'enkida was also waiting for us, dressed in simple but splendid robes of soft, coppery cloth. As with many older Zida'ya, her age could be guessed only by subtle signs, but I knew that she had guided the folk of the Summer City for many Great Years. Sunoyatta was one of the so-called Landborn, the first generation of Hikeda'ya and Zida'ya birthed in these lands after the flight from the Garden. She had the same pale purple hair as her son, swept up and piled high on her head, held in place with pins of lavender bloodwood. Her expression was cool but not unkind as her son Minasao presented me. I bowed low to her, then began the Six Songs to show my respect, but she stopped me after the first one with a graceful gesture. "That is salutation enough, Armiger."

"Yes, let us not wait on ceremony," said Minasao as I rose to my feet. "Tell us everything that has happened."

"My master," I asked, "—how is he?"

"Sleeping, but he spoke to the healers when he briefly awoke. He knows where he is."

I said a silent prayer of thanks to the Garden. "That is good to hear, my lord. I will do my best to tell you all you wish to know."

"First give the armiger a bench so he will have some comfort." Lady Sunoyatta's voice was deep, like the lowest notes of a harp. "And bring something so he can break his fast."

The young Zida'ya who had led me there hurried out but returned a very short time later with a platter of honey-bread and forest fruits. I ate as slowly and politely as I could, though I was nearly starving; still, half my answers must have come while I was chewing.

I did my best to describe everything that had happened since the day the mortal Hernsmen had come in embassy to Asu'a. I could not guess why Sunoyatta and her son wanted to know so much about our travels other than their love for my master and sadness over his afflictions. Of course, they were relatives of Amerasu and Iyu'unigato, and thus of my master and Lord Ineluki, but that is true for most of the highest families in the Nine Cities. They stayed mostly silent as I spoke, though they exchanged many glances, and from time to time they asked me to say more about certain things, especially our time atop Sesuad'ra. To my surprise, though, the things they seemed most interested in were not that strange interlude, or the fight with the dragon, or even our time with Xaniko the Exile, who seemed to fascinate everyone else we met, but our journey to Nakkiga and the doings of my master's brother during that time.

"Tell again what you recall of that first day inside the mountain," Minasao asked me. "You said Ineluki met first with High Celebrant Hikhi, and you also mentioned Lord Yedade. Do you recall the names of any others?"

I shook my head. "I stayed mostly by Hakatri's side, as I told you. Many of Queen Utuk'ku's advisers came to us—they went in and out of my master's chamber like priests going to prayers. But I understand that Lord Ineluki met with Queen Utuk'ku herself."

The questions about Nakkiga went on for some time, but at last the Zida'ya allowed me to tell the rest of my tale, ending with our trip across the grasslands and our arrival at Enki-e-Shao'saye's gate.

After I had finished, we all sat for a while in silence, although it seemed to me that Minasao and his mother were able to come to agreement about something even without speaking. They thanked me, then the young Zida'ya who had brought me led me back to Goldenleaf House.

Lord Hakatri was either asleep or barely awake for several days afterward. The healers bustled in and out of his chamber, dutiful as parents, but one of them confessed quietly to me that they could do little but tend to his comfort, because the curse of dragon's blood was so seldom seen these days. My explanation of what had happened on Sesuad'ra—leaving out the actual things that Hakatri and the mysterious presence had said to each other, because I would not breach my master's confidence—only puzzled and disturbed them.

"Sesuad'ra is known as a very dangerous place to use a Witness," one of the healers told me. "I cannot imagine how much more dangerous for one so badly burned by wormsblood."

Despite my master's hopes, what he experienced on the Leavetaking Stone did not seem to have helped him and might even have made his problems worse. I chided myself for standing by and letting him risk such harm, but in all truth, I still cannot imagine what else I could have done, short of trying to drag him away from the place by force, which would likely have ended with one of us badly hurt or even dead. I had never forgotten awakening to find my master caught up in night-visions, swinging his deadly sword at dream-enemies.

When Hakatri finally awakened in full, and had drunk deeply from the water pitcher, like a man who has been crawling through a barren desert for days, I asked him what he remembered of Sesuad'ra.

"Only a little," he told me, blinking his eyes as though the light in the dim room hurt them. "And much." I must have frowned, because he said, "Do not look so unhappy, loyal Pamon—I am not playing games with words. I am trying to tell you the truth as I recall it."

I did my best to clear my face of all expression, as though I were one of my master's own folk. "I am listening, my lord."

"When I looked in the Witness, I . . . fell into it, or so it seemed. I saw a hundred Hakatris—a thousand! I saw myself in all directions, a world made only of my own reflections."

That was nothing like my own vision, and I wondered whether I should tell him about it, but I held my tongue. That was the closest to lying to my master I would ever come, and I still agonize over it. "A thousand Hakatris?" I asked.

"Who knows? Perhaps more! Countless reflections of my own face, but each slightly different. And then a voice spoke to me, a woman's voice I did not know. It told me that a day was coming—or a time a thousand years in the future, or the time might not come at all—and that in that time to come, I would be forced to a choice. And as it spoke, I saw all those shadows of myself moving, speaking, living—each separate, each with a life of its own, but none of them had anything to do with me, except that somehow they were *all* me."

The female voice at least seemed the same as what I had heard, but I still did not tell him my story. I did not want to admit that I had been privy to my master's innermost thoughts in the *Kosa'ajika*—it seemed like a breach of his trust at a time of his greatest vulnerability, and I feared he would feel betrayed. "This is very hard to understand, Master."

"I find it so, too," he said. "But whoever or whatever spoke to me offered me no cure for my suffering, or even respite. It only told me, 'suffering is.'"

"Then it was a bad oracle, my lord." About this I felt certain. How could anyone, mortal or immortal, see my master's torment and ignore it, much less dismiss it so callously?

"No, Pamon, I do not think there is either good or bad to be learned from the wisdom of the Earth-Drake's Eye." He winced as he changed position in the bed. "I do not say that its every word must be obeyed or even believed, but I think such a power can only show us truth. What is left is a question of how much truth, and of what truth was *not* shown."

Such fine distinctions were beyond me. "I only want to see you well, Lord Hakatri. I do not think you should brood overlong on this."

My master smiled, but it was such a sorrowful expression that it made my heart ache. "And what should I brood about instead, good Pamon? The family I cannot touch? The little daughter who fears me? My unending pain?" He shook his head. "That doom the voice foretold, the fate it believes hangs over me, at least has the virtue of waiting for me in some future time. I think I prefer that to anything I am living through now."

Lord Hakatri soon sank into another long fever. I attended him every day, though he seldom realized I was there. But even when I left him to fall into an exhausted sleep of my own, it felt as if I still attended him, so much did my own dreams seem to be ruled by my master's. Once I even asked one of the Enki-e-Shao'saye healers, a female Zida'ya whose name I no longer remember, whether being so close to Hakatri touched her dreams as well, and she seemed frankly astonished.

"You dream his dreams?" she asked me.

"How should I know? But I never dreamed of burning before the dragon's blood burned him, and I never wandered so far on the Road of Dreams, either. On Sesuad'ra I heard . . ." I stopped myself then. If I could not admit to my own master that I had overheard his Crossroad visions, how could I share it with a stranger? "In my dreams I shout names I do not know," I said instead, "as if I have seen old friends who cannot quite hear me, or old enemies I must fight who are always beyond my reach."

The healer looked puzzled, but said at last, "Perhaps it is in your blood."

"My blood? But I am not the one who fought the worm. I am not scarred by the black ooze that sprang from its wicked heart when it died."

"You are Tinukeda'ya, are you not? One of the Vao out of the Garden."

Again my heritage was thrown at me. "What of it?"

"Your people are strange in that way," was all she said. "Alive to the Dream Road."

Because of my master's slow return to anything like health, we stayed in the Summer City as several moons slipped past. By the time the Fox Moon was waxing, I was beginning to feel that I had been stolen out of my own life. Even as I write this, I am ashamed to have been so selfish, but I must confess that I wondered many times if the folk back at Asu'a still remembered me, or if they thought only of Hakatri. I wondered also if my friends at Ravensperch talked of me from time to time. As the days sped past, I considered the marks my own life had left and was overwhelmed by how little difference I had made in the world, except to my master. I was a nullity, something that only existed where my life touched the lives of more important folk.

With my master being ably cared for in Goldenleaf House, I wandered the Summer City, exploring its ancient gardens and the forest. I talked to some of the folk I encountered, both my master's kind and my own, and soon learned that I had not been wrong: many of its inhabitants had already left Enki-e-Shao'saye. The trade routes on the eastern side of Old-heart Forest had fallen out of use since Tumet'ai was abandoned, the remaining Zida'ya settlements in that part of the world were too small to

make up for the disappearance of that once-great city of the North beneath the encroaching ice. Many I spoke with confessed that they, too,
would likely leave soon for Asu'a or Mezutu'a or some other, easier place
to live. I had known little of the Summer City before our arrival, but after
spending so much time there, I had begun to mourn it like a beloved elder
who was soon to die. Again, Ineluki's gloomy predictions came to me. If
the Zida'ya faded away, I could not help wondering, would my people
finally be free, or would we fade with the immortals we served?

On one of the days when I had been out walking in the city, I returned
to my master's chamber to discover he was still sleeping, but the Protector
Minasao Redwing was sitting at his bedside. By the reckoning of the Zida'ya, Minasao was young for his responsibilities—he looked to be in the
first bloom of youth though, as with my master, I knew he was older than
his appearance. But the look on his face as I entered was not that of a carefree youth, but someone bowed beneath worries.

"Hakatri has not awakened in all the time I have waited here today,"
he told me.

I gently set my hand against my master's forehead, which was warm but
not fevered. "That is often the case, my lord," I said. "Sometimes the pain
is so grave that he can do nothing but sleep—and in fact, at those times,
sleep is a welcome escape." I hesitated. "But for his dreams."

"I have heard something about this from the healers," he said. "Tell me
about these dreams."

"If they can even be called that." I offered Minasao refreshment and he
accepted a cup of wine. As he drank, still watching my master, I described
the strange things that Hakatri had seen and felt since the dragon's death,
the bizarre journeys he described to me on waking.

"So these dire dreams began even before you climbed Sesuad'ra?"

"Long before. Almost from the moment my master was first splashed
with Hidohebhi's heart-blood, though they changed after our night on the
sea with the false healer, Fen Yona. But they were always more than just
dreams. He has sworn to me that he floats helplessly from the past to future
days and back again."

"Not even the wisest of our elders truly understands the Road of
Dreams," Minasao acknowledged. "But what do you mean, past *and* future?"

"I know only what my master tells me, my lord, but there have been many times when he was certain he witnessed events yet to happen." I hesitated. "Once he saw ruins where this place, Enki é-Shao'saye, stands— broken stones that the trees and brambles had all but swallowed. Other times he said he spoke to mortals who remembered the Zida'ya people only as an old story. Was that simply fever-madness? How could he speak to people still unborn?"

Minasao shook his head. "If he saw our city in ruins, I fear he saw the future in truth—or at least one likely future. Jakoya herself, the great Gatherer of the Garden, once said that what is to come might extend before us like a road with many branchings, and each time you or I choose one direction, a ghost of ourselves takes the other one."

"A ghost?" I did not like the sound of that. "A spirit of the dead?" Ghosts were a thing the mortals believed, but I had never heard it from a Zida'ya before.

"Not precisely. I doubt such a twin of ourselves, if Jakoya spoke rightly, thinks of itself as a ghost. *That* Minasao—or that Hakatri, or even that Armiger Pamon—would be oblivious to its twin. It continues with the only life it has ever known and thinks itself the real one—just as we all do on our own journeys."

I could make no sense of this. In fact, the idea made me a bit queasy. "So we all have a twin?"

Minasao smiled. "Not merely one. Hundreds, if you take Jakoya's idea as truth. Thousands. Every time we choose, the other choices are also made, and all those versions—all those twins—go forward from there."

I could not help recalling my master's vision of a multitude of Hakatris, each living a life of its own, each separate but nearly the same as every other. That idea led to the sudden thought of thousands of Kes-reflections— an army of them—all scattering in countless directions, choosing different courses and making different lives for themselves. This made my heart clutch in sudden unhappiness, and not only because those shadows would lead lives I could only dream of, lives of choice and freedom. "I do not understand it, my lord. In truth I find it . . . painful to contemplate."

"Painful?" He stood, perhaps having decided that he could wait no longer for my master to awake.

"Because it suggests there must be a mirror-twin of Lord Hakatri who did not stand against the dragon." My master had turned in his sleep and sloughed off the bedclothes. I looked down at the terrible scars on his belly and chest. "*That* twin is hale and whole, without pain," I said. "Because that twin's brother did not make a dreadful oath."

Minasao nodded. "Perhaps that is why your master sleeps so much. Perhaps in dreams he is trying to find another life where Ineluki did not swear that oath, a life where none of this happened."

It was all too much for me to understand and I told him so.

"Perhaps such thoughts should be left alone," he said. "We have enough to worry about in our own world and time—and with our own Ineluki, who *did* swear his oath. And who also seems to grow stranger and more desperate with each passing moon."

"Why this talk of my master's brother, Protector? Ineluki escaped without any wounds, unlike my master. In fact, my master and I have not even seen him for more than half a circle of seasons."

Minasao looked down at sleeping Hakatri. "Perhaps it is only me, Armiger. I have been thinking and worrying much about your lord's younger brother since the killing of the Blackworm." Now he turned back to me, startling me with the directness of his stare. "Ineluki is angry. He is angriest with himself, of course, but he is the sort that turns that fury outward as well as inward. I hear from friends in Asu'a that he rages every day about the mortals, though his mother Amerasu has made it clear she wants no threats against the short-lived Hernsmen or any of their kind over Hakatri's wounding. She does not think what happened is their fault, but Ineluki's fire burns too hot to be so easily extinguished. And he has looked beyond Asu'a for those who share his anger."

"Beyond Asu'a?" I was puzzled. "Do you mean Lord Enazashi of Silverhome? His grudge against the mortal Hernsmen is ancient, but surely he and Ineluki—"

"No, I do not mean Enazashi. I mean Nakkiga. I mean Utuk'ku Silvermask, who calls herself the queen of the Hikeda'ya."

I was startled, but Minasao's words made new sense out of Ineluki's long absences when we guested in the deeps of Ur-Nakkiga. "But Lord Ineluki must know that the Queen of the North cannot be trusted," I said. "His own mother and father have contested with her since long before he was born!"

"Still, a fanatic heart will ignore what it does not want to know," said

Minasao. "It will excuse even that which cannot be excused in the need to find someone to share its bitterness."

"No—he is good," said a weak, raw voice. My master had awakened. "Ineluki's spirit is good. Do not misjudge his hurt."

Minasao kneeled beside the bed. "It is good to hear you, Hakatri. Do not tire yourself."

"My brother loves me."

"Yes," said Minasao. "Yes, he does. And that is one reason why he is so fierce, so desperate."

"Water, Pamon," said my master. I hurried to bring him a cup. He tried to take it from me, but his hands were trembling too badly, and he spilled more than he drank. "I dreamed just now that time turned widdershins," he said as he wiped his chin with the back of a trembling hand. "The sun rolled backward across the sky, west to east, and the years drained away. And all the time, I thought I heard my brother crying out, *'The three! The three will avenge us!'*"

Minasao was shaking his head. "Leave these dreams behind, Hakatri, so that you may attend my words. It is time for you to go back to Asu'a."

My master looked at the Summer City's Protector as though he had never seen him before. "What does this mean, Minasao? I can barely move. The dragon's blood still scourges my flesh every moment. I do not blame you for being tired of my useless presence—"

"No, Hakatri. You mistake me. It is not that we wish you gone. Rather, my mother and I fear what your brother may do in your absence."

This angered my master so that he tried to sit up, his face contorting with the anguish of his movements. I dared not touch him, but I wanted to hold him down, because I knew that he would pay a steep price later for trying to raise himself now. "Even you must be careful how you speak of my brother, Minasao," Hakatri said through pain-clamped teeth. "You are my friend and kinsman, and your mother is beloved of my mother, but I cannot hear you speak about Ineluki this way."

Minasao remained silent until my master gave up his futile attempt to rise and fell back, gasping with discomfort. "I am sorry, Hakatri," he said at last. "But truth, even a fearful truth, must be told. I have waited until you were better to speak to you about it, but I can wait no longer. Your brother has become very close to Utuk'ku's folk since your fight with the worm. Do you remember blind Jikkyo, the Hikeda'ya cleric who attended you when you first came back to Asu'a?"

My master shook his head. "I remember little of that time."

"He is one of the highest of the mountain queen's Lords of Song, a magician of great skill."

Hakatri gave out a strangled laugh. "Then his powers failed him, for he certainly brought me no cure."

"If that was his intent he surely failed, yes. But perhaps he had other goals. As it is, I have learned that Jikkyo has gone back to Nakkiga—alone."

My master was grimacing with another tidal rush of pain, leaving it to me to ask the question. "Alone? What does that signify, Lord Protector?"

"The other high master of Utuk'ku's Order of Song did not return with him but remains in Asu'a and is constantly with Ineluki," Minasao said. "Her name is Ommu. She is only a little less than Jikkyo in her abilities, but no less in her pride or ambition."

"I saw her," I said. "Many times. But she never speaks."

"She speaks to Ineluki, it seems. They are always together these days." He now dropped his voice, which made me uneasy. Why should the heir of Goldenleaf Clan have to speak softly in his own house? "Those I know in Asu'a say that Ommu has become your brother's shadow—that she goes everywhere with him and whispers constantly into his ear. How can we not wonder what it is that she tells him? The words may come from Ommu's lips, but do not doubt they are Utuk'ku's words and Utuk'ku's thoughts. The queen of the Hikeda'ya hates the mortals even more than she despises those of us who do not agree with her, and she seems to have found an attentive listener in your brother."

Minasao had caught my master's attention. "You may go now, Kes," Hakatri said abruptly. "You have no doubt been sitting with me a long time."

I had not—I had only just arrived—but I understood he wanted to speak to Minasao privily, and in fact I had already heard more than I wanted to hear.

Part
Five

The Green Sea

We left Enki-e-Shao'saye to return to Asu'a as the first crescent of the Lynx Moon crept into the night sky. My master was determined to ride, and he honored the horses we had brought out of the mortal lands by refusing the other steeds that Goldenleaf Clan offered him. His Enki-e-Shao'saye kinfolk would even have carried him home in a litter had he wished, but my master did not want to return that way after such a long time apart from his people—he was determined to return in his own saddle or not at all. Such was his way, the way of all truly high and noble folk. We who are less important need think only of ourselves, and sometimes of our families, but I have seen that the great ones—the high ones—are different. They know that the things they do and the way they appear while doing them are matters larger than themselves—the stuff of omens, the foundation of their people's fears and hopes. After so long away, Hakatri was determined to show a brave face to the folk of Asu'a.

But as I feared it might, his bravery cost him. Once we reached Asu'a he had to be carried to his chamber in the palace, and for many days afterward he was prisoned in his bed. Ineluki came to see him that first day and so did his parents. Ineluki was troubled to find his brother no better than when they had last been together and even wearier than before, and I am certain that Amerasu and Iyu'unigato must have felt the same, but they all spoke only of their gladness at seeing him again, and their sorrow that he still struggled with the pain of his wounds.

To my surprise (and secret delight) a letter from Ravensperch was waiting for me when I arrived. I waited until my master was once more in the
care of the Asu'a healers before I took myself aside and read it.

> *To the Armiger Pamon Kes,*

it began,

> *We who live atop the Beacon send our good wishes to you and your
> master. We hope that your travels were not too wearying or painful for either
> of you. We do not know when you will read this but pray it will not be too
> long after we have sent it, since our news is nothing exciting even now while
> it is fresh and will be even less so later.*
>
> *The "we" is, of course, the two of us, Lady Ona (who is writing this)
> and Lady Sholi (who has included her own message).*
>
> *As I sit here looking out my window, I of course cannot see Asu'a, but
> I often look to the east and think of you and your master. It almost seems as
> if that first visit you made to Ravensperch took place in another life—
> another world. That is one thing about living an exile life, so far from the
> crowded places of the world. It sometimes seems as though time itself, a
> constant force against which all others strive like rowers fighting the tide, has
> passed this place by. Nothing changes but the seasons, and even those—it is
> now winter here—seem like pale, uninspired recreations of a more whole-
> hearted past.*
>
> *Forgive me, Kes, if my words are less than inspiring. I have been unwell
> of late, but I am improving, and with better health I think my mood will
> also rise.*
>
> *Little has happened of late here in Ravensperch, and I have not the skill
> or the wit to make a great poem out of the ordinary days that have passed.
> In truth, I confess that I write this largely in hope that you will tell us, in
> return, something of the wonders you must have seen among the mortals of
> the Southlands, where you said you were bound. Are the mortals there
> small, almost dwarfish in stature, as they say of the troll folk in the frozen
> north? I have also been told that huge, hungry lizards called cockindrills live
> in the southern marshlands. Did you see any? And more importantly, did
> you learn anything in your travels that has brought your master some relief
> from his afflictions?*

Please write to us if you are able, Kes. Surely some of the mortal men who visit Asu'a must travel back toward these lands and could carry a message for you. Or—I hardly dare ask it—might you again come to visit us here atop our tall, lonely Beacon? For the days hang heavily here. I do not say this to complain about my husband—I knew his ways, his pains, and what our life would be when we married. I confess, though, that I did not realize how small our company would be here, or how few diversions there would be to make the days pass. Sholi and I find each day much the same as the one before. I walk often on the rooftops. Sholi reads. Of late she has spent many hours studying the words of our people's ancient bard Ta-Hindae, whose poems she has lately discovered.

Looking at what I have written here, I see clearly that I have done nothing in this missive but complain; and what is worse, I have made you a tool of our salvation. No one should have to bear up beneath such a burden, especially a spirit as unassuming as yours, dear Kes. And now, having spoken again of Sholi, I should leave you to discover what she chooses to send along.

I assure you I will be happier on another day and will write a more agreeable letter then. It could be you will even read that one first and never dream I could be as tiresome as I have been here.

She ended the letter on that abrupt note, closing it with, *"Your friend."* Underneath it she had signed her full name in fine, careful curlicues—*Lady Sa-Ruyan Ona, Mistress of Ravensperch*—as though she wished to put off sealing the letter.

I opened the missive from Sholi that had been folded inside Ona's. To my surprise, the parchment was blank, its only contents a single white blossom, pressed and dried—the flower of a hawthorn tree. I stared at it for no little time, trying to understand. Lady Ona had written of Sholi's sending, so the dried bloom had not been included by accident, or merely because it was close by when Ona finished her letter.

I was puzzled and even a little disappointed. I had hoped to at least hear some words of friendship or regard from Sholi after so long, but instead she had sent only the desiccated remains of a flower that must have been picked during the previous year's Nightingale Moon.

I asked some of my master's healers about hawthorn blossoms, and was given a long, thorough lesson in its use against many illnesses, from catarrh

of the chest to heart pains and even disorders of the liver, but I could not
think of any reason for Lady Sholi to be concerned for the health of my
inner organs. I read the letter again and saw that Lady Ona had mentioned
a poet Sholi had been studying, Ta-Hindae, a name I did not know. I was
about to ask some of Asu'a's fabled scholars and chroniclers about it until
one of the older Tinukeda'ya grooms pointed out that it was a Vao name,
so I should ask among our own people, not the Zida'ya. I felt more than a
little foolish that I had not realized this, but I had been very busy tending
my ailing master.

Young Nali-Yun overheard this conversation and said, "You should
speak to my great-gran. She's a healer too, or she was before she came
here, and she knows books and many other things. In the old days our folk
called her '*Val Adai*'—wise woman."

I had not heard this before, though I knew old Nali-Pina tolerably well.
Most of the Tinukeda'ya in Asu'a knew each other, at least those bound to
the lords and ladies of House Sa'onserei. "Is that true?" I asked. "I have
never heard her called that."

He shook his head in disgust. "Sometimes you don't even seem to
know your own kind, Kes."

I was beginning to think he was right.

"Ta-Hindae!" said the old woman when I went to her, and gently
clapped her hands. "I have not heard that name in many years. Back in
Senditu's day, he was called by many the 'Voice of the Dreaming Sea.' He
was a great maker of songs, especially songs about our people's story in the
Garden and afterward, in exile."

Nali-Pina lived with the rest of Nali-Yun's large family in what was
called the Servants Hall, a warren of chambers that crouched beside the
Visitors Court of Asu'a. She was likely the oldest living Tinukeda'ya in the
city, wizened as a dried apple, the white hair on her head so thin that I
could see much of her scalp, but her wits were nimble enough. This only
pointed up the distance between Lord Hakatri's people and my own: my
master's mother Lady Amerasu must have been twenty times Nali-Pina's
age, but showed none of the same outward signs of decline.

"Tell me what this flower means," I begged her.

"It depends on who sent it to you and when," she said, showing her
few remaining teeth in a teasing grin. "It is known to be dangerous to

bring hawthorn into the house during the Nightingale Moon. If an enemy sent this, they might mean to wish you bad luck."

I shook my head, though even the merest idea that the ladies of Ravensperch might have purposefully sent me a symbol of ill fate made me queasy. "It is not an enemy who sent it," I said firmly. "It comes from a woman of the Tinukeda'ya, and I have believed her to be a friend."

She gave me a look that I swear was mostly amusement. "Ah! But that shows that you, like so many others in these sad days, do not know Ta-Hindae's poetry."

"You know I do not. That is why I came to you, Grandmother." Among the Tinukeda'ya, all are considered part of the same family. Every old person is a grandmother or a grandfather to the young, whether they share blood or not.

She nodded. "And you were right to do so. I am likely one of the few of our kind here in Asu'a who can guess at the meaning. Another part of our history, all but lost." She shook her head, frowning, but did not say anything else for so long that it was all I could do to stay silent. "If this . . . friend of yours has been reading Ta-Hindae," she said at last, "then I think it most likely the flower is meant to speak of his song, *The Haw-Twig*."

"Recite the song to me, then, if you please."

"Do you think I carry all the poems and stories that ever were in my head?" She swatted gently at me, as though I were a troublesome child. "I am not the Voice of the Dreaming Sea, Armiger, I am just an old Vao woman who wants her dinner. But once all our folk knew his songs, and I can remember at least the lines I think you would want to know. But do you speak your people's tongue?"

Again, my ignorance turned to bite me. "I do not."

"I will try to put it in Zida'ya words, then, but it will be a poor copy of the original." She leaned back and closed her eyes, taking so long that I was half-certain she had fallen asleep. At last, after an agonizing pause, she lifted her cracked voice and sang.

> *Forever floating*
> *In the dream we share*
> *I dreamed a path*
> *I dreamed a woman*

And as she went
I could not catch her
Because she would not be caught
Unless by her own will
And as she ran
Lightly, lithely
She let drop a haw-twig
On the path before me
It had buds like stars
And barbs like spears
And these words she called
Back to me
"If you pass it by,
You will not be pierced
You will not suffer pain
No blood will flow
From thorn's sharp point
But neither will you know
The sweetness of its scent . . ."

I waited to see if she had finished, thinking there must be more. "But what does it mean?" I finally asked.

Nali-Pina shook her head. "You are a good person, Pamon Kes, and a hard worker, but I suspect you are also a bit of a fool."

By now I was almost beyond shame at having my failings discussed. "So I have been told, over and over. But what does this bit of poetry mean? Why a hawthorn flower?"

"Come now—it is there to be heard in the song if you have ears," she said. "The hawthorn flower signifies affection and fidelity—even the mortals know that. What it *means* is that someone has made you an offer. If you accept it, you risk what all lovers risk—pain and heartache, because love does not always go smoothly. And if you let the haw-twig lie, for fear of thorns, you will not be hurt but neither will you smell its fragrance."

But I am not escaping pain, I thought, *because this itself is painful.* The old woman's words resurrected the earlier hurt I had tried to bury. Whatever we might think of each other, Sholi and I were both caught in webs of duty, separated by our loyalties to others—my master, her mistress—and I had believed we agreed on this sad truth when we first met. Now she seemed to be telling me that I had misunderstood, that she was still waiting to hear what my feelings were, and so I despaired. How could I answer her hawthorn blossom? What could I say? I was sworn to serve my master Hakatri, who needed me now more than ever. Why would she set me a cruel task that I could only fail?

I stumbled out of the Servants Hall without thanking Nali-Pina, full of pain and muddled thoughts. I wondered whether I had given Lady Sholi some encouragement that I could not remember or had not recognized. Could I have unwittingly made some promise to her?

If I had, she seemed to have believed it. And what was more—and far stranger too—she seemed to have welcomed this misperceived affection, this unintended vow. How could that be? How could a clever and comely lady of good family, used to fine things and the company of high folk like Ona and Xaniko, favor a mere servant like Pamon Kes, with the dirt of the stables beneath his fingernails? I could not even feel flattered. The weight of someone's affections, especially someone as admirable as Sholi, felt like an unsupportable burden. I was already carrying so much.

I immediately wrote a reply, though I confess my hands trembled more than they should have. I thanked Lady Ona and told her that Hakatri and I had only lately arrived back at Asu'a after a long journey. I related a little of what we had seen and experienced, as well as the sad truth that we had found no cure for my master's suffering. I wrote of Sholi's gift only to acknowledge it with gratitude, but I dared not presume on Nali-Pina's learning enough to say more about it, let alone how it made me feel.

But as I finished, I saw that I had spoken of Sholi too little, so I added at the end of my missive that I held both ladies in the very highest regard. I asked Lady Ona to please give her friend my very best wishes and to thank her for the kindness of her gift. Then I took the letter to the post riders' hall near the stable and left it for the next rider who could carry it on its journey west.

That night, with my master sleeping, I agonized again over the letter I had written. It was graceless, I feared, and it said nothing useful. Several times I almost got up and claimed it back. What right did I have even to think of my own happiness, in any case? Asu'a's healers had exhausted their knowledge and medicaments, and my master was already beginning to talk about another journey in search of new help. Could I expect a lady like Sholi to trudge around the world with me, to put up with the filth of the mortal cities or the hardships of swamps and forests? And even if Lord Hakatri decided to stay in Asu'a, for us to be together Sholi would have to leave her beloved friend Lady Ona behind in that lonely castle of exile, with only her bitter, burned husband for company.

It all seemed impossible, though I agonized over it through many long nights, so at last I put it from my mind as best I could and fixed my attention on trying to help my master.

The circle of seasons continued, of course. The Moon Spirits chased one another, each swallowing the one that had gone before. The Season of Growth passed, then Gathering, with Lord Hakatri still showing no signs of true improvement, and his spirit sinking even lower. The letter I had written to Ravensperch had gone on its way long before, but it drew no reply. My master had not mounted a horse since coming back from Enki-e-Shao'saye, so I had little work to do in the stable, and I spent days upon days at his side instead, waiting for his infrequent moments of wakefulness. But when he was awake he hardly seemed to notice me, his mind so full of dreams and ghosts that the true world around him must have seemed only another realm of fogs and shadows. He had rallied for a while, but now he seemed to be sinking again.

As for me, I was waiting, but I could not guess what I waited for.

Almost two full circles of seasons had passed since Lord Hakatri had been burned by the worm's blood, and because they saw him so little, his family and the people of Asu'a mourned for him almost as if he had died. Still, life in the great city continued, and not just the season-circle, but the Great Year of the Gardenborn was almost ended as well. The arrival of the Rooster Moon meant that only a short time remained until the Year-Torch would appear and set the sky alight, proclaiming the arrival of a new Great Year. That sacred moment came only once in every sixty or so of the season-circles that mortals called a year, and preparations for the Year-

Dancing celebration had been underway in Asu'a for a long time, so the city was full of anticipation.

Even though the Zida'ya live longer than my folk and much, much longer than mortal men, the changing of a Great Year is an important occasion, especially in Asu'a. Deep in mirror-lit caverns beneath Asu'a, the witchwood grove where the ceremonies would take place was made as tidy as the throne hall, and special flowers were planted between the ancient, silver-gray trunks. The trees themselves were ritually trimmed of white-weave vines and festooned with silken ribbons of many colors, like ancient relatives dressed in their finest garments for a feast. Soon the Sa'onsera herself would begin the sacred rituals to welcome the new Great Year.

But I could not enter too much into the spirit of celebration. As the time of change advanced on us, Hakatri's dreams began to overspill his tortured sleep once more and wash into my own. And what had been a trickle as we crossed the Whisperwaste now increased manyfold, until scarcely a night passed for me when I was not captured by some powerful, often painful dream that did not seem to be my own. I ran beneath alien skies, chased by things I could hear but not see. I writhed in the grip of agony I could not escape. Sometimes I was myself but with my master's afflictions, my skin afire, my bones smoldering inside me like hot coals. Other times I felt that I *was* Hakatri, that I could see the ancient history of my bloodline stretching behind me but could discern only phantoms ahead, as though the entire heritage of the Zida'ya would fail because of my weakness. At such moments a deep, overwhelming fear seized me, but it also seemed that nothing I could do would make things better: the mistakes had already been made, or so the dreams seemed to suggest; the wrong turns taken, and I was lost beyond salvation.

Strangest and most frightening of all, though, were the dreams I had about Asu'a itself. Whether they sprang from my master's imaginings or my own growing fears I could not tell, but they were truly terrible. I dreamed of our ancient home in flames, of dark, distorted shapes running through the halls and of blood dripping down marble stairs. I heard frightful screams and cries for help, all in the Zida'ya tongue. Over it all I saw again and again a shadow wearing the ancient birchbark crown of Asu'a's Protectors, with branches that spread from it like the antlers of a stag. I dreamed that a ghastly horned shadow sat in the Protector's chair, but the Sa'onsera's chair beside it was empty, and the sky beyond the high windows was tinged with the red light of fire.

Jingizu, a voice said, echoing through those Asu'a dreams, a voice that hissed like the Blackworm but that I could almost recognize. *Sorrow.*

Were the dreams only Hakatri's, or were they mine as well? Sometimes I saw my master in these visions, bent in pain at the railing of a ship or staring out at endless ocean swells, and at those moments I thought the visions must be my own, for my master and I had traveled by water many times during my life. But at other moments, as I watched dim, armored shapes struggling against beasts stranger than any dragon, I felt sure I gazed on something I had never seen, something from the long-lost days of the Garden itself.

It became a fearful exercise merely to lay myself down on my bed in those days, though I was always weary. Sometimes I drank wine until I fell into sleep sitting upright, but even that did not protect me from most of the invading visions, and it never saved me from the dreams of burning.

Many nights I slept in my master's chamber because I did not want to leave his side, though there was little I could do for him except to let him know that he was not alone. It was on such a night in the Wolf Moon, only days before the first celebration of the new Great Year, called the Feast of Exodus, that I awakened to hear my master thrashing and groaning in his bed. In his agony he had thrown off his bedclothes, so that they had fallen over me where I lay on my pallet on the floor, and as I first awakened I struggled against them, blind and fearful, until I realized what had happened and stopped fighting. Hakatri's breath was short and harsh—*ha, ha, ha, ha*—and that frightened me. Then, just as I was about to go to him, he calmed again and fell into a gentler rhythm. As I paused, half-upright, I became aware of a shadow in the doorway of the chamber. I peered out of the coils of blanket and saw that it was not a single silhouette but two, one tall, one less so, and that they both were looking at Hakatri in his bed.

Assassins! I thought, but as quick as the terror came, I thought again, *No, never in Asu'a.* I stayed silent, a heartbeat from shouting for the rest of my master's household, but the twin shapes did not move past the threshold.

"It tears at my heart," said the taller one, and though he spoke quietly I recognized Ineluki's voice. My fear ebbed but was replaced by a troubled curiosity. What did he want in his brother's chamber? And who was with him? "He lives, but he suffers every day," Ineluki said. "There are moments when I think it would have been better if he had perished in Serpent's Vale."

I did not hear what, if anything, his companion said, then Ineluki spoke again. "Of course I do. No punishment could be enough to pay for his suffering. For what they did to him, I would happily see every one of those cowardly vermin driven from our lands."

As I peered from the shadows, I saw the shorter figure lean close to Ineluki, but all I heard was an almost silent murmur, like dry leaves blowing across the ground. The figure was hooded, but I thought I could guess the name of Ineluki's companion, and my heart sank a little.

"No!" Ineluki still did not raise his voice, but his reply was full of shock and disgust. "Never! He is dearer to me than anything. But I see no way to go forward with him this way. How can he be Protector when the time comes?"

Again I heard the dry rattle of a whisper.

"You run ahead of all sense, Ommu," Ineluki said. "That day will never come. I have told you so before and told your mistress as well. He is my brother. He is my blood."

The hooded figure muttered a few more words, but this time Ineluki did not answer. A moment later they turned and their shadows slid from the doorway, leaving me shivering on the floor. When I rose to make certain they had gone, I saw that though my master's face was hidden in the shadow cast by the open door, his eyes were open, as though he had been awake the whole time. Then he shut them again.

The next day, Hakatri sent for me to meet him in Asu'a's garden gallery, which girdled the bottom of the Yásira's great dome above Thousand Leaves Hall. The gallery was a score of paces in width, and planted with trees and other greenery, a circular, mid-air forest fitted out with benches and paths.

As soon as I arrived, I saw my master, but did not immediately approach him because he was with his wife, Lady Briseyu. I waited a discreet distance away, but after no little time had passed it became clear to me that the conversation would be a long one, so I found a bench among the greenery of the dense garden. A light rain was falling through the open spaces of the domed roof. Fern leaves bounced as the drops fell on them. I looked down at the people of the court in the levels below me, tiny figures as oblivious to my existence as they might be to a pigeon gazing at them from a high branch. The air was chill now that the Season of Withering was upon us, and I pulled my tunic closer around me: I feel the cold more deeply than do my master's folk.

Hakatri and his wife were deep in conversation. I had of course picked a spot where I could not accidentally overhear them, but I soon realized my error: they were not speaking aloud, but in the gestures that are so much a part of Zida'ya discourse. I wondered at this until I saw their daughter Likimeya tumble out of the bushes beside them, pause only long enough to sneak a glance at my master, then speed away again before Briseyu could capture her. Now I understood why they were talking without speech, and I wondered what they might be discussing that they wanted to keep from their child.

In the moments before I turned away, I could see that there was contention between them. Hakatri's hand-gestures were weary, as though they had been at it for some time. Briseyu's seemed pained, abrupt as startled birds taking flight.

Little Likimeya soon returned to the bench. She kept her mother between her father and herself, and when she did look at Hakatri it was only quickly, like a grazing deer keeping an eye on a distant wolf. I could not understand this. My master had been badly scarred by the dragon's blood, but there were other Zida'ya almost as cruelly marked by hunting mishaps and other sorts of bad luck. But Hakatri's daughter seemed to treat her father like an unknown quantity—like an envoy sent by a potential enemy.

My master and his wife paused even their silent gestures while Likimeya was beside them, but the child soon leaped to her feet and vanished back into the garden tangle.

I should have looked away. Spying on Hakatri and Briseyu with my eyes was just as ignoble as eavesdropping, but it seemed clear that some large matter was between them and I was fearful of what that might be and what it might mean for me.

To look on Lady Briseyu of the Silver Braids is to be half in love with her, even for one of a different kind, like myself. She is tall for her folk, tall as any male, and even her most gentle, graceful movements carry a suggestion of strength. She is of the Star's Path House, age-old allies of my master's Year-Dancing House, known for their loyalty to the Sa'onserei and Asu'a. My master married her for love, I was told, but I feel sure that his mother and father approved of his choice.

Now, though, I watched Briseyu, usually as poised and perfect as a statue, struggling with her composure. She made a series of signs—*lost fledgling, stars misread, tumbled walls*—and her face was imploring. My master only clasped his hands in the gesture that meant *necessity*, then separated his hands and spread them in another movement that signified a stronger version of the same—*cannot be changed*.

Briseyu stared at those hands as if she had never seen them before, then drew two fingers across her eyes—the sign for *jingizu*. *Sorrow*. I could see such misery on her face that my heart plunged inside me like a stone dropped into a well. From her expression, I would not have been surprised—although I would also have been astounded at the same time— if Briseyu had begun to weep like a mortal woman. A moment later my master made the same sign she had, passing his hand before his own gaze. *Sorrow*. I turned away, unhappy and ashamed to have seen their naked pain. A mist of rain drifted down from the open roof of the Yásira, dampening my face and hands.

Something appeared at my feet then, startling me. It was young Likimeya, who had crawled out of the greenery beside my bench. She rose and came to me in a meandering way that suggested she planned to speak to me but would choose her own time. Like most Zida'ya children, her white hair had not yet been colored with the flower dyes and mineral essences her elders favored. She was still very young, but it was clear she took her looks from her much-admired mother, though little Likimeya had a restlessness I had never seen in either parent. Her eyes continued roaming the forested gallery even as she spoke to me.

"Greetings, Arm'ger Pamon," she said with a very good imitation of queenly condescension. "It's Year-Dancing soon."

"That is true," I said. Little Likimeya and I did not talk very often, but when we did our conversations often began like this, with her explaining things to me as though I were witless. To be fair, she spoke this way to most of her elders.

"Grandmother said I can carry the lamp in the Procession of Light. That's very important."

"You must be proud."

She frowned. "Why aren't you in the stables?" she asked. "You're supposed to be taking care of the horses."

"Because Lord Hakatri asked me to meet him here."

"Ah." She nodded, chewing on her lower lip as she considered. "Swan tried to throw me off yesterday. I was riding in the woods by myself. She is very wicked."

Swan was Likimeya's own horse, a surpassingly gentle creature who would not have thrown even a rider wearing a suit made from burrs. "You must have been frightened," I said.

"Never!" She was so outraged by this that she made the sign the courtiers used for *untrustworthy gossip*, which made me laugh, and for an instant I could almost forget the unhappiness on the faces of my master and his wife sitting just a short distance away. A moment later the child's indignation was forgotten. She gave me a long, curious look. "Why aren't you with my father, Arm'ger?"

She only called me by my title instead of my clan-name when she was annoyed by something. "Because your parents are talking and I don't want to interrupt."

Her face showed childish disgust, as well as something else I could not quite fathom, something opaque, hidden. "No, I mean my *real* father." And then she abruptly turned and scurried back into the tangle of greenery once more, leaving me to wonder what strange ideas must be in her mind, and feeling inexpressibly sad about the events that had brought us all to this point.

I turned back in time to see Lady Briseyu rise from my master's side. She called for Likimeya, who appeared from behind a curtain of aspens, and together they made their way around the gallery toward the long, spiraling staircase that led down to Thousand Leaves Hall. I waited a respectful time, then at last got up and went to my master.

I could tell by Hakatri's pallor and the tightness around his eyes that his talk with Briseyu had been very difficult. "The Year-Dance is coming soon," he said.

I nodded. "So your daughter informed me." I did my best to amuse. "I couldn't possibly have known if she hadn't."

My very small jest might as well not have been shared; my master's expression remained drained and distant. "After the ceremony," he said slowly, "we will be leaving Asu'a."

I was more than surprised—I was stunned, as by an unexpected blow to the head. Words caught in my throat, and more than a few moments passed before I could get any of them out. "Leaving, my lord?"

"I see no other way. Now we must find a ship, Pamon, and I give that important task to you. A small, sturdy ship, with a crew to sail her. Make certain to choose mariners without families—we may be gone for a long time."

My innards clenched, and I felt bile rise in my throat. But the habit of duty was strong. "A long time? How long, my lord?"

"As long as it takes to find an answer."

"And where are we bound, my lord?"

"I do not know, Pamon. Westward, across the great ocean, that is all I can tell you."

Stark terror clutched at me. "West across the ocean? But there is nothing out there, Lord Hakatri. Only empty water. Only storms and unending waves."

He shook his head, almost violently. "The mortals came from there long ago. And there are islands far out from shore that our people have seen as they prowled the coasts. Somewhere beyond the horizon there must be another land, perhaps one even greater than this, the place of our exile. I have seen its shadow in my fevered sleep."

"But why, my lord? Why go in search of . . . of a dream? Remember how the last dream disappointed you when you found it." I was too astonished to take much care with my words.

"Sit down, Pamon." He gestured to the bench with a trembling hand. "Listen, now. There is nothing here for me in Asu'a. Year-Dancing is an empty masquerade. In my dreams I have seen what was and what will be—or at least what might be. But down every road, on every path that stretches out before me, nothing waits for me but torment."

Not really understanding, I could only shake my head in despair.

"It is true. I feel it," he said. "In only one direction does anything else wait, and that is to the west. I do not foresee my salvation there, but I sense that if anything can bring an end to the horror I live with, it lies beyond the sunset. So find a ship for us, Pamon. Make sure she is strong and swift. I must grab at this chance, small as it may be, because if I stay here in the place of my birth, I know to a certainty that darkness and destruction will be the only result."

I wept then but did my best to hide it from him. If Hakatri saw, he did me the courtesy of pretending not to. "Oh, master, if you command me, of course I will do it, but my heart is breaking for your family."

"It is my family that will break if I do not go," he said. "It will collapse beneath the weight of my affliction and my failure."

"Failure?" A surge of anger pushed me back onto my feet again. "Punish me for insolence if you want, my lord, but I cannot stay silent. Do not use that word, 'failure,' in front of me. You have not failed. You did everything you could. You stood alone and killed the Blackworm! The fault belongs to your—"

"Do not say it!" Hakatri's eyes turned up to mine, and his face was filled with a sudden misery that matched my own. "Do not speak his name. My brother made a mistake, but he need not be cursed for it eternally. He has a chance to redeem his error—but only if I go."

I suddenly understood, and the brief moment of anger turned icy cold in my breast. "You mean to remove yourself. You mean to let Ineluki become the next Protector of Asu'a."

"That is where his salvation lies, if he can seize it. The dreams have shown me." My master's stare had become distant, as though he looked across not just the space between us but across centuries still unborn. I shuddered, remembering when he had promised his brother that all would be well, and how wrong he had been. "But my salvation," he continued, "if such a thing exists, lies elsewhere—in the unknown West."

All that night my thoughts clashed like warring armies. I did not want to leave Asu'a, but I could not desert Hakatri. I had come to desire some kind of life of my own, but that was impossible without betraying my debt to my master. No matter what I did, I would fail someone I cared about. Back and forth the struggle raged, both sides desperate, both sides bone-weary, but neither able to get the upper hand.

At last, after struggling for hours alone in the sleepless darkness, I decided that my first obligation was to my master Hakatri, and always had been. I had to give up even the unlikely hope that one day I might follow a road chosen by myself alone. Honor and duty had been the foundation of my life. I could not give them up now, though it likely condemned me to dying in some unknown land, a mere afterthought in the greater story that was Hakatri's. I tried to console myself that even in exile with my master, I would be part of something more important than I could ever achieve by myself. It was not much comfort, but comfort is not usually part of a servant's life.

As the days until Year-Dancing wore down, I pursued all the tasks my master had set for me, though I confess I performed my duties with a heavy heart.

No sailor who cared for his home at all wished to go on such a voyage as my master proposed, even though Hakatri was greatly loved. I only succeeded in my mission after invaluable help from Iyato the Mariner, the greatest and most venerable of Asu'a's ship commanders. Though Ju'ujo Iyato was now long past his greatest days, he still knew the seafaring world better than any other of his race, and he found a small but worthy craft called *Petrel's Wing* that would serve my master's needs. She was an ancient but well-kept vessel, long and low and trim, with two masts rigged fore and aft. Masts and hull were made of sturdy, hammered witchwood, the rest of its appointments of hand-carved and lovingly polished silverwood, and its bow swept upward in a steep curve, like a seabird taking flight. With Iyato's aid, I was also able to find enough brave or reckless souls from the docks of Asu'a to fill out the modest crew, but I could nowhere find a captain of sufficient skill. When the ceremony ushering out the old Great Year was only a short time away, I went to Iyato in despair.

"What can we do?" I asked him. "No Zida'ya will take the helm of *Petrel's Wing*. And even if we could find a captain among the Hikeda'ya who could be trusted to protect my lord Hakatri, Nakkiga is too far away, as is their harbor at Black Cliffs on the coast." I felt empty inside. Time had run out, and I had failed my master in his only remaining hope.

Iyato's great age was beginning to show in the boniness of his features and his slowing movements, but his eyes were still bright and his wits sharp. "Then I will do it," he said. "I will be the captain."

I thought I had not heard him correctly, but when I asked, he said it again. "Lord Hakatri is the Sa'onsera's firstborn, one of the worthiest of all our people," he explained. "And even if his voyage is folly, what a glorious folly it will be to sail beyond the sunset!"

I never imagined this aged hero, whose record of deeds was already so lengthy, might decide to undertake such a perilous, ill-omened voyage. A part of me thought I should try to dissuade him, because if evil did befall the ship, the loss of Iyato would be almost as dire for the Zida'ya folk as the loss of my master. But at the same moment I was hard-pressed to have a ship ready for Hakatri, and no other captain could be found.

When I told my master of what the Mariner had said, he was grateful but troubled. "I desired a crew with no family," he said. "The whole of Asu'a is Iyato's family, and he would be fiercely missed."

"Then it is for you to talk him out of it, my lord."

He sighed. "Compromise is a very slow poison. I have already sipped from that cup too many times, and I cannot abide staying here any longer."

"But why, Lord Hakatri? Why must we go at all?" It seemed to me as though we stood at the edge of some precipice, our only choices either to turn back or to leap into the unknown, but I still could not understand what had brought us there. "You are with your family now, surrounded by the folk who love you. The best healers in the world are here, and if they have not cured you of your suffering, neither has anyone else, mortal or immortal. Why would you leave it all behind for the hardships and dangers of a journey whose end no one can guess?"

Hakatri stared at me, then reached out his hand and put his fingers on my arm. It was so rare for me to feel my master's touch since the dragon's blood burned him that I held my breath, startled. "I do not know if I can explain, faithful Pamon," he said. "In my waking thoughts these days everything is shadows and noise, but my dreams are even worse, full of dreadsome visions. I cannot bear the idea of existing like this any longer. If I do nothing, if nothing changes, one day I will end myself. If such a day should come, I do not want to be in the midst of my loved ones and all our folk. If I leave Asu'a now, then I will either find salvation or pass into history quietly, as a wayward, wounded spirit instead of an object of horror and pity."

I wept. I dared not clutch his hand as he withdrew it—I had learned the lessons of the last year too well for that—but it was all I could do not to sink to my knees and beg him to change his mind. It was not my own fear of the voyage that made my heart go cold in my breast, though I truly did not want to go, did not want to turn my back on what my own small life might have become to follow my master on his terrible journey. It was my master himself I mourned, and all he might have been. But if there was even the smallest chance his future could be saved, how could I set my own happiness at an equal value?

That night I prayed to the Garden, as my mother had taught me to do when I was still very small.

> *Green sea, full of light*
> *Green hills, pointing to the sky*
> *White stars and white sands, each a world in itself*
> *Each a fleck of the Great Dream*
> *Hear us, the scatterlings from your sacred shores and shallows*
> *Hear us, the fireflies in the long night*
> *Watch over us for we are ever faithful*
> *Faithful to your memory*
> *O, Garden that birthed us, O, Sea that receives us*
> *Hear us, for we are your children*

Only in that very hour, near the end of a Great Year and after a lifetime of daily prayers, did I finally stop to wonder why I had been taught to pray in the Zida'ya tongue instead of the tongue of my own Tinukeda'ya folk. Had my mother or father learned and then lost our people's speech, or had they never known it?

Did anything but my name belong to me and to me alone?

At the last sunset of the Wolf Moon, the fiery star known as the Year-Torch appeared in the sky, heralding the new Great Year.

That night, the courtyards, balconies, and rooftops of Asu'a were crowded as the Sa'onserei and the rest of the Zida'ya gathered to greet the arrival of the fiery star. Almost alone among his people, my master did not join the celebration. Hakatri spent the Days of the Torch by himself—or

at least with only me for company. Even Ineluki and his silent Hikeda'ya
shadow joined in the festivities. The people of Asu'a did not find Ommu's
presence any less disturbing than before, but they were hungry for the
presence of Asu'a's heirs, so they welcomed Ineluki back into their midst.
My master's younger brother drank much and deeply, but it did not seem
to make him as moody as at other times. Instead, he showed the people a
heedless, merry face. Although some might have wondered at it, they were
grateful for the chance to forget tragedy and look toward a new and better day.

On the first of the nine nights of Year-Dancing, Lady Amerasu held the
Invocation of the Garden, and the witchwood grove echoed to the sound of
singing voices. I could hear them even in my chambers in the Servants Hall,
where I was alone. When the Zida'ya gather for Year-Dancing their servants
and mortal guests are not part of the celebration, but are free to make holiday
in their own ways, but I was not in a festive mood. All I could think was
that when the nine nights were finished, I would be leaving Asu'a behind
me, and not just Asu'a but all the lands and people I knew. No more letters
had reached me from Ravensperch, and although that saddened me, I had
come to feel it was for the best. What if they begged me to come to them?
What if pretty, clever Sholi sent some new token of affection, one that could
not be courteously overlooked? It would have been a torture to me. I decided to write to them to explain that I was leaving with Hakatri on a voyage into the unknown west, and that they would likely not see me or hear
from me again. Nobody was likely to ride out of the city during Year-
Dancing, so I knew I would need someone to carry my message to Ravensperch after I had gone. When I finished writing, I folded it and slipped it
into my tunic until I could find a trustworthy courier.

The Starry Crown, the Progress of Light, the Pledge of Root and
Bough, each sunset brought a different part of the Year-Dancing ceremony. Beneath the strange, frosty gleam of the Year-Torch, as the world
hung each night in its net of stars, the voices of the Zida'ya floated up from
the witchwood groves hidden in the caverns beneath Asu'a as if the earth
itself sang, and I mourned the home I was about to lose. Full of restlessness,
I hurried back and forth between the palace and the dock where the *Petrel's
Wing* was anchored, asking the same things over and over until the sailors
begged me to leave them alone.

On the last night of those nine sacred days my master's people gathered again to sing the Hymn to the Garden and the Songs of Renewal, invoking the names of Jakoya the Gatherer and the first Sa'onsera. My master, his preparations completed, finally joined his people that night and, as I learned later, was welcomed by them with relief and joy, since many had feared he would not be able to attend any of the ceremony. But I could barely stand to hear the singing, which seemed to follow me wherever I went. I walked through the palace until I could scarcely hear the celebration any longer, and the sound of my own footfalls echoed through empty halls.

It was in the Garden of Songbirds, the hour well past middle-night, that my master found me.

"Pamon! Here you are." Hakatri's voice was strange, loud and full of cheer that seemed forced. He was limping a little, but otherwise did not show the pain he always carried, and he held a large and ornate cup in his hand. "I have been looking for you all through the palace."

"Why have you left the grove, Master? Are you unwell?"

"I have had worse days," he said. "But I have seen better, too." He laughed. I did not like the sound of it.

"And why on your last night among your family and folk have you come looking for me, my lord?" It was an unusually blunt question, but I was deep in mourning for what I was about to lose and my master seemed more than a little drunk, the first time I had seen him so since before the dragon died. "Tell me and I will do my best to serve you."

"Then drink this, loyal Pamon." He held out the cup. "It is the least I can offer you."

I did not particularly want to cloud my thoughts with wine, but another part of me suddenly welcomed the idea of drawing a curtain of drunkenness between the world and myself. I took the cup from him and lifted it but was made to pause by the strange scent that rose from the drink, dank moss, cloying spices, and an odd tang like hot metal. It was a combination I had smelled before, in Lord Enazashi's grove on the night we stole the tree.

"It smells a little like a witchwood forest," I said.

"Ha!" Now my master sounded more feverish than drunken. "Your nose is as wise as your heart is loyal, Pamon. It is my share of the *Kei-t'si*." He gestured vigorously. "Go, drink. It is for you."

This shocked and frightened me. Drinking the *Kei-t'si*—the blood of the witchwood—was the most sacred part of the Year-Dancing ceremony. The sublime liquor was made from the flower and fruits of the witchwood, things much rarer in these fallen days than gold or jewels. It lengthened the lives and strengthened the blood of all who drank it. Almost everything about it was kept secret from my kind, but I knew with certainty that *Kei-t'si* was meant only for the Zida'ya themselves and was forbidden to Tinukeda'ya like me. As far as I knew, no one of my kind had ever tasted it, and I did not want to be the first.

"I . . . I cannot take it, my lord." I held out the cup. "Here. It is meant for you and your folk, not mine. Why do you not drink it yourself?"

He did not accept the cup but turned from me and took a staggering step or two, staring up into the sky at the dying glow of the Year-Torch. I finally realized that my master was not drunk from any wine or liquor. He was drunk with his pain, but he had forced himself out of his bed to attend the final night of Year-Dancing. "Why do I not drink it?" he asked, still staring upward. "If you were me, would you wish to add to your years of suffering? If we somehow find a cure for my torment in the unknown west, there will be more ceremonies, more Great Years, and I can again take the *Kei-t'si*. But if, as I expect, there is nothing out there for me but more disappointment, why prolong a ruined life?" He finally turned back toward me. "But you, Pamon—I could not bear to see you grow old beside me, a sacrifice to my misery. If you drink the blood of the trees and are made strong, you might even return here someday after I am gone, your life still to be lived."

I was both touched and horrified. I had reconciled myself, or thought I had, to several score of years spent at my master's side, of leaving all I knew or even hoped, to sail into mystery for the rest of my life in search of a cure for him. But ten times that? A hundred times? A life stretched far beyond what any but a tiny few of my kind had ever known, as long as that of the great Navigator himself? And always in service to someone else, even someone as kind and honorable as my master? Hakatri's plan for me was meant as an act of kindness, I knew, an act of love and loyalty, but it seemed more like a curse.

I did not drink from the cup, though I will admit that not all my thoughts in that instant were against it. Who could contemplate a span as long as the lords of the Zida'ya and be completely indifferent? A small part of me was even excited by fleeting thoughts of the power and honor that would accompany such a far-stretching life, of the riches I could gather, the things I could see and do. But in the end, even those very real temptations were not enough to persuade me.

"You do not drink, Pamon," my master said.

"I must consider your gift carefully," I told him, because I did not want to refuse him outright.

His wild mood seemed to subside. "You are keeping something from me, Pamon," he said. "After all this time in each other's company, that feels strange."

It felt strange to me too, but in all the days since he was struck down by the dragon's blood, I had told him almost nothing of my own thoughts, my own worries and fears, let alone my feeble imaginings of having a life of my own. I had not wanted to trouble him with any of it, and I still did not. As I hesitated, I could hear the last singing voices in the distant grove bidding the old Great Year farewell and welcoming in the new one. "It is nothing, Master," I said.

But Hakatri had lost the feverish excitement that had brought him to me. I saw him wincing in pain once more, which he usually hid when he could. "Tell me what troubles you, loyal servant. Tonight of all nights, our last in Asu'a, you must not hide anything from me."

But I could not tell him, of course. He had suffered so much. I told him another small untruth—not for my own comfort this time, but for his. "Nothing troubles me, Lord Hakatri. I am content."

For a while after that we stood in silence. "Time for you to take a little sleep," he said at last. "Tomorrow will be a hard day for both of us."

"Will you be well here, Master, if I leave?"

"I will. Go to your bed, Armiger Pamon. You have always been more than a servant to me."

"Tomorrow is not far away, my lord. What time should I come?"

"*Petrel's Wing* is docked beneath Greenwatch Tower. Meet me there in the last hour of the dark." He reached out a hand and briefly, carefully, touched my arm. "I will never forget your kindness to me during these terrible times."

"Nor will I forget yours to me, my lord." But it felt as if some nearly invisible fracture had weakened our bond, the strongest attachment of my life. Without it, what was left to me? I felt dizzied. If I did not serve my master, did I even exist?

Thus we parted, my master to wander the gardens a little longer, saying his farewells to the home he had known for so many years, but knew he might never see again. I did not do the same. Exhaustion and dismay had fallen on me like a heavy cloak, and I could barely stay upright. When Hakatri was not looking, I set the cup down in the grass, the wine of immortality still untasted, and went off to my bed.

This night my life changes forever, I thought. The stars looked down. I could not imagine they cared one way or the other what might become of me. *I must go forward from this homely, familiar place to a future I cannot guess. May the Garden wait for me.*

I made my way down to the water in the hour before dawn, to the slip where *Petrel's Wing* floated on the unseasonably calm waters of Landfall Bay. I did not realize as I climbed the gangplank that the letter I had sat up so late writing to Ona and Sholi—my letter of farewell and apology—was still tucked in my tunic. Overwhelmed by all that was happening, I had forgotten to leave it in the post-riders' guardroom. In truth, so many thoughts were racing through my head in that hour that I scarcely acknowledged the sailors as I made my way to my master's cabin and set down my things. To my surprise, Hakatri was lying in the narrow bunk as if he had slept there.

"Are you unwell, my lord?" I asked him.

He opened his eyes and gave me a wan smile. "It was a bad night, Pamon."

"Your wounds? The burning?"

He shook his head. "Saying farewell to my wife and child. My little daughter would not even let me put my arms around her. 'No, you'll burn me.' That was what Likimeya said, though she must have known it wasn't true."

He was unhappy enough; I did not tell him what his little daughter had said about him not being her real father. "I am sorry, my lord."

"It cannot be helped." He closed his eyes again. "I cannot do anything

for them. I cannot live with their helpless love. I will find aid somewhere—
a cure, perhaps, or at least something to dull this cursed, unending pain
and the madness of my dreams. One day I will return and make things
right for them—for my family and all the folk I have disappointed." That
sounded more like a fading dream than something he truly believed, and
my heart ached for him. I ached for myself, too, but that was not something I could afford to think about until we had left Asu'a far behind.

Several streams empty into Landfall Bay, but the water that leaves it flows
out in one great river—*Tinuk'oro*, the Ocean Road. As placid as a pond in
some places, in others fast-flowing and treacherous, full of hidden rocks
and surprising cross currents, the Ocean Road is a challenge even to experienced sailors, but with Captain Iyato at the helm we swiftly made our
way down to the ocean.

I watched from the stern rail as Asu'a's bright towers and walls vanished
into the morning mist. Later, as we approached the river's mouth, I watched
the jade expanse of the sea spreading before us, its swells shimmering with
the trail of the setting sun, and my mother's long-ago words came back to
me again: *"One day you will feel the heartbeat of the Dreaming Sea."* This was
not that day, but I did feel something as we left the river behind, a sudden
sense that I was on the verge of something important. *Ocean Children*—that
was what Tinukeda'ya meant. Children of the Ocean.

We did not set our course immediately toward the west. Iyato had seen
clouds that he did not like along the horizon before darkness fell, so we
swung the bow northward and made our way a short distance up the coast
before anchoring in a shallow bay for the night. The captain had been
right to wait: before an hour had passed, a storm swept down on the coast-
line with high winds and rain so hard it stung the skin, while the skies
echoed with distant thunder. Even in the sheltered bay, *Petrel's Wing* rocked
and pitched against the hawser as though it were only a child's plaything.
I tumbled from side to side on a straw-stuffed pallet in my master's cabin,
trying not to think of all that I was leaving behind and all the things that
would never come to be. I had chosen duty, I reminded myself. I had
chosen honor, which was eternal, over mere happiness.

My master, I am sorry to say, had one of his worst nights, moaning in his
sleep and even shouting sometimes, though I could not understand his

words. Whatever dreams plagued him must have been terrible. I had to wrap my cloak around my head to shut out his cries, but still I had little sleep.

With the dawn, the skies cleared. The winds were strong but not dangerous, so the captain ordered the sails unfurled and we began to make our way west. But even Iyato the Mariner could be fooled: the storm that seemed to have spent its fury returned shortly before sundown. The waves rose swiftly until the ship rolled and bobbed like a piece of corkwood. Iyato ordered storm sails, and for a little while we beat on against the winds, the snap and flap of canvas so loud that it hurt my ears. Iyato ordered me to leave the deck so, as the sailors struck the storm sails and tied down everything that might move, I made my way to my master's cabin. When I entered, he opened his eyes.

"Do I still sleep?" he asked. His voice was ragged, plaintive. "Pamon, is that you? I can scarcely see you."

What he said frightened me more than a little, because my master's eyes had always been so much better than mine. "Let me light the lamp," I said. As the wick caught and I replaced the fish-skin hood, I saw that Hakatri had flung his blankets aside and his face and neck were gleaming with sweat.

"You must leave me, Pamon." He said it as flatly as a sentence of death. I had never heard that harsh tone of voice from him before, and for a moment I was speechless. "You must not make this journey."

"I have only just come into the cabin, Master," I told him. "Let me cover you up again first. I fear you are still ensnared in dreams."

"No," he said. "No, Pamon. I have been dreaming again, yes— dreaming of my thousand reflections, of a thousand different lives—and I have seen something that has frozen my heart."

I still thought he was babbling, as he sometimes did when he first awakened. "Dreams, even the dreams brought by the dragon's blood, are still only dreams, my lord. I am here with you now. You may rest."

To my surprise Hakatri forced himself upright on his narrow bunk, clinging to the pallet with straining fingers. His golden eyes were wide in the shadowy cabin, like those of some hunted creature turning at last to fight to the death. "No! By the Lost Garden itself, no! *Listen to me!* In all those dream-lives I saw you *die*, Pamon. It was a torture as great as anything the worm's cursed blood has brought me. I lay helpless and saw it—saw your death—over and over, in more terrible ways than I could count. In every life where you were beside me as we sailed into the west, I saw you die. If you accompany me, your doom is written."

The pitching of the *Petrel's Wing* was now becoming even stronger, so that Hakatri lost his grip on his pallet and fell back on his bed. The wind howled like a wolf pack beyond the cabin walls. I grabbed the edge of the bunk to keep myself from toppling, but even the ship's fearsome wallowing could not distract me. "No, Master, no," I said. "These are only dreams, you know that! And even if they were true, what then? You will live much longer than I will. I knew that when I swore to your service. But I will die serving you, whether it is tonight or ten years from now or a hundred. I reconciled myself to that long ago."

He shook his head roughly, like someone beset by stinging insects. "No! I cannot allow it, Pamon. I cannot stand by and see you die when I know I could prevent it. We will return to land tomorrow and put you ashore."

"But I will not go." I had never before defied him, or even contemplated it, but I knew I could no longer stay silent. "You do not know all that I have turned my back upon for you, my lord. You cannot be so unfeeling, my lord, as to send me away now—"

"Enough! I order you to leave me, Armiger Pamon." He was struggling to sit up again, but the rolling of the ship prevented it. I could scarcely hear him now for the thunder that rattled the skies. "Do you hear me? As your master, I order that you leave this ship!"

I had fought with myself so fiercely over what to do and had suffered so much unhappiness to make my decision that his words provoked a kind of madness in me. "No and no, Lord Hakatri. I refuse your order. I would do anything else, my lord—I would gladly give my life for you—but in this one thing I must defy you. If you would rid yourself of me, you will have to summon Captain Iyato to put me in chains first. I will not leave your side in any other way."

"Get out!" Hakatri cried, sounding as pained and miserable as I had ever heard him. "If you will only go in chains, then chains you shall wear. I will not have your death on my conscience, Pamon—I have done enough damage to those around me. My back is nearly breaking under the weight of my mistakes."

"I am here to care for you—" I began.

"*Out!*" He was shaking with anger now—and fear, too, I could see. "Go and summon Iyato. If you will not obey me, he will. You say you have given up much for my sake. If my suffering made me selfish and blind to *your* pain, then that is a curse I must bear." And indeed, I could see a dreadful shame on his damp, tormented face. "But that is all the more reason for you to leave me now. I pray it is not too late to undo some of the hurt I have done—at least to you, Pamon, most faithful of servants. Go. Summon the captain so I can tell him to head to shore. I have no strength left to argue." He fell back on the bed as though he had been pierced by an arrow.

Heartbroken and full of rage, I got to my feet, fell as the ship yawed, got up again and stumbled a few steps before crashing against the cabin door, then managed at last to get it open and stumble out into the narrow passage. I was overwhelmed to think that my master could feel so deeply about my unimportant life, but I was also furious that he should so badly fail to understand my loyalty, as well as all that I had sacrificed for him.

The growing tempest seemed to echo the near-madness that filled me, thunder cracking and booming. As I climbed the swaying ladder to the deck the ship pitched and rolled like a wounded animal. When I opened the hatch and clambered out, rain flew at me like arrows, so I could scarcely see a thing. Thunder seemed to make the entire sky shake as *Petrel's Wing* heaved and rolled in the storm's fierce grip.

I have turned my back on everything for Hakatri's sake, was all I could think. *And now he would send me away to protect me, as if I were a child—as if I had not long ago given my life over to him.* I clung to the rail as I looked around for the captain, but the few sailors I could see were all desperately at work, struggling with ropes, trying desperately to stay upright as great surges of water rushed from one side of the deck to the other. I was so battered by the thunder and the driving rain and my anguish that I did not even stop to think about my own safety. I leaned into the fierce wind of the storm and waded across the deck, still looking for Iyato—still, even in this mad moment, trying to do my master's bidding.

One of the Zida'ya sailors had noticed me. As lightning split the sky, I saw his eyes widen. He was roped to the mast to keep from being washed overboard. "*What are you doing up here, changeling fool?*" he cried, his voice nearly swallowed by the howling wind. "*Get below decks!*"

"Where is the captain?" I shouted, but the shrieking gale obliterated my words. I gripped the rail and took in breath to try again, but at that moment *Petrel's Wing* crested a wave and suddenly the bow tipped down. For a moment I felt my feet rise off the deck, then we hit the bottom of the trough and a massive wave leaped out of the darkness. I saw only its edge, white with foam, as it struck me and sent me spinning. A moment later I was struck again. Everything was cold and black then, and my mouth was full of salt water.

At first I thought I had only swallowed too much of a wave crashing over us, but the ship's wildly swinging lanterns were suddenly above me and swells were pounding me, one after another. I had been swept from the deck into the sea.

I tried to call out, but a wave swept over me and left me spluttering. Even as I managed to spit the salty water from my mouth and take a breath, another, even larger wave thundered down on top of me, and I went spinning down into the cold darkness, limbs thrashing slowly, helplessly against the ocean's powerful grip. My first thought as the sea closed over me was a strange one.

I am free—!

The larger part of me flailed in utter terror, fighting to reach the surface again as the air began to burn in my lungs, but I had been tossed and turned until I had no notion of which way might be up, and the heavy blackness of the stormy ocean crushed me from all sides.

I am drowned, I thought.

Then, a moment later, as the darkness around me passed into me as well, and life began to sputter out, I thought again, with sorrow but also relief, *I am free.*

When the blackness at last rolled away I was astounded to find myself alive and floating in a wind-whipped nighttime sea, clutching a broken yardarm that must have been torn free by the storm. I could see no lights from *Petrel's Wing*, and storm clouds had effaced the stars. In truth, I was not entirely certain that I lived, but until it was proved otherwise to me, I determined to stay afloat.

I bobbed on the gradually calming ocean for the rest of the night. I think I went mad after a while, because I thought that my master came to me and said, *"I am sorry I never called you by your true name, Kes."*

"You always treated me well, Lord Hakatri."

"I did not see you when I should have. I did not hear you when I should have been listening. The terrible singing in my blood blinded and deafened me. Forgive me, if you can."

"I will never leave you," I told him, but of course I had left him already: I was talking only to myself.

As the hours of darkness crept past, I slipped in and out of a sort of dreamy wakefulness. After the storm had spent its ire, the movement of the waves felt almost soothing. When the sun rose again it first turned the swells pink along the eastern horizon. As it climbed higher, I could see myself at the center of an endless desert of water, little dunes of green topped with white foam stretching as far as I could see. Much of the ocean's surface was covered with a thin cloak of mist, and I saw no sign of either the ship I had lost or of land. A part of me thought it might be better to simply let go of the broken yardarm and thus of life, to slide into the depths and take a deep drink, but I was not yet ready to die. My mother's words again came back to me.

"Someday, at a moment you most need it, you will feel the Garden inside you—you will feel the heartbeat of the Dreaming Sea."

And as I hung between the sky and the deeps, floating like an unhomed spirit, I began to understand what she meant. Time passed, but it also stood still. The waves splashed me, but were they different waves each time? Or was the same wave slapping at me over and over? Why had I thought I was saved when I was drowning? Saved from choosing my master's orders over my own loyalty to him? Or simply saved from the confusion and disappointment of being alive?

I could not answer these riddles, and I still cannot to this day, but my mother's long-ago words soothed me: there *was* something in me that was more than my thoughts, my breath, my beating heart. That was all I knew, but during that timeless time it seemed to be enough.

It was Tinukeda'ya fishermen—my own people, but of the Niskie folk— who found me bobbing among the waves like an empty but sealed jar. And like an empty jar, when they pulled me onto their boat, I could not tell them who I was or how I had come there, and only said *"I feel the heartbeat"* over and over. I know this because they told me so after they had taken me back to land and nursed me back to health in their small seaside village. I remember nothing of the moment of my rescue except the feeling of hands pulling me out of the water—a rebirth.

No, I can remember one more thing: I mourned the sea when it no longer surrounded me.

Here is where the story of my master ends, because I have no more to tell of him—or little, in any case—and the rest of my own story will be of little interest to those who study great matters.

After my rescue from the waves, I spent a good while among those Niskie-folk of the western coast, staying with them through all the Season of Withering. *Petrel's Wing* did not return for me. My master and Iyato must have believed me swept into the sea and drowned. While I stayed with the fisher-folk I helped them on their fishing boats, learning a little of their hard lives and their old stories, but when the Season of Renewal came I felt the urge to move on. Fate had given me my freedom: now I had to decide what I would do with it.

I could have returned to Asu'a, but though I greatly admired and re-spected my master's family, it was Hakatri who had chosen me and lifted me up, and without him I knew my life there could never be the same. I would be permitted to live among them, I knew, and even treated kindly, but it would be the sort of forbearance shown to an old horse who has long passed his useful days. Instead, I decided I would go to Ravensperch. I still had the letter I had meant to send on the day we left. The ocean's waters had made it unreadable, but I conceived a desire to deliver it in person to those for whom it had been intended. And that is what I did.

Years have passed since the sea almost swallowed me, but I have never regretted seeking out my new life, and I write these words from my cham-ber in the castle atop the Beacon, the smells of heather and hawthorn wafting to my window from the green mountainside. Two floors below me, my wife and Lady Ona are watching the baby learn to crawl.

But no matter how different my current life is from my old, and no matter how long I live, my master Hakatri will never be far from my heart. He still lives, this I know and will always know so long as it is true, because at times I still share his dreams. Hakatri's visions can be painful, frightening, and difficult to bear, but I hope by sharing them I might take a small share of his pain on myself. I will never know if that is true, of course, but I can hope. He was good to me, and even if I were to live as long as one of the highest Zida'ya, I still could never forget the glad sight of Hakatri and his brother Ineluki as they rode side by side in days that are now gone—swift as a storm, so fair and full of laughter, the Brothers of the Wind. I wish my onetime master only happiness and an end to his suffering, that he might someday find his way back home—as, in my own way, I have done.

Despite the unknowable distance between us—both the distance between then and now and the distance between dream and waking—it seems I will remain bound to Lord Hakatri until his death or my own finally cuts our ties.

I am content with that.

Appendix

PEOPLE

ZIDA'YA

Aisoga the Tall—a warrior of Hikehikayo, dragon fighter

Amerasu, Lady—the Sa'onsera, mother of Hakatri and Ineluki; also known as "First Grandmother" and "Amerasu Ship-Born"

Athuke, Lady—Asu'a's greatest healer

Azosha, Lady—the former mistress of M'yin Azoshai who bequeathed her land to Hern's folk

Benayha-Shonó—a great bard of Kementari, originally named Shonó, who took the nom de plume "sparrow"

Briseyu—wife of Hakatri, originally of Roe Deer Clan; also known as "Briseyu of the Silver Braids"

Diritu—a chronicler and poet

Dunyadi, Lord—the master of Snowdrift settlement; known as "the Ram"

Enazashi, Lord—Protector of Mezutu'a

Geniki—a wise healer of Snowdrift

Gondo, Lord—a noble of Silverhome

Hakatri—the elder son of Amerasu and Iyu'unigato; a noble of Asu'a

Himuna—Birchwood Clan's High Celebrant

Ineluki—the younger son of Amerasu and Iyu'unigato; a noble of Asu'a

Initri—the late Protector of Tumet'ai; husband of Jenjiyana

Isiki—the fabled lord of all birds

Iyu'unigato—Protector of Asu'a; husband of Amerasu and father of Hakatri and Ineluki

Ja'aro—the father of Briseyu and Nidreyu; once known as "the Silent"

Jenjiyana—the first Sa'onsera after leaving the Garden, also known as "the Nightingale"

Ju'ujo Iyato—a great Zida'ya captain, also known as "Iyato the Mariner"

Kuroyi, Lord—a noble

Likimeya—the young daughter of Briseyu and Hakatri

Lilumo the Poet—one of Hakatri's hunting companions

Minasao—Enki-e-Shao'saye's Protector; son of Sunoyatta no-Sha'enkida

Mezumiiru—a fabled moon woman; in myth, the ancestor of all Keida'ya

Nenais'u—Jenjiyana's daughter, wife of Drukhi; killed by mortals

Nidreyu—Briseyu's sister, Ineluki's friend

Rukiyo—one of Hakatri's hunting companions

Senayana—a character from a song or perhaps its composer

Senditu—Amerasu's mother and granddaughter of Jenjiyana; Sa'onsera ruling on the legitimacy of giving M'yin Azoshai to Hern

Shuda—a young armiger (squire) and one of Hakatri's hunting companions

Soniso—the first lord of Kementari, who lost his wits

Sunoyatta no-Sha'enkida—the lady of the Goldenleaf Clan and Sa'onsera of Enki-e-Shao'saye

Tariki Clearsight—a friend and companion of Hakatri

Tuya—a poet

Uaye—one of Hakatri's hunting companions

Uzu'una—the late wife of Lord Dunyadi

Vinadarta, Lady—the mistress of Skyglass Lake

Vinaju—the daughter of Lady Vinadarta

Yizashi—the son and heir of Lord Enazashi; called "Little Grayspear"

Yohe—Ineluki's armiger

HIKEDA'YA

Drukhi—the son of Queen Utuk'ku and Ekimeniso; called "the martyr"

Ekimeniso Blackstaff—Queen Utuk'ku's long-dead husband
Hikhi, Lord—the Queen's High Celebrant
Jikkyo, Lord—an important magister of the Order of Song
Karkkaraji—a member of the Order of Song
Ommu—Jikkyo's acolyte
Nerudade—Yedade's father; the philosopher who released Unbeing and thus destroyed the Garden
Utuk'ku, Queen—the oldest being in the world, Queen of the Hikeda'ya; called "Silvermask"
Xaniko sey-Hamakha—a noble called "The Exile"; lives at Ravensperch
Yedade—leading philosopher-cleric of Nakkiga; tends Hakatri while he is in Nakkiga

TINUKEDA'YA

Fen Hasha—a Niskie; Fen Yona's nephew
Fen Yona—a Niskie healer
Kai-Unyu—"co-ruler" of Silverhome
Nali-Pina—Nali-Yun's great-grandmother
Nali-Yun—a young stable hand at Asu'a
Pamon Kes—a horse groom in Asu'a; Hakatri's armiger, the narrator of this story
Pamon Enla—Pamon Kes's mother
Pamon Sur—Pamon Kes's father, well-known in Asu'a for his horse-handling abilities
Sa-Ruyan Ona—the mistress of Ravensperch castle; wife of Xaniko
Ta-Hindae—a poet and great maker of songs, called "The Voice of the Dreaming Sea"
Tur Sholi—a Niskie from Goblin Rock; lady-in-waiting of Lady Ona

HERNSLANDERS

Cormach, Prince—a nobleman and envoy to Asu'a
Dermod—a servant of Prince Cormach
Gorlach-ubh-Grainh, King—the ruler of Hernsland
Hern—called "the Hunter"; the first king of Hernsland, gifted with the land by Lady Azosha
Rian, Prince—Cormach's father, called "Prince of the Coastlands"

OTHERS

Hamakho Wormslayer—the founder of the Hamakho clan and Utuk'ku's ancestor; killed during the fall of the Garden
Hurma—a mortal healer who lives in the Wran
Jakoya—one of the Garden's most important leaders; called "the Gatherer"
Rinno—of Clan Kaura; leader of Hamakho's dragon-hunters, executed by Utuk'ku's Hamakha clan
Third Garden Poet—a bard from the Lost Garden, his name lost to history

PLACES

Anvi'janya—a Zida'ya settlement north of Asu'a
Asu'a—the greatest of the nine Keida'ya cities
Azosha's Garden—old name for the hilly region north of M'yin Azoshai
Beacon, the—a tall peak at the northernmost end of the Sunstep Mountains
Birch Hill—a hill near the Silver Way on which the Snowdrift settlement stands
Black Cliffs—a Hikeda'ya harbor on the far northern part of the coast
Court of Fowls—a part of Asu'a
Cruel Winds—the mountainous uplands south of Ur-Nakkiga
Dazzling Way—a road leading to Kementari

Dancing Pavilion—a part of Asu'a

Dreaming Sea—the mysterious and life-giving ocean that surrounded the Garden

Enki-e-Shao'saye—one of the nine chief Keida'ya cities, located on the southeastern fringe of Old-heart Forest; called "the Summer City"

Fernlight Passage—an underground river entrance into Mezutu'a from the east side of Skyglass Lake

Garden of Songbirds—a part of Asu'a

Garden, the—the ancient, now lost homeland of the Keida'ya

Goblin Rock—a coastal town in Hernsland, called Crannhyr by mortals and Da-Yoshoga by the Niskies

Goldenleaf House—the chief residence of Minasao's clan in Enki-e-Shao'saye

Great Redwash—one of the largest rivers in the middle-lands around Asu'a

Greenwatch Tower—the dock in Asu'a where Petrel's Wing is berthed

Grove, the—the fabled sacred witchwood grove in the Garden

Hernsland—a nation of mortals in the west,

Hikehikayo—one of the nine Keida'ya cities

Jhiná-T'seneí—one of the nine Keida'ya cities, destroyed in a great earth-shake

Kementari—one of the nine Keida'ya cities, now almost deserted

Kestrel Gap—the flatlands between the Redwash River and the Whitewake Fells

Kwan-To-Po—a waterfront city on the edge of the Wran

Lake Starless—the lake that surrounds the underground entrance to Mezutu'a

Landfall Bay—the body of water beside which Asu'a stands

Limberlight—the lands northeast of Shi'iki's Wood

Little Redwash River—a fork of the Great Redwash

Mezutu'a—one of the nine Keida'ya cities, located in the Sunstep Mountains; called "the Silverhome"

Mountain's Milk—a fork off the Great Redwash; Birch Hill is between the two rivers

M'yin Azoshai—the land given to Hern's people by Lady Azosha

Nakkiga—one of the nine Keida'ya cities, located in the far north; main home of the Hikeda'ya

Nightingale Tower—the highest tower in Asu'a, with a statue of Jenjiyana looking back toward the Garden on its top

Ocean Indefinite and Eternal—the body crossed by the Keida'ya fleeing the Garden on their way to the west

Oldheart—the huge forest northeast of Asu'a

Old Gate—entrance to Mezutu'a on an island in Lake Starless, cut into the hull of one of the Eight Ships

Old Whitecap—a mountain in Hernsland, site of Lady Azosha's witchwood grove

Omeiyo Hamakh—Queen Utuk'ku's palace in Nakkiga

Protector's Chase—a hilly area between Asu'a and the Westmarch Road

Ravensperch—the castle of Lord Xaniko and Lady Ona atop the Beacon

Royal Way—the road leading to Nakkiga

Seaswell Hills—western hills that contain Serpent's Vale

Serpent's Vale—the valley where the worm Hidohebhi dwells

Servants Hall—buildings near Visitors Court; home to Asu'a's servants, including many Tinukeda'ya

Sesuad'ra—a rocky tor on the southeastern fringe of Oldheart Forest, called "the Leavetaking Stone" because it was the site of the Parting of Zida'ya and Hikeda'ya

Shi'iki's Wood—a forest north of Landfall Bay and Asu'a

Silver Sea—a sea in the west

Silver Way—a major thoroughfare between Westmarch Road and Mezutu'a

Site of Witness—the chamber of the Shard in Mezutu'a

Sithmead—the Hernslander name for the meadow below Skyglass Lake

Skyglass Lake—a narrow but long body of water along the base of the Sunstep Mountains

Smoke Gardens—a part of Asu'a

Snowdrift—a small but important Zida'ya settlement west of Asu'a

Snowfields, the—a sparsely-inhabited, cold region between the Great Redwash and the lands of the
    Hikeda'ya
S'un Hinakta—a fiery mountain in the southern ocean near Nabban which destroyed Jhiná-T'seneí;
    called "the curse of the southern islands"
Sunstep Mountains—the western mountain range, located between Mezutu'a and The Beacon
Tan'ja Stairs—a great staircase in Asu'a, leading down to the Pool of Three Depths
Tapu—an island in the ocean near Nabban
Tearfall, the—a gigantic cascade in Nakkiga
Temple of Witness—the former home of the Breathing Harp in Kementari
Thousand Leaves Hall—the great central hall of Asu'a, beneath the Yásira dome
Tinuk'oro River—the Ocean Road, the river that connects Landfall Bay and the sea
Tumet'ai—one of the nine Keida'ya cities, located in the far north
Ur-Nakkiga—the mountain above Nakkiga
Vastmire—the Zida'ya name for the southern marshland that the mortals call the Wran
Visitors Court—a set of buildings in Asu'a where visitors are housed
Westfold, the—the lands immediately west of Asu'a
Westmarch Road—a major road that connects Asu'a and Westfold to the Silver Way on the west side
    of Tinuk'oro River
Westwood Track—a road that runs along the foothills (and through forests) roughly parallel to the
    Sunstep Mountains
Whisperwaste, the—the endless grassy plains southeast of Asu'a
Whitewake Fells—the hilly country south of the Sunstep Mountains
Wran, the—the marshland in the southern lands
Yásira, the—the sacred congregation of butterflies at Asu'a; spiritual center of chief Zida'ya settlements

CREATURES

Blackbird—Likimeya's horse
Boots—Pamon Kes's horse during the journey back to Asu'a
Bronze—Ineluki's horse
Frostmane—Hakatri's war horse
Gray—Hakatri's horse during the journey back to Asu'a
Harcha sunbird—a bird native to the south
Hidohebhi—a dragon also called Blackworm or Drochnathair
Khaerukama'o—an infamous dragon, thought to be the sire of many others; also known as "the
    Great" or "the Golden"
Lambkin—Lady Sholi's cat
Poem—a filly ridden by Pamon Kes
Seafoam—Hakatri's courser horse
Snareworm—a dragon slain by Xaniko
White Drake—a fabled dragon killed by Aisoga the Tall and other warriors

THINGS

Breathing Harp, the—the Master Witness in the city of Nakkiga, brought from Kementari
Chronicles of History in the New Land—a book by Diritu
Eight Ships—the vessels on which the Keida'ya fled the Garden and Unbeing
Exile's Letter—an infamous poem by Xaniko, the cause of his banishment from Nakkiga
Feast of Exodus—part of the Year-Dancing celebrations
Garden of Memory—a Zida'ya song about the death of Drukhi and Nenais'u
Gatherer's Questions—a social game of the Zida'ya
Gathering Bell—Mezutu'a's great central bell that tolls the time of day
Great Year—a Gardenborn time span, approximately 60 mortal years

Green Column, the—the lost Master Witness of Jhiná-T'seneí

Haw-Twig, the—a poem by the ancient Tinukeda'ya bard Ta-Hindae

Hymn to the Garden—a song from the Year-Dancing ritual

Indreju—Hakatri's witchwood sword, also called "Thunderstroke"

Kimeku—Ineluki's witchwood sword, also called "Gleaming"

Kei-t'si—witchwood blood; a liquor made from witchwood flowers and fruits which gives the Zi-da'ya and Hikeda'ya long lives

Master Witnesses—objects which allow passage to the Road of Dreams

Parting, the—the ceremony at Sesuad'ra which sealed the separation of Zida'ya and Hikeda'ya

Petrel's Wing—Hakatri's ship, captained by Iyato the Mariner

Pool of Three Depths—the Master Witness in the city of Asu'a

Protector—the title of the male half of the ruling Zida'ya dyad in the nine cities

Road of Dreams, the—a place that can be reached in dreams where thoughts can be communicated through space and time; some think it borders the lands of death, others that it exists beyond both death and life

Sa'onsera—the title of the female half of the ruling Zida'ya dyad in the nine cities and also the title of the ruling female descendant of Jenjiyana, in charge of the Year-Dancing ritual

Senayana's Ode—a Zida'ya song

Shard, the—the Master Witness in the city of Mezutu'a

Shent—a Zida'ya game of strategy, called "Shaynat" by the Hikeda'ya

Singing Fire—the Great Ship which carried Queen Utuk'ku and her clansfolk out of the Lost Garden

Songs of Renewal—songs from the Year-Dancing ritual

Whiteweave—a creeping vine that only grows on witchwood trees; also called "yedu-ame" by the Zida'ya

STAR CONSTELLATIONS

Korinu's Shield—a star called the Summer Lantern's precursor

Light of Joy—a star that shone on the Lost Garden

Lu'yasa's Staff—a line of three stars in the sky's northeast quadrant

Mezumiiru's Net—the great froth of stars that stretches across the nighttime sky from south to north

Night-Heart—a star that stays visible until dawn; also known as "the Heart"

Year-Torch—a fiery bearded star that heralds a new Great Year

SEASONS

Season of Renewal, Season of Growth, Season of Gathering, Season of Withering

MOONS (MONTHS)

Raven (Ice-Mother)

Serpent

Hare (Wind-Child)

Dove (Grieving Sister)

Nightingale (Cloud-Song)

Otter (Lantern Bearer)

Fox (Stone-Listener)

Lynx

Crane (Sky-Singer)

Tortoise

Rooster (Fire-Knight)

Wolf (Moon-Herald)

CLANS

Birchwood—a Zida'ya family
Hamakha—Queen Utuk'ku's ruling Hikeda'ya family
Kaura—a Keida'ya family in the Garden
Silverhome—the Zida'ya family in Mezutu'a
Skyglass—a Zida'ya family
Tur—a Tinukeda'ya family
Year-Dancing—the ruling Zida'ya family, called Sa'onserei

WORDS AND PHRASES

KEIDA'YASAO

A't'si—the smell of living witchwood; called "earthblood"
Benhaya—"sparrow"
Haká-sho—what Ineluki calls Hakatri
Inka-sho—what Hakatri calls Ineluki
Keida'ya—"children of the witchwood"
Nidi-sa—what Dunyadi calls Nidreyu
S'huesa—"my lady"
Ske'i, Sudhoda'ya!—"Beware, you mortals!"

TINUKEDA'YASAO

Din so-nosa beya Vao-ya ulluru—"You, too, are most welcome here, Child of the Garden."
Val Adai—"wise woman"
Sha-Vao—"Niskie"
Yanum dok sin ro danna bir?—"What is your name?"

OTHER

Cockindrill—archaic word for "crocodile"
Prehan—Hernslandish for "crows", and also for reavers and bandits
Quiet Folk—Hernslander name for Zida'ya and Hikeda'ya